D1324259

Larissa Ione is a *USA Today* and *New York Times* bestselling author. She currently resides in Williamsburg, Virginia, with her husband and young son.

Please visit her website at www.larissaione.com
www.facebook.com/OfficialLarissaIone
www.twitter.com/Larissa Ione

PLEASURE UNBOUND

LARISSA IONE

piatkus

PIATKUS

First published in the US in 2008 by Grand Central Publishing,
A division of Hachette Book Group, Inc.
First published in Great Britain as a paperback original in 2011 by Piatkus
Reprinted 2012

A CIP catalogue record for this book
is available from the British Library.

ISBN 978-0-7499-5562-5

Typeset in Times by M Rules
Printed and bound in Great Britain by
Clays Ltd, St Ives plc

Papers used by Piatkus are from well-managed forests
and other responsible sources.

MIX
Paper from
responsible sources
FSC® C104740

Piatkus
An imprint of
Little, Brown Book Group
100 Victoria Embankment
London EC4Y 0DY

An Hachette UK Company
www.hachette.co.uk

www.piatkus.co.uk

This book is dedicated to every single person who came to the aid of my family after Hurricane Katrina ... you were instrumental in getting me back on my feet and writing again. Without you, this book would not have been possible. I will never be able to thank you often enough or well enough, but know that I will not forget.

To my parents, who never stopped encouraging me, who supported my dream from the beginning. I love you very much.

To my husband, Bryan, and my son Brennan, who put up with countless nights of hearing, 'You're on your own for dinner,' while I was under deadline. You mean the world to me.

To Roberta Brown, for being an incredible agent and having faith in my writing, and Melanie Murray for being patient, helpful, and enthusiastic about this project.

To HelenKay Dimon, Alison Kent, Lynn Viehl ... you know why.

To my fellow Gnippers, who have been rooting me on for years.

Last but not least, to Karen Boss and Dee Knight, who took time out of their busy schedules to provide last-minute reads and the best advice ever, and Stephanie Tyler, Jaci Burton, and Lara Adrian, for more than I have room to list.

GLOSSARY

The Aegis – Society of human warriors dedicated to protecting the world from evil. See: Guardians, Regent, Sigil.

Council – All demon species and breeds are governed by a Council that makes laws and metes out punishment for individual members of their species or breed.

Dresdiin – The demon equivalent of angels.

Guardians – Warriors for The Aegis, trained in combat techniques, weapons, magic. Upon induction into The Aegis, all Guardians are presented with an enchanted piece of jewelry bearing the Aegis shield, which, among other things, allows for night vision and the ability to see through demon invisibility enchantment.

Harrowgate – Vertical portals, invisible to humans, which demons use to travel between locations on Earth and Sheoul.

Infadre – A female of any demon species who has been impregnated by a Seminus demon.

Maleconcieo – Highest level of ruling demon boards, served by a representative from each species Council. The U.N. of the demon world.

Orgesu – A demon sex slave, often taken from breeds bred specifically for the purpose of providing sex.

Regent – Head of a local Aegis cell.

S'genesis – Final maturation cycle for Seminus demons. Occurs at one hundred years of age. A post-*s'genesis* male is capable of procreation and possesses the ability to shapeshift into the male of any demon species.

Sheoul – Demon realm. Located deep in the bowels of the earth, accessible only by Harrowgates.

Sigil – Board of twelve humans known as Elders, who serve as the supreme leaders of The Aegis. Based in Berlin, they oversee all Aegis cells worldwide.

Ter'taceo – Demons who can pass as human, either because their species is naturally human in appearance, or because they can shapeshift into human form.

Classification of Demons, as listed by Baradoc, Umber demon, using the demon breed, Seminus, as an example:

Kingdom: Animalia
Class: Demon
Family: Sexual Demon
Genus: Terrestrial
Species: Incubus
Breed: Seminus

ONE

ॐ

**The demon is a prince of the air and can
transform himself into several shapes, delude
our senses for a time; but his power is determined,
he may terrify us but not hurt.
– Robert Burton, *Anatomy of Melancholy***

Had Eidolon been anywhere but the hospital, he would have killed the guy pleading for his life before him.

As it was, he'd have to save the bastard.

'Sometimes, being a doctor blows,' he muttered, and jabbed the demon in a human suit with a syringe full of hemoxacin.

The patient screamed as the needle passed through mangled thigh tissue, releasing blood sterilization medication into the wound.

'You didn't numb him first?'

Eidolon snorted at his younger brother's words. 'The Haven spell keeps me from killing him. It doesn't prevent me from dispensing a little justice during treatment.'

'Can't escape your old job, huh?' Shade pushed aside the curtain separating two of the three ER cubicles and stepped fully inside. 'The son of a bitch eats babies. Let me wheel him outside and waste his sorry ass.'

'Wraith already offered.'

1

'Wraith offers to waste all the patients.'

Eidolon grunted. 'Probably a good thing our little brother didn't go the doctor route.'

'Neither did I.'

'You had different reasons.'

Shade hadn't wanted to spend that much time in school, especially since his healing gift was better suited to his chosen field, paramedicine. He was all about scraping patients off the street and keeping them alive long enough for the Underworld General staff to fix them.

Blood dripped to the obsidian floor as Eidolon probed the patient's most serious wound. A female Umber demon, the same species as Shade's mother, had caught the patient sneaking into her nursery, and had somehow impaled him – several times – with a toilet brush.

Then again, Umber demons were remarkably strong for their petite size. The females were especially so. Eidolon had, on several occasions, enjoyed the application of that strength in bed. In fact, when he could no longer resist the final maturation cycle his body had entered, he planned to make an Umber female his first *infadre*. Umbers made good mothers, and only rarely did they kill the unwanted offspring of a Seminus demon.

Putting aside the thoughts that plagued him more frequently as The Change progressed, Eidolon glanced at the patient's face. The skin that should have been a deep reddish-brown was now pale with pain and blood loss. 'What's your name?'

The patient groaned. 'Derc.'

'Listen, Derc. I'm going to repair this unsightly hole, but it's going to hurt. A lot. Try not to move. Or scream like a cowering little imp.'

'Give me something for the pain, you fucking parasite,' he snarled.

'*Doctor* parasite.' Eidolon nodded at the equipment tray, and Paige, one of their few human nurses, handed him clamps.

'Derc, buddy, did you eat any of the Umber's young before she caught you?'

Hatred rolled off Shade's body as Derc shook his head, sharp teeth bared, eyes glowing orange.

'Today isn't your lucky day then. Didn't get a meal, and you aren't getting anything for the pain, either.'

Allowing himself a grim smile, Eidolon clamped the damaged artery in two places as Derc screamed vile curses and struggled against the restraints that held him on the metal table.

'Scalpel.'

Paige handed him the instrument, and he expertly sliced between the clamps. Shade crowded close, watching as he shaved away the shredded artery tissue and then held the newly clean ends together. A warm tingle wound its way down his right arm along his dermal markings to the tips of his gloved fingers, and the artery fused. The baby-eater would no longer have to worry about bleeding out. From the expression on Shade's face, however, he would have to worry about surviving more than two steps outside the hospital.

It wouldn't be the first time he'd saved a life only to have it taken once the patient had been released.

'BP's dropping.' Shade's gaze focused on the bedside monitor. 'Could be shock.'

'There's another bleed somewhere. Bring up his pressure.'

Reluctantly, Shade placed his large palm over the bony ridges in Derc's forehead. The numbers on the monitor dipped, raised, and then stabilized, but the change would be temporary. Shade's powers couldn't sustain life that wasn't there, and if Eidolon couldn't find the problem, nothing Shade did would make a difference.

A rapid assessment of the other wounds revealed nothing to explain the drop in vitals. Then, just below the patient's twelfth rib, a fresh scar. Beneath the razor-straight mark, something bubbled.

'Shade.'

'Hell's fires,' Shade breathed. His gaze snapped up as he raked his fingers through nearly black hair that, at shoulder-length, was longer than but identical in color to Eidolon's. 'It might be nothing. It might not be Ghouls.'

Ghouls. Not the cannibalistic monsters of human lore, but the term for those who carved up demons to sell their parts on the underworld black market.

Hoping his brother was right but not ripped from the womb yesterday, Eidolon pressed softly on the scar.

'Derc, what happened here?'

'Cut myself.'

'This is a surgical scar.'

UG was the only medical facility in the world that performed surgery on their kind, and Derc hadn't been treated here before.

Eidolon caught the pungent stink of fear. 'No. It was an accident.' Derc clenched his fists, his lidless eyes wild. 'You must believe me.'

'Derc, calm down. Derc?'

Monitor alarms beeped, and the baby-eater convulsed.

'Paige, grab the crash cart. Shade, keep his vitals up.'

An eerie wail seemed to leak from every pore in Derc's skin, and a stench like rotting bacon and licorice filled the small space. Paige lost her lunch in the garbage can.

The heart monitor flatlined. Shade removed his hand from the patient's forehead.

'I hate it when they do that.' Wondering what had frightened Derc so badly he'd felt the need to stop his own bodily functions, Eidolon opened the scar with a smooth slash of a scalpel, knowing what he'd find, but needing to see for sure.

Shade dug through his uniform shirt pocket and pulled out his ever-present pack of bubble gum. 'What's missing?'

'The Pan Tai sac. It processes digestive waste and returns it to the body so his species never has to urinate or defecate.'

4

'Handy,' Shade murmured. 'What would someone want with it?'

Paige dabbed her mouth with a surgical sponge, her complexion still greenish, though the patient's death stench had largely dissipated. 'The contents are used in some voodoo curses that affect bowel movements.'

Shade shook his head and passed the nurse a stick of gum. 'Is nothing sacred anymore?' He turned to Eidolon. 'Why didn't they kill him? They've killed the others.'

'He was worth more alive. His species can grow another organ in a matter of weeks.'

'Which they could harvest.' Shade let out a string of curses that included some Eidolon hadn't heard in his hundred years of life. 'It's gotta be The Aegis. Sick bastards.'

Whoever the bastards were, they'd been busy. Medics had brought in twelve mutilated bodies over the last two weeks, and the violence had escalated. Some of the victims showed evidence of having been carved up while still alive – and awake.

Worse, demons as a whole couldn't care less, and those who did wouldn't cooperate with other species' Councils in order to organize an investigation. Eidolon cared, not only because someone with medical knowledge was involved, but because it was only a matter of time before the butchers nabbed someone he knew.

'Paige, have the morgue fetch the body and let them know I want a copy of the autopsy report. I'm going to find out who these assholes are.'

∞

'Doc E!' Eidolon hadn't taken more than a dozen steps when Nancy, a vampire who'd been a nurse since before she was turned thirty years ago, shouted from where she sat behind the triage desk. 'Skulk called, said she's bringing in a Cruentus. ETA two minutes.'

Eidolon nearly groaned. Cruenti lived to kill, their desire to slaughter so uncontrollable that even while mating they sometimes tore each other apart. Their last Cruentus patient had broken free of his bonds and destroyed half the hospital before he could be sedated.

'Prepare ER two with the gold restraints, and page Dr. Yuri. He likes Cruenti.'

'She also said she's bringing a surprise patient.'

This time he did groan. Skulk's last surprise turned out to be a dog struck by a car. A dog he'd had to take home with him because releasing it outside the ER would have meant a fresh meal for any number of staff members. Now the damned mutt had eaten three pairs of shoes and taken over his apartment.

Shade seemed torn between wanting to be irritable with Skulk, his Umber sister, and wanting to flirt with Nancy, whom he'd already bedded twice that Eidolon knew about.

'I'm going to kill her.' Clearly, irritability won out.

'Not if I get to her first.'

'She's off-limits to you.'

'You never said I can't kill her,' Eidolon pointed out. 'Just that I can't sleep with her.'

'True.' Shade shrugged. 'You kill her, then. My mom would never forgive me.'

Shade had that right. Though Eidolon, Wraith, and Shade were purebred Seminus demons with the same long-dead sire, their mothers were all of different species, and of them, Shade's was the most maternal and protective.

Red halogen beacons rotated in their ceiling mountings, signaling the ambulance's approach. The light splashed crimson around the room, bringing out the writing on the gray walls. The drab shade hadn't been Eidolon's first choice, but it held spells better than any other color, and in a hospital where everyone was someone's mortal enemy, every advantage was critical. Because of that, the symbols and incantations had been modified to increase their protective powers.

Instead of paint, they'd been written in blood.

The ambulance pulled into the subterranean facility's bay, and Eidolon's adrenaline shot hotly into his veins. He loved this job. Loved managing his own little piece of hell that was as close to heaven as he'd ever get.

The hospital, located beneath New York City's bustling streets and hidden by sorcery right under the clueless humans' noses, was his baby. More than that, it was his promise to demonkind – whether they lived in the bowels of the earth or above ground with the humans – that they would be treated without discrimination, that their race was not forsaken by all.

The sliding ER doors whooshed open, and Skulk's paramedic partner, a werewolf who hated everyone and everything, wheeled in a bloodied Cruentus demon that had been securely strapped to the stretcher. Eidolon and Shade fell into step with Luc, and though they both topped six feet three, the were's extra three inches and thick build dwarfed them.

'Cruentus,' Luc growled, because he never made any other noises even while in human form, as he was now. 'Found unconscious. Open tib-fib fracture to the right leg. Crush wound to the back of the skull. Both injuries are sealing. Nonsealing deep lacerations to the abdomen and throat.'

Eidolon raised an eyebrow at that last. Only gold or magically enhanced weapons could have caused nonsealing wounds. All other injuries closed up on their own as the Cruentus regenerated.

'Who summoned help?'

'Some vamp found them. The Cruentus and—' he cocked one long-nailed thumb back toward the ambulance, where Skulk had rolled out the secondary stretcher '—*that*.'

Eidolon halted in his tracks, Shade with him. For a moment, they both stared at the unconscious humanoid female. One of the medics had cut away her red leather clothes that lay like flayed flesh beneath her. She now wore only restraints, matching black panties and bra, and a variety of weapons sheaths around her ankles and forearms.

A chill went up his double-jointed spine, and fuck no, this would not happen. 'You brought an Aegis slayer into my ER? What in all that's unholy were you thinking?'

Skulk huffed, looked up at him with flashing gunmetal eyes that matched her ashen skin and hair. 'What else was I supposed to do with her? Her partner is rat chow.'

'The Cruentus took out an Aegi?' Shade asked, and when his sister nodded, he raked his gaze over the injured human. Average humans posed little threat to demons, but those who belonged to The Aegis, a warrior guild sworn to slay them, weren't average. 'Never thought I'd thank a Cruentus. You should have turned this one into rat chow too.'

'Her injuries might do the job for us.' Skulk rattled off the list of wounds, all of which were serious, but the worst, the punctured lung, had the potential to kill the fastest. Skulk had performed a needle decompression, and for now, the slayer was stable, her color good. 'And,' she added, 'her aura is weak, thin. She hasn't been well for a long time.'

Paige drifted toward them, her hazel eyes gleaming with something close to awe. 'Never seen a Buffy before. Not a live one, anyway.'

'I have. Several.' Wraith's gravelly voice came from somewhere behind Eidolon. 'But they didn't stay alive for long.' Wraith, nearly identical to his brothers except for his blue eyes and shoulder-length, bleached blond hair, took control of the stretcher. 'I'll take her outside and dispose of her.'

Dispose of her. It was the right thing to do. After all, it was what The Aegis had done to their brother, Roag, a loss Eidolon still felt like a hole in the soul. 'No,' he said, grinding his teeth at his own decision. 'Wait.'

As tempting as it was to let Wraith have his way, only three types of beings could be turned away at UG, according to the charter he himself drafted, and Aegis butchers weren't among those listed, an oversight he intended to correct. Granted, as the equivalent to a human hospital's chief of staff, he had the final say, could send the woman to her death, but they'd just been handed a rare opportunity. His personal feelings about slayers would have to be put aside.

'Take her to ER one.'

'E,' Shade said in a voice that had gone low with disapproval, 'catch and release in this case is a bad idea. What if it's a trap? What if she's wearing some sort of tracking device?'

Wraith looked around as though he expected Aegis slayers – 'Guardians,' they called themselves – to pop in from nowhere.

'We're protected by the Haven spell.'

'Only if they attack from the inside. If they find out where we are, they could go Bin Laden on the building.'

'We'll fix her and worry about the rest later.' Eidolon wheeled the human into the prepared room, both paranoid brothers and Paige on his heels. 'We have an opportunity to learn about them. The knowledge we could gain outweighs the dangers.'

He removed the restraints and lifted her left hand. The silver and black ring on her pinky finger looked innocent enough, but when he removed it, the Aegis shield engraved on the inside of the band confirmed her identity and sent a chill through his heart. If the rumors were true, any jewelry bearing the shield was imbued with powers that bestowed slayers with night vision, resistance to certain spells, the ability to see through invisibility mantles, and gods knew what else.

'You'd better know what you're doing, E.' Wraith whipped the curtain closed to shut out the gawking staff.

Judging by the number of onlookers, they'd probably been paged. *Come see the Buffy, the nightmare that lurks in our closets.*

'Not so scary now, are you, little killer?' Eidolon murmured as he gloved up.

Her upper lip curled as though she'd heard him, and he

9

suddenly knew he wouldn't lose this patient. Death despised strength and stubbornness, qualities that radiated from her in waves. Unsure if her survival would be a good thing or a bad one, he cut away her bra and inspected the chest lacerations. Shade, who had been hanging around while waiting for his medic shift to start, managed her vitals, his gifted touch easing her labored, gurgling breaths.

'Paige, type her blood and get me some human O while we're waiting.'

The nurse set to work, and Eidolon widened the slayer's most serious wound with a scalpel. Blood and air bubbled through damaged lung and chest wall tissue as he inserted his fingers and held the ragged edges together for fusion.

Wraith folded his thick arms over his chest, his biceps twitching as if they wanted to lead the charge to kill the slayer. 'This is going to bite us in the ass, and you two are too stupid and arrogant to see it.'

'Ironic, isn't it,' Eidolon said flatly, 'that *you* would lecture *us* on arrogance and stupidity.'

Wraith flipped him the bird, and Shade laughed. 'Someone got up on the wrong side of the crypt. You jonesing for a fix, bro? I saw a tasty-looking junkie topside. Why don't you go eat him?'

'Screw you.'

'Shut up,' Eidolon snapped. 'Both of you. Something isn't right. Shade, look at this.' He adjusted the overhead light. 'I haven't been to med school in decades, but I've treated enough humans to know this isn't normal.'

Shade peered at the woman's organs, at the tangled mass of veins and arteries, at the strange ropes of nerve tissue that wove in and out of muscle and spongy lung. 'Looks like a bomb went off in there. What is all that?'

'No idea.' He'd never seen anything like the mess that had scrambled the slayer's insides. 'Check this out.' He pointed to a blackened blob that resembled a blood clot. A pulsing, morphing blood clot that, as they watched, swallowed healthy tissue. 'It's like it's taking over.'

Eidolon peeled back the gelled mass. His breath caught, and he rocked back on his heels.

'Hell's rings,' Shade breathed. 'She's a fucking demon.'

'*We're* fucking demons. She's some other species.'

For the first time, Eidolon allowed himself a frank, unhurried look at the nearly naked woman, from her black-painted toes to matted hair the color of red wine. Smooth skin stretched over curves and lean muscle that even in unconsciousness conveyed coiled, deadly strength. Probably in her midtwenties, she was in her prime, and if she weren't a murderous fiend, she'd be hot. He fingered her ruined clothing. He'd always been a sucker for women in leather. Preferably, short leather skirts, but tight pants would do.

Wraith tipped the woman's chin back and inspected her face. 'I thought Aegi were human. She looks human. Smells human.' His fangs flashed as his tongue swiped at the bloody punctures in her throat. 'Tastes human.'

Eidolon probed a peculiar valve bisecting the transverse colon. 'What did I say about tasting patients?'

'What?' Wraith asked innocently. 'We had to know if she's human.'

'She is. Aegi are human.' Shade shook his head, making his stud earring glint in the light from the overhead. 'Something's wrong here. It's like she's infected with a demon mutation. Maybe a virus.'

'No, she was born this way. She's got a demon parent. Look.' Eidolon showed his brother the genetic proof, the organs that had formed from a human-demon union, something that occurred more frequently than most knew, but that human doctors diagnosed as certain 'syndromes.' 'Her physical abnormalities could be a birth defect. Or maybe these two species aren't compatible genetically. She was probably born with some unusual traits, ones she's been

11

hiding or that haven't been blatantly noticeable. Like better-than-average eyesight. Or telepathy. But I'll bet my stethoscope this is causing problems now.'

'Like what?'

'Could be anything. Maybe she's losing her hearing or pissing herself in public.' Excited, because this kind of thing made his corner of hell interesting, he glanced up at Shade, who palmed her forehead and closed his eyes.

'I can feel it,' he said, his voice rough with the effort he expended to go deep into her body at the cellular level. 'Some of her DNA feels fragmented. We can fuse it. We could—'

Wraith let out a disgusted snort. 'Don't even think about it. If you fix her, you could turn her into some sort of uber assassin. That's all we need hunting us.'

'He's right,' Shade agreed, the glossy black of his eyes going flat. 'Depending on the species, it's possible that we could turn her damn near immortal.'

Sedating and medicating could also prove difficult, given the unidentified demon DNA. Something as seemingly innocent as aspirin could kill her.

Eidolon studied her for a moment, thinking. 'We'll take care of her immediate injuries, and deal with the rest later. She should have the choice about whether or not she wants the demon half to be integrated.'

'Choice?' Wraith scoffed. 'You think she gives her victims a choice? You think Roag had a choice?'

Though Eidolon often thought about their fallen brother, hearing his name out loud was a punch to the gut. 'Do you give your victims a choice?' he asked softly.

'I have to feed.'

'You need to drink blood. You don't need to kill.'

Wraith pushed away from the wall. 'You're an asshole.' Lashing out with one arm, he sent a tray full of surgical instruments flying and swept out of the room.

Shade crouched to help Paige pick up the mess. 'You shouldn't provoke him.'

'You're the one who brought up the junkie.'

'He knows I was yanking his chain. He's been clean for months.'

Eidolon wished he could share Shade's certainty. Wraith liked to escape his life now and then, but since their species was immune to drug and alcohol highs unless the substances had been processed through human blood, eating a human druggie was Wraith's only path to blotto.

'I'm tired of coddling him,' Eidolon said, pulling another tray of instruments to him. 'Let alone constantly yanking his ass out of trouble.'

'He needs time.'

'Ninety-eight years isn't enough time? Shade, in two years he's going to go through his transition. He's not ready. He'll get us all killed.'

Shade said nothing, probably because there was nothing to say. Their brother was out of control, and as the only Seminus demon in history to have been conceived by a vampire female, he was alone and had no idea how to handle his urges and instincts. As a male who had been tortured in the most heinous ways imaginable by the vampires who'd raised him, he had no idea how to live life at all.

Not that Eidolon had room to judge. He'd spent the last half-century concentrating on nothing but medicine, but unless he found a mate, in a few months his focus would shift and narrow until he became a mindless beast that functioned on instinct alone.

Maybe he should let the Buffy kill him now and get it over with.

He looked down at her, at the deceptively innocent face, and wondered just how easily and remorselessly she'd take him down.

Before she could do that, though, he'd have to fix her.

'Paige, scalpel.'

∽

Awareness came slowly, in a haze of black blotches punctuated by points of light. Warm, elastic darkness tugged at Tayla, luring her toward slumber, but pain prodded her into consciousness. Every inch of her body ached, and her head felt heavy, too large for her neck to support. Groaning, she opened her eyes.

Fuzzy, shadowy images swirled and pulsed in front of her. Gradually, her vision came into focus, and whoa . . . she must be in another realm, because the dark-haired man staring down at her was a god. His lips, glistening sensuously as if he'd just licked them, were moving, but the buzz in her ears drowned out his words.

She narrowed her eyes and concentrated on his mouth. Name. He wanted her name. She had to think about it for a second before she remembered. Great. She must have hit her head. Which, duh, explained the headache.

'Tayla,' she croaked, and wondered why her throat hurt so much. 'Tayla Mancuso. I think. Does that sound right to you?'

He smiled, and if she weren't dying on some type of table, she'd have appreciated the sexy curve of his mouth and the flash of very white teeth. The guy must have a fab dentist.

'Tayla? Can you hear me?'

She could, but the buzzing lingered. 'Uh-huh.'

'Good.' He put a hand on her forehead, allowing her a glimpse of one muscular arm adorned by intricate, swirling tribal tattoos. 'You're at a hospital. Is there anything I need to know? Allergies? Medical conditions? Parentage?'

She blinked. Had he said 'parentage'? And could eyelashes hurt? Because hers did.

'This is a waste of time.' The new speaker, an exotic-looking man, Middle Eastern, maybe, glared down at her.

'Go handle your own patients, Yuri.' The hot doctor with the espresso eyes shoved Yuri aside. 'Can you answer my question, Tayla?'

Right. Allergies, parentage, medical conditions. 'Um, no. No allergies.' No parents, either. And her medical condition wasn't something she could share.

'Okay then. I'm going to give you something to help you sleep, and if it doesn't kill you, when you wake up you'll feel better.'

Better would be good. Because if she felt a little less like she'd been run over by a truck, she could jump on Dr. Hottie.

The very fact that she wanted to jump Dr. Hottie told her more about the state of her head trauma than anything else, but what the hell. The pretty nurse had just injected her with something that totally rocked, and if she wanted to think about boinking a bronzed, tattooed, impossibly handsome doctor who was so far out of her league she needed a telescope to see him, then screw it.

Screw him. Over and over.

'I'll bet you could make a woman throw out all her toys.' Had she said that out loud? The cocky grin on his face told her that yes, she'd verbalized her runaway thoughts. 'Drugs talking. Don't get excited.'

'Paige, push another milligram,' he said, in his rich, smooth doctor voice.

A warm, burning sensation washed through her veins from the IV line in the back of her hand. 'Mmm, trying to get rid of me, huh?'

'That's already been discussed.'

Damn, this guy was saying some weird shit. Not that it mattered. Her eyes wouldn't open anymore, and her body wouldn't work. Only her ears still seemed to function, and as she drifted off, she heard one last thing.

'Wraith, I already told you. You can't kill her.'

Aww. Her hot doctor was protecting her. She'd have smiled if her face hadn't frozen. And clearly, her hearing had gone, too, because he couldn't have tacked on what she thought he tacked on.

'Yet.'

TWO

Someone was having sex nearby. Eidolon could feel it. Smell it. The ability was part of his breed's gift; any Seminus demon within thirty yards would sense the same thing. As he walked, the scent of arousal grew stronger, making his body tighten and his balls throb. At any given time someone was screwing in the hospital – usually Wraith – but this time he scented only a female.

Normally, such arousal was a beacon for any incubus, but Eidolon had always fought the urge to seek out the horny female and take advantage of her lust. At least, he had resisted the urge until a few months ago, when he'd entered his hundredth year and had begun The Change. Resistance had grown increasingly hard and painful. As his dick was at this moment.

Dammit, Wraith or Shade had better find the female and satisfy her cravings before they became too much of a distraction – or temptation – for him.

He moved swiftly through the dim corridors, nodding greetings to passing staff members, and as he approached the slayer's room, the scent of arousal became almost overwhelming. A low, drawn-out moan forced him to bite back his own sound of need.

Muttering obscenities, he brushed past the two imps stationed outside her chamber and armed with enough sedatives to bring down a Gargantua demon, and entered.

Tayla lay on the hospital bed, fists clenched, her chest heaving with her panting breaths. His own breath froze as she cried out and tilted her hips as though taking some imaginary lover inside her.

Standing at the foot of the bed, his brother smirked. Eidolon should have known.

'Get out of her head, Wraith.'

'You're just jealous because you don't have this power.'

Eidolon inhaled deeply and prayed to the Two Gods for patience. Wraith's mercurial moods made it difficult to deal with him in any circumstance, but throw any of his primal instincts – sex, violence, blood-hunger – into the mix, and Wraith went from difficult to impossible.

'Wraith . . .'

'Chill, eldest male sibling. She kills our kind. I'm seeing how she feels about screwing us.' He shot Eidolon a sideways glance. 'Screwing you, anyway. I'm a little more selective about my partners than you are, so I'm feeding her your images.'

Eidolon almost laughed. The words 'Wraith' and 'selective' canceled each other out. Both Shade and Eidolon preferred humanoid sex partners, though his preferences would soon change. But with the exception of humans and vampires, Wraith would nail anything that breathed. Though even that seemed to be optional.

Tayla's head thrashed back and forth, and suddenly he pictured her under him, doing the same as he pounded into her. He'd tangle his hands in fistfuls of her fiery hair and fuck her until she climaxed so hard she'd beg him to stop, and then he'd make her come again just to show her he could. His cock twitched, and he ground his teeth because this line of thinking was one that could only lead to No Way In Hell.

'Knock it off,' he growled, knowing his brother would catch

the scent of his own arousal if this didn't stop. 'She'll tear her stitches.'

The reasoning was weak; it had been twenty-four hours since Eidolon had patched her up, and in addition to his healing touch, she'd been bathed in regenerative waters and had received recuperative potions and spells from other, specialized staff members. She'd be up and running and killing demons as soon as the sedatives wore off. Which reminded him that they needed to fit her with restraints immediately. The Haven spell would prevent her from hurting anyone, but she could still tear the hospital apart.

'You know, I thought the *s'genesis* would loosen you up. It's only wedged that stick farther up your ass.' Wraith elbowed Eidolon on the way to the door, and then halted with a knowing grin. 'Or maybe not. E, man, you smell like a virgin male in a brothel who can't decide which whore to hump.' He grimaced. 'And eew. Dude, she's a Buffy. I'd sooner shove my dick into a month-dead corpse.'

'You probably have.'

Wraith snorted. 'Eliminates the obligatory cuddling afterward.' He reached for the door handle, but drew up short. 'Oh, Gemella called. Wants you to get in touch. Lucky bastard.'

'It's not like that.'

Gem, a demon masquerading as a human intern in a human hospital, regularly checked in with Eidolon, mainly to share intel on the types of demon activity that came through her hospital. He'd tried to talk her into working for him, but she felt her duty was to follow in her parents' footsteps, using her skills to intercept human-demon issues that would create questions if discovered by human physicians.

'Whatever. You ought to make it *like that*. She's hot.'

Wraith sauntered out of the room, and Eidolon turned back to the slayer. Wraith had gone, but Tayla still squirmed. Her sheet had fallen to the floor, and the hospital gown had ridden up to her waist, revealing her silky black panties. He didn't need to touch to know they were soaked. Her scent, her sexual perfume, hung so thick and heavy in the air that it was only a matter of time before he became drunk with it.

'Damn you, Wraith,' he muttered, and moved to Tayla's side.

Stay detached. Professional.

Yeah, because the erection popping a tent in the front of his scrubs was real fucking professional.

Willing his pulse to idle out, he lifted her gown and methodically checked her most serious injuries, which looked good, nearly healed. Only one of the wounds had required sutures, and her writhing hadn't disturbed the stitches.

'Yes,' she whispered, and grasped his hand where it rested on her ribcage. Her needs came to him in a rush of visions, a riot of tangled limbs and sweaty skin, and gods help him, a surge of excitement rocked his entire reproductive system.

Tamp it down, E.

He tried to pry her fingers loose with his other hand, but her iron grip tugged him upward to her breast. Beneath his palm, her flesh felt tight, hot, fevered in a way no thermometer would register. Her areola puckered at his touch, and his own body hardened in response. If he were made of stone he couldn't be any harder.

Eidolon exhaled slowly, reaching deep for control. He'd been born to the Judicia, demons known for cool, calm logic, something that didn't come naturally to him, but that he'd honed to perfection over the years both while growing up and later, when he'd served as all Judicium did, as a Justice Dealer.

But all those years fell away as he looked at Tayla. Even half-asleep, seductive, deadly power bled from her pores. She could crush him between her thighs and he'd beg her to make it hurt. *Idiot.* His brothers might like to mix it up with females like her, but Eidolon's tastes in bedmates ran more on the civilized side.

'Tayla.' He struggled with her strength and his own desire as he drew his hand back. She was a killer of his people. A butcher. '*Slayer.* Wake up.'

She shook her head and reached out blindly. He grasped her face between his palms and held her still. Using his thumbs, he lifted her eyelids. Pupils were equal and responsive when he turned her face toward the overhead light, though she didn't seem to see him.

Damn, she had beautiful eyes. Green rimmed with gold, and so expressive that he doubted she could shield her thoughts from anyone. Pale freckles shimmered just beneath the surface of her creamy skin. High cheekbones added definition to her slightly rounded face, marred by the faintest tinge of a healing bruise. He let his gaze travel to her mouth, her pouty lips that parted slightly to let out the sounds of wanton desperation.

He wanted to take that mouth. Wanted to feel it take him.

Human medicine demanded ethics. Here, at Underworld General, if he, or any doctor, screwed every patient who came through the doors, few would care.

Eidolon happened to be one of the few.

Moral codes were not his concern; doctors didn't screw patients in his hospital not because it was 'wrong,' but because the hospital teetered in a precarious position. Demons weren't a trusting sort. Most held a distrust, even contempt, for those with power. Doctors with scalpels could kill. If word got out that the doctors were raping their patients, even fewer demons would trust the hospital's services.

As a result, most of the staff had agreed to keep their paws, claws, and teeth off the patients. Naturally, there had been exceptions and indiscretions.

Hell, he'd be willing to make an exception with the right woman, but an Aegi killer wasn't the right woman, no matter how much his throbbing cock argued that she was.

'Doc.'

Tayla was looking at him, her eyes glittering with a combination of determination and lust so potent that he drew a startled breath. Her hand came up, grasped a handful of his hair near the nape, and pulled his head down with such force that he barely had time to brace his hands on either side of her head before his mouth came down hard on hers.

Her tongue pushed past his lips to tangle with his, and he growled at the taste of her. Her flavor was bold and wicked, like the scent of her lust, but beneath it all lurked a faint sweetness, as though innocence had been buried.

Buried under the corpses of his brethren she'd killed, most likely.

An icy blast speared his chest and he reared back, his control balancing on a scalpel's edge. This was his greatest fear, the loss of restraint as The Change took him – the *s'genesis* had to be the reason he was on the verge of mounting the enemy like a beast in rut.

But when her hand brushed his shaft, the beast suddenly didn't care who she was or what she'd done. He was a Seminus demon, after all, a breed of incubi that lived for sex, existed to deceive and cause misery through intimate means once the *s'genesis* was complete. Perhaps now wasn't the time to fight his nature. Perhaps his nature *was* his weapon against an age-old enemy.

Her fingers closed around his sex through his scrub pants, and fuck, he was tired of analyzing his body, his emotions, and his instincts. It was time to just feel.

He rocked his hips into her touch as desire rocked the rest of his body.

'Please,' she begged against his lips, 'please. Touch me.'

Groaning, he dropped a hand down to one hip and lifted her so that his erection nudged her other hip.

So much for remaining professional.

ର

Never had Tayla dreamed anything like this. It had to be a dream, because she'd never been this turned on in real life. And she'd certainly never hoped to get it on with a doctor. Especially not a doctor as totally mouthwatering as the one who was kissing her blind and stroking her hip so masterfully that some women would already have come a dozen times from that alone.

She lifted her knees, hooked one leg around his waist. The move knocked him off-balance, and he grunted as he brought a leg up on the bed to brace himself.

'Shit.' Doc Hottie dragged his mouth away from hers. 'Tayla, are you awake?'

'Shut up and let me have this,' she muttered, and tugged on the waistband of his scrubs.

He hissed when she grasped his erection. Oh, my. She measured his length and thickness with her fingers, and for a moment she wondered if there would be any pain when he entered her, but then she remembered that this was a dream, and nothing hurt in a dream.

'Tayla,' he whispered against her neck, 'you're injured. We have to be caref—'

She squeezed his shaft, and his words cut off with a strangled moan. Slowly, she stroked, rubbed her palm over the velvety head and then took him in her fist again. His ragged, sharp breaths feathered over her skin as she worked him, and when she trailed a fingertip through the drop of moisture that welled at the tip of his cock, something seemed to break inside him. The wall that had restrained him crumbled, and suddenly his hands were everywhere at once, his mouth devouring her cheekbone, her jaw, her throat.

Intense hunger, as though she'd suffered years of famine, rushed through her veins at the way his hand caressed her flesh. He skimmed over places she thought might hurt, but the memories danced at the edge of her mind, shimmering away altogether when the doctor's tongue traced a wet circle on her neck.

His decadent touch strayed lower, over her thigh and between her legs, where he languidly, maddeningly, stroked the crease of her leg and her sex. She arched against his hand, needing his touch in the right place, but he didn't comply, his torture deliberate. Devious. Delicious.

She wanted to see his eyes, but he'd buried his face in her throat as he nuzzled her skin, worked lower to her collarbone, nipped lightly there. Threading her fingers through his dark hair, she held him against her, reveling in his touch, in the feel of a man worshipping her flesh, if only in a dream.

Here, in a sleeping world of fantasy, perhaps she'd find the pleasure that had always eluded her in real-life sexual encounters. Here, her past didn't matter. Her fears held no sway.

The deft touch of the man on top of her was her whole world in her dream, and when his fingers moved to trace the hills and valleys of her swollen sex through her panties, she welcomed the hot tingle of excitement that buzzed through her.

'Yes, oh, yes.'

She threw her head back and spread her legs wider. His fingers tunneled beneath the cotton, and she trembled as he circled her entrance, once, twice, her slippery juices enhancing the erotic massage. It was good, so good that she nearly came off the bed when he plunged a finger inside her. He drove it deep, slid it slowly out, and then thrust again, pleasuring her with his finger in a way no man had ever done even with his dick.

'You're so wet.' His gravelly voice shot through her like an electric current. 'You smell raw, ready.'

Oh, God, she was ready. 'Now.' She angled her hips upward, unashamedly inviting him inside. 'Please.'

The sound of fabric tearing made her heart pound in anticipation. He shifted above her, guiding his erection between her legs. The bed wobbled and her senses did the same as he rocked against her, sliding his shaft between her labia. Each stroke rubbed her aching nub with a perfect amount of pressure and slick, molten friction.

She whimpered, but he smothered the sound with his lips and surged inside her. Her eager walls clasped his cock as it stretched

24

her, filled her until she thought she'd unravel into a quivering ball of lust. Nothing had ever felt so wonderful.

Desperate to reach the ultimate peak, she wrapped her legs tightly around his waist and dug into the backs of his thighs with her heels. He growled in response, braced his elbow at her head, and moved faster against her. Slipping her hands beneath his scrub top, she caressed the hard ridges of his spine, the flexing muscles of his back, the taut buttocks that tightened further beneath her fingers.

'Harder. More.'

He tore his mouth away from hers. 'More?' With one powerful, dominating thrust, the bed scooted forward. 'Tell me how much more.'

Speaking seemed like an impossibility when he lifted her hips against him and rode her harder and deeper, fueling the fire in her blood. 'Like that,' she said between panting breaths. 'Do it like that.'

He lifted his head, and though his eyes were closed, he'd bared his teeth, his expression a savage mask of ecstasy. So absorbed in the beauty of his pleasure, she barely noticed when something bounced against her throat. A pendant. A necklace had come free of his shirt's neckline, and the silver dagger encircled by snakes dangled against her skin, a cool, sharp caress.

Then suddenly, he was on his feet, still sheathed inside her, and she was wrapped around him as he carried her across the room. Her back slammed up against a wall. Medical equipment rattled with the force of his enthusiasm.

The doctor had one hell of a bedside manner.

He rocked against her, sometimes fully withdrawing before plunging inside her again, sometimes going deep and driving short, hard strokes all the way to her womb. Pleasure ripped through her, almost shocking her with its severity. His fingers dug into her butt where he held her to him, and his teeth sank into her shoulder, holding her upper body immobile.

It was the most erotic thing she'd ever experienced.

Heat spread through her pelvis as his cock stroked and rubbed and if this weren't a dream, she'd not believe how his shaft pulsed inside her.

Pressure built, squeezed her organs, and knotted her muscles. *No man could feel this good.*

She seized his hair and dragged his head up, made him look at her. Her breath caught. Passion and raw hunger and something even darker lurked in his eyes, but what stole the air from her lungs was the color. They'd been brown before, a bold, rich coffee.

Now, they were gold. Hypnotic, decadent. Twenty-four karat sex.

Oh, she loved this dream. This dream where her lover was walking sex, from his magic penis and hypnotic eyes to his skilled lips, fingers, and even his scent, which was something like dark chocolate, as though it had been designed to attract women.

'Come, slayer,' he growled. 'Ride me. Drench me.'

He twisted his hips, drove deep, and she cried out, so close to the summit that her entire body shook. There, there ... yes! Oh, yes, she was almost there.

He jerked, his roar of release ringing in her ears and rocketing her need even higher. Hot, shivery spurts of semen jolted her sensitive internal tissues until it seemed as though millions of tiny fingers were stroking her with so much pleasure she could only tremble and pant.

And yet, she didn't peak.

She should have. Dream or no, this man had done something to her no woman should be able to resist.

He kept thrusting, even though his muscles quivered and his bronzed skin glistened with sweat. The tattoo that covered his right hand and arm, all the way to his throat, rippled like a living thing, angry at not getting what it craved.

'You can stop now.' She wanted to scream with frustration. She should have known better, and now her body felt bruised, alien, and so tightly coiled she needed to strike out at something to achieve some sort of release.

'You didn't come,' he said, and plunged into her again. Ruthlessly.

'I never do.'

'It's impossible to not orgasm for me.' He doubled his efforts. 'Must be your injuries . . . '

'So I didn't get off. Tuck your ego back in your pants and deal with it.'

Criminy. Even in dreams men were crybabies when it came to their sexual prowess. In dreams . . . her thought trailed off as her mind finally registered what he'd said.

Injuries? She reached between them and winced when she touched a sensitive spot over her ribs. What had happened?

'Doc?' He didn't respond, was too deep inside her, stroking, threatening to bring her back to the place that walked the terrible line between orgasm and frustration. 'Stop. Please. What happened to me?'

He looked down at her with dark eyes. What had happened to the gold? Where had the dream gone?

'Cruentus demon.'

The answer slammed her back to reality, and this time, when the breath caught in her lungs, it hurt like hell. Images flashed through her brain. The sewer. Blood. Pain. *Janet.*

No. Oh, no. This was real.

Her heart kicked against sore ribs as she took in the shadowy room and medical equipment. The strange designs on the walls. No, not designs. Writing. Not a language she recognized. Odd, ancient-looking objects adorned shelves inside locked glass cabinets. Was that one thing mounted on the wall a . . . *skull*?

Where was she?

Her sex contracted around the still-engorged penis inside her. And who was this man who had so thoroughly screwed her?

Narrow whips of air seared her throat as she tried to take in

27

enough oxygen to remain clear-headed. He must have realized how close she was to panic, because he withdrew and set her down gently. Her bare feet hit the cold stone floor – what kind of hospital had stone floors? – and her hospital gown dropped down to cover her.

'Where am I?' she croaked.

'You're in a hospital.' The dream doctor who'd just given her the most pleasant injection of her life guided her toward the bed with a firm grasp on her elbow. As she walked, the indisputable proof of their union dripped down her thighs, and why did it tingle, sensitizing her skin so that she wanted to rub it all over? 'You were injured during a fight with a Cruentus demon.'

She jerked out of his grip. 'How do you know about demons? What kind of hospital is this? Who *are you*?'

'Have a seat. I'll explain everything.'

'Oh, no. Don't give me that soothing bullshit tone.' She backed away as he moved toward her, trying to herd her toward the bed. He towered over her, eclipsing the crimson-tinted overhead lights. 'Stay away from me.'

'Tayla, you need to listen to me.' His voice morphed into something deep and ominous, rattling what was left of her nerves.

The door opened, and someone, no, some*thing* dressed in scrubs, stepped inside. 'Doctor,' it said through a mouthful of tusks, 'you're needed in the ER.'

Demon. Cold sweat broke out on her skin. 'What in God's name is this place?'

She whirled back to Eidolon and saw his eyes as they had been in her dream. Only it hadn't been a dream. The room spun as realization bitch-slapped her. 'You,' she rasped. 'You're a demon, too.'

He moved in a blur, and the prick of a needle stung her arm. Suddenly, she couldn't move, couldn't so much as scream as monsters surrounded her, strapped her to her bed.

Inside her head, though, the screams wouldn't stop.

28

THREE

༄

Darkness fell like a guillotine blade, severing Tayla and her part-ner from the daylight. Somewhere nearby, a dog barked, and gunfire erupted, probably another gang drive-by, but Tay and Janet weren't cops, and they didn't care. Hell, even the cops wouldn't give a rat's ass. This part of New York City was a third-world country at war, and the cops had long ago gone U.N. and with-drawn from the battle.

Standing next to the sewer access, Tay fingered her jacket pocket where she kept her stang, an S-shaped, dual-ended blade, each end coated with a different metal. The gold side made short work of demons like the Cruentus they were hunting, and she wanted the weapon at the ready.

'Looks clear,' Tay said, and Janet lifted the heavy grating.

With a final glance into the night, they hurried down the ladder into tunnels ripe with the acrid stench of decay and waste. There were no lights, but the darkness posed no problem, not for any Aegis Guardian.

Out of habit – habit in the face of danger – Janet played with her necklace, a crucifix marked on the back with an etching of the Aegis shield. Tayla wiggled her pinky ring out of the same habit, but the protective talisman wouldn't help her in this instance; her night vision had always been exceptional even without magic.

She crouched at the base of the ladder, touched her fingers to a dark smear on the tunnel's brick wall. 'Blood,' she whispered. 'It's here.'

The sound of blades clearing their leather wrist housings echoed through the narrow passageway. Tayla held her spiked blade in one hand and her stang in the other as they followed the trail of blood. She ignored the squishing noises beneath her feet, ignored the rats and the sound of moisture dripping down the walls. Her focus narrowed to take in only the sights, sounds, and smells that would lead her to her target. Her eyesight sharpened, her ears tamped down her internal noises and picked up the most delicate sounds, like those of the cockroaches skittering behind the walls.

Down here, she was the predator.

Tay lived for this. Lived for the high, the rush of adrenaline that coursed through her veins during the hunt.

Lived for this because hatred was all that kept her heart beating.

Shadows shifted inside a tunnel ahead, and the hairs on the back of Tay's neck prickled. In front of her, Janet sank into a crouch. Tay flattened herself against the brick and eased next to the opening.

Heart pounding, she wheeled into the tunnel arch.

Three red eyes met hers. Two rows of sharp teeth flashed. The demon's high-pitched screech blasted through her brain, and son of a bitch, the thing wasn't a Cruentus.

'Croucher demon,' she shouted back to her partner, who cursed and surged next to her.

'What, you can't find a house to terrorize, you ugly piece of shit?' In one smooth motion, Janet drew an air claw from her belt pouch and launched it.

The demon shrieked, clutched the throwing star buried deep in one eye, hatred burning in the remaining two. Tay worked her stang into a spin that would sever the Croucher's head, but motion in her peripheral vision brought her around. Janet tumbled awkwardly through the air and landed in a crumpled heap. In the space where she'd stood, the Cruentus demon growled deep in its skeletal chest.

'Not. Nice.' Tay hurled her spiked blade backward even as she lunged forward with the stang. She didn't need to look to know the spike had buried itself in the Croucher's throat.

One down, one to go.

The gold razor edge of her stang found its target and sliced a thin line across the Cruentus's stomach. The thing stumbled back, one hand covering its belly like it expected its guts to fall out. She spun, struck it in the pelvis with a roundhouse kick.

The creature slammed into an access ladder. Tay moved in, stang whirling. The Cruentus's claws lashed out, catching Janet in the shoulder.

'Ow! Bastard.' Janet brought her favorite weapon, a hatchet, from beneath her jacket. The demon sidestepped her attack, and the blade landed only a glancing blow to its shin.

'Hey, asshole!' Tay charged, but she drew short with a cry. Her right leg tingled, the muscles turned to water. Her hand went numb, and her stang clattered to the ground just before her body landed in the slime.

Not again. Not now!

'Tayla!' Janet screamed as the demon's thorny fingers closed around her throat.

Gnashing her teeth, Tay dragged herself toward the demon, which was shaking her partner like a terrier with a rat.

'Hey!' Tayla's fingers closed around a jagged chunk of brick. 'You disgusting sonofabitch, look at me.'

She hurled the brick with her good arm, and a sharp edge crunched into the back of its head. Black fluid spurted from the *wound. Snarling, it released Janet and turned, its eyes little more than orange balls of rage.*

'Whore,' it rasped. 'Filthy human whore. I'll feast on your organs, suck them out through your cunt while you scream.' It slipped its narrow tongue between its fangs and slurped obscenely at the air.

'Men,' she muttered, stretching for the stang she'd dropped. 'Doesn't matter what species, you always make everything about sex.'

Baring its teeth in a smile that wrinkled its blunt, hairless snout, it picked up Janet's hatchet. 'Not sex. Death.'

It swung. The sound, the dull thud of a blade sinking into flesh tore through Tayla like a werewolf's claws. Janet's head, nearly separated from her body by her own hatchet, lolled to one side, caught against her shoulder only by a strip of sinewy muscle and skin. Surprise flashed in Janet's blue eyes, and then the cloudy mist of death settled in them.

'Janet! No!'

'No!'

Tayla's eyes flew open. Terror swept through her in a series of quakes. Sweat dripped down her forehead and into her hair as she took in the hospital equipment, the darkened, cool room. She was safe.

No, not safe. After the Cruentus killed Janet, it had attacked her, landed her in some sort of facility run by demons. She'd been patched up. Bathed. *And, oh, God.*

She'd had sex with a demon.

Tayla swallowed bile and tried to keep her stomach from heaving. She needed to shower. And douche. Maybe sterilize her skin by burning it off.

Not that she could do any of those things, seeing how she was chained to a bed and could have been for days as far as she knew.

She made a fist, wiggled her toes. At least function had returned.

But for how long? The episodes had been occurring more frequently, had gotten Janet killed and had nearly done the same for Tayla.

Next time, she might not be so lucky.

'Good evening.' A petite blonde woman in godawful fuchsia scrubs stood next to the bed. How she got there without Tayla hearing, she had no clue. 'You look better than you did when you came in, what with all the blood and bite marks and Cruentus bits splattered all over. And you really should rethink the red leather. It clashes with your hair.'

'The red hides the bloodstains, and who the hell are you? The fashion police?' Her voice sounded scratchy, unused.

The air-headed twit shook her head as if Tay had been serious. 'Nurse Allen. I brought food, but you can't eat until Dr. Eidolon removes the restraints.' She smiled, revealing shiny fangs. 'Obviously, the restraints are necessary, seeing how your kind are merciless murderers and all.'

Tayla stared. 'Pot, meet kettle.'

'Thanks, Nancy. I've got it. Go home. We'll see you tomorrow.' The masculine voice shivered through Tayla like a forbidden pleasure. Vodka for the alcoholic. Cheesecake for the dieter. Orgasm for the monk. 'Hello, Tayla.'

'Hey, Dr. Evil.' She didn't look. What if she'd dreamed up his good looks? What if he had horns, hooves, and porcupine quills?

Nancy's bubbly laughter followed her out the door, and what kind of vampire chatted and giggled like a brain-dead cheerleader? Didn't really matter, though. The vamp would die in a rain of embers and ashes just like any other bloodsucking fiend. Tay just wished the remains weren't so greasy. Washing that crap out of clothes was a bitch.

But then, such was the life of a member of The Aegis, the unsung protectors of the world. The secret guardians of humanity. The slayers of demons and things that went bump in the night.

And all the other bullshit that was supposed to make Tay feel warm and fuzzy, but that only reminded her how she had nothing better to do with her life than hang out in monster-infested alleys that smelled like rancid piss.

After all, it was hard to find a legitimate job when you had an arrest warrant for murder hanging over your head.

Then again, even if she had a perfect record and a freakin' doctorate to her name, nothing would change. She'd still spend her nights patrolling the New York City underground she knew more intimately than anyone should, searching for evil filth to squash.

Evil filth like the doctor whose footsteps grew louder as he approached. She closed her eyes, still unable to face him. It wasn't until she felt the head of the bed jack up that she dared to peek.

Chills shivered over her skin. Dressed in green scrubs, he was just as she'd remembered, all muscle and angular features and brown eyes that flashed with intelligence and confidence. That wicked tattoo on his right arm shimmered, its sharp, curved lines blurring when she looked too closely.

She'd fought demons for eight of her twenty-four years, but never had she encountered one whose devastatingly powerful presence filled her with a sense of awe. It was as though he was pure sexual energy contained in a wrapper of smooth, bronze skin, and damn, it wasn't fair that a demon should be so cover-model handsome.

Too bad she'd have to ruin his looks with the bruising end of her right hook.

'I'm going to release your wrist restraints so you can eat. Don't try to fight me. The hospital is under the protection of an antiviolence spell.'

Sure. She waited until he'd freed her hands. Then she smiled. And took a swing at his jaw.

Pain nearly sheared off the top of her skull. She fell back, clutching her head with both hands.

'I warned you.'

'My ass,' she groaned. 'You wanted me to try something.'

34

'Maybe a little.'

When the pain dimmed, she narrowed her eyes at him.

'That's why I'm still alive, isn't it? The spell. You probably want to kill me but can't.'

He shrugged and marked something on her chart. 'I also want to be inside you again, so I wouldn't read too much into my instincts.'

She nearly choked on her own saliva. 'I could have done without the reminder.'

Did he mean what he'd said? About being inside her? Not that it was a possibility, because clearly, she had to kill him at the first available opportunity.

'Oh,' he said, his voice rumbling through parts that had no business being rumbled, 'you remembered all on your own.' He set aside the clipboard and put his long, slender fingers to the pulse in her wrist. 'You didn't come, but you wanted to. And I wanted to make you come. Wanted to feel you spasm around me.'

His eyes darkened as he took in her face, her throat, her breasts beneath the hospital gown. 'I can still smell what we did. Smell your desire.' He pressed more firmly against the skin of her wrist, where her pulse throbbed harder with every word. 'I can *feel* your desire.'

So could she, in the ache between her legs, the sweet pinch of puckered nipples, the rush of moisture that funneled through her sex.

'I wonder,' he purred, 'how your desire would taste.'

Good God. The effect he had on her, the way he made her crave things she'd never wanted ... it shouldn't be happening. Not only was the man an enemy, but the lust itself ... it shouldn't be there at all. Sex had always been a weapon, a tool, the only form of currency that never ran out. Sex with a man was certainly not recreational. The times she'd tried to make it so had ended in anger, frustration, and emptiness. She faked orgasms like everyone else faked laughter at dumb jokes.

'Stop touching me,' she said a little too breathlessly, 'or the only thing you'll be tasting is my fist.' An idle threat, given the stupid spell, but threatening him made her feel better.

To her relief, he released her and stepped back, his arousal straining the front of his scrubs. Averting her gaze, she reached for the ankle restraints, but he shook his head.

'Leave them. Your hands are free so you can eat, but you aren't at liberty to walk around.'

'Okay, Hellboy,' she said. 'What if I have to go to the bathroom?'

'A nurse will assist you.' His voice pitched low with dark amusement. 'Unless you'd rather I helped.'

'Thanks, I'll pass.' She dragged her fingers through her tangled hair and cast a longing gaze at the food the vamp nurse had brought. 'Do I get to eat, or what?'

He handed her the tray, and even though her stomach growled at the sight of what appeared to be an egg salad sandwich, she hesitated. 'What kind of eggs are in this?'

'Could be anything. Rusalka. Harpy. Bone devil.'

She had a feeling he was messing with her, but it didn't matter. She couldn't take a bite. Not until she asked the vital questions that had been bugging her since she woke up.

'So, uh, where am I, exactly? And what do you plan on doing with me?'

'You're at Underworld General Hospital. As you can probably guess, we specialize in nonhuman medical care. Our location is secret, so don't ask.'

'UGH? Your hospital is called, "*ugh*"? Oh, that's precious.'

Doc Humorless gave her a flat stare, and she sighed. 'How did I get here?'

'Ambulance. We have our own.'

'Of course you do.' She wished she could remember even the smallest detail of the trip here, but her mind was a black hole. 'What about the Cruentus? Is it dead?'

36

'He'll be released tonight.'

Rage burned like acid in her belly. 'It killed my friend.'

'Your colleagues have killed many of mine,' he shot back.

She ground her teeth and forced herself to take control of her emotions. Truthfully, she'd never considered Janet a friend – she'd learned long ago to avoid attachments to people who risked death daily, but if he wanted to talk about loss, she could go toe to toe – or hoof, paw, whatever he had – with him. But right now, she had to play smart. And smart meant intel. She just hoped Guardians had already found Janet's body. The thought of an Aegis warrior rotting in a sewer made the acid in her gut bubble.

'So where do you get training for something like this? Because I'm thinking a lot of you wouldn't blend real well in anatomy class.'

His pager went off, but he ignored it. 'Anyone who is human or can pass as human trains in human medical schools. I'm a medical doctor with a degree from Harvard, for example. We train all others ourselves.'

He brushed his fingers over the medical symbol on the pocket of his shirt as though making sure what he'd said was true. At least, she thought it was a medical symbol. The familiar winged staff encircled by two serpents had been replaced by a sinister-looking dagger. The vipers wrapped around the blade looked ready to strike. And the feathered wings had been replaced by batlike, tribal wings in a pattern similar to those on his arm. She frowned, because she'd seen it before . . .

His necklace. His pendant matched the design on his scrubs.

'It's a modified caduceus,' he said, and she tore her gaze away from the design because now the image of the silver blade caressing her skin while he'd been inside her was burned into her brain. 'My youngest brother designed it. We couldn't very well use a human medical symbol.'

'I still don't understand how demons can get into medical

37

school. Don't you have to have good college grades, or hey, here's a novel idea – proof that you're human?'

'Not everyone who looks human is, Tayla. Friends in high places can arrange anything. Including getting demons who didn't grow up in human society into med school.'

The idea that demons had come together to do something so organized and not blatantly evil blew her mind. Almost enough to make her forget that he hadn't answered her second question. Almost.

'And? What about me? You just going to keep me tied to the bed as your personal sex toy?'

'I should point out that *you* begged *me* for sex. Not the other way around.'

There he went with the unnecessary reminders again.

'And what? You couldn't resist the injured, weakened human having a sexy dream?'

Something in his gaze went all smoldering and hot, and her body answered with an inappropriate return of heat. 'Call it a peculiarity of my species. I couldn't resist your scent. You had a need. I responded.'

'But you didn't fulfill it.' A cruel blow, meant to injure since she had no other way to do so, but he merely frowned, looking troubled.

'Could have something to do with your biology. I could run tests ... try again ...'

'No!' She wondered if his apparently keen sense of smell would pick up the odor of her failing deodorant. She knew why she hadn't climaxed, but she wasn't about to share. 'Just answer my question. What are you going to do with me?'

He finally glanced at his pager and then back at her. 'Some of my colleagues want to take you elsewhere and torture you until you talk.' The way he said it, all calm and matter-of-fact, frightened her more than the actual words did. 'I'd rather they didn't do that. I worked too hard to save you.'

Tay poked at her mystery egg sandwich, knowing she wouldn't eat now. 'Yeah, I can see how torturing and killing me after all your efforts would be a bummer.'

'Then give me something, slayer.'

'And what? You'll let me waltz out the front doors?'

'I'll make sure no one tortures you.'

'If you think I'm going to say one word about The Aegis, you're on crack.' She looked down at her hand. 'Where's my ring?'

'Consider it a partial payment on your hospital bill.'

'You ... bastard,' she sputtered. 'That ring has sentimental value.'

Upon joining The Aegis, every Guardian chose a piece of jewelry – rings, watches, necklaces, anything personal – to have imbued with magical enhancements, and her ring had belonged to her mother.

'Much of what The Aegis took from me had sentimental value.'

Great. Just great. If the enemy learned how the sorcery attached to her ring worked and what gifts it bestowed upon the human wearer, demons could find a way to neutralize the Aegis magic.

Clenching her fists, she cursed the antiviolence spell. 'I'm not telling you anything.'

'Tell me about your parents.'

She blinked, caught off-guard by the change of subject. 'Why?'

'If you won't give me anything about The Aegis, tell me something about yourself. What can it hurt?'

Surely it was a trick, but she didn't see the harm in discussing people who no longer existed. 'I never knew my dad. My mom died when I was sixteen.'

'Did you ever see your father? Pictures, maybe?'

'What the hell kind of question is that? And not that it's any of your business, but no. My mom never even gave me a name.'

Tayla doubted her mom had known the guy's name. Tay had been born addicted to heroin, so her old man could have been one of any number of losers her mom screwed while doped up.

Hellboy looked thoughtful, as if what she'd said had been fascinating. He must not have a life beyond patching up other evil demons and boinking human patients.

'How did your mom die?'

Memories she'd battled for years twisted and rolled like a living thing inside her head. She didn't bother to tamp down the rage. The bitterness tasted too good, and she needed the reminder of why she hated this man. 'She was killed,' Tay said. 'By a demon.'

ଓ୬

Nancy Allen had no intention of taking the life of the man standing at the junction of a shadowy sidewalk and a dark alley, even though he deserved death for being so stupid. His expensive trench coat, slacks, and dress shoes all but screamed, 'Rob me, beat me, and then stab my liver.'

No, she wouldn't kill him. The Vampire Council imposed strict guidelines regarding the butchering and disposal of humans, as did the councils for most demon species, and though the rules allowed her one kill per month, she hadn't killed in several.

Perhaps her reluctance to take lives had something to do with the fact that she'd been a nurse since before she turned vamp. Or maybe it was because she rarely achieved the high her kind experienced at the moment of death.

She simply didn't have an addictive personality, as long as chocolate didn't count.

Even when she had killed, the victims had been woman-abusing scumbags and child molesters who deserved to die. Now, *that* gave her a high.

Unfortunately, she rarely dined on scumbags anymore. They had a tendency to drink or do drugs, and ingesting either left her dizzy for days. Smokers were the worst; their blood tasted nasty and gave her migraines.

Her intended victim tucked his hands in his coat pockets and watched the traffic light two blocks away, probably expecting a ride. He looked as if he might be heading to one of the upscale Manhattan hangouts where the electric-blue drinks cost more than she'd made in an entire month as a human nurse.

Nancy smiled and moved toward him, let her hips sway in her tight hunting dress, the classy red one that showed lots of skin and attracted both men and women. She'd changed out of her scrubs before she left the hospital, as per policy, though she didn't usually dress to kill.

She giggled at her own wit, suddenly glad she'd decided to catch her own snack tonight instead of raiding the hospital's blood bank. Doc E didn't mind if staffers tapped a bag every once in a while, but she'd already sucked down two units of A-neg this week because she'd been too lazy to hunt.

'Are you waiting for a cab?' she asked, and her snack-to-be turned, startled. 'I called for one an hour ago, and it never showed up. I have a very important party to get to.'

He watched her through narrowed eyes. Maybe he wasn't as stupid as she'd thought. He was good-looking, though ... chin-length brown hair, full lips, five-o'clock shadow. Maybe she'd do him while she fed from him. Shade wasn't always available for a rendezvous in the hospital's supply closet, and Wraith acted as if she had a disease.

Now, Doc E ... she'd pay to wrap her legs around that brother. Too bad he was a freak of nature, probably the only Seminus demon in history who didn't bang everything he touched. As far as she knew, he took his pleasures outside the hospital, because no one on staff admitted to screwing him or catching him screwing anyone else.

The man raked his gaze over her body, and she sensed him relax, though a low-pitched, unclean energy buzzed in the air around him. This one might be a Dark Soul, a killer of his own kind. A serial murderer, maybe a sociopath. His dark energy wasn't strong; he hadn't killed another human yet, but someday he would.

41

Perhaps she would dispatch the man, after all. Do humanity a favor.

'You can share my ride if you let me buy you a drink.' He stepped closer, touched her elbow.

'I'd like that.'

Glancing over his shoulder behind him, she took note of the passing vehicles, the people down the street. None paid any attention. Mouth watering, she shoved him into the alley, slammed him against the building wall. He grunted and tried to wrench his hand free of his coat pocket.

Her fangs ached, throbbed in time with the pulse in his jugular. She went up on her toes, sank her canines deep into his neck, and waited for him to stop struggling against her superior power.

The sharp sting of a needle in the back of her neck came as a total surprise. So did the knee to the groin.

The dark-souled one yanked her head away from his throat and hurled her to the pavement. Weakness turned her limbs to noodles, leaving her at the mercy of the man who crouched next to her, rage burning in his eyes.

'Filthy bloodsucker.' He reached up, put pressure to the bite wounds in his throat, and if her heart hadn't already been shriveled, the sight of his ring, turned so she could see an Aegis shield etched into the band, would have done the job. 'Do you know what people will pay for vampire parts? Bitch, it's time to reap what you have sown.'

He smiled, and for the first time since becoming a vampire, Nancy knew terror.

FOUR

❧

On the surface, Eidolon wasn't opposed to torture. Most demons weren't. Besides, his former career had demanded a certain amount of pain-giving, though it had been his duty to make sure the individual on the receiving end actually deserved the pain.

And really, he could respect torture as an art form – a skilled master could keep his subject alive indefinitely. Someone trained in medical sciences knew how to inflict the maximum amount of pain with the maximum amount of effectiveness.

So yeah, on a superficial level, he could appreciate his colleagues' discussion. Deep down, though, the part of him that had built UG from concept to the third-wing lava bath would rather see a body heal than be slowly taken apart.

'I have the perfect place to torture the Aegi scum,' Yuri said, kicking up his feet onto the break room couch. 'My basement is extremely uncomfortable.'

Eidolon couldn't agree more. He'd seen the basement in Yuri's three-story Suffern home, and while he hadn't been shocked to learn of the shapeshifting hyena's fondness for BDSM, he had been surprised at the size and contents of the dungeon.

'You wouldn't want to get blood all over that shiny rubber floor.'

'It hoses off.'

Blaspheme, a False Angel who truly enjoyed her ability to fool humans into thinking she was the real thing, shoved Yuri's feet aside so she could sit, and then took a sip of the iced tea in her hand. 'So, Yuri, how often do you have to wash your floors?'

'Two or three times a week. It's not always blood. Petroleum jelly, honey, urine ...'

Eidolon folded his arms over his chest and braced a hip on the snack counter. 'Nice.'

Yuri shrugged. 'The females are almost always willing.'

'The slayer won't be.'

'That's the point. I can make her talk. A few hours of hanging from my razor cuffs while I flog her will have her spilling her guts.' He grinned, revealing slightly elongated canines. 'Which will also hose off the floor.'

A low growl brought Eidolon's gaze around to the doorway, where Wraith stood, his eyes burning gold. 'No one told me about the staff meeting.'

Yuri didn't spare Wraith a glance. 'Because you aren't staff, phlegmwad.'

'This isn't a formal meeting, Wraith,' Eidolon told him, before his brother could go off on their chief of surgery.

Dressed in low-slung jeans and a Jimmy Buffet T-shirt, Wraith bared his fangs and stalked into the break room, and Eidolon knew his anger had nothing to do with feeling left out of a staff meeting.

'You aren't going to torture the Aegi.' Wraith grabbed a Styrofoam cup and reached for the coffee pot.

'For once, I'm with my brother,' Eidolon said. 'We don't need to torture her for information. We can turn her loose, watch her.'

More than watch. Touch, take, taste. The thought blasted through his brain, along with images of Tayla's naked body sliding against his. He'd move inside her, deep, hard, and she'd find her release if he had to spend hours getting her there.

His failure with her ate at him, ripped into his most basic

instincts and told him to try again, to take her over and over until there was no doubt that the other day was a fluke.

Gods, he was *losing it.*

'So that's your idea? Spy on her?' Yuri rolled his eyes, black marbles spinning in their sockets. 'Yawn.'

'That'll take too long,' Blas said. 'Yuri has these thorny flails . . . ' She shivered, and Eidolon caught the scent of lust, which made his own ramp up a notch. 'Let's just say that fragile human skin won't stand up to them.'

Wraith hurled his fresh cup of coffee into the sink, splattering it on the walls and counters. 'You two can beat yourselves into pulps all you want, but you are not torturing the woman. Kill her outright or let her go, but no burning of limbs or peeling of skin or hanging from hooks. We clear?'

Yuri bounded to his feet, nearly knocking Blaspheme's glass out of her hand. 'Who made you chief of staff? You need to shut the fuck up and go back to being a gofer.'

The writing on the walls began to shimmer and pulse. Had it not been for the Haven spell, the room would have erupted in fists and claws. Instead, Wraith collected himself, his hands clenching reflexively even as he smiled. 'E, did you tell them she's half-demon?'

'She's *what*?'

'A half-breed,' Wraith drawled. 'You know, one parent is human, the other is demon? Dickhead.'

Yuri shot Eidolon a confused glance. 'Aegi are human.'

'That's what we've always assumed. But I don't think she knows.' Yesterday, Eidolon had intended to tell her, before her revelation about her mother being killed by a demon. At that point, mentioning that her father might have been a demon as well didn't seem prudent. 'She'll know soon enough. The demon DNA is taking over. She'll need our help to survive. We can wait until she comes to us. Take her while she's weak and bring her over to our side. Having a spy inside The Aegis would be invaluable.'

Yuri considered that for a moment, then shook his head. 'Our people are dying, being cut up by some barbaric butcher. The Aegis is involved. We can't wait.' His eyes glazed, his thin lips stretched into a toothy grin, and Eidolon once again caught the odor of lust, this time musky and bitter. 'The slayer will look good in chains. Helpless. Bleeding . . . '

Wraith's irises went gold again, and Eidolon alone knew why. Nearly eighty years ago, Wraith had been tortured nearly to death, a fate their sire hadn't escaped.

Their father, by all reports half-insane, had been made to pay for his obsession with Wraith's mother, for impregnating her during her transition from human to vampire and holding her captive until she gave birth.

Wraith had paid for their father's transgressions as well, and some would say that in comparison, their father had gotten off easy. Eidolon and Shade *knew* their father had gotten off easy. They'd been the ones to put Wraith back together, literally, after finding him strung up by vampires in a Chicago warehouse they'd been led to by Wraith's distress, which Shade, Roag, and Eidolon had felt like a homing beacon.

If only they'd found him sooner. But Shade, Eidolon, and Roag had found each other years earlier, had been content to wait for Wraith to come to them if he wanted to. Had Eidolon known the reason Wraith hadn't come to New York was that his own mother had held him prisoner until he broke out of his cage at twenty, Eidolon would have gone to him. Instead, Wraith had gone on the run until the vampires caught up with him in Chicago, and by then, it was too late.

Before the threats began, Eidolon dragged his brother into the hall.

'E, don't let them take her.'

'I won't.'

'Let me put her down. I'll do it now.'

'No,' he snapped, and then, aware that his brother was offering mercy, not getting off on killing, Eidolon took a calming breath. 'I meant what I said. We can use her.'

Wraith brushed his shoulder-length hair back from his face with a sharp, impatient shove. 'Bro, in case you hadn't noticed, everyone in this hospital is ready to either string her up or slit her throat, so whatever you do, it had better happen fast.'

☙

The door to Tayla's room flew open. Hellboy stalked inside, looking unfairly sexy – and human – in tan cargo pants and a black button-down shirt that hung loose at the waist and clung to his broad chest to reveal sharply defined pecs.

'You're being discharged.' He tossed a folded set of green scrubs into her lap.

'What, no hello?'

His expression tight, he freed her wrists from the restraints. 'We don't have time.' The ankle restraints popped loose with a deft flick of his fingers. 'Get dressed.'

She glanced down at the scrubs. 'What happened to my clothes?'

'Cut off.'

'Crap.' The Aegis issued an allowance for battle garb, but the next sum wouldn't come for another four months and she was down to the dregs.

She eased off the bed, her stiff muscles protesting with twinges of pain. The only exercise she'd had for – days? hard to tell when there were no windows – had been to shuffle in chains to the bathroom to bathe or brush her teeth, and her body was telling her all about it. She didn't bother asking him to turn around while she dressed; she'd never been modest, and besides, he'd seen – and touched – pretty much every inch of her body, inside and out. For his part, Hellboy watched with such intensity that she finally snapped as she tugged the pants up over her bare ass.

'Like what you see?'

If she thought she could shame him into looking away, she'd been dead wrong. His gaze snapped up to hers. 'Yes.'

'I swear, I've never met any demon as annoying as you are.'

'You haven't met my youngest brother.'

'Oh, good. There are more of you to kill.' She tied the drawstrings on her pants. 'Speaking of which, where are my weapons?'

'Do you truly believe we'd return the tools you use to slaughter us?'

Yeah, dumb question, and man, were her bosses going to be pissed at the loss. 'Did you cut off my boots, too?'

'They were destroyed. You'll go barefoot.'

'What about my ring?'

'I told you—'

'Yeah, yeah. I'd so sue you if this was a human hospital,' she muttered. She didn't need the ring for the powers it bestowed – she had great hearing and night vision without it, and she'd always possessed a natural and rare ability to see through the invisibility cloak that prevented average humans from seeing the demons among them. But dammit, she didn't want demons keeping anything that had been her mother's.

'Hurry up.'

Reluctantly, she followed him out of the room and down the hall.

The same black floors and graffiti-scarred gray walls she'd had in her room were everywhere, except that out here, deep drains ran along either side of the corridor, and every so often they passed an iron cage or a stretcher. Nearby, the steady beeping of medical equipment droned; somewhere else, someone or something screeched over the grating sound of metal on metal. Tayla suppressed a shudder. If Castle Dracula screwed a hospital, this would be the bastard offspring.

'Where are we going?'

'Parking lot.'

'Parking lot?' Sounded so normal.

'You were expecting to ride out on a river of fire? On hell-hounds, maybe?'

Heat seared her cheeks, because that was exactly what she'd been thinking. 'No.'

'We do have means for regular patients to leave, but the exit points are all in territory unfriendly to you, so I'm taking you home.'

'In a car?'

'Only because my flaming chariot is in the shop.'

'You don't have to be such a smartass.' She paused to gaze at a row of skulls lining the walls, some suspiciously human in appearance, others clearly demon, the bony protrusions and wicked teeth hinting at dozens of different species. 'How do you keep this place hidden from humans?'

'I'll tell you if you tell me how The Aegis keep their headquarters hidden from demons.'

'Nice try.'

A Sora demon nearly ran into them as she rounded a corner. Eidolon grasped Tayla's elbow and spoke into her ear, deep and low. 'You need to be quiet now. Look miserable.'

Miserable. No problem. Besides, the intensity in his voice warned her not to argue, and she had little choice but to trust him.

Trust a demon. The thought made her want to hurl.

The Sora's sangria-colored skin flushed even darker, becoming dried-blood black as she gazed up at Eidolon, ignoring Tayla in favor of batting her spiky lashes. 'I'd say I'm sorry, doctor,' she purred, 'but I'd be lying if I said I had not wanted to run into you.'

Her tail whipped like a playful cat's around her feet, and before Hellboy could answer, she sauntered away, her species one that had always reminded Tayla of sexy cartoon devils perched on people's shoulders.

'She was ... interesting.'

'New nurse.'

They hurried along dimly lit hallways made darker by the black floors and populated only by the occasional nurse or maintenance worker, all of whom eyed her warily. Tayla took note of the rooms, some clearly for patients, some very lablike in appearance, and she was more than a little surprised to see a workout area complete with weight benches, treadmills, and punching bags. The hospital was larger than she would have expected.

Finally, as they entered an area of the hospital that went from sterile and weird to sterile and weirder, he slowed, drawing a set of car keys from his pocket.

'Where are we?' She trailed her fingers over the paw of a gargoylelike statue guarding the arched entrance.

'Administrative offices. The parking lot exit is ahead.'

The sound of her bare feet slapping the floor echoed as they walked past the small rooms and cubicles that resembled any other corporate offices she'd seen on TV. She almost expected to see men in suits behind the desks.

'Which one is yours?'

'Ahead on the right. We're going to duck inside.'

They slipped through the doorway, and the door clicked shut behind them. Moving quickly, he closed the blinds on the only window, which faced out into the hall. With a few taps on his computer keyboard, he brought up a video feed of an underground parking lot.

'No one there.' He turned off the monitor. 'We can go.'

'Wait a second,' she said, turning away from him.

Employee parking lot. In a demon hospital.

None of this made sense or connected in her head. She felt as if she'd read a book from cover to cover, but couldn't remember anything but the first and last chapters. The last eight years of her life had been spent learning about demons, how to hunt them, fight them, kill them.

No Aegis lesson had ever prepared her for *Life in the Everyday World of Demon Doctors.* Demons were supposed to live in sewers and fiery netherworlds. They didn't hold jobs. They didn't save lives. They tormented, raped, and killed.

There were exceptions, what The Aegis called *corporate hellspawn,* fiends who masqueraded as humans, living among them to gain power and control over her race, but they were supposedly few and far between. And beneath their human skins, they were ugly beasts, with fangs and claws like any other.

'Slayer?' His voice was close, so close that his breath stirred her hair. How had he moved so silently?

Maybe he hadn't. Things had been happening to her lately ... loss of strength, hearing, sometimes, even, her sense of taste.

Worse, her libido seemed to have careened out of control, was even now firing up in his close proximity. She stepped away, but his hand came down on her shoulder and spun her around.

'What is your deal?' she snapped.

'Why are you stalling?' Suspicious dark eyes drilled into her. 'My brother said your being here could be a trap. Was he right?'

'You're paranoid.'

He pushed her against the wall, held her there with the weight of his body so she could barely wiggle. 'I'm cautious, and not all that patient, so answer the question.'

'I'm not stalling. I'm freaked out. Happy?' She glared up at him. 'And do you get off on manhandling women?'

'I get off on handling them. But you don't get off, do you?'

'Shut up.'

'Do you have a problem with men? What about women?'

At her sudden intake of air, he grinned, the devastating one that made her shiver in pure, feminine appreciation despite what he was. 'You've been with women?'

She shook her head, but her denial lacked conviction. She'd never gone all the way, but her frustration at being inorgasmic with men had driven her to see if her inability to come while being touched by someone else extended to the other sex. A few humiliating minutes with a bisexual Guardian had proved without a doubt that women just didn't do it for her.

'Why the interest in my sex life?'

He dipped his head to her throat and inhaled deeply. 'Your scent is dark, drugging.'

Oh, God. She wriggled to escape his seductive presence, but he tightened his grip. 'You didn't answer me,' she said with as much force as she could muster. 'Why the interest in my sex life?'

Hot breath feathered over the skin of her neck as he spoke, his voice dripping with erotic promise. 'Because you are possibly the only female in history who hasn't achieved orgasm with a Seminus demon.'

'Ah. So your pride is bruised.' And just what was a Seminus demon? She'd thought she knew them all.

'My curiosity is piqued.' He let his hand drift to her flank, where he stroked slowly. His erection, a thick bulge behind his fly, pressed into her belly. She tightened her abs as though to shrink away from it, but the resulting hard flesh on hard flesh only made her more aware of the intimate contact. 'Can you bring yourself pleasure? When you touch yourself, do you come?'

Heat flushed her face. 'That's none of your business.'

'That would be a yes.' His fingers slipped behind her until he was probing her cleft through the thin scrub material. 'I can picture you pleasuring yourself,' he murmured. 'Your legs spread wide, your sex swollen and wet, your fingers coated in your slick arousal. What do you think about when you come, Tayla?'

'Stop,' she choked out.

'Why? Because I make you hot?'

'Because you disgust me, demon.'

He laughed, because he didn't believe her words any more than she did. Pressure between her legs made her squirm, seeking more of his touch while at the same time trying to escape.

'I wonder what disgusts you more, the fact that I'm a demon, or the fact that when I touch you, it doesn't matter.'

Growling, she brought her knee up, but he stepped back in time to avoid a shot to the groin. Pain shot through her head once more, spreading like a spiderweb of cracks in glass until she thought her skull would shatter.

The door creaked open. *'Hell's fucking bells.'*

Hands pressed to her temples, she glanced at the doorway, where a huge guy who looked a lot like Eidolon right down to the arm-length tattoo stood, his face a stony mask. He was bigger than Eidolon, nearly as tall, and his dark hair fell like a thick, wavy curtain to his shoulders. His black uniform, some sort of short-sleeved military BDUs, enhanced his sinister appearance despite the stethoscope around his neck. Or maybe because of it. He looked as if he could take a life as easily as save one.

'Let it go, Shade.'

'Like hell.' Shade closed the door a lot more quietly than she'd have expected, given that the guy looked homicidal. 'What are you doing with her?'

'Wraith already told you, or you wouldn't be here.'

'Dammit, E, I should have been brought in on this decision. It's my hospital, too.' Shade moved toward her, and she instinctively sank into attack position. 'I have a say regarding her disposal, and I say we give her to Yuri.'

Disposal?

Eidolon angled closer to her, putting his big body between her and the other demon. 'Wraith doesn't want that.'

'No, he wants her dead. And since when do you give a shit what Wraith wants?'

'Enough, brother. We'll talk about this later.' Eidolon's words, sharp and edged with menace, fell like a cold blade.

For a moment it appeared that Shade would heed the warning, but then he sniffed the air, nostrils flaring, and his eyes, which she just realized were darker than Eidolon's, turned molten gold. 'Unbelievable. I'd have expected this of Wraith, but you?' He made a harsh sound of disgust. 'I take that back. Even Wraith wouldn't touch an Aegi whore except to put her down.'

Tay didn't have time to take offense. Eidolon's fist connected with the other demon's face. A crack rang out, and blood splattered on the walls. She watched in morbid fascination as the paint absorbed the thick fluid like a thirsty sponge.

'This is my hospital and I have the final word.' Eidolon's jaw clenched so hard she heard the pop of bone. 'No one harms the Aegi but me.'

'The Aegi whore thanks you,' she muttered, but neither demon seemed to hear.

'You are so damned thick-skulled.' Shade touched the back of his hand to his bleeding nose. 'You aren't a Justice Dealer anymore, E. You don't have to play fair.'

The tension seemed to drain out of Eidolon as he looked at the other man. 'You have no idea how much I wish it were that simple.'

'It's the *s'genesis,* isn't it? Messing you up, screwing with your judgment.'

There was a long silence, and then Shade opened his mouth to say something else, but Eidolon cut him off by grasping the side of his brother's face. The hold reminded her of a scene from a *Star Trek* movie she'd once seen, where Spock probed some Vulcan chick's mind. Shade closed his eyes, and a few seconds later, blood stopped trickling from his nose. Feeling like a voyeur, Tayla wanted to look away, but couldn't. How had the two brothers gone from violent bloodshed to some sort of intimate bonding so quickly?

The throbbing in her head finally subsided, and she cleared her throat. 'Hey, is the touchy-feely homo moment over? Because I'm wondering how Minion of Darkness One got to hit Minion of Darkness Two without his skull fracturing.'

Eidolon's mouth twitched in a half-smile. 'I had the Haven spell altered so it didn't apply to me or my brothers.'

'So you guys can beat anyone you want?'

'No. Just each other.'

They came to blows so often that they'd designed an antiviolence spell around their sibling rivalry? 'Growing up in your house must have been fun.' A lot like growing up in foster homes, probably, something she knew way too much about.

Shade stepped back from Eidolon and speared her with a look of pure malice. 'We weren't raised together.' He turned to his brother. 'Nancy didn't show up for work today, and she's not answering her phone. Watch your back.'

Nodding, Eidolon opened the door and ushered Shade out. 'Come on, slayer. I'm taking you home.'

FIVE

ೲ

The trip through the underground parking lot proved uneventful, though once they'd settled into Eidolon's sporty but unassuming silver BMW, he forced some sort of gem into Tayla's hand. Instantly, she went blind, but for some reason, she couldn't drop the stone.

Clammy sweat coated her skin as he started the car. 'What did you do to me?'

'The effect is temporary. I'll take back the artifact once we're clear of the hospital.'

The BMW slid into motion, the smooth ride angling up some sort of steep incline. Once they leveled out, she wondered if they were out of range of the Haven spell, and then decided that pummeling him while she was blind and he was driving might not be the best idea she'd ever had.

Silence descended on the leather-scented interior like a shroud. Tay bounced her legs. Tapped her fingers on the arm rest. Chewed her lip.

Anything to keep her breathing even and steady when all she wanted to do was fight the darkness, silence, and unknown.

'I should have sedated you.'

'I'm sure you'll regret it soon enough.' Like when she drove a blade through his throat at her first opportunity.

'I already do.'

She really wanted to glare at him. 'Anything else you regret? Like saving me? I mean, why didn't you let me die?'

'I'm a doctor.'

'Bullshit.'

'I'm not a doctor?'

'You're a demon, smartass, so you can't tell me that the hypocritical oath applies to you.'

'Hippocratic, and it doesn't.'

'A, I was being sarcastic, and B, you didn't answer my question.'

She felt the vehicle take a sharp turn and sensed that he'd steered a little harder than he needed to. 'I don't owe you any answers.'

'Christ,' she muttered. 'I hate demons.'

His bark of laughter made her jump like a twitchy cat. 'I didn't let you die because doing so would go against hospital policy, which I wrote and can't violate without losing the respect of my staff.'

He sounded as if he might be telling the truth, but then, demons lied as easily as they killed. 'Know what I think?'

'Please,' he said drolly, 'do tell me.'

Ass. 'I think you kept me alive to get information about The Aegis. You'd have been stupid not to.'

'That was part of the original plan, yes. But since you aren't hanging from razor wire in a dungeon with rubber floors that hose clean, you can assume the plan changed.'

His tone told her there was a story behind the rubber floored dungeon, a story she figured belonged shelved alongside the only books she owned, tattered, used copies of Stephen King novels. 'Does the change of plans have something to do with the play-fair-Justice-Dealer thing your brother was talking about?' When he didn't answer, she pressed on, because the dark silence was making her nuts. 'What's a Justice Dealer?'

'My former career. I was raised by the Judicia.'

'Ah. Vengeance demons.'

'Justice demons,' he corrected. 'Vengeance demons can be summoned by anyone, human or demon, to take revenge on another. Justice demons serve only other demons – generally species and breed Councils. And, unlike vengeance demons, Judicium must investigate the complaint before taking action.'

Interesting. Demons had their own cops. 'What happens after the investigation?'

'Sentences are meted out based on the crime. But if we find that the petitioner is in the wrong, it's the accuser who is dealt the punishment.'

'We? So you still do the job?'

'No. Since I'm not Judicium, my JD powers weren't inherited and had to be bestowed upon me as a fledgling.'

'Did you like being a demon cop?'

'Are you always so nosy?'

She shrugged, making her scrub top rasp against the warm leather. 'You got something better to do than talk? Besides drive, I mean.'

There was a brief silence. 'I hated being a Justice Dealer. But because I grew up in a Judicium household, it was expected of me. My species' innate gifts make us naturals in the field of medicine, so as soon as I earned my doctorate, I relinquished my JD powers.'

'Your brother said you weren't raised together. How many brothers do you have?'

'Total? Dead and alive?'

Well, this was awkward. 'Um . . . both?'

'I had forty-four.' Another sharp turn had her sliding in the leather seat. 'I'm down to two. I'm the eldest.'

'Firstborn?'

'No. Twenty were born before I was, but only one survived to *s'genesis*. Roag was killed two years ago. Now, if I take back the artifact, will you shut up?'

'You betcha.'

He pried the stone from her fingers. Bright, noontime sunlight nearly blinded her as effectively as the darkness.

'Obviously, daylight isn't an issue for you.'

'My species isn't heliophobic.'

Of course not, because sensitivity to the sun would be a weakness, and from what she could tell, there was nothing weak about Hellboy. Not with those muscles, that jaw-line, those eyes. Everything about him screamed strength. Intelligence. Sex. Definitely sex. Her body reminded her of that fact with a wave of hot tingles across her skin.

'You got the heater on? It's like a furnace in here,' she muttered, and he smiled as if he knew exactly what had jacked up her body temperature.

She huffed and glanced out the side window, where people were taking advantage of the mild spring day, dining in outdoor cafés and chatting on corners, clueless about the horrors that took place right under their noses. She didn't recognize the part of the city they were in, but she did make note of the street names. His vile hospital couldn't stay hidden. Not from The Aegis.

'Where do you live?' he asked.

'Like I'm going to tell you.'

'Stubborn human. You can think about it on the way.'

'The way where?'

'One of my nurses didn't show up for work today. I'm checking on her.'

'Human?'

'Vampire.'

She kept to herself the thought that maybe a Guardian had cremated the bloodsucker.

Sliding a glance at Hellboy, she wondered if killing him would

59

be as easy as driving a stake through a vamp's chest. Sure, he didn't look weak, but every demon had a vulnerability. Maybe his tattoos were his. The way they snaked around his hard, muscular arm, all the way to his throat ... she remembered how they'd writhed when he was inside her, and yeah, they were part of him. Not inked tattoos, but extensions of his tan skin. Special features were often the heart of a weakness, and she intended to find his.

'What do your markings symbolize?' Before she could stop herself, she reached out and skimmed her fingertip over the clean lines of the top one, an oddly crooked set of scales, on his neck.

A sound broke from deep inside him, a rush of air through slightly parted lips. 'Unless you want me to pull over and take you where you sit, you'd better remove your hand.'

She drew back so fast her elbow clanked against the passenger window.

Gripping the steering wheel hard enough that his knuckles turned white, he brought the vehicle to a smooth stop at a red light. When he spoke, his voice sounded as if his larynx had gone a round with sandpaper. 'It's called a *dermoire*. It's a history of my paternity. The symbol on my throat is my own. The one below it is my father's. The one below that is his father's, and so on, all the way to my fingers. When we meet others of our species, one glance will tell us all we need to know about our relationship to each other.'

The knowledge that he could trace his paternal roots back more than a dozen generations while she didn't even know the name of her father clawed at her. He'd probably grown up all happy in his special little demon family, Mom baking freakin' cookies and Dad teaching him how to ride a bike. Tayla's upbringing had been less rosy, sleeping on cots if she was lucky, getting secondhand toys for Christmas ... if she got a toy at all, spending most of her days hungry and hiding from drunks.

Oh, yeah. Way to feel sorry for herself. Christ, she hadn't felt sorry for herself in years, and she wasn't about to let a demon change that. She wouldn't let anyone change that. Her survival depended on her ability to lock out the past and people. No one was getting in, especially not Doctor Evil over there in the driver's seat.

He made a left turn, making those tats undulate on ropy muscle. If he were human, she'd run her tongue along every one of them . . .

Focus, Tay, focus. Well, the tats were the focus, but not like that. 'So, um, you were born with the markings?'

'Yes, though my individual symbol didn't appear until I reached my first stage of sexual maturity.'

'First stage?'

He studied her with a cool, measuring gaze, probably trying to decide how much to reveal. 'There are two,' he said finally. 'The first hits around the age of twenty. The second, *s'genesis,* occurs during our hundredth year.'

It's the s'genesis, *isn't it? Messing you up, affecting your judgment.*

So that was what Shade had been talking about. Which made Hellboy three-quarters of a century older than her.

'What's your true form?'

'This is it.'

She gaped. 'Your species looks like Playgirl models? It's not fair.'

'What's not?'

'You. You're a demon. Evil should look . . . evil. Ugly. Wouldn't hurt if you smelled bad, either.' Heck, she'd be happy if he just didn't smell *good.* The air around him smelled faintly of spiced dark chocolate and man, making her mouth water and her libido kick into high gear.

'I'm not exactly evil.'

She snorted. 'All demons are pure evil.'

'What about half-breeds? Are they evil, too?'

'They're abominations that deserve to die the same as any other demon.'

61

He turned and looked at her, wearing a grin that was about as evil as any she'd seen. 'This is going to be fun.'

⌒

Doctor Gemella Endri was up to her elbows in condoms.

Which was what made hearing the man of her dreams' voice so incredibly mortifying.

'Gem!'

She extracted herself from a thirty-gallon tub of prophylactics in the back of the ambulance and smiled. Shakily.

Kynan Morgan was crossing the street, his easy, powerful stride ratcheting her pulse up a notch. Tall and lean, with thick, muscular arms and a broad chest made to crush a woman beneath him, he invited wicked fantasies that didn't stop between the sheets. Gem pictured being with him on the floor. On counters. In pools and hot sulfur baths.

He halted on the sidewalk behind the ambulance and peeled off his sunglasses. He was dressed like always; worn jeans, a brown leather bomber jacket, and combat boots. Another human male, ten years younger than Ky at twenty, maybe, stood next to him.

'Hey.' She gestured to the little yellow baggies filled with condoms and safe-sex pamphlets, hoping her nerves didn't show too much in the way her voice wavered. 'Obviously, it's my day to run the "come prepared" campaign with Judy.'

Judy, the woman in charge of the public service, waved over her shoulder but didn't miss a beat as she finished stuffing a bag. 'Gem is always happy to give up a day off to make sure people on the streets can have protected sex.'

'A noble cause,' Kynan said, and graced her with one of his heart-stopping grins.

God, he was fine. At least six-two, with spiky dark hair and eyes the color of new denim. He filled out his clothes as if they were custom-made for his athletic build, which she'd seen nearly unclothed. He was a regular at the hospital where she interned,

62

Mercy General, where his best friend, Dennis, a man who'd saved his life during his military days, headed the emergency department. Usually, when Kynan came in, it was to have one of his halfway house residents treated, but sometimes he needed a little patch-up work himself.

He was such a good guy to take in street kids, clean them up, and give them a chance in the world. Kynan even smelled good . . . not just the natural, earthy male scent that clung to him, but the pure, fresh rain aroma of someone who was truly . . . decent. She never encountered that in the demon world, and rarely in the human one. Such purity should have repelled her, but instead, it drew her, fascinated her . . . and sometimes, it made her demon half long to corrupt it.

Her demon half could be a real bitch.

'Did you notice that Gem changed her hair?' Judy gave Gem an exasperated look and handed a passerby a baggie of condoms. 'Again.'

Kynan nodded. 'The black and blue is much better than the red.'

'Well, people kept saying I looked like a Goth Raggedy Ann doll.'

He laughed, a rich, deep sound that hit her in every one of her erogenous zones, and Judy sniffed. 'Don't encourage her. Now she looks like a Goth bruise. It's not seemly for a doctor.'

'I think she looks great,' Kynan said, and then winked at Gem. 'Don't let this old biddy talk you out of being who you are.' He shot the old biddy a mischievous look. 'You should take some pointers from Gem. I'll bet you'd look hot in chains and leather.'

Judy blushed. 'You are a such a flirt, Kynan Morgan. Does Lori know that about you?'

'It's why she loves me.' He lit up, as he always did when he talked about his wife, and Gem sighed. His bone-deep loyalty to Lori was one of the most attractive things about him. She couldn't fathom how it would feel to have someone love her like that. Being a half-breed in a world where both humans and demons valued pure blood over all else left her on the lonely outskirts of society.

Even her own parents liked to pretend she was pure demon, and when small things reminded them of her mixed parentage, their unintentionally hurtful comments left her longing for the company of someone who understood.

A commotion at the bus stop up the block snapped her out of her pathetic musings. A man was shouting at the people waiting with him. They were backing up, he was advancing ... and then he turned and looked directly at Gem.

'What choo lookin' at, bitch?' He swaggered toward the ambulance, his loose-limbed gait a theatrical show of arrogance.

'Go back to what you were doing, buddy,' Kynan said, his voice low and soothing, but edged with warning.

The guy whipped out a gun from the waistband of his sweatpants and leveled it sideways at Ky. 'Fuck you, man.'

Gem held her breath. She could handle this, but doing so would reveal secrets best kept that way.

Kynan's pleasant, *let's-deal* expression turned into something deadly and cold. A shiver of both unease and feminine appreciation rippled through her, and she realized that even after knowing him for two years, this was the first time she'd seen the military man he'd once been.

'Give me the gun,' he said, 'and you might walk away from this.'

'I ain't stupid, you motherf—'

Kynan struck, a serpent uncoiling in a lethal blur. The man's shocked curse ended in a grunt as Kynan took him to the pavement, face-down. In a matter of seconds, Kynan was standing over the man, holding the gun, one booted foot crunched down on his neck.

'Call the police,' he said in a honeyed, easy drawl. As though he disarmed lunatics every day.

Gem sprang into action like a seasoned soldier following a superior's command. Geez, she had it bad for him. The cops must have been a block over, because by the time she hung up with the 911 dispatcher, a cruiser was rounding the corner. The cops spent about five minutes taking a report, and then they gathered up the stunned thug and took off.

'You're kinda handy to have around,' Gem said, after the cops were gone, and Judy, her hands shaking visibly as she stuffed condoms into baggies like a robot on an assembly line, agreed with an enthusiastic nod.

Kynan shrugged. 'That guy was so out of it he probably couldn't have pulled the trigger if he'd wanted to.'

He was being modest, but his take-down had probably prevented disaster.

Her cell phone rang with a jaunty jingle. 'One second.' She flipped it open, hoping Eidolon had finally gotten off his ass and called back. She'd left him several messages, though most had been with Wraith, who was about as reliable as a witch doctor's miracle cure. 'Doctor Endri.'

'Hello, Gem.'

The voice froze the fluid in her spine. With forced casualness, she turned away from the others and lowered her voice. 'I told you, no. I'll never help you.'

'Your parents would like you to reconsider. They're begging, in fact.'

The air exploded from Gem's lungs in a painful burst. The ability to speak went with her breath, and for a moment it was all she could do to stand upright.

Shock made her fingers clumsy, and she fumbled the phone, nearly dropping it.

'You bastard,' she whispered. 'What did you do to them? Where are they?'

The line went dead, and she sagged against the ambulance, cold sweat beading on her skin. What now? God, what now?

'You okay, Gem?' Kynan was watching her, concern darkening his eyes to nearly black. 'Anything I can do?'

She pasted on a fragile smile. 'I'm fine. Thank you.' She turned to Judy, whose expression of worry matched Kynan's. 'Can you take me to the hospital so I can pick up my car? I have a family matter to attend to.'

SIX

⁓

Tayla and Eidolon had ridden through the city in silence for half an hour, since she'd grown tired of arguing. Eventually, he made her hold the gemstone artifact again until they arrived at a run-down apartment complex, that, as scroungy as it was, didn't compare to the slum where she lived.

He parked around back, between a rusted-out Gremlin and a lowered El Camino, and gestured for her to get out. She did, her bare feet barely registering the flattened cigarette butts and cracked asphalt as they crossed the parking lot. They entered the building, taking steps down to an area she wouldn't have thought housed apartments. He made her go first, a smart move. It had occurred to her that she could take him from behind and escape, except that if she killed him she'd never learn the location of the hospital.

As they entered the dank bowels of the building, the gurgle of boilers and the smell of mold brought back memories of being homeless and alone, when survival had depended on sleeping in places fit only for rats. She scowled into the darkness lit by a lone, caged bulb at the end of the hall.

'This is the basement.'

'Vampires and apartments with windows don't mix,' he said,

stopping at one of three steel doors. A sensation like ants crawling up her spine made her shiver. She'd always trusted her gut, and her gut told her that something wasn't right. When Eidolon rapped on the door, she instinctively reached for her stang, too late remembering she was unarmed.

'Do a lot of vampires live here?' she asked.

'Do I look like the landlord to the undead?' He knocked again and cursed before testing the knob and finding it locked.

He stepped back, and then, in one smooth, powerful move, he kicked in the door. Metal twisted as though a bomb had gone off, and the door jamb splintered. The strength he must possess to do that ... it was definitely for the best that she hadn't taken him on without a weapon. She'd put her fighting skills up against his any day, but with the strange losses of muscle control that always struck at the most inconvenient times, she wouldn't want to risk an attack on him unless she was sure she had the advantage.

'She'll be pissed if she was just napping.'

Eidolon snorted at that. They entered the apartment, which, though small, proved that vampires weren't all grim and Goth. No, this was worse. The stuff of nightmares.

Shades of purple and yellow assaulted her vision, from the lavender carpet to the baby-duck-colored, fuzzy lamp-shade. Even the walls had been slathered with lemon paint. Christ, the place looked like a Muppet slaughterhouse. The nurse who lived here was truly not right in the head. She deserved to die for her horrible taste in décor alone.

Tayla sidestepped to avoid a particularly vile throw rug. 'What did she do? Skin Barney?'

Eidolon's sexy mouth twitched in a relaxed half-smile, though his movements were nothing but lethal grace as he moved swiftly down the hall. She watched him go, disgusted at herself for admiring how nicely his ass fit in his cargos, but unable to look away until a soft thump drew her attention to the kitchen. Once again, she reached for her stang, clenching her fist in annoyance at its loss. Whatever. She was dangerous without it, and after being held prisoner by demons, she was ready to kick some ass.

A scratching noise got her blood pumping a little faster. She followed the sound to a door just off the lilac-accented cubicle of a kitchen. A muffled moan drifted through the door. Bracing herself for battle, she turned the knob.

The door opened into some sort of dark corridor, a tunnel allowing passage for nightwalkers during the day. Blood smears left a trail from as far as she could see to the door, where a naked, mutilated woman lay at Tay's feet.

The vampire nurse. The bubble-headed one who'd worn the fuchsia scrubs.

The nurse – Nancy – tried to speak, her lips forming words that never made it past the blood gurgling out of her swollen mouth. Her abdomen lay wide open, a gaping hole from her hipbones to her sternum. *Dear God.*

Tay grasped the woman's wrists, bloody stumps with no hands, and dragged her inside. The smell of vampire blood, pungent and metallic, clogged her nose and throat until she nearly gagged.

'Hellboy!'

Nancy curled in on herself with a whimper. Tayla's heart had hardened a long time ago, but now the shell around it cracked at the sight of the undead nurse's suffering. Who would do this, even to a vampire? Who would disembowel her, and sever hands from limbs? Even her teeth ... the vampire canines had been removed.

Eidolon burst into the kitchen. He came to a sudden halt, as though he couldn't process what he was seeing. A heartbeat later, his expression became a savage, hardcore mask of everything she'd ever associated with hell. Death, pain, rage. This was the demon behind the man.

'Get away from her.'

Tayla bristled at the snarled command, but yeah, she got it; she was the enemy even if she hadn't been the one to hurt Nancy.

He crouched beside the vampire, spoke in some language she

didn't know but understood nevertheless. The words were urgent, guttural, straight out of the Demon Dictionary of Cuss. The vamp moaned when he lifted her, carried her to the living room and laid her gently on the Barney pelt.

'Hey, Nancy,' he said, his voice no longer a nasty growl but deep and soothing, the one he'd used on Tayla when she first woke up at the hospital. An appreciation for his dedication and skill had her inching forward to watch as he framed the vampire's face with his hands to keep her from thrashing. 'It's Eidolon. You're safe now.'

Tayla thought she had long ago lost the ability to feel pity for the monsters she hunted, but this ... this threatened to shatter her defenses. The oddness of the emotion and what it meant didn't have time to register before Nancy's lips moved, spilling blood down her chin. Eidolon put his ear to her mouth.

The muscles in his back grew more and more rigid the longer he listened. 'I'm going to help you, Nance. Hold on.' He rapidly ran his hands over her body with gentle efficiency, pausing to probe the edges of the smooth gash in her belly. When she cried out, he drew back.

'I need my medical kit, but I'll be right back,' he said to her, and she shook her head, her eyes going wide with panic. 'It's all right. I'm not going anywhere. Just a few feet, okay?'

Wondering what he was up to, because he hadn't brought a medical bag inside, Tayla watched him fetch a cleaver from the kitchen. He shot her a keep-your-mouth-shut look as he knelt beside Nancy once more, the wicked blade concealed at his thigh.

He tenderly ran a finger across her cheek and then bent, brushed his lips across hers in a gesture so touching that Tayla swallowed a lump of emotion. 'I'm going to make it better, *lirsha*. Close your eyes.'

Nancy relaxed, utter trust softening her expression, and for a moment, her pain seemed to melt away. She did as he'd asked.

The realization of what Eidolon was about to do struck Tayla like a roundhouse kick to the gut, knocking the air from her lungs. 'No,' she gasped, without even knowing why.

In a blur of motion, he brought the knife down on Nancy's throat. Blood exploded in a fine mist as her head separated from her neck. Her entire body flamed and burst into ash. The burning hot dog odor of vamp flambé swamped the room like invisible smoke.

Shoulders slumped, Eidolon hung his head and remained so still Tayla wondered if he breathed. And for a moment, she could almost pretend he was human, mourning over the loss of a loved one. It didn't seem possible that he could love, but there it was, and something inside her wanted to reach out to him. The need to do so, the warm, subtle glow of it, bloomed like a poisonous flower, a terrifying yet beautiful weed to be destroyed before it spread. She'd never reached out to anyone either for help or to offer comfort. Doing so exposed weakness, got people killed.

Eidolon's head snapped up, eyes glowing gold. Silver flashed; he launched the cleaver, impaling it in the wall. Forget surgery. The guy wielded a knife with deadlier skill than any OR required.

Still on his knees, he threw back his head and roared, a furious, raw sound that drove her backward until the backs of her knees struck the couch. Rage and danger emanated from him in scorching waves she could feel on her skin, and the hair on the back of her neck stood up.

Her gaze cut to the knife. Just a few steps . . .

Her hand closed on the hilt; his hand closed on her arm.

'Sonofa—' In an instant, her spine cracked against the wall and his forearm crushed her throat.

'What do you know about this?' She couldn't speak, could barely breathe thanks to his choke hold. 'Tell me!'

He emphasized his last words with more pressure against her windpipe. Fury burned her blood as badly as the lack of oxygen burned her lungs. He'd caught her off-guard, but it wouldn't happen again.

She struck. Hard, fast, in the ribs. A hook to the leg knocked him to the ground. He was up in a flash, and she had to hand it to Hellboy, he had moves.

He swung. She blocked, buried her fist in his gut.

'I do this for a living, asshole, so you don't have a chance.'

As though he hadn't heard, or didn't care, he lunged, and she flew back against the wall again. The whole wall thing was getting old.

'Is The Aegis responsible?' He spun her, took her to the floor. The impact rattled her teeth and made her abdomen throb at the site of her stitches.

'I don't know what the hell you're talking about!' She elbowed his jaw and rolled so she was on top of him, squeezing him between her thighs. 'What's your problem?'

His snarl vibrated through her as he roughly jerked her beneath him, pinning her with his weight. 'My problem is that someone, probably The Aegis, is slicing up my kind and selling their parts in the human and demon magical black markets.'

And that's a problem, why? Probably something she shouldn't say out loud. She wriggled and tested his grip. 'If The Aegis was involved, I'd know. They aren't.'

'That's not what Nancy said.'

'And you believed her? A vampire?'

He watched her, peered so intently into her eyes that she suddenly felt stripped bare of all her thoughts. The sensation was disturbing as hell, and she bucked, trying to dislodge him. When she struck at his face, he pressed down with his body and muscled her arms into place above her head.

'You're a better fighter, little killer, but I'm stronger and you're injured, so don't fuck with me.'

She glared, tempted to spit in his face. She hated being restrained, despised the feeling of helplessness and vulnerability. She especially hated that he was stronger, because they should have been an even match, but in recent weeks she'd lost the freak-ish strength she'd been born with.

'Get off of me.'

'So you can hit me?' he asked. 'I don't think so.'

'You just going to keep me like this forever, then?'

'I should kill you. Here, with no Haven spell to keep me from wringing your neck.'

She had no doubt he meant it, but she'd never backed down from a threat. 'Try it, asshole.'

He watched her, his eyes still glowing gold. Even when he was threatening her, he was hypnotic. She watched right back, slowly becoming aware of how his body pressed down on hers, one thigh between her legs. His muscular chest crushed her breasts, and her scrub top had ridden up so the crisp cotton of his shirt rasped against her stomach.

'How many demons have you slaughtered, Aegi?' he asked softly. 'Have you even kept count?'

She snorted. 'How many humans have *you* killed?'

One dark eyebrow arched. 'None.'

'I don't believe you.'

'Because I'm a demon. So I must kill humans for sport.'

'Pretty much.'

'Your ignorance is disgusting.'

'Everything about you is disgusting.' She tried to pretend that hadn't been as childish as it sounded.

'I could remind you—'

'Don't.'

The gold faded out of his eyes, replaced by the dark chocolate of desire that sucked her in like a whirlpool she couldn't fight. She had to, though, because they were engaged in a war, and her side had to win. That it suddenly didn't feel like a battle didn't escape her notice.

One of his fingers stroked her wrists where he held them over her head, and she wondered if he realized what he was doing. It felt good, much better than it should, considering the situation.

'What are you going to tell your Aegis buddies about my

hospital and what happened to you?' More fingers joined the first to caress the sensitive spot where her palm met her wrist.

'Nothing,' she said smoothly. 'If they find out that I was held by the enemy, they might think I talked, and they'll never trust me again.' Which could be true, but she did have to tell them.

One long swipe of his thumb over a pulse point nearly made her moan. 'And what would they do to you, these *friends* of yours?'

'I don't know. Maybe assign me to research instead of hunting.'

But something niggled at her, because she vaguely remembered another Guardian who had been captured and tortured by a brutal clan of vampires. When he escaped, mutilated and a pint low on blood, he'd gone straight to Aegis HQ.

For days they'd kept him sequestered, and when he finally went out on a routine patrol, he didn't return. Everyone assumed he'd been killed in battle, but Tay hadn't been so certain. What if they'd transferred him, processed him out of The Aegis, or even sent him to the Berlin Sigil to be watched or interrogated? Now that she was in a similar situation, the tiny sliver of doubt about his fate had grown into a two-by-four that was about to knock her upside the head.

She needed an insurance policy. A way to prove her loyalty if it ever came down to that.

The demon lying on top of her, his heart pounding strong and steady against her chest, was just the ticket. She could turn him over to them, if she had to.

'Look, Hellboy, what do you say we call it a draw and you let me up?'

The suspicion in his penetrating gaze made her lose hope. 'What are you up to?'

His thumb still ran over the sensitive skin of her wrist in slow, rhythmic circles, and his thigh rocked against her core with every tiny movement from either one of them. It wasn't fair, the way he could make her so aware of her body, of every inch of skin that touched his. It was almost as though her concentration had turned inward, so much so that nothing around her existed.

And because of that, she didn't hear the scrape of claws on flooring until it was too late.

৬৯

Eidolon was rarely caught off-guard, his instincts too honed, his experience with danger too vast. But the *s'genesis* had hijacked his senses, his thoughts, and Tayla distracted him with her curves and her voice and her scent, and as a result, they'd just been taken by surprise.

Hell's fucking bells, as Shade would say.

Still stretched out on top of Tayla, he turned to the creature lurking just inside the kitchen passage doorway. 'There's nothing for you here, carrion-eater. Leave.'

The Obhirrat shuffled into the living room, its pale snout sniffing the air. The foot-long, razor claws on one hand clacked together in a spine-tingling, steady beat. Beneath its transparent skin, maggots writhed, the grind of squirming bodies so nauseating that few could look upon the creature for more than a few seconds, but Eidolon steadied his gaze even as he swallowed bile.

Slowly, casually, he pushed off Tayla. He didn't help her up; any show of weakness would set off the creature. Tayla must have known, came to her feet smoothly and moved with deliberate arrogance as she squared her stance next to him.

As if they were a team.

Given the situation, he wasn't about to complain or analyze.

'*I ... hunger ...*' The Obhirrat's snakelike tongue slipped between long teeth, tasting the air.

'I destroyed the injured vampire you trailed,' Eidolon said, focusing on the beady red eyes that kept shifting to Tayla, 'so there is nothing for you here.'

The creature's claws clicked faster. The maggots beneath its skin writhed anew and even the air seemed to shimmer with its agitation. '*She was mine . . .*'

Eidolon stepped forward, and Tayla moved with him, a show of unity and power, but the Obhirrat's burning concentration on her made him wish she'd stayed back. 'Tell me where you picked up her scent.'

'*Why should I help the one who stole my meal?*'

The knowledge that the creature would have started feasting on Nancy's flesh while she was still alive set Eidolon on fire.

'Ever met an Aegis slayer?' he said with a deadly calm he didn't feel, and the Obhirrat hissed, the hunger in its eyes replaced by alarm. 'I'm a doctor, you ugly fuck, and I can tell her exactly how to take you apart so your little maggots can't do a damned thing.'

It wasn't true, but the creatures were big on size, small on brains, and Eidolon had always been a good liar. Cutting into an Obhirrat released its primary means of defense, the maggots, which made them one of the three species that would never be treated at UG.

'*Crossroadsss . . . ssssweeeeet blood.*'

Without taking his eyes off the creature, Eidolon inclined his head at Tayla in a silent message. She had warrior instincts, read him like a battle plan, and immediately edged around the Obhirrat to wait at the kitchen entrance. Eidolon palmed the cleaver he'd parked in the wall, skirted the beast, and then they both slipped into the dank passage. For an instant, he regretted not finding shoes for her, but she padded unimpeded down the tunnel. If the sharp stones beneath her feet bothered her, she didn't show it. The darkness posed no problem for Eidolon, and Tayla seemed to have little difficulty, as well.

The crude passage opened up into a wide brick tunnel. Tayla made no sound as they followed the blood trail, though he suspected that she'd manage the same silence in boots. Even injured, she moved with a deadly, powerful grace that he admired when she wasn't looking. Which was often, since her attention focused on their surroundings, her sharp gaze taking everything in, cataloging, planning.

'What did you get us into, Hellboy?' she whispered.

'Isn't this what you do for a living? Skulk around in sewers to find demons?'

'I don't skulk, and I've certainly never done it *with* a demon.'

Oh, you did it with a demon, and did it well . . .

Abruptly, his skin grew warm, which cracked him up in a *this-is-pathetic* way. He'd always prided himself on being more civilized than his brothers, but so much for that; he was becoming aroused in a damned *sewer*.

Cursing, more at himself than at her, he caught her arm and dragged her around. 'Then why? You could have avoided all of this. You could have left me alone with the Obhirrat and escaped through Nancy's front door.'

Her gaze went steely, a hard challenge. 'You accused The Aegis of torturing the vampire. I'm going to prove it wasn't my people.'

'Why?'

'Because I'm tired of being accused of things I didn't do.'

He wanted to ask more, but instead, he released her. 'For your sake, I hope you're right.'

'Is that a threat?'

Truthfully, he wasn't sure. And he was rarely unsure about anything. This human was a menace to everything that made him a demon. 'Take it as you will.'

She muttered something about hating demons and started moving again. The trail ended at a crossroads in the tunnel. Someone must have carried Nancy to the junction, then left her to the carrion-eaters like the Obhirrat. There were four possible directions from which the person had come, because the fifth wasn't a possibility.

The Harrowgate.

One of hundreds in New York City alone, it shimmered across the width of the north tunnel like a gossamer curtain, visible only to demons. Humans would pass harmlessly through it and continue down the tunnel.

'What is that?' Tayla asked, staring at the gate.

He scented the air for danger, detected nothing but the usual rancid currents of sewer rot. Tayla waited, her thick hair falling in soft, feminine waves around her shoulders, at odds with the hard, alert stance she'd taken.

'What do you see?' he asked.

'Outlines. Sort of fuzzy. I've seen them before, but I always thought they were a trick of the light. This one is clearer. What is it?'

Eidolon got an instant, alarming vision of Tayla, her demon DNA fully integrated, leading Aegis slayers through Harrowgates, and dread shivered over his skin. Only dark-souled or unconscious humans could pass through the gates, but no doubt The Aegis would find a way around that limitation. Once they learned how to use the gates for travel, there would be nothing to stop them from locating his hospital, traveling anywhere in the world in seconds, and invading the demon realm deep inside the earth. Most demons, especially those that didn't appear human, adhered to strict rules when venturing topside where the humans dwelled, but humans had no such restrictions.

The possibilities were terrifying.

When he didn't answer, Tayla nodded as if she'd put the last piece in a jigsaw puzzle. 'It's a gate, isn't it? An entrance to hell,' she murmured, and he didn't bother to contradict her. The less she knew about his world, the better. 'Fine. Ignore me.' She noted the blood smears at the crossroads and looked down the passageways. 'Someone carried your vamp to this point.'

'Looks that way.'

'Or they came from that gate thing.'

'Those responsible for what happened to Nancy were not demons.'

She rolled her eyes. 'Back to how The Aegis is involved.'

'They are involved often enough,' he ground out, because even though demons were their own worst enemies, were more than capable of killing each other, Roag's fiery death at the hands of The Aegis had left scorch marks on his soul.

The hair on the back of Eidolon's neck prickled a split second before a blinding light flashed from the gate.

Shielding her eyes, Tayla leaped aside, and he spun between her and the gate. 'What happened?'

'The gate activated,' he said, pushing her fully behind him, because whatever was going to come through that portal wouldn't be happy with the welcoming party. 'The light should have been invisible to you.' To all humans, actually, but as he'd discovered, Tayla wasn't entirely human.

'Yeah, well—'

Four male Nightlash demons emerged from the gate, their human appearances broken only by their misshapen, clawed feet and hands. And the daggerlike teeth.

Tayla shifted forward, glaring at him. 'Oh, look,' she snapped, as she sank into a fighting stance, fists clenched, back leg bearing her weight. 'Demons. And me without any weapons.'

Pale silver eyes gleamed in the darkness, a good twelve inches above Eidolon's eye level, as the largest's mouth spread into a gluttonous sneer. 'We're in luck, brothers. A short hunt tonight.'

'Seminus demon,' another growled, as he took in Eidolon from head to toe. 'No markings on face ... he's still a whelp. We'll get no credit for killing him.'

The big one moved closer, bringing his putrid swamp stench with him. 'We'll take the human,' it said to Eidolon. 'Go, and we'll let you live.'

Eidolon smiled tightly. 'The human is mine. Find your meals elsewhere.'

'I have a better idea,' Tayla said. 'Why don't I kill you all, and then no one will need supper?'

'As long as "all" doesn't include me,' Eidolon said, 'I'm all right with that plan.' He thrust the cleaver into Tayla's hand. No doubt she could handle herself without a weapon, but her injury compromised her more than he liked, and more than she'd probably admit.

The demons attacked, mouths gaping wide, claws extended. Tayla met them, moving like a dancer, blade flashing, and though he was no slouch when it came to fighting, thanks to his Justice Dealer background and lessons with Wraith, Tayla left him in the dust. She ripped through the demons, punching, slashing, death on sexy legs.

Moving in what felt like slow motion compared to her, Eidolon took down the largest of the enemies, smoothly, efficiently, breaking the demon's neck. Tayla took a hard hit and slammed into him, and they both crunched into the wall.

One of the brothers lay writhing nearby, his head nearly severed by Tayla's blade. The other two advanced, limping, bleeding, one holding his forearm awkwardly. Light flashed in the Harrowgate, and son of a bitch, a Cruentus burst from it. And, as if things couldn't get worse, a clicking noise came from behind them.

'*Hunger . . . slayer . . .*'

'Shit,' he muttered, because now the remaining demons knew what they were fighting.

The Nightlashes pounced, their fury billowing from their pores in clouds of bitter scent. Eidolon spun, lashed out with a foot, and knocked one of the brothers off his misshapen feet.

'I've got the Obhirrat,' he shouted, as Tayla opened up a deep gash in one Nightlash's chest.

'Don't break its skin!'

Breaking the skin was the idea.

In a quick series of moves, he shifted behind the slower creature and shoved. The Obhirrat slammed into the Cruentus, which yelped and scrambled backward. Even Cruenti were smart enough to avoid injuring an Obhirrat.

'Tayla! Cut it!'

She paused for a split second to stare at him as if he was insane, a pause that cost her. The Cruentus raked its claws across her face, laying open her cheek. Snarling, Eidolon plowed his fist into the beast's snout, reveling in the crunch of cartilage beneath his knuckles.

'Do it,' he yelled, and though indecision flashed in Tayla's eyes, she buried the knife in the Obhirrat's belly and yanked up, opening the creature like an unzipped coat.

It screamed, a high-pitched, ear-shattering sound. Tayla leaped back as squirming, ricelike grains spilled from the wound. The maggots moved with unnatural speed and purpose; unlike their nondemon counterparts, these fed on living flesh.

Eidolon seized Tayla's arm and yanked her up the tunnel that led to Nancy's lair, leaving the sounds of battle and pain behind.

When they burst into Nancy's purple nightmare, Tayla slammed the door shut, and he bolted it. Blood dripped down her face from the Cruentus's clawmarks, but she didn't seem to notice.

'We took a risk, cutting that thing open,' she said, doubling over to catch her breath.

We. Interesting. 'You okay?'

Immediately, she straightened, her chin jutting out stubbornly. 'I'm fine. Been through worse.'

'You never stop fighting, do you?'

She watched him warily as he slid his palm over the curve of her cheek and pinched her torn flesh between his fingers. The familiar warm tingle traveled down his arm. Her lids flew up as the power ripped into her flesh. Beneath his fingertips, her tissue knitted together, the torn blood vessels fusing. In moments, he wiped the blood away from new, unmarked skin.

'How . . . how do you do that?'

'Members of my breed share three different gifts, all with some healing ability.' The healing abilities were, however, secondary to the primary purpose . . . which was to aid in reproduction once the *s'genesis* was complete. Shade could use his gift to stimulate early

81

ovulation, Wraith practiced mind-seductions, but could also heal mental disorders. Eidolon could create favorable conditions for fertilization of eggs.

She touched her face, awe reflecting in her expression. Man, she was beautiful, all wild-haired warrior with the scent of battle clinging to her skin. The sight of her, the smell of her, triggered a primitive reaction deep in his core, one that both disgusted and intrigued him. He hated everything about her. But he wanted to bed her. Over and over.

She'd been spot on when she'd said his ego had taken a blow because he hadn't brought her to climax, but his desire to take her again went beyond patching his pride or even slaking the ever-present lust that plagued his breed. He'd never encountered anyone who radiated such a fierce will to live. Her life force drew him, her fire fascinated him, and her sensuality held him in an iron grip he couldn't break.

He wanted to fuck her when what he should do was kill her.

Her eyes flared, as if she knew what he was thinking, and his focus slammed home.

'I'm taking you home now.'

'You can drop me off in the general vicinity.'

Despite the fact that they'd fought together, saved each other's lives, and he'd healed her wounds, she still couldn't make this easy. Not that he blamed her.

But she still wasn't going to win this round.

'Not an option. I'm walking you to your door.'

'Why?' She stepped back. 'So you can tell all your demon buddies where I live?'

He closed the distance she'd put between them, used his size and height to deliver the message that if she wanted to fight, he was ready to throw down. 'Remember how I told you that my colleagues wanted to torture you for information?'

'Kinda hard to forget, and hello, personal space.'

'You don't have the luxury of personal space right now, because

82

you're in danger. I want to make sure my colleagues *don't* know where you live. As in, they aren't there waiting for you.'

'That would suck.'

Call it a curse of his species that the word 'suck' would turn him on, but there it was, a sexual stirring in his gut that was so powerful he had to grind out, 'Is that a yes?'

'Yeah.'

'Fine.' Gods help him, he was going to take her home. He'd be walking into the lion's den.

ॐ

Nothing possessed a hair trigger like a werewolf on the eve of a full moon, so when Shade rounded a corner on his way to the hospital's administrative offices and collided with Luc, he expected a snarling backlash. Instead, the were smiled, actually *smiled,* and clapped Shade on the shoulder.

'See ya next week, incubus.'

Luc would be locking himself away for the duration of the full moon, which usually made him grumpier than a Cruentus with a fangache, but today he was downright cheerful.

'Luc, you okay, man?'

'Oh, hell, yeah.' Luc sauntered off, the strike of his boots on the stone floor echoing through the halls.

Weird. Shade made a mental note to check the ambulances' drug boxes and continued down the hall to admin. He propped himself against the door jamb of Wraith's office and watched his brother throw on a worn leather jacket. 'Where are you off to?'

'Mongolia. E wants some special mana crap for his collection of "what ifs."'

Laughing, because Eidolon was always sending Wraith to retrieve rare artifacts, potions, and materials for the hospital on the off-chance that they might be needed, Shade entered the room, which was little more than a junk closet. Wraith's job at the medical center was, in truth, to acquire nontraditional supplies unique to demon medicine, and his office reflected his haphazard method of researching and locating said supplies.

As Shade was a control freak, Wraith's utter lack of organization in any aspect of his life gave him heartburn.

Wraith shoved a set of knives into his chest harness and a Glock into his thigh holster. Two more blades slid into ankle holders, and various vials of poisons and holy waters got tucked into the dozens of hidden coat pockets. The guy didn't screw around when it came to a mission, especially since he made enemies wherever he went.

'I'm worried about E,' Shade said abruptly. 'He introduced my face to his fist a little while ago.'

Wheeling around, Wraith let out a low whistle. 'He decked you? E? That's not like him.'

No, it wasn't. Shade and Wraith regularly went at it, but Eidolon usually kept his fists to himself. 'I think the *s'genesis* is making him unstable.'

Wraith snorted. 'Just because he healed the slayer when he should have killed her, boned her, and then instead of giving her to Yuri – which I was against but really, it would have been the smart thing to do – he's giving her a lift home?'

Shade digested that for a second, and then it all came back up like acid in his esophagus. 'Eidolon had sex with the Aegi butcher? *In the hospital?*'

'Yep. I caught a whiff of him right afterward.' Wraith plopped down on the edge of his desk, spilling papers and pens all over the floor. 'Who would have seen that coming? Mr. Stick Up His Ass finally getting laid in the hospital. With a patient. And an enemy to top it off? I'm not sure if we should throw him a party or throw him into a firepit for being so stupid.'

Shade pinched the bridge of his nose to stave off what was going to be a killer headache. Fuck. This was worse than he'd thought. Clearly, The Change was messing with Eidolon's judgment and sex drive, and that meant they were all in a lot of trouble.

If Eidolon couldn't control himself, there wasn't a whole lot of hope for Shade or Wraith.

'He needs a mate.' A mate wouldn't stop the *s'genesis,* but it would stop the out-of-control need to impregnate every female in the underworld.

'Yeah, right. How often do we find females who are willing to spend the next six hundred years with us? I don't know about you, bro, but there isn't a female in the universe I'd tie myself to for that long.'

And there was the rub, the reason so few Seminus demons mated. Mating was for life, and the only way out was to kill the other. The fear of mating often outweighed the fear of *s'genesis.* Shade had never known a single Seminus male who had mated. Only Eidolon had ever shown any desire to do so, but worthy females were rarer than fallen angels, and so far, he'd come up empty.

'E just needs to stop fighting it. Maybe it won't be that bad. We've known Sems who didn't change much after the transition.'

'Name one,' Shade said, and then silently screamed, *Don't say it, don't say it* –

'Roag.'

Hell's fires. He hated talking about Roag, hated how he and Shade had been at odds before his death. Roag had never understood Eidolon's need to protect Wraith, even though Roag had been there in the Chicago warehouse nearly eighty years ago. When Roag died, Eidolon had been devastated, but Shade had been more relieved than anything.

'Roag doesn't count. He was such a bastard that he didn't have a lot of room to turn into—'

'A dick?' Wraith offered. 'You're right. He was always that. What about Otto?'

Shade sighed. 'He's the only one, and he did have to give up his vet practice.'

'He still worked there part-time. Maybe E can keep working

here so Yuri the Asshole doesn't have to take over once you've gone over, too.'

'We can't count on that,' Shade said. 'And even if he's stable enough to keep working, he'll have to limit himself to admin crap, stay in his office.' A post-*s'genesis* male couldn't control himself in the presence of fertile females, would immediately change form to match theirs and try to seduce them. If seduction didn't work, force often did.

'This is bullshit.' Wraith pushed to his feet. 'We're all going through the transformation, and you two whining about it won't change anything.' He ran his finger over his rack of weapons, snagged a flail, and grinned as he slammed it home through a loop in his leather harness. 'I can't wait. Bring it on, baby.'

Gods, Wraith had issues. Sure, Shade wasn't going to fight the *s'genesis* like Eidolon was – fuck if he was going to store blood for transfusions in hopes it would hold off The Change – but he also wasn't looking forward to it. He just wished he could take a mate. If not for the –

'Damned curse?'

Shade scowled at his brother. 'I hate it when you do that.'

'I can't help it. Your thoughts invade my head sometimes.' Wraith finished loading himself with weapons, probably adding another twenty pounds to his already large frame.

'My. Ass.' Shade fisted his hands to conceal the slight trembling that always followed one of Wraith's mind invasions – the same gift Roag had possessed.

'Seriously, man. That one just popped into my brain.'

'You being straight with me?' Two big secrets drifted around in Shade's brain, secrets that could destroy his little brother, and son of a bitch, it made him nervous when Wraith went on an expedition inside his head.

'I always am, bro.' Wraith hoisted a backpack off the floor and slung it over a shoulder. 'Hey, you still seeing that human female? Runa?'

'Sort of.' Shade doubted their month-long relationship would last much longer, partly because she was growing clingy, and partly because he was tired of holding back with her during sex. Humans were fragile, which was why bonding with them was out of the question. They'd never survive the bonding rituals. Even if they could, the offspring would be half-breeds, so bonding would be pointless.

'I know she's not the only one. A human female couldn't meet your needs.'

Shade grinned. No single female of any species could meet his needs. 'I get off work in an hour, and I'll be getting off with Vantha and Ailarca about an hour after that.

And Nancy, if she ever shows up ... ' At Wraith's rumbling growl, Shade sighed. 'Let's skip the vampire lecture.'

'You can't trust them.'

'You're a vampire, and I trust you.'

'I'm not a true vampire, and you shouldn't trust me.'

'There's no one I trust more,' Shade said quietly. He loved E, trusted him with his life. But he had a strong mental bond with Wraith, knew his mind even when his brother's mind was scrambled. E always followed the rules even if his personal feelings didn't match up with them; Wraith always followed his heart and instincts even – or especially – if they went against the rules. In a way, E was far more dangerous simply because he didn't stray from the straight and narrow, and often that path didn't make allowances for family.

Wraith cursed. 'Don't start with me. I'm outta here. Locked, cocked, and ready to rock.' He strode to the door. 'Do yourself a favor and forget Nancy. Go find that new nurse, the Sora demon. The things she can do with her tail ... '

'I know.'

Shooting Shade a toothy grin, Wraith sauntered off, his boots falling like hammers on the stone. Shade rubbed his jaw, thinking that seeking out the Sora might be a good idea. Work off a little stress. He'd accomplished nothing in his chat with Wraith about Eidolon, and as time wore on, he grew more and more anxious.

He'd lost too many brothers. He wasn't prepared to lose the last two.

SEVEN

❧

Eidolon couldn't decide whether Tayla had caved in too easily to his request to take her home. He hadn't smelled deception on her, but then, his olfactory senses were designed more to pick up on the scent of lust than anything else.

And lust was something that rippled off her in subtle undercurrents, often when she was in the middle of hating him. Or when she was beneath him.

Welcome to my world, slayer.

His own desire pumped through him as he glanced sideways at her in the passenger seat of his BMW. He'd have been attracted to her anyway, but the *s'genesis* was jerking him around, was making the right side of his face throb, just below the surface of his skin, where the marking would appear when the change was complete. The marking that would identify him to the entire demon world as a menace to all things female, and a threat to all things male.

The Change was coming on fast, and he only hoped his experimental treatment would hold off the worst of the effects, or at least make the transition less dangerous and painful. With any luck, he'd find a mate and wouldn't have to worry about any of it. Then again, he wasn't likely to find a mate if he filled his days with hospital work instead of courting females.

Not that he hadn't tried. But few females were willing to commit to a lifetime with a Seminus, knowing the only way out of the bond was death. The females who *were* willing left Eidolon thinking that whatever the *s'genesis* did to him would be preferable to a life sentence with them. Then again, he didn't have much choice.

He was running out of time, and he had no way of knowing if his treatment would delay the transition long enough to allow him to find a worthy female. He needed to act now. Preferably, the moment he dropped off Tayla.

'Out of curiosity,' she said, shifting her focus from the police car ahead of them to him, 'why did you kill the vampire? Why not take her to your hospital?'

Fury blasted through him once more, and he had to take three long, deep breaths to keep from lashing out at Tayla. 'Most of her circulatory system had been removed. I couldn't save her.' He rubbed his chest as though doing so would relieve the ache there, the one that was starting to grow as his losses piled up.

She caught her lower lip between her teeth, the action tamping down the embers of his anger and sparking a different fire. 'I don't get it. Vamps are dead. Undead. Whatever. Why do they need a circulatory system?'

He didn't want to talk about Nancy, but talking kept him from thinking. Or feeling. 'The transformation from human to vampire alters their internal makeup. The stomach takes over for the heart when it stops beating. New arteries and veins carry ingested blood throughout the body. Without those veins, a vampire will die as surely as it will when a slayer jams a stake into its chest. It just takes longer.'

'Why would someone do that?' she asked, her curiosity genuine as far as he could tell, and damn her, he was starting to think she didn't know anything about the killings.

'Vampire circulatory systems must be worth something on the black market, for use in spells or rituals or some crap.' And the person doing the cutting enjoyed misery, because he or she could have spared Nancy by killing her once her organs had been removed.

'So she fingered The Aegis for what happened to her? Is that what she was saying to you before you—'

'Yes.'

Tayla shook her head. 'It's not us. It's not The Aegis. Our job is to protect humans, not give evil more weapons by selling potentially useful body parts.' When he said nothing, she stared at him with such intensity that he damn near squirmed in his seat. And he *never* squirmed.

'What?' he snapped.

'What did you call her? You know, before you . . . '

'*Lirsha.*' He gripped the steering wheel a little tighter. 'Loosely translates to lover.'

There was a slight pause before she said, 'She was your lover?'

'Not mine. Shade's.' But she'd been at UG almost since the beginning, and he'd always liked the quirky nurse. Shade's sister, Skulk, had once said that Nancy's aura burned bright, more colorful than that of other vampires, which hadn't been a shock. He'd never seen the nurse in a bad mood.

Wrapping her arms around herself as though cold, Tayla braced her shoulder against the window. 'Turn here and park anywhere.'

He looked around the area in disgust. He hadn't been sure what to expect from the slayer's neighborhood, but the ghetto wasn't it. Not even the cheery April sunlight could put a shine on the graffiti-tagged, run-down character of the neighborhood.

'You won't want to leave your car for more than thirty seconds, or it'll be stripped or ripped.'

'It'll be fine.' He parked between a furniture truck and a lowered pickup riddled with bullet holes, and they got out of the car.

When Tayla glanced hesitantly at the vehicle and then back at

91

him, he shook his head. 'Trust me. People will walk by like they don't even see it.' The BMW wouldn't literally be invisible, but the Deflection spell that came standard on demon-dealer autos meant his BMW didn't attract human attention. They'd see it, but it would register only in their subconscious.

'Whatever. Your loss. My keys are at HQ, so I hope the super is around.'

She led him to a building roaches wouldn't call home, and after picking up a key at the office, they climbed two flights of rickety stairs. When she opened her door, she swore.

'*Mickey!*'

Eidolon stepped inside the apartment, not bothering to hide his shock. The place was a dump. Not filthy – Tayla obviously cleaned – but she didn't have a lot to work with. The ceiling, stained by generations of water leaks and mold, bowed as though on the verge of collapse. Gray paint peeled like shredded skin from the walls, and holes the size of his foot pockmarked the vinyl flooring.

And scattered throughout were bits of foam that had once belonged inside one of the cushions on the orange seventies-style sofa.

'What happened?'

'Mickey. My ferret.'

'You have a pet weasel?' Said weasel poked its brown head out of the ragged hole in the cushion.

'He's a ferret.' She moved into the kitchen, which could barely be called such. The fridge, more rust than metal, rattled like it was on its dying breath, and if the ancient stove worked, he'd sell one of his brothers into Neethul slavery. He might do that with Wraith, anyway.

Maybe The Aegis wasn't involved in the demon organ ring, after all. If they were, they could afford to pay their people more.

'He must be starving,' she said, pouring what he assumed was weasel food into a plastic margarine container. 'How long was I in the hospital?'

'Three days.'

'My poor baby.' Her voice was a soothing croon but it did the opposite to him, and when she bent to place the bowl on the floor, he watched the way the scrub pants molded to her rounded ass. His mind fuzzed out, and he realized he'd taken three steps toward her. The way she stroked the weasel's narrow head, yeah, if she'd touch him the way she was touching the little animal . . .

Shit. He halted in his tracks, feeling flushed and hot and way too short-fused to be anywhere near any female, let alone a female like Tayla.

The weasel tackled the bowl, flinging pellets everywhere. Tayla straightened and turned, a smile curving her full lips that he was suddenly picturing on his.

He had to get out of there.

She dug an orange out of a bag on top of the stove, which was pretty much her only counter space, and then grabbed a bag of marshmallows from one of the two cupboards.

'Three days that felt like three years.' She bit into a marshmallow and watched him, her gaze secretive, and he wondered what was going on in that pretty head.

He knew what was going on in his, and she'd probably kill him for it.

'Look, I have to go. If you need anything—'

'Like what?'

Like, for instance, help when you grow horns and scales as your demon DNA kicks in.

'Your wound. The stitches will need to be removed.'

'I'll do it myself.'

'I'd like to follow up with you.' He drew a card from his pocket and placed it on the TV tray that must serve as her kitchen table. 'Here's the hospital phone number. Say the words on the back before you dial.'

'An underworld communications system?'

'Something like that.'

'Are you this dedicated to all your patients? Or am I special?'

'Both.'

Under normal circumstances, he couldn't have cared less if a human lived or died. But the half-demon mating-gone-wrong thing fascinated him, and the Aegi issue guaranteed that he wasn't going to let her go that easily.

Then there was the fact that just looking at her made his blood run hotter than his normal body temperature of one-oh-nine.

Gods, she was thin, but as hard and sleek as a Trillah demon, but he knew firsthand how soft and pliant she could go beneath his touch. Knew how her slim hips could take his thrusts, how her long legs wrapped around him to hold him deep.

And her scent ... *damn.* Her scent, deceptively appealing, the way cyanide smelled like sweet almonds, drove him mad.

He burned. He ached. He had to get back on track and fast, because he needed to find a mate before it was too late, and every second spent with Tayla was a second wasted.

'I have to go,' he repeated, but his feet didn't move, because she was striding toward him.

He gazed at her, at the blood smears still darkening her cheek, at the smooth, tight skin everywhere else, and his own skin tightened and shrank as if it no longer fit.

'Thank you for saving my life.' She halted a foot away, close enough to smell the marshmallow on her breath. 'But don't think this changes anything.'

'Everything has changed, Tayla,' he said softly, reaching for her. He put two fingers to her throat, told himself he was probing for any signs of illness, fever, progression of her DNA transformation. Told himself whatever lies he had to in order to pretend he wasn't touching her for the sheer pleasure of it.

'I hate it when you put your hands on me,' she whispered, but the way her pulse ticked violently beneath his fingers betrayed her.

He breathed deep, seeking her scent like a hellhound on the track of a hellbitch in heat. He slid his thumb down along her clavicle. Fragile. Delicate. He could break the bone with a flick of his wrist.

Or he could run his tongue over the silky skin there. It was insane the way he wanted her, the way his body sought the thrill of something as forbidden and dangerous as an Aegi killer. The instinct was so strong that images of the ways he'd take her swamped his brain, short-circuiting his control.

Against the wall ... in a hot shower ... bound and helpless, laid out like a sacrifice ...

His gaze snapped up, caught hers. His temperature spiked and his thoughts hemorrhaged, bleeding out until there was only primal instinct to guide his actions.

He licked his lips. The knowledge of what he was about to do made her jaw drop as he dipped his head and slanted his mouth over hers. For a moment she stiffened, and then, oh, yeah, she caught his waist in one hand and melted against him.

Sticky, marshmallow sweetness coated his tongue as it sparred with hers. The soft recess of her mouth drew him deep, made him want to spend all day enjoying the wet, hot kiss. But his body wanted more, and he could find better uses for his tongue.

He tangled his hand in her thick hair, holding her firmly as he dropped his other hand to her ass to press her against his aching sex.

The subtle tightening of her body was his only warning.

A flash of silver arced near the extreme border of his vision, and the sting of metal bit into his throat. Hissing, he wrenched Tayla's wrist and grabbed the knife.

'Son of a—' She bit off the curse and spun out of his grip.

There was nothing wrong with her reflexes, and she proved there was nothing wrong with her speed either, as she bolted toward a closed door. He dived, hit her as she reached for the handle, and they both tumbled through the bedroom doorway. She landed awkwardly, half on, half off the bed, and he came down on top of her.

'Remind me not to save your life again, if that's how you repay small favors,' he growled.

'I don't need you to save my life.' She clocked him in the jaw hard enough to make his teeth crack together. 'And FYI? I wasn't going to kill you.'

In one smooth move, he pinned both of her wrists with one hand, forcing her to buck beneath his weight. Which, of course, gave him a hard-on. He could blame the *s'genesis,* could blame the fact that he was an incubus. Could blame those things, and would, because the idea that Tayla herself could jumpstart him like a defibrillator was unacceptable.

'No? Was this your idea of foreplay?' He held the knife in front of her face, and though her eyes flared wide, she looked more curious than afraid as he brought it down to the collar of the scrub top. 'Because I'm into this kind of sex toy. It's a demon thing.'

'I know what you are,' she ground out, and he might have believed she was as pissed as she sounded, if it weren't for the way she'd angled her pelvis to meet his erection.

'What were you going to do with the knife, little killer?' He drew the dull reverse edge along the skin just above her collar, leaving a trailing white line. Still, she didn't look afraid, didn't smell of fear. That turned him on as much as the fact that if she wanted to, if she really wanted to, she could kill him. Any doubt about that had been squashed during the battle with the Nightlashes.

'I was going to cut off your clothes.'

'You're a terrible liar.' He slid the blade beneath the fabric.

A flick of his wrist sliced the scrub top down to her breasts, and her breath hitched, but she didn't protest. He didn't have Shade's powers, couldn't measure her internal systemic responses. But he could see the rapid rise and fall of her chest, the dilating pupils, the flushed skin. He could feel the pounding thud of her pulse in her wrist and could hear the thump of her heart as it raced. She could deny her arousal all she wanted, but her body spoke the truth.

Clenching the knife hilt between his teeth, he hauled her onto her bed, which was nothing more than a twin-sized mattress and twisted sheets on a metal frame. Using his weight, he imprisoned her beneath him, his long legs trapping hers between them.

'Bastard.'

Lightning fast, she escaped his grip and landed a blow to his cheek, but her strike lacked the strength and conviction he knew she was capable of. Adrenaline surged in his veins, hot, potent, the line between battle lust and sexual lust blurred. A cry escaped her as he flipped her onto her belly and straddled her thighs. He held her down with one hand pressed between her shoulder blades and took the knife from between his teeth with the other.

'What's the matter, Tayla?' He slashed through the length of the top. 'Are you going to tell me you don't want this?'

'I hate you,' she snarled into her pillow.

He moved his hips in a slow, circular grind against her buttocks. 'We've established that.'

She bucked angrily, and he pressed her even more firmly into the mattress. 'Be still, slayer, or you'll have a knife through your kidney.' He could fix it, of course, but a punctured organ would ruin the mood.

'Fuck. You.'

'Yeah, that's the plan.'

He shifted his weight and pushed the flat of the blade between her spine and the waistband of the scrub pants. Cold steel rasped against hot flesh, and she arched up with a groan that shot straight to his cock. Greedily, he sliced through the trousers, and this time, she didn't move a muscle as he ran the blade down the pant legs until she lay before him, gloriously naked.

Dropping the knife, he spread her legs and knelt between them, let his palms drift from the backs of her knees up along her muscular thighs.

'I can't do this with you,' she whispered.

'We've done it before.'

'But I can't—'

'I'll make sure you do.' He bent over her, pressed a lingering kiss to the base of her neck. 'You'll come, Tayla. I'm dying to make you scream for me.'

Her response was muffled by the pillow, and she started to wriggle, but he slid his hand between her legs, cupped her, and she settled down.

'You're wet. Gods, you're wet.' He pushed a finger between her swollen lips and started an easy rhythm.

There was nothing easy about how his lungs worked hard to draw air in as he stroked her. Adding another finger, he squeezed her knot of nerves between them, gently rolling it with alternating light and firm pressure. Slow passes of his thumb over the sensitive flesh behind her sex made her squirm and push against him, and when he eased his thumb inside her slick heat while working her with his fingers, she cried out.

'This won't work,' she whimpered, but her hips were pumping as if she couldn't stop.

A powerful mix of lust and the need to possess Tayla made him shudder as he scraped his teeth down her spine and murmured against her skin, 'But it feels good, doesn't it?'

'Yeah.' She fisted the pillow with white-knuckled force. 'Oh, yeah.'

'I can smell your need.' Her scent made his nostrils flare, and suddenly he had to taste her, to take all of her into his body. His body that was screaming for release, aching for this woman he should hate but desired in the most primal way.

Unable to wait any longer, he rolled her onto her back. Surprise flickered in the drowsy depths of her eyes, and for a moment he thought she'd resist as he lowered his mouth to her breast. Tremors shook her body, and she held her hands in fists at her sides, but as he drew one dusky nipple between his lips, a soft sigh loosened her to a boneless puddle.

He caressed her breasts, held them so he could divide his attention between them, licking, sucking until she was writhing and her hands had come up to tangle in his hair.

This was what he'd missed out on at the hospital when he'd been in a rush to take her. The slow windup of tension. The building heat. The sweet, citrusy taste of her skin as he licked a trail from her breasts down her abdomen.

He paused to rim her navel with his tongue, felt her sleek, honed muscles flex beneath his palms. Her fingers caressed his scalp, sending tingles to the base of his spine and sparking fiery bolts of pleasure into his balls.

Inching lower, he let her soft feminine curls tickle his cheek as he spread her legs wide, opening her to him. He shifted, admired the sight before him, her swollen flesh served up for him and him alone.

'This . . . I don't . . . ' Her gaze met his, and his breath caught at the sight of fear tangled with desire in the depths of her beguiling green eyes. 'I—'

'Shh. Easy, slayer.' He buried his tongue in her folds, swiped up her hot valley in one long, slow, motion. She tasted sweet and salty. Honey and hellfire. Forbidden fruit.

Her sultry moan drifted down to him, fueling his hunger. He kissed her deeply, sucked her bud between his lips and flicked his tongue lightly over the protruding tip. Her hips came off the bed, and she whispered something incoherent as he lapped at her and then plunged his tongue deep inside.

'This is wrong,' she panted, but she arched against his lips and dug her nails into his scalp, holding him there in the place he'd like to stay for a long time. But what had been a slow burn under his skin became an inferno, and if he didn't dip into her hot center quickly, he'd turn to ash.

'Please . . . '

Please make me come.

She hadn't said it, but he filled in the blanks, and although he wanted to make her come in his mouth, he reared up, tore off his shirt and sent buttons pinging off the walls. Too impatient to shed his pants, he yanked open his fly with one hand and entered her with a hard thrust. Tight, silken heat surrounded him, a mix of intense sensation that made his arms shake as he covered her.

She clung to him, wrapped her legs around his waist and rode him with a strength and enthusiasm he'd never encountered. He'd taken a lot of females in his life, females who played at sex like a contact sport, but Tayla ... she rocked his underworld. She rode him as if she had something to prove, and suddenly he found himself beneath her, squeezed between her iron thighs.

Her pulse leaped in her throat, in time with the small spasms that clenched his shaft and had him on edge and ready to spill inside her. He punched his hips upward, drove so deep her knees came off the bed. Dropping one hand, he spread her wide, used his thumb to rub her rigid button.

'Come,' he panted, his voice harsh, as if he could make her climax with a command.

'I want to, God, I want to ... ' She increased her pace, sliding up and down on his shaft so hard that the slap of wet flesh striking wet flesh nearly drowned out the fleeting, confusing voice in his head that told him to use the knife.

On himself.

Use it to draw a few precious drops of bond-blood. If she was his ...

For all that was unholy, what was he *thinking*? The *s'genesis* should come with a warning label.

'I can't ... ' Tayla's cry of frustration took him down a notch, back to where he needed to be. A tear rolled down her cheek, and fuck, he couldn't take it. She quivered with the need for release, her jaw clenched so tight her lips had turned pale.

'Please.'

Grasping her hips with both hands, he steadied her against him. 'Touch yourself. Make yourself come.'

100

Her fingers dipped between them, and she threw her head back as she circled her bud. Her abs flexed, and her breasts, flushed and heavy with arousal, bounced as she rode him as if they were oiled. The sight of her riding him and pleasuring herself was enough to push him past his limit, and he had to bite his lip until he tasted blood to keep from climaxing.

'Won't work. It won't work!' She shook her head wildly, her hair a tangled mess that covered her face. 'Dammit!'

She was a mystery. A beautiful, ferocious mystery, the way she was so tough, so dangerous, and at the same time, vulnerable in ways he'd never have expected and couldn't understand.

'I *will* get you there,' he swore, and flipped her, pulling out so fast she didn't have time to look surprised. Taking his cock in his fist, he pumped, imagined it was her hand squeezing his hard length. Seminus demons couldn't masturbate to orgasm, making sex with females a necessity to relieve the intense, constant sexual cravings, but he could get himself close enough for Tayla to take over. Her slippery juices lubricated him perfectly, and in half a dozen pulls, he walked the line between heaven and hell.

'Spread yourself with one hand,' he panted, 'and touch me with the other.'

Reaching between their bodies, she obeyed. The moment she closed her fist around his shaft, he came. Legs shaking as he strad-dled her thighs, he bent, spurted hot bursts of seed over her center, coating her quivering flesh, her swollen lips, her pulsing nub.

'Oh!' Tiny whimpers escaped her, and she threw her head back, her hips tilting toward him.

Son of a bitch, she was gorgeous, her hair whipping over the pillow in a cascade of fire, her skin slick with sweat, her muscles rippling. He held himself away from her, his breathing still not settled as he watched her approach orgasm. She didn't need manual stimulation now. His semen was too powerful, a stimulant in its own right.

'That's it,' he whispered. 'Let it happen.'

Her gaze flew up, as if she remembered he was still in the room. A sob escaped her, and then her eyes went wild and a scream of frustration tore through the air and, apparently, the paper-thin walls, because someone on the other side pounded against them and shouted vile curses about Tayla's sexual habits that made him want to punch through the plaster and rip out the man's throat.

Another sob wracked her body. What the hell? No female could withstand a topical aphrodisiac of that nature ... unless her father's species possessed some sort of natural immunity, something he'd never heard of.

Something was wrong. Very wrong.

∾

Never in her life had Tayla been so miserable. She writhed, clenching her thighs together. Her body was a powder keg, lit and ready to blow, but unable. It was as though she were being licked, sucked, caressed, held on the very edge of ecstasy until the need for relief became torture.

'Please, make it stop!'

She flailed around on the bed, humiliating herself with the begging, until she felt the cool, wet rasp of a washcloth between her legs as Eidolon washed away what he'd done to her.

'I'm sorry, Tayla ... gods, I'm sorry.' He knelt beside her, his gentle ministrations the most intimate thing anyone had ever done to her. 'I don't understand this,' he muttered. 'This shouldn't happen.'

None of this should have happened, but she didn't have the energy to say that.

When the lust finally eased, she lay limp, trembling, barely able to move. Her sex tingled, felt tender and warm, but at least the maddening arousal had gone.

As with all her sexual encounters with men, she hadn't been able to climax, had never even been aroused enough to come close.

102

But whatever Hellboy had done when he pulled out and let loose his potent –

Oh, God.

'You.' She sat up in the bed, her head spinning. 'Seminus demon ... you're an incubus, aren't you?'

The lean angle of his jaw grew sharper as he speared her with an unreadable look. 'Yes. A rare breed.'

Which explained her unnatural vulnerability and attraction to him. Incubi were opportunistic creatures that used sex as a means to an end. Some fed on sexual energy until the victim died, some stole souls through sex, some planted their offspring inside –

Her stomach heaved. 'What did you do to me? Did you suck my energy? I swear, if you impregnated me ...'

'Don't worry. I'm incapable of impregnating anyone until my *s'genesis* is complete. After that, only other demons need fear me.'

'Other Seminus demons?'

'There are no females of my breed,' he said, tossing the washcloth into her hamper beside the bed. She'd trash it later. Burn it, maybe. 'We have to impregnate other species. The offspring are always male, always pure-blooded Seminus demons, though every individual shares some minor traits with his mother's species.'

She tugged a sheet up to cover herself, because the way he was watching her made her feel like a science experiment. Besides, she was shaking like a leaf. 'Like?'

He shrugged. 'Shade can turn to shadow in the presence of a shadow. Wraith possesses extraordinary speed and needs to ingest blood to survive. I suffer from a terrible sense of fair play that my brothers lack.'

'Why not impregnate humans?' She couldn't believe she was asking these questions as though they were bonding over beer and peanuts, but hey, the more she knew, the more efficiently she could kill them.

'Breeding with humans results in *cambions*. Sterile half-breeds. We need to mate with other demons to keep our species from extinction.'

'And these other species ... they don't mind giving birth to yours?'

The bed creaked and sagged beneath his considerable weight as he stretched out beside her, uncomfortably close, as if they were lovers. Real lovers and not the most mismatched pair of fuck buddies ever. The wolf and the rabbit. The predator and the prey.

A shudder shook her because she was dangerously underestimating him. They were both predators.

'They mind. Which is why, when the *s'genesis* is complete, we have the ability to shapeshift into the male of any species.'

'So you're parasites who trick the females into having sex with you.'

'Essentially. The females have no idea what they've slept with.'

'And what happens when Junior pops out and he doesn't look like Mom?' Now her questioning had nothing to do with the job and everything to do with her curiosity. She found it interesting that demons scammed other demons as well as humans.

'Most Seminus demon offspring are abandoned, slaughtered, or eaten within hours of birth.' She could have sworn his expression softened with sadness for a moment, but it was gone by the time he said, 'Less than 10 percent survive to adulthood.'

She winced. 'Harsh. Is that why so many of the brothers you were talking about are dead?'

'Most of them.'

'What about the one you said survived to the *s'genesis*? What happened to him?'

'He didn't have a chance to die from the usual things, like angry males of other species avenging their females' seductions. Roag was killed by Aegi.'

Shit. She should have seen that one coming. 'I, ah—'

'Don't,' he said softly. 'Don't say you're sorry, because you aren't.'

She wasn't sure she had been going to offer condolences, but she was glad she hadn't. When she'd told him about her mom, if he'd said he was sorry, she'd have blown a fuse. Yeah, a change of subject would be good right about now. 'Your brother said you weren't raised together . . . so how do you know how many brothers you've had?'

'We feel them. We're aware of every birth, we stay connected during their lives, and we feel them die.' He averted his gaze. 'Every death leaves a hole.'

For the first time, she knew the feeling. Her mother's death had carved a canyon through her soul, and Janet's death had cut it deeper. Tay had known foster kids who had been beaten to death, street kids who had ODed, Guardians who'd been torn apart, but she'd never allowed herself to feel sorrow. Not until Janet. Now Tayla encouraged the pain, intentionally maintaining it because although she and Janet hadn't been close, her death had been Tay's fault.

'Have you ever met your father? Your real father?'

'He was killed when I was two, shortly after Wraith was born.' She didn't want to ask, afraid he'd say The Aegis was responsible again, but he seemed to know what she was thinking, and said, 'Vampires. Revenge for what he did to Wraith's mother.'

This time she did want to ask, but her mind had already moved onto the math calculations . . . Eidolon had said he had over forty siblings, twenty born before he was . . . so if the father died when he was two, twenty more had come between Eidolon's birth and his second year.

'Sounds like your species is pretty prolific.'

He folded his arms behind his head and stared up at the ceiling. 'Exactly. That's why, once the *s'genesis* is complete, unless we have bonded with a single mate, we are overcome by the urge to seduce and impregnate as many females as possible.' His voice changed, went low, and something told her he wasn't happy about this change. 'It's all we can think about. And yet, we still face extinction.'

'That would be too bad.'

He narrowed his gaze at her with such intensity that she sucked a harsh breath. 'Be careful, little killer. The Fates can fuck with you in ways you can't even imagine.'

Sitting up, he swung his legs off the bed and started to button his pants. The muscles in his back and arms flexed, and she admired them even as she reached beneath her pillow, grasped her handy-dandy steel pipe – she had a duffel bag full of fancy weapons, but nothing felt as good as heavy piece of basic metal in the palm.

He was beautiful, terribly beautiful. Which made what she was about to do that much more difficult.

She brought the pipe down on his skull. It cracked sharply, and he slumped to the floor.

'Looks like the Fates really fucked with you, Hellboy.' She peered down, almost feeling sorry for him, but she tucked that foolish sentiment away and wrote it off as near-orgasm warm fuzzies. 'And they aren't even close to being done.'

෨

Gem burst into her parents' Upper West Side house, hoping the call had been a hoax. The broken vase filled with her mother's prize orchids and the blood on the floor in the formal sitting room said otherwise.

'You sons of bitches,' she whispered to no one in particular, though most of her anger was directed at herself.

If only she'd taken the threat seriously. If only she hadn't answered the phone the first time the bastards asked her to cut for them. If only she hadn't told them no when they called back three days later. If only . . .

Didn't matter. The damage had been done.

But if it didn't matter, why did the second phone call, two weeks ago today, keep replaying over and over in her head?

'Well, Gem, what is your answer?'

She looked over at her parents, who were busy serving guests in their backyard – the annual spring barbecue they hosted for the clinic staff they worked with. As Sensor demons, her parents were ter'taceo, *demons who lived and worked in the human world, and none were the wiser. Life in the earthly realm came at a price for their particular species, though; every six months they were forced to return to the underground demon realm, Sheoul, and endure a painful, two-week-long regeneration ritual.*

'I've thought about your offer,' she said in a hushed voice, 'and the answer is no. You can't pay me enough to do what you want.'

'I'd urge you to reconsider.'

'Never.'

'Never say never, doctor.' Insane laughter crackled over the airwaves. The bastard hung up, leaving her shaking and feeling ill.

'Gemella, darling, you don't look well.'

Startled by her mother's voice, Gem yelped and spun around. 'It's nothing. Work issue.'

'Must be some work issue.' Her mother, whose human name was Eileen, handed Gem the margarita in her hand. 'Looks like you could use this more than I can.'

Gem had practically inhaled the cocktail, even though she rarely drank alcohol. Too much liquor negated the effect of the protective spells she'd had tattooed on her body in order to control her demon half. She'd stopped after that one margarita, but now, as she searched her parents' house, hoping they were here despite the bloody evidence to the contrary, she thought about breaking into their wet bar and drinking everything they had. Right now, letting out her inner demon might not be a bad thing.

She saved her old room for last, the one her parents kept exactly as she'd left it when she moved out almost five years ago to attend medical school – two years early, thanks to her parents' militant homeschooling that had put her ahead of schedule in college. They'd always hoped she'd come back home to live after graduation as many Sensor demon offspring did until they'd been mated off by their parents. But Gem wasn't a Sensor, and while she loved the family that had adopted her instead of killing her as an infant, she'd needed her own space to discover who she was and where she truly belonged.

She also had no desire to suffer an arranged mating.

Her room, decorated in black, crimson, and blue, had driven her mom nuts, which had pretty much been the point. Rebellious from the start, Gem had probably, on several occasions over the course of her twenty-four years, made her parents regret their decision to raise her. But they'd also loved her, and she had no doubts about that. Her mom never once let her go to bed without a good night hug, and her father had set aside the third Saturday of every month to take her someplace special, just the two of them. Knowing she'd need to blend in, they'd provided her with a very normal human childhood that included church, sleepovers, and camping. As long as she avoided the securely locked basement, she could almost pretend she – and they – were human.

Though she didn't expect to find anything, she searched her bedroom and found exactly what she'd expected. Nothing. The Ghouls really had nabbed her parents, the sons of bitches. She moved toward the door. Halted as she passed the dresser.

No.

But she had to. She'd avoided this for far too long.

Heart pounding, she opened the top drawer and fumbled around until her fingers found the thin photo album duct-taped to the underside of the top. She removed it, her hands shaking so badly that she nearly dropped the small leather-bound book.

She almost didn't open it. The thing felt heavier than it was, the phantom weight of memories that should have been but never were.

God, she was such a drama queen.

Disgusted with herself, she opened the book and flipped through the two dozen pictures. All of people who didn't know they'd been captured on film. All taken at a distance.

All of Tayla Mancuso and the slayer's now-dead mom.

EIGHT

୭ଢ

It took three minutes to secure Eidolon to the bed. As tempting as it was to kill him, Tayla knew The Aegis might benefit more from his survival. At least, that's what she told herself. Anything to keep from thinking too hard about the fact that he had saved her life, and she owed him.

Afterward, Tayla showered, dressed in ratty jeans and a tank top, and checked his breathing and bindings once more. She'd laid him out spread-eagled on his back, his arms stretched over his head and chained to the bed frame.

Lying there, unconscious, he was beautiful. She'd been hesitant to look too closely before, when he was awake and would know what she was doing. Now, she could spare a moment to admire a body so perfect she could only compare it to an athlete's.

Thick layers of muscle cut valleys across his bare chest and down to ripped abs that spoke of hours of sit-ups. His caduceus pendant had slipped to the side, pointing to a thin, almost invisible scar on his shoulder. When she leaned closer, she saw more of them, so faint she doubted they could be seen in anything but the most perfect conditions, like now, with the afternoon sunlight pouring through her window.

Geez, he looked like he'd been scored by a thousand paper cuts that had healed but left shadows.

Tentatively, she trailed a finger along his shoulder and up his right arm, tracing the tribal tats, firm muscle, and pulsing ropes of vein. That arm had wrapped around her. Held her. No one had held her. Not since her mother had died.

Dammit.

Chastising herself for letting her thoughts take her in a direction she had no business going in, she darted out of the apartment.

It was cooler outside than it had been earlier – apparently Mother Nature hadn't gotten the newsflash that it was spring and should be warm in the afternoon – but she didn't waste time going back for a jacket. She wanted to get back before Hellboy woke up, if possible.

She took two trains and a bus, and forty-five minutes later, arrived five blocks south of Aegis HQ.

Headquarters sat on the remote outskirts of a New York City suburb, a large three-story house where the two Regents, the married heads of the New York City cell, lived and sheltered dozens of Guardians. The nearest neighbors were nearly half a mile distant, but standard operating procedure required an approach from the rear, through a secret entrance hidden in a copse of trees a quarter-mile away from HQ. An underground tunnel brought Tayla into the wooded, enclosed backyard, where two male Guardians were engaged in crossbow target practice. Trey couldn't hit the ocean if he were in the middle of it, but the straw vampire didn't stand a chance against Warren, a recently transferred Guardian from a London cell. Another Guardian, Cole, fiddled with something in his hand.

An explosion rattled her eardrums, Body parts whistled through the air. She ducked in time to avoid being struck in the head by a flaming foot.

Near the guest house that was home to nine male Guardians, the burning remains of a mannequin smoldered.

111

Tayla jammed her fists on her hips and scowled. 'What are you guys doing now?'

Cole grinned. 'I'm testing a new explosive that's odorless and practically invisible. Really cool. Works with electronic devices.'

'Stephanie must have developed it,' Tayla said, and Cole nodded. Steph was their cell's chief spellcaster, but because her specialized talents worked best – or only – with electronics, they'd had to adapt.

'We just blew the hell out of that mannequin with an MP3 player.'

'Why do we need an explosive like that?'

'In case we ever get into a situation we can't get out of.' He shrugged. 'Take out a lot of scum with us. And obviously, we can remotely detonate.'

Tayla grimaced. Sounded a little too suicide bomber to her.

'Call me old-fashioned, but I'd rather go down swinging a sword.'

She mounted the steps to the rear deck and entered the house without knocking. Laughter met her, the usual playful banter that filled the three-story house twenty-four-seven. An outsider would see a disciplined, happy group of teens and young adults living in the well-kept facility, but Tayla knew better, knew everyone here could turn into focused, deadly warriors in an instant.

As usual, someone was baking. Lori, fondly nicknamed June Cleaver, taught everyone to cook and assigned baking days to ensure healthful treats would always be available. Even now, the mouth-watering aroma of banana bread nearly had Tayla detouring to the kitchen. Instead, she cut through the living room that was as large as her entire apartment. Four Guardians looked up from playing video games, and one, a high-strung eighteen-year-old named Rosa, jumped to her feet.

'Tayla! Lori and Kynan have been worried.'

Tay strode past the TV, ignoring the curious faces. 'Where are they?'

'In the library, I think.' Rosa tagged along. 'Where's Janet?'

'Dead.'

Tayla supposed she should feel bad for being so blunt, but the answer had the desired effect; Rosa stumbled to a stop in the hallway, and Tayla sped up to escape the shock and questions. She pounded down the stairs to the giant multiroom basement. It had, sometime before Tayla became a Guardian, been expanded from a small, unfinished cellar to an underground facility complete with its own security systems and escape tunnels. Should anything attack the house, Guardians could shut themselves in the basement indefinitely, and could use the two exits as well.

Two Guardians were sparring in the brightly lit workout area, their bare feet thumping softly on the padded floor, and two more lifted weights near the rock wall. She hurried past them, through the darkened lab, which was empty except for the mystical relics, weapons, and magic supplies. The door to the library was closed.

She opened it and immediately wished she hadn't. Inside, Kynan had his wife bent over the arm of the couch. He drove into her from behind, his jeans bunched around his thick thighs, one hand playing between her legs. Lori whimpered, digging her nails into the cushions Tayla would never sit on again.

Quietly, Tayla closed the door and sagged against the wall to wait. The sounds of their lovemaking made her wince in remembrance of the noises she and Eidolon had made, though what they'd done had been anything but making love.

No, their romp had been raw and rough, sex born of anger, hormones, and wicked magic. Because what she felt for him when he was near had to be a result of some sort of incubus enchantment. Now she could sit back and be disgusted to the point of wanting to kill him, but when he touched her, heck, when he *looked* at her, she fell under his spell.

Yeah, he was a poster boy for hot doctors, but the memory of her mother, writhing in pain beneath the demon that raped and killed her, raked her brain like the back end of a claw hammer.

113

She pressed the heels of her palms into her eyes and shook her head, willing the memories away.

Only to have the fresher memories of being naked with Eidolon crash into her head.

Stop. She could tell herself that his incubus sorcery was still affecting her, but a tiny part of her, the part that had come closer to finding the ultimate pleasure with him than with any man, didn't care why she kept thinking about him. In any case, she needed to be stronger.

Eidolon had to die.

When the door finally opened, Kynan stepped out, graced her with one of his killer smiles, though his blue eyes darkened with concern. He didn't miss much, always appeared to be reading a situation about ten seconds into the future. Before she'd laid eyes on Eidolon, she'd thought Kynan was the most gorgeous man she'd ever seen.

'Sorry,' he said, his voice a gravelly mix of Afghan battlefield vocal cord damage and sexual afterglow. 'We sometimes forget to lock doors.'

Sometimes? Lori had once confessed that when she and Kynan got into it, things ignited so quickly that they'd started up while people were in the room with them. Only when they'd finished and found the room empty did they realize how carried away in each other they had become.

Tay couldn't even imagine being so into someone. Especially not someone like Eidolon, who wasn't even a someone. He was a some*thing*.

He held the door wider and motioned for her to come in. 'Where have you been? Where's Janet?'

Tears unexpectedly stung her eyes. Guardians died all the time. But guilt over Janet's death plagued her . . . if only Tayla had come clean months ago about her strange symptoms. If only she'd taken herself off active duty status. *If only, if only, if only.*

Her self-lashing was pointless, but it was a family trait, an addiction as powerful as any other. When she'd been clean, Tayla's mom had beat herself up daily for the things she'd done while under the influence.

The self-abuse had been as damaging as the drugs.

Tayla collapsed into one of the two overstuffed chairs, glad to rest the shaky noodles that were her legs. 'Janet and I ran into some problems.'

Lori hurried over, squatted at her knee. 'Tell us,' she said gently, her comforting, maternal presence at odds with the warrior-woman who could wipe out a den of man-sized Croix vipers with nothing more than a hatchet.

Her nickname, June *Cleaver*, definitely had its roots.

Kynan ran a hand through the spiky brown hair she knew from pictures hadn't changed since his Army days. 'She's dead, isn't she?'

'Yeah.'

'Goddammit.' He sank onto the couch and sprawled backward, legs spread, head back as he stared at the ceiling fan that spun in lazy circles. 'Where? We need to retrieve what we can.'

'We went into the sewers at the Aspen entrance. She's a few blocks north of that.'

Her stomach churned. The Guardians wouldn't find much, if anything. Janet's body had probably been taken or eaten by now. Every Guardian knew and accepted the risks of dying in demon territory. But it was the survivors who suffered when their comrades fell.

'We'd flushed out two Cruenti doing the nasty behind a Dumpster. We killed the female, but the male tucked tail. We gave chase, tangoed with a Croucher demon, and the Cruentus ambushed us.'

Lori and Kynan exchanged looks. It didn't take a Velma to figure out what they were thinking. A Cruentus shouldn't have been able to take out two experienced fighters. No way could she mention the truth of what had happened, how she'd lost the use of the right side of her body during the battle. The Aegis had doctors in their service, and Kynan, a former Army medic, performed most of the patch-up work, but despite her feelings of guilt, deep down she knew she had to keep her strange symptoms a secret. If the truth came out, she might be taken off the streets and relegated to training or paperwork. Or worse, kicked out of The Aegis altogether.

This was the only family she had left, and she wouldn't lose it. Couldn't. An ex-Guardian with no job prospects and without the tools and protection of The Aegis could measure her life expectancy in days. No, she'd keep her condition to herself, and she'd continue to hunt, but from now on, she was a solo act. No way would she risk another Guardian's life.

'I'm not sure how it all happened,' she said, 'but I saw her die. The Cruentus attacked me. That's all I remember until I woke up in a hospital.'

'Hospital?' Kynan shot forward like he'd hit a brick wall doing ninety in his Mustang. Tayla half-expected him to rub his neck from the whiplash. 'What hospital? We'd have heard.'

Lori stood, and ice formed in the room. 'You know, Tay, you don't look worse for wear.'

Yeah, as family-oriented as The Aegis was, a healthy dose of suspicion kept everyone alive. Tayla understood that, but the Regents' reactions stung. The Aegis was all she had, and she'd felt secure in the knowledge that she soldiered on a team where everyone relied on each other, where everyone put aside personal differences while in battle. You might hate your partner on a personal level, but at least he or she was human, and in a fight with a demon, that was all that mattered.

But now a crack had formed in the brittle bubble in which she'd been living, and a frisson of insecurity shivered through her veins.

Slowly, Tayla lifted her shirt, revealing her well-healed scars and the one wound that still festered. 'It was a demon hospital.'

❧

Lori and Kynan said little as Tayla told them what she knew about Underworld General. She left out the fact that she'd knocked boots with a demon.

Twice.

And a niggling sense of ... something ... told her to, for now at least, leave out how said demon was tied to her bed, his big body dwarfing the twin mattress.

'That's just what we need,' Kynan said, as he pushed off the couch. 'Demons treating the wounds we give them. Infiltrating our medical schools. Learning our physiology and weaknesses.'

'We've got to destroy it.' Lori paced the hardwood floor so quickly Tay expected to see sawdust fly. 'We can appeal to the Sigil for help. They won't ignore something this big. Maybe they can ask the government for assistance, as well.'

The government might help, indirectly, of course. From what Tay had gathered, officials in very high places knew of the underworld threat and worked closely with the Sigil, twelve Aegis members who prevailed over all cells worldwide. And in every city, ex-Guardians and Aegis sympathizers could be found working as doctors, cops, taxi drivers ... all willing to lend a hand.

'We can try appealing to them.' Scowling, Ky ran his hand over his hair, his frustration evident in the abrupt move. The Sigil was famous for refusing requests for assistance, forcing Regents to contact other Regents from nearby cells for help. 'Tayla, can you hazard a guess on a location for this hospital?'

'New York, maybe. But really, it could be anywhere. Another realm for all we know, with the parking lot exit at a gateway between our world and theirs.'

Kynan cursed and checked his watch. 'You two hammer out a battle plan. I'm going to assemble a team and retrieve Janet's remains before it gets dark.'

He gave Lori a peck on the lips and left, and Lori continued to pace. 'How did you get out of the hospital?'

Well, a demon doctor gave me a lift to a vampire nurse's

apartment, where we fought demons together, and then he took me to my place, where we had sex and chatted like old friends. Yeah, *that* would go over well. She thought she'd been prepared to give up Eidolon to them, but the truth could only go so far, and until she knew she wasn't going to be shipped off to the Sigil for interrogation, she was going to keep the fine details – and Eidolon – to herself.

'I convinced one of the doctors to let me go.'

'And this doctor just . . . let you?'

Tayla fought the urge to squirm. 'I told him I was a Screamer, that if they killed me, my spirit would call out to all Guardians until they found the hospital and destroyed it.' She licked her dry lips and hoped Lori bought the story. 'You know how stupid demons are. He believed me. Figured it was safer to let me go than keep me and risk my death.'

To her relief, Lori nodded. 'Good thinking. They can't know how rare Screamers are.' She pivoted in midstride. 'What was the doctor's name?'

Tayla didn't think it mattered, but what the hell. 'Eidolon.'

'And do you know what kind of demon he was?'

No way was she going to reveal that little detail. Lori would assume, and rightly so, that an incubus would use its powers on a weaker human, and Tayla couldn't afford to be thought of as compromised. Even though she had been.

Her body heated, because yeah, she'd been *very* compromised.

'Some sort of corporate hellspawn, looks human. But he gave me a way to get in touch with him. He was stupid, but smart enough to try to gain my trust,' Tayla said, knowing neither was true. 'I'll bet he thinks I'll give him info.'

Lori's bright green eyes grew brighter. 'Excellent. You've done great, Tayla.'

The door opened, and Jagger, a life-hardened Guardian with an extraordinary number of kills under his belt and a string of demon teeth hanging from said belt, sauntered inside.

Her gaze locked with his dark one, the battle of wills never-ending. They had been rivals for years before either one of them had even heard of The Aegis, bumping into each other in the revolving doors of the foster care system and then later, on the streets where they'd lived like rats. A police raid on one of their mutual hangouts had sent them scurrying into an alley together, where demons had ambushed them. Fortunately, Kynan and two other Guardians had been there, and Ky'd taken Jagger and Tayla back to HQ, later saying that he'd seen promise in their lack of fear and their fighting abilities. She and Jagger had been sworn in as Guardians together, but nothing had changed. She trusted no one, but him least of all. Damned Scorpios.

'You're getting sloppy,' she said, taking note of the twin punctures in his throat. 'Got yourself tapped.'

So did you, by a demon.

Jagger shot her the finger, his Aegis ring flashing. Cocky bastard was the only Guardian who didn't bother to hide the shield symbol on his jewelry. No, he liked to show it off, to strike terror into the hearts of the demons he encountered. Idiot didn't care that it made him a target for demons, said he welcomed the challenge.

'Ky said you might need some brainstorming help. Some BS about a demon hospital.' He stroked his chin, his fingers rasping over whiskers he kept trimmed into a permanent five-o'clock shadow, while she brought him up to speed. When she finished, he glanced at Lori. 'You thinking what I'm thinking?'

'Tracking spell?'

'Yep.'

How interesting that Jagger was so plugged into the cell's leaders. Tayla really needed to start hanging out at HQ more. She'd gotten an apartment to maintain the emotional distance she required, but she definitely didn't like being kept out of the loop. And sure, she could admit to a little jealousy where Jagger was concerned. He was such an ass.

The ass turned to Tayla. 'If you can contact your demon and

tag him, we can track where he goes. We might be able to locate the hospital.'

Your demon. Eidolon wasn't her demon. He was her captive. Visions of him chained to her bed clouded her brain again. She shivered and tried to tell herself it wasn't from pleasure.

Liar.

'Sounds good.' She smiled, but her joy felt halfhearted. The hospital needed to be destroyed, and Eidolon with it. All for the good of mankind.

She repeated that to herself as she hoofed it to the weapons room to replace those Hellboy had confiscated at the hospital, but for some reason, 'for the good of mankind' didn't ring as true as it had just a few days before.

NINE

ೲ

Tayla arrived at her apartment as darkness began to swallow the red glow of the sun on the horizon. Hardcore executives were just now leaving their Wall Street offices. Drug dealers were hitting the streets. Vampires were waking from their sleep and getting ready to suck innocent humans dry.

Her own blood sang, ran like a wolf pack through her veins as the hunt called to her. Oh, how she wanted to be tracking and destroying hellspawn. But her wound ached, and she had a demon tied to her bed.

She entered her apartment cautiously, in case he'd pulled a Houdini. Once inside, she peeled the tracking sticker – nothing more than a spell-saturated black paper dot – from its backing and concealed it in her palm. She eased around the door frame to her bedroom, and her jaw dropped at the sight of Eidolon lying on the bed, one arm nearly free from the chain still attached to the twisted mass of metal frame. He'd obviously gone on a rampage to get loose, but what shocked her was how Mickey lay curled on Eidolon's washboard abs, looking content as the fiend petted the traitorous animal.

'Oh, hey, Tayla,' he drawled, as though he were lounging on a

121

beach and not being held prisoner. 'I hope you picked up some Taco Bell while you were out. I'm starving.'

She dropped the bag of weapons she'd taken from HQ. 'You eat fast food?'

'Only when there's a shortage of live sheep and small children.'

Smartass. At least, she hoped he was being a smartass. 'I'm fresh out of those things, but I have stale marshmallows and oranges.'

His eyes caressed her, half-lidded and glittering with hunger that had nothing to do with food – or affection, which was something she'd do well to remember. 'I can think of something else I'd like to—'

'Don't say it.' The dark, sultry note in his voice hit her right between the legs, and she gritted her teeth to keep from falling into the incubus trap. 'Is that all you think about?'

'Lately? Yeah,' he said, and he didn't sound happy about it, either.

'Does it have something to do with that *s'genwhatever* you were talking about?'

'*S'genesis,* and yes. I'm close to the change.'

He scratched Mickey on the belly, and the ferret rolled onto its back, practically purring. The weasel was in so much trouble, though if she were being honest with herself, she'd admit that Eidolon's touch had made her purr, too.

The bastard. She moved to the bed and pretended to check his bonds. When she leaned across his big body to test the loose one, she casually applied the sticker to his pager, a necessity since Stephanie's magic worked only when attached to electronics. Tayla's breasts brushed his chest, the light contact sending up a violent tingle through her body.

God, he felt good, even when he wasn't trying.

'You going to release me any time soon?'

Straightening, she peered down at him. 'I was thinking I'd hold you prisoner for as long as you held me in the hospital. Why? You have some other patient to screw?'

'I need to feed my dog.'

'You have a dog? To eat?'

Eidolon stared at her.

'What? Why are you looking at me like that?'

He snorted. 'My kind has been terrified of you for centuries, and now I realize how stupid we've been.'

'Excuse me?' The demon was chained to his mortal enemy's bed, vulnerable, and calling *her* stupid?

'Aegi. You kill indiscriminately. You have no idea what you kill or why. You know nothing about us.'

'I know exactly what I kill,' she shot back. 'Evil. I don't need a reason to do that.'

He kept petting Mickey, the silence growing thick until he finally said, 'We've always assumed The Aegis is all-knowing, highly trained and organized,' he mused, one corner of his mouth turned up as if he'd uncovered a great secret. 'But it's nothing but a cult, isn't it? The weak and uneducated being led by those with their own agendas. Brainwashed lemmings following orders without question.'

'So you think I'm brainwashed. That I blindly do the bidding of some David Koresh because I'm ignorant about the underworld?'

Overwhelming rage pummeled her like the fists of foster parents from so long ago. The knife he'd used to cut off her scrubs lay on the floor, and she picked it up, tested the edge with one finger. Hellboy watched her warily, but if he was frightened, it didn't show.

She suddenly wanted him to be afraid, to hurt as much as she did. But she also knew that what she wanted wasn't possible. She could skin him alive and he wouldn't feel the pain she felt on a daily basis. Still, she put the blade to the pulse at the base of his throat.

'I knew the nature of demons long before I became a Guardian.' Her gravelly voice cut out. She had to swallow several times before

123

she could continue, but not before putting more pressure on the knife, until a drop of his blood welled at the tip. He didn't even flinch.

'When I was sixteen, I watched a demon torture my mom for hours before he killed her. After that, I lived on the streets and fought them when they would have taken me as a meal. Or worse, because I happen to know there *is* worse. So don't you *dare* tell me I know nothing about evil, you sonofabitch.'

'You think you're the only one who's experienced loss at the hands of the enemy? Have you heard of a pub called Brimstone? Yes, I can see you have. Two years ago, Aegis slayers slaughtered everyone there, including the brother I told you about, Roag, who had done nothing to deserve death. You haven't cornered the market on pain, slayer.'

Brimstone. Two years ago. A cold sweat broke out on her skin. She'd been there. She remembered going in through the rear of the secret lair, remembered how the place had reeked of smoke and worse, a coppery, rotten stench like decaying blood. Demons had been drinking, fighting, gambling. In the center of the room, several demons had been involved in an orgy while others placed bets. On what, she'd had no idea.

The Guardians had swarmed over the demons like mosquitoes, drawing blood. The entire cell had been there, and not one demon had escaped. Especially not after they set fire to the place.

Tayla could have been his brother's killer.

Mickey scampered off his belly and out of the room, and Eidolon put his hand over hers, not threateningly. 'You say I'm wrong about you. If I am, then can't you accept that you might be wrong about me?' His voice was surprisingly calm, given that she could kill him with a flick of her wrist. Given that she'd hit him over the head, tied him to the bed, and probably slaughtered his brother.

'If I'm wrong about you, then everything I've lived for . . .' Was a lie. She shook her head, because the beasts she'd killed over the years had been just that. Beasts with no redeeming qualities. And yet, she couldn't get the image of Eidolon caring for the dying nurse out of her head. 'I'm not wrong.'

Holding her gaze, he tilted his head, exposing his throat, making blood drip down the smooth skin there. 'Then you have to kill me.'

Just three days ago she'd have believed that. Three days ago, if not for the orders to send him packing with a tracking device on his pager, she'd have put him down where he lay. But he'd saved her life. He'd healed his brother and shown mercy to the nurse. Her long-held beliefs had been challenged, and now her resolve wobbled. She tried to pretend she didn't feel relief at the fact that she didn't have to kill him. That would be some other slayer's job.

'You didn't let me die,' she said, pulling the knife away and tamping down the desire to find him a bandage, 'so I won't kill you today.'

'How generous.' He tugged at the chains holding him down. 'Are we done with these now? Or are you going to pay me back for keeping you in the hospital?'

'I should. You destroyed my bed.'

'I could think of more ways to destroy it.'

She huffed. 'Demons.'

He winked, and she wheeled away, refusing to be charmed. She retrieved the key to the cuffs from where she'd hidden it beneath the music box – the only gift besides the ring her mother had ever given her. Sweat popped out on the bridge of her nose in an ominous warning, instantly followed by a wave of dizziness. Eidolon's face blurred.

'Tayla?'

'I'm fine.' She stepped toward the bed, but her right leg went rubbery and her arms turned into lead weights. Oh, yeah, she was going down.

Swaying, she sat on the floor before she fell. She was getting so tired of this.

'Tayla, what's wrong? Look at me.' He jerked on his chains

125

with such force that the rattle of metal echoed off the inside of her skull. 'Look at me, dammit,' he said, the commanding tone in his voice irritating but effective, because she swiveled her head in his direction.

'Shut up,' she groaned.

'Your eyes aren't tracking. You're pale.'

The room spun in a pudding-smooth mix of pale grays and browns. She really, really wanted to fall over and go to sleep, maybe after throwing up.

'Hand me the key and I'll help you.'

Yeah, like she'd let him loose while she was weak and vulnerable. He couldn't kill her in the hospital, but he could do it now. That smooth doctor voice he was using didn't fool her or comfort her in the least. Not when his words at Nancy's apartment kept replaying in her ears. *'I should kill you. Here, with no Haven spell to keep me from wringing your neck.'*

'This'll pass.' She pushed to her feet, only to stumble. Eidolon caught her forearm with his loose hand, and she dropped the key.

Her legs gave out, and she found herself face-down on the floor, unable to move.

ॐ

The key had fallen just beyond Eidolon's reach. He rocked his body, jiggling the mattress until the key slid into range of his fingers. Once he had it, he quickly released himself.

'Tayla.' Ignoring his stiff joints and aching muscles, he crouched beside her and turned her face toward him. 'Can you hear me? Blink once if you can.'

She blinked, her terror shining through the glaze of confusion in her eyes. He knew how it felt to be helpless and vulnerable, and for someone as strong as she was, the sting would go deep. He shouldn't care, was still pissed as hell that he'd allowed himself to be knocked out and tied up, but he was a physician and this was his job.

'It's okay,' he murmured, and gently brushed her hair back from her face. 'Just answer my questions. Can you move at all? Two blinks for no.'

She blinked twice.

'I'm going to roll you onto your back. If I hurt you, blink.' Carefully, he rolled her. 'I'm going to check your vitals, so just relax and breathe, okay?'

A rapid assessment revealed a clear airway, a regular pulse, and rapid but steady breathing. Her skin felt too cold, but her capillary refill was satisfactory. Until she could speak again, he wouldn't know what was wrong, but he suspected that her demon half was having a tantrum.

It wanted out.

'Does this happen often?'

No response at all, though the fingers on her left hand began to wiggle. Grasping her arm, he closed his eyes, wishing he possessed Shade's power to affect bodily functions and detect systemic malfunction. Instead, all Eidolon could do for Tayla was send a generalized healing wave into her and hope that any damage would reverse.

Warmth washed over his skin, seeping from his fingertips into her arm. 'This won't hurt,' he said, because the bitter scent of fear was rising from her and her pulse had gone tachy. 'I'm trying to heal you.'

A low moan wracked her body, and her feet twitched. He reached down, pressed his palm to one sole. 'Push against my hand.'

She did, a good sign.

'I'm getting better,' she rasped, and he pulled back his healing powers, uncertain if they had anything to do with her recovery.

She grasped his hand, her grip strong but trembling. 'Do you know what's wrong?'

Sixty years ago, he'd gone to Africa to rescue Wraith from yet another incident, and he'd come across a lion dying from a festering bullet wound. The animal, once strong and proud, had been reduced to a weakened shell, but its eyes still burned with the will to live.

Tayla reminded him of the big cat, dismayed at how its powerful body had failed it, yet wanting to survive. Something inside Eidolon buckled, and fuck, nothing should be buckling or unbuckling for this woman. There had already been way too much of the latter.

If anyone in this room was weak, it was him.

'Does this happen often?' he repeated, more sharply than he intended.

She hesitated. It couldn't be easy revealing vulnerabilities to a mortal enemy. 'It's happening a lot more lately.'

'When did it start?'

She still hadn't released him, as though she needed comfort and had forgotten who – and what – he was. Just as he had.

'A few months ago. It started small. Numb fingers and toes. Then I'd lose the use of a hand or foot for a few minutes.'

'And now?'

She closed her eyes and took a deep, shuddering breath. Without thinking, he covered her free hand with his, stroked the cold skin. 'Tayla? I need to know.'

'Sometimes both legs go out. Or one side of my body. This has been the worst so far. I've never been completely immobilized.' She opened her eyes, tried to lift her head, but failed. 'I haven't been to a doctor.'

'I don't think a human physician could help you.'

'Why?' She struggled to sit up, but he held her down with gentle force. *'Tell me!'*

'Calm down—'

'Oh, my God,' she breathed, struggling even harder against his hold. She was growing stronger by the second. 'I've been infected by some kind of demon disease, haven't I?'

'Something like that . . .'

'What will it do to me? Can you cure it?'

128

'I took blood samples at the hospital. I won't know the results for a couple of days. We can go from there.' It would definitely be helpful to know her sire's species.

She relaxed, but her eyes shifted wildly in their sockets as her mind worked. 'It started after an Alu demon bit me. They carry disease. I'll bet that's what happened.' She rolled her bottom lip between her teeth and worried it in a way that stirred him in an extremely inappropriate manner considering the situation. 'Do you think that's it?'

'Alus do carry disease,' he hedged. The bite of the Alu had been known to trigger dormant illnesses and diseases in remission. Contact with the creature could have activated her demon genes.

She nodded as though relieved at having pinpointed the source of her malady. 'The Aegis has doctors. Good ones who used to be Guardians, so they understand this kind of thing.' The pitch of her voice climbed a notch, and her words fell out in a tumble of excitement and hope that would have broken his heart if he'd cared about her on more than a professional level. Which he didn't. 'They probably see stuff like this all the time.'

Infections, curses, demon bites, yes. Half-breeds gone wrong? He doubted it. If an Aegi doctor learned the truth, she would probably wind up dead after a lot of torture or painful medical experiments.

'You can't see a human doctor, Tayla.'

'Why not?' The familiar wariness had crept back into her eyes, shadows that flickered in the green depths. She scrambled to sit up, and this time he let her, though when she jerked out of his grip, he felt a slight twinge of regret. 'I can't trust a demon to help me.'

'You're right.' He hated it, but demons weren't the most trustworthy beings, though many, like his mother's species, did live by a code of honor that had influenced his upbringing and had instilled in him a sense of moral principles. Which was something his brothers lacked, and was why he didn't fully trust anyone. Not even his own siblings. Wraith was too unstable, and Shade ... he had a curse to deal with.

'You can't trust any demon,' he said. 'But that doesn't change the fact that you might have to rely on one to save your life.'

She pushed to her feet, a little wobbly. Standing, he reached out to steady her. For a moment, she swayed toward him. Then, as though realizing what she was doing, she pivoted out of his reach, her movements fluid despite her weakness. Even when not in top form, she radiated deadly strength and determination. She was a fantastic specimen, a perfect female, and his body hardened in response.

Her gaze locked onto his, and this time he was the one who swayed. His world tilted as he pictured her beneath him, begging him to relieve her ache. But he hadn't. Couldn't. His inability to do so had him cracking his knuckles in frustration.

'You think I'm going to rely on you? Do I look like an idiot?'

'I could have killed you while you were helpless just now.'

'I'm sure there's a reason you didn't,' she said. 'I just don't know what it is yet.'

There was no point in denying her accusation; not only was it true, but he couldn't convince her otherwise. She was too smart, too street-savvy and well-trained to believe anything else.

'Your condition is more serious than you think.' The panicked light in her eyes flared again, and he didn't wait for her to speak before blurting, 'You are half-demon, Tayla.'

She stared. Blinked. Stumbled back a step. 'What did you say?'

'One of your parents, likely your father, was a demon.'

'You son of a bitch,' she said softly. 'How stupid do you think I am?'

'It's true, Tayla. Think back to when you were a kid. You were different in some way. Your nutritional requirements were probably odd. You craved certain things.'

Hatred came off her in sizzling lashes that practically peeled away his skin. 'Shut your lying, filthy mouth. My mother—'

130

'Slept with a demon.'

'She wouldn't! She would never willingly have sex with something so . . . so *vile*.'

Vile? 'It was easy enough for you.'

She punched him, knocking him back a step. Shit, she had a killer right hook. He'd feel that one in his cheek for hours.

'Get. Out,' she snarled. 'Before I change my mind about letting you go.'

Her pain, anger, and fear hit him like another blow, and he knew there would be no more talk. 'You know how to contact me should you need help.' He strode into the living room. 'And you *will* need help.'

'Don't hold your breath.'

Not holding his breath was impossible when she looked the way she did, even as pissed as she was, standing in the bedroom doorway, the neckline of her tank unbuttoned enough to show cleavage. The hem had ridden up to reveal a creamy expanse of skin between the top and her extremely low-slung jeans. Lust shot through his blood, throbbing through him with the same beat as the pain in his cheek.

He cursed, long and loud. The human was a menace to his control. Control would keep him alive. Lack of it would land him as dead as Roag.

And his control was being slowly stripped with every hour he drew nearer to his change.

❧

Gem checked her watch for what had to be the millionth time as she sat on the hood of Eidolon's car and watched the entrance to Tayla's apartment building.

What was going on in there? Gem had come to have a little chat with the slayer, had arrived just in time to see the other woman enter her building a half-hour ago. Gem had been poised to follow . . . until she saw the other doctor's BMW.

It was too much of a coincidence to assume he was in this part of the city on business unrelated to the slayer, so she'd held back, growing more agitated by the minute.

Her suspicious nature was running amok.

A gang of humans approached from the north, their sleazy banter ringing out over the honking horns, distant sirens, and the sounds of domestic violence from the dwellings above. Humans like Tayla should worry less about the evil brought about by demonkind and focus on the evil and violence their own species perpetuated. Violence like what she witnessed today while handing out condoms. What she witnessed every day in the human emergency room where she worked while covertly assessing patients for suspicious injuries, illness, and impregnation with demon spawn.

The men passed by without noticing her, thanks to the spell surrounding Eidolon's vehicle. She breathed a sigh of relief, not because she'd been afraid, but because defending herself would have been messy.

For them.

Yet another reason she was glad Kynan had neutralized the earlier threat. Had she done it, her secret would have been exposed.

Exposed not only to humans, but to the demons from whom she hid her identity, as well. As far as her demon brethren were concerned, she was a full-blooded Sensor, just like her parents. Because to many demons, slaughtering half-breeds was considered sport.

Movement in the shadows across the street drew her attention, and she sucked in an appreciative breath at the sight of Eidolon exiting Tayla's apartment building, his shirt wrinkled and missing most of the buttons. The man was fine. Smokin'. Why hadn't she bedded him before now?

Oh, right. Because she was in love with a married human who hardly knew she existed.

She shook off thoughts she had no business thinking when her parents were in such grave danger and hoped to hell Eidolon wasn't in league with The Aegis in the demon organ ring.

She respected the Seminus demon and his brothers for what they'd done with UG. The hospital was one of the few places a demon could go for help. UG had had a rough start, but as the word spread, suspicion faded and there was even talk of opening a similar facility in Paris, where the demon population was nearly double that of New York.

If Eidolon had anything to do with the black market killings, or if the hospital was being used ... the damage done to all medically trained underworld beings would be irreparable.

Eidolon crossed the street, his easy, powerful stride ratcheting her heart rate up a notch. Incubi did that to her, even incubi as uptight as he was. Son of the devil, she'd never met an incubus with such self-control. Then again, he had grown up with Justice demons, a species that couldn't be more opposite. He was the ultimate experiment in Nature Versus Nurture, and she imagined he must be engaged in a constant battle between what he was and what he wanted to be.

He didn't miss a step when he saw her sitting on his hood, but his gaze narrowed and the angular line of his jaw hardened.

'Gem.' He stopped next to the driver's-side door. 'What are you doing here?'

'I could ask you the same.' Could ask, but given the state of his clothing, the answer was obvious. So much for his famous self-control.

His expression shuttered. 'I gave a patient a ride.'

'Oh, please.' She barked out a laugh. 'There's no way in Hades you'd treat an Aegi.'

'Why are you here?' He crossed his arms over his broad chest, the flexing muscles making his dermoire dance. 'To see me or the slayer?'

'I was hoping to have a chat with Tayla.'

A blast of scent came from him, sweet yet acrid, like burnt

133

chocolate. It was a potent cocktail of lust and unease, an arousing combination for the demon in her.

'How do you know about her?'

She slid from the hood on the passenger side. 'You know my mother works at an East Side free clinic? Well, she took care of Tayla's mom when she was pregnant with Tayla.'

'Then you know she's half-demon.'

'My mother had sensed a demon pregnancy,' she said carefully.

Eidolon smiled, nearly taking her breath away. 'Get in the car. We have a lot to talk about.'

ॐ

Tayla sagged against the front door, shaking uncontrollably, as though she was coming off a drinking binge to put college kids to shame. She covered her mouth with her hand as her stomach rolled and rebelled. Why would Eidolon lie like that?

Because he's a demon. Duh.

So why had his words hit her on a level so deep she couldn't climb back out of the pit she'd sunk into?

Think back to when you were a kid.

She didn't want to, but everything that had separated her from the other kids came crashing back. She'd been stronger. Faster. She'd read others' emotions by the odors they gave off. Her need for vitamin C had been overwhelming and crippling at times, something doctors had never understood or explained.

Not that any of those things were proof of what Eidolon claimed. No way was she the spawn of hell. It wasn't possible. She'd have felt it somehow. She'd have known.

So why had she kept her exceptional vision, hearing, and strength a secret from everyone including her mother and, especially, The Aegis? Deep down, had she suspected?

No.

Fury exploded inside her, and she put her fist through the flimsy door. Eidolon had made her question her beliefs about demons, her loyalty to The Aegis, and now, her very heritage.

'You bastard,' she shouted, but she didn't know if she was cursing at Eidolon or whatever had fathered her, human or demon.

All she knew was that she needed to kill something. And unlike earlier when she hadn't taken Eidolon down where he stood, this time, she'd show no mercy.

TEN

ᏧᏫ

Eidolon gripped the steering wheel hard and tried to ignore his body's needs as he worked Gem for information. He'd left Tayla mired in confusion, rage, and harsh truths, but the image of how she'd looked was burned into his brain, leaving him in a state of sexual frustration. It was a curse of his species that once they were aroused, release was all they could think about.

'Tell me everything you know about Tayla,' he said, pulling onto the interchange that would take him toward Greenwich Village where Gem lived. 'Was her mother human?'

'Yes, she was.'

'Then, if your mother sensed the demon pregnancy, why was Tayla not destroyed or fostered at birth?' As Sensor demons, Gem's parents' ability to detect demon blood in humans allowed them to sense pregnancies that would result in half-breeds. They then took care of the infants accordingly.

'When Tayla was born, there was no indication that she was part demon. Once her mother gave birth, the demon vibes disappeared.' Gem smoothed her hands down her thighs as though her black fishnets were wrinkled. Her micromini leather skirt wasn't, for damned sure. 'Eidolon, I've been checking up on Tayla for years. I've never sensed the demon in her. I thought maybe Tayla's mother had some demon blood in her from way back in her family tree, and that's what my mom had sensed. But tonight I felt it in Tayla.' She paused for a moment. 'Something's not right.'

No, something wasn't right, including Gem's explanation, but for now, he let it go. 'I think her demon DNA never fully integrated with the human. A bite from an Alu probably triggered activation of dormant genes.' He glanced over at her. 'Why would you be checking up on her over the years?'

'Curiosity.'

Again, her explanation didn't ring true. 'Why so curious tonight?'

She sank her teeth into her lower lip in a way that reminded him of Tayla. Which set off a blast of heat in his body that couldn't be hotter if he were standing next to a lava beast.

'My parents are missing,' she said. 'I think The Aegis is involved.'

Gods, The Aegis had its fingers in more pies than a baker. 'And you were what? Going to kidnap Tayla?'

'If that's what it took to get some answers,' she said, pinning him with a look that said he'd best not lift a finger to defend Tayla. 'And I *will* get those answers.'

Son of a bitch. The list of those who wanted Tayla strung up grew longer by the hour. And that didn't make him happy, dammit. 'Why do you think The Aegis took your parents?'

'Because someone is killing demons and selling their parts on the underworld market, and you know damned good and well The Aegis is responsible. My parents are being held as leverage.'

A chill ran down his spine. 'Leverage for what?'

Her ominous pause made the chill spread to the rest of his body. 'They want me to work for them. To remove the parts that'll be sold. Obviously, they've expanded their operation and need more help to harvest the parts. That's why I've been trying to contact you. To see what you knew. But I ran out of time today when they called and said they had my parents.'

'Bastards.'

'That's a nicer word than I've been using to describe them.' She threw her head back against the headrest and stared at the roof. Her small breasts jutted forward, the dark valley just visible beneath the neckline of her crimson corset top. Creamy, lightly freckled swells pushed up with each breath, the way Tayla's had when he had her on the bed, working her into a passionate frenzy.

The temporary cool-down his body had experienced a moment ago only made the sudden flare of heat even more marked. Flames licked at his skin and burned deep into the muscle, the bone.

'Eidolon?'

Clenching his teeth, he concentrated on driving and not on the erection popping at his fly.

Gem settled her palm on his thigh, and he jerked. 'Eidolon, are you okay? Eidolon?'

Tayla's voice rang through his ears. *'Hellboy, are you okay? Hellboy?'*

The palm on his thigh squeezed. He willed it to go higher. To squeeze harder. A low growl erupted in his throat as he turned to the woman in the passenger seat, her blue-streaked black hair pulled into twin ponytails, her profile so like Tayla's . . . his head fuzzed and his vision swirled and he knew the woman wasn't Tayla, but in his mind she looked like her, smelled like her, and he couldn't wait.

Yanking the wheel so hard that vehicles behind him honked and slammed on brakes, he whipped the BMW to the side of the road.

'What the hell are you doing?' Tayla yelled, and he didn't bother to kill the engine before he pounced on her, his control shattered.

Lust buzzed in his head, and through it, he heard the sounds of fabric tearing, of buttons pinging off the vehicle interior, of Tayla moaning. He would give her a release this time. He had to. It's what he did, what he was born to do.

He closed his eyes and breathed deeply, taking her into his body. She smelled good. Dark, yet sweet, like cloves and citrus, the scents he'd forever associate with her. 'I should hate you, Tayla,' he said as he wedged one thigh between her legs and used the other to brace himself against the dashboard.

She stiffened. 'Eidolon.' Her palms shoved hard against his chest. '*Eidolon!* Shit.'

It wasn't Tayla's voice. It wasn't Tayla's breast he was caressing. Blinking, he looked down through eyes he knew had gone gold. He frowned. Tayla gazed up at him, concern in her expression. Her skin . . . no, not hers. Gem. Fuck.

Didn't matter. His loins were heavy and full, his cock so hard it could break, and his entire body was so wired for sex that she could be a mannequin for all he cared.

'You're going through The Change, aren't you?' she said quietly, and that fast he snapped out of the sexual haze.

Groaning, he untangled himself from the knot of flesh he'd created with Gem and settled back in his seat. 'I'm sorry.' He scrubbed a hand over his face, feeling the fevered sheen of sweat that coated his skin. His right side throbbed, and a glance in the rearview mirror revealed a shadow on his cheek, a design pulsing just beneath the surface as though trying to get out.

'Don't be. No one's made a pass at me in so long I've forgotten how nice it can be.' She fastened the few remaining buttons on her top. 'But calling me Tayla is one hell of a mood-killer.'

He groaned again. What had made him think Gem was Tayla? And why had it mattered? The slayer was nothing to him. He shouldn't desire her like this. The *s'genesis* was really fucking with him. He hadn't been this out of control since he was twenty and going through his first maturation cycle. At least then he'd had the comfort of knowing that once the days of nonstop lust were done, he'd come out of the transition stronger, bigger, more focused. Better.

That wouldn't be the case this time.

'I have to get to the hospital. Can you drive?' His hands were too shaky to even want to try.

She nodded. 'Are you okay?'

Not even close. 'I'm going to transfuse myself. I've been saving up blood, hoping that if I transfuse when the *s'genesis* gets tough, the fresh blood will hold it off.'

'Even if it works, it's just a temporary fix,' she said, in that know-it-all voice every doctor inherited upon graduating from medical school.

'I'm aware of that,' he snapped, unspent lust and harsh fact mixing into one caustic brew. 'Just get me to UG. And Gem, do me a favor and leave Tayla alone.'

'No way. She knows something about my parents. She has to.'

He thrust his fingers through his hair. 'Even if she does, she's not going to talk. Nothing you can do to her will break her. Trust me on that,' he muttered.

'So what's your great plan, then?' She made a sound of disgust and flicked the front of his shirt where a button had torn loose. 'Pleasure her into admitting The Aegis is involved? How do I know I can even trust you? Boinking the enemy doesn't say a lot for your reliability.'

That much was true. 'I'm an incubus. Sex is a weapon for my kind.' Except, even he didn't buy that, because he wasn't sure sex with Tayla had been about hurting her, about making her feel self-loathing for seeking pleasure with a demon – a demon she should, by all rights, kill.

'Don't give me that load of crap. Your breed of incubus doesn't turn all evil-demonic until after *s'genesis*. Well, mostly. Your brothers aren't exactly stand-up little Sems.'

'Leave her alone, Gem,' he growled softly.

'That's not going to happen.'

He could feel Gem's fear and anger as if it were his own. But his anger was darkly possessive and not at all welcome. 'Tayla's mine.'

'Yours?'

'To deal with.' He ground his molars. 'Mine to deal with.'

'Very reassuring. But my parents' lives are at stake. I'm not letting this go, and no offense, but your thoughts seem to be originating from below the belt when it comes to her.'

'Just for a few days. She's growing weak. She might cooperate if she's sick and isolated from her human colleagues.'

Gem's upper lip peeled back as she leveled a look of grave promise at him. Normally, she hid the demon well, but with her emotions ramped up, her human exterior had begun to unravel.

'I'll give you twenty-four hours. After that, all bets are off. Tayla will be *mine*. And my way of dealing with her won't be nearly as pleasant as yours.'

ରଦ

The seductive pull of the full moon had nothing on the lure of a she-warg in her season, and with both mistresses tugging at Luc, the next three nights promised to be both heaven and hell.

He closed the door to the reinforced steel cargo container in his basement and set the timer that would prevent the door from being opened from the inside. Ula, the female he'd won in a bloody battle with five other males, pressed her naked body to his bare back as the clank of the outer metal bar falling into place echoed through the room.

'I still don't see why we must lock ourselves away,' she murmured against the skin of his neck. 'We could have gone to the country. We could run free. We could hunt.'

Hunt. The very word made his blood fire. Luc would love to run wild like Ula, who was a pureblood, whelped by warg parents and more animal than human. As a born warg, she lived by different rules than Luc, belonged to a different social order.

Luc had become a warg – a werewolf, to the ignorant – at the age of twenty-four, the victim of a warg attack in 1918, while fighting as an American soldier in World War I France. Every passing year chipped away at his humanity, but he retained enough to want to live among humans even if he didn't associate with them. Living with the humans came at a price, however, and to keep from tearing them apart during the most powerful three nights of the moon phase, he imprisoned himself, something he swore to do until the last of his humanity had withered away.

At that point, Wraith had a promise to keep.

'We don't need to hunt,' he said, turning into her so all six feet of her curvy body molded to his. 'We'll keep busy in other ways.'

Besides, two halves of a cow carcass hung from the ceiling, double his usual monthly order and delivered fresh from the closest slaughterhouse. They wouldn't starve.

Her hand, already elongating, tipped with claws, closed around his cock, and a low growl escaped him. 'This union will produce young. I can feel it.'

He drew a sharp breath. Wargs didn't take mates unless a female became pregnant, and then the bond would become permanent. He sifted his fingers through Ula's waist-length, silver-blonde hair. Should his seed take root, she would be his.

One hundred years of loneliness would vanish.

'The Warg Council won't be happy.' Not that he gave a shit, not when she rolled her hips against him like that.

'Only if the cubs are not born wargs.'

He tangled his fist in her hair and wrenched her head back. 'We will not put down any that are born human,' he growled.

The silver flecks in her eyes sparked, but with annoyance or the impending transformation, he wasn't sure. 'But the law—'

'Is meant to be broken.' He released his grip and dropped his hand to her perfect, round ass. 'We'll nip the human cubs, turn them into wargs. No one will ever know they weren't born that way.'

'And if someone suspects?'

'I'll take out that someone before he can voice his suspicions.'

She grinned, her canines glistening. 'Ruthless. Strong. Protective. That is why I wanted you to win.' She dragged her tongue over the claw marks on his clavicle, where one of his opponents had slashed him. 'I haven't forgotten what you did for my pack.'

Nor had he. They'd met in Austria three years ago, when he'd gone with Wraith to literally sniff out a relic made from warg hide. Wraith had returned to the hospital, but Luc had remained with Ula and her pack. He'd intended to make the move a permanent one, his longing for relationships with his own kind a factor. But a rival clan had attacked them, and when Ula had gone down beneath three enemy warriors, her family abandoned her in favor of saving their own cowardly skins. Luc alone remained, standing over her and defending her until the battle ended, her pack proving victorious.

But her family's abandonment of her when she needed them had made him realize he wasn't ready for pack life, and he'd returned to New York, disillusioned and more alone than ever.

Ula hadn't forgotten him, and when she felt her season coming on, she'd sought him out, arriving two days ago on his doorstep. Other males had challenged him; a shewarg's season attracted males from miles around. He'd battled the other males, unable to resist the draw of her heat.

Nor could he resist the draw of the moon, and his muscles began to stretch tight under his skin. Ula shoved away from him, her expression one of ecstasy and misery as her own body trembled, her muscles writhing.

Blood pounded through his veins. His joints popped and contorted, the discomfort always on the verge of overwhelming the pleasure of the transformation.

But no, the real pain would come after he'd made the change and then realized his human side had locked him away, unable to hunt, unable to feel the tear of flesh and bone between his jaws, the warm tang of blood pouring down his throat.

Ula completed her change before he did, and she stood on two strong, silver-furred legs, watching him with silver eyes. Her lips peeled back from her sharp teeth in a snarl, and he snarled back, willing his body to hurry. Her mating scent had grown stronger, making his mouth water and his sex throb.

Throwing back his head, he howled as the last of the transformation took him, and then Ula was on him, snapping at his shoulder, claws digging into his chest. He took her down to all fours, more than ready to mount her, but she didn't give in. He had beaten his opponents, but he had one more test to pass in order to prove himself worthy of fathering her cubs.

He would have to subdue her by force, and once she was satisfied with his performance, she would allow him to take her. They would mate in beast and human form for three days, and then, exhausted, would probably sleep for another three.

It would be the first time he'd ever asked Eidolon for so many days off work in a row.

Grasping her haunches, he covered her as she crouched on the straw-strewn floor. He closed his powerful jaws over the back of her neck, pinched her scruff between his teeth.

She growled, twisted, raked her claws over his flank. He felt nothing, was too deep in the feel of her body, the rasp of black fur on silver, the heat radiating from between her legs. With every motion, the tip of his shaft inched closer to the place he wanted to be.

The sound of the door opening didn't register until it was too late.

'Shit,' shouted a male voice. 'There's two of them!'

Luc wheeled around.

Humans.

The Aegis.

He launched at the man standing in the doorway, crossbow readied, but Ula was a split second ahead, and she struck the slayer full in the chest. The extra-narrow crossbow bolt pierced her neck, and even as her claws tore open the slayer's rib cage, she shifted to human form.

'Morph dart,' she gasped, rolling off the dead man. She came easily to her feet, but as a human, she was weak, and she didn't stand a chance when the female slayer at the base of the stairs shot her through the heart with a silver-tipped killing bolt.

Ula crumpled to the floor in a pool of blood.

Bastards! Roaring with rage, Luc body-slammed the female slayer to the ground so hard he heard the unmistakable and satisfying crack of spine. Two more slayers, males, came at him with stangs. Luc pounced on the closest, claws ripping, teeth snapping, and then pain, white-hot and searing, exploded in his gut when one of the man's blades found its mark.

'Get him,' the guy screamed, and Luc felt another stab of pain in his side. The other male had injected him with something, silver nitrate, probably. Agony like a million razor cuts spread through his veins and sucked the air from his lungs.

His vision grew fuzzy, dimmed to a pinpoint. He had to get out of there. He lurched toward the stairwell, barely avoiding the swing of a cudgel aimed for his head.

'Goddammit, Cole, don't kill him! He's worth thousands.'

Chills shivered over his skin, ruffling his fur. Their goal was to take him alive. No way in hell. Panting with pain and effort, he scrambled up the stairs, the sounds of cursing following him. He didn't bother opening his front door; burst through it in a shower of wooden shards. Dropping to all fours, he sprinted down the street. The night air revived him, gave him a temporary burst of strength and speed.

He had no idea how long or far he ran, keeping to the shadows and ducking behind parked cars, but when the adrenaline ran out and he began to fade again, he was in unfamiliar territory, caught on the edge of the city and well out of his suburban neighborhood.

Fire seared his lungs with each breath, and nausea tumbled in his stomach.

Ula.

A scream ripped from his throat, ringing as a howl through the darkness. Going up on two legs, he opened his mind, sought the nearest Harrowgate. North. Several blocks away. Too far, but his only hope.

He loped toward it, no longer bothering with concealment. Operating on instinct alone, he rounded a corner and slammed into a woman. She smelled of rage and hurt that veered instantly to stark, icy terror. The emotions collided with his identical ones, intensifying them in a massive explosion.

Out-of-control hunger, the need to take something apart, made him tremble as he towered over her.

'Run, Little Red Riding Hood.'

In beast form, his words came out as a snarl, and she screamed like a fucking B-movie horror actress. The slayers would hear. Panic eroded what little remained of his humanity, and he struck, sinking his teeth into the soft spot between her shoulder and neck. She pounded against his chest, kicked wildly in futile defense as he shook her like a terrier with a rat.

'This way!'

A slayer's voice broke him out of his murderous rage. The woman moaned, hanging limp from his jaws. In the distance, the sound of pounding footsteps echoed off the surrounding buildings. *Time's up.*

With a toss of his head, he flung the woman's unconscious body behind a Dumpster and sprinted down the sidewalk, bouncing off light posts and street signs in his insane bid to get to the Harrowgate. To the hospital.

Suddenly, something like a fist to the kidney knocked him off his feet. Another crossbow bolt. Blood splashed all over the pavement, and it took all his strength to stand, to limp toward the sewer grate ahead, all the while holding on to his beast form, which was far stronger than his human one.

Each breath was like breathing water, each step was agony. He welcomed the pain, encouraged it, because it kept him from passing out.

If he passed out, The Aegis would have him.

And he had a sneaky suspicion that if they took him alive, he'd wish he were dead.

☙

Demons and netherworldly creatures rarely gave up the ghost without a fight, and tonight, Tayla was glad for that. She needed to cause pain. She needed to purge herself of everything that evil, lying demon doctor had said.

But no matter how much she pummeled the *drekavac,* a spindly, long-limbed demon with an oversized head and fangs as long as her forearm, she couldn't get Eidolon's words out of her head.

You are half-demon.

'No!' she shouted, and drove her heel into the *drekavac*'s midsection. The ugly creature crumpled to the floor of the abandoned warehouse, a shooting gallery for drug addicts, where she'd found it searching for humans to sicken with its breath. Beneath the demon, a dark stain marked the floor, and she wondered if it had been made by birth blood.

Hers.

Letting loose a roar of rage, she kicked the demon, kept kicking it, long after it was dead, until the sound of footsteps broke her out of her mindless violence.

''Sup, honey.'

A man was walking toward her, his gait ambling but predatory, as though his body couldn't quite keep up with his intentions. His glazed eyes gave nothing away except that he was stoned off his ass.

'You got some sort of dog, there?' Then he blinked, and she knew the *drekavac*'s body had disintegrated. Aboveground, all demons disappeared within moments of their deaths unless they

147

died in an area specially designed to keep bodies intact. Aegis labs, for example.

'Worse,' she muttered, and stepped around the junkie as she headed toward the exit. She'd always hated this place, but it was a demon magnet and made for a rich hunting ground.

The man's grimy hand closed on her shoulder. She froze, her fists clenched at her sides.

'Get your fucking paw off me.'

'Or what?'

'Or you lose it.'

The guy yanked her backward, and her tenuous hold on her temper snapped. She grabbed him by his ragged Army jacket collar and lifted him off the ground. With a hard shove, she drove him into the warehouse wall. He laughed, too shitfaced to realize the danger he was in.

'Take it easy, bitch. You want me, you only gotta ask.'

A shudder ran through her. This was the kind of guy her mother used to hang out with, the kind she'd always assumed had fathered her. She'd thought this was as bad as it could get. But now she knew the truth could be far worse.

'Shut up. Just shut up.'

'Bitch ain't playin' nice.' He started to struggle, but she shoved harder, felt the strain of his clavicle bones as they bowed, on the verge of breaking. 'Ow, fuck!'

The scent of his anger, tainted with a touch of fear, got her heart pumping faster. Good. Because someone else should feel the way she did, as if their world had crashed in. Misery loved company.

'Does this hurt?' she whispered, and his glassy eyes went wide with terror.

The sound of multiple footsteps barely registered in her mind, but her body revved with adrenaline. She was ready to throw down and take no prisoners.

'Tayla?'

Frowning, she looked over her shoulder. 'Kynan. Did you find—'

'Janet's body was gone.' The three Guardians with him lagged behind as Ky moved toward her, his eyes on the junkie, his hand hovering over his stang holster on his chest. 'Demon?'

She gasped. '*What? What did you say to me?*'

'Is that a demon? Tayla? Are you okay? Do you want me to finish it off?'

Oh, right. He wasn't talking about her. *Finish it off.* She was an *it.* Because demons were *its.* So really, in a way, he was talking about her.

She turned back to the man in her clutches. His face had gone bloodless and pasty, his breaths rapid and shallow thanks to the pressure on his clavicle and trachea. Oh, God, what had she been about to do? He was human, not a demon.

You are half-demon.

'No!' she shouted, but she wasn't sure if she was talking to the voice in her head or to Kynan. Still, she released the junkie, watching numbly as he slid to the ground. 'No. He's human. Scum, but human.'

The guy crawled off, muttering, 'You're crazy. Fucking certifiable.'

Kynan approached, cautiously, as though she might bite. 'Why don't you stay at HQ for a few days? Janet's death has hit us all hard, and I think we need to be together.'

'You mean I shouldn't be alone.'

'We're all here for you, Tayla.' The warmth in his smile was meant to comfort, but it didn't make her feel any better. If anything, it only emphasized how disconnected she felt right now.

Disconnected to what made her human.

'I – I have to go.' She brushed past him, turning a deaf ear when he called out to her.

'No hunting, Tayla. Not alone, and not until we clear you for duty.'

She fled. Fled her fellow Guardians, fled the warehouse where she'd been born. But the one thing she couldn't get away from were Eidolon's words.

You are half-demon.

ELEVEN

൙

The transfusion worked. As the last of the second unit of blood drained into Eidolon's body, the terrible lust eased, the maddening itch just beneath the surface of his skin died away.

Gods, he'd been strung out by the time he arrived at UG, his mind taking him back to being inside Tayla and then firing him up with new scenarios, all involving the slayer. He must have been writhing in the car seat, because twice Gem offered to ease him, her proposal nothing more than a physician's obligation to relieve suffering, though the scent she gave off spoke of her state of arousal. He knew his body was giving off fuck-me pheromones in copious quantities, a fact that had been confirmed the moment he walked through the ER doors. Every female he'd passed had been drawn to him, some touching themselves without seeming to realize it. He'd been tempted, so tempted to take them all ... individually, at once, he didn't care.

Though he knew in his mind, he'd be thrusting into Tayla. Sex with her was pure adrenaline. Untamed. Raw. The kind of sex the demon in him had always wanted, but his logical, civilized brain had never allowed him to have. Entering her had been exquisite, a freefall of sensation that demolished coherent thought and left him with the ability to do nothing but feel when in the past, sex had been more about satisfying his body's demands while his mind remained detached. He hadn't known his mind could join in the sex act like that, so wholly.

It was amazing. Shattering. Terrifying.

He'd used a freaking *knife* on her.

He'd damned near gone back to her apartment.

Instead, he'd grabbed Yuri, made him promise not to allow Eidolon to give in to his needs. Not while the glyph was trying to break through on his face. Though he had no proof to back it up, he suspected that sex during *s'genesis* pangs would hurry the change along, if not complete it altogether.

So Yuri sat across from him in the lab, arms crossed, one foot propped up on a technician's stool. 'You got it together? Because I have better things to do than babysit you.'

'Yeah, I'm good. Thanks.'

Yuri stood and adjusted the stethoscope around his neck. 'You should probably take time off work until all of this is under control.'

'Until the transformation is complete, you mean.'

'You gotta admit, it's making you twitchy and unpredictable, and you've never been either. You're acting like Wraith. Well, Shade, anyway.'

Eidolon removed the catheter from his arm and stanched the blood with a cotton ball. 'This isn't about my duty schedule, and you aren't concerned about my performance. It's about Tayla.'

'Tayla? You two so buddy-buddy that she's not just the Aegi whore anymore?'

'Let it go, Yuri. Now.'

Yuri barked out a laugh, a high-pitched hyena yip. 'See what the *s'genesis* is doing to you, Sem? It's turning you into a pussy.'

'Excuse me?' Growling, Eidolon came to his feet.

'You didn't want to turn her over to me. I get that.' Yuri moved forward, right up in Eidolon's face. 'But she wasn't yours to turn

152

loose. This was a matter for the Maleconcieo, and you should have taken her before it.'

The Maleconcieo, the demon U.N., a council formed of members of the most powerful of all demon species, would have salivated over the opportunity to question Tayla. Yuri was right, but that fact only angered Eidolon more. He'd told himself that he had let Tayla go so she could be watched, so she would come to them for help, but was it the truth? Had he been lying to himself and following his dick instead of his brain?

'Back off, shapeshifter. I know what I'm doing.'

Yuri grinned, his sharp teeth gleaming wickedly, but before he could say anything, the door to the lab burst open. Dr. Shakvhan, an ancient succubus who practiced Druidic medicine, gestured to Eidolon.

'It's Luc.'

Yuri and Eidolon raced to the ER, where Luc was writhing on an exam table, blood flowing from various wounds as Gem and half a dozen nurses attempted to strap him down. His form kept changing from beast to human, flickering like a dying fluorescent bulb.

'What happened?' Eidolon nudged a nurse aside while Yuri ordered a vitals check and gloved up.

The nurse next to him cursed when Luc jerked his arm out of the restraints. 'He came in like this. Stumbled through the ER doors and hasn't said anything.'

Eidolon grasped Luc's furry face, narrowly avoiding his snapping jaws. 'Someone get a muzzle!' He tapped Luc's cheek with his fingers. 'Luc. Luc! Focus. Look at me, man.'

Slowly, awareness peeked through the pain in his dark eyes, and he turned human. 'Aegis,' he rasped. 'Killed . . . her. My mate.'

Mate? He hadn't known Luc was mated, but then, he didn't know much about the reclusive warg. Eidolon used the pads of his fingers to make long, soothing strokes along the skin of Luc's neck, which seemed to calm him. 'You're safe now. But I need you to hold human form so we can talk. Can you do that?'

Luc roared, his wail rattling the equipment. '*They killed her! Fucking animals . . . they smelled like animals . . . apes. Bastards!*'

Eidolon nodded at Yuri, giving the unspoken go-ahead for sedation. 'Luc, I need you to tell me what they did to you.'

Luc's body thrashed, but his eyes caught and held his. 'They weren't going to kill me,' he said, and a tremor of dread shot up Eidolon's spine. 'They wanted me alive, doc. They wanted me *alive*.'

TWELVE

❧

Tayla didn't bother going in to Aegis HQ the next morning. Unable to sleep in the bed that still smelled like Eidolon, she'd curled up on the couch with Mickey. As the first gloomy rays of cloudy daylight peeked through her kitchen window, the phone had started ringing.

She'd ignored it. But she couldn't ignore the pounding on her door hours later. Kynan's knocking had been soft at first, but had grown rapidly more violent, until he was threatening to break down the door.

She'd opened it, and immediately wished she hadn't.

'We lost Trey and Michelle last night.'

Oh, God. Numb, she backed away from the door and collapsed onto the couch. 'How?'

'They were tracking a pack of werewolves with Bleak and Cole. Got ambushed inside a house. They took out a female, but lost the others.'

Despair settled over her like a chilled blanket. With Janet's death, that made three Guardians lost in the span of a week when they hadn't lost even one in over a year. And Tayla ... she'd been compromised.

'We're losing, aren't we? The battle. We're losing.'

Kynan dropped to one knee and clamped a hand on her wrist. 'Do not say that. Don't even think it. The fight against evil has always been a marathon, not a sprint.' She tried to jerk away from him, but he held her in place, his grip firm but gentle. 'Everyone is feeling the same way, Tay. But you're a veteran fighter. You can lead the others and help our cell through this. Come stay at HQ, just for a few nights. It'll be good for you. For everyone.'

For a moment she was tempted. Though she'd never been a social creature, right now, she felt more alone and out of place than ever. Still, she had a feeling that being among the other Guardians would only emphasize her loneliness. When she was by herself, no one looked at her as if she were a black sheep. No one talked through her instead of to her. Certainly, no one would look at her as if they knew what Eidolon had said and were trying to figure out for themselves if he had been telling the truth.

Join the club.

'I can't,' she finally said. 'I need to be alone.'

She also needed to be able to get up in the morning, check the mirror, and make sure she hadn't turned into a demon overnight.

And on the subject of demons, she wondered if the tracking device she'd planted on Eidolon had led The Aegis to the hospital. Then again, if it had, Kynan would have told her by now.

'Ky ... do you think there is such a thing as good demons?'

He blinked, taken aback. 'Ah, well, there are eudaimons, benevolent spirits, but in most cases these are thought to be guardian angels.'

'But can other demons, like Cruenti, ever be good?'

'What? Tayla, what has gotten into you?'

Eidolon had. Twice.

'I guess ... I just ... what if they aren't all bad?'

He felt her forehead with one hand, checked her pulse with the other, his medic training taking over. 'I'm going to take you to the hospital. You're tachy and a little warm.'

'I don't need to see an Aegis doctor—'

'Tayla, you're talking crazy. And it isn't a bad idea to have you checked out. Who knows what was done to you at that demon hospital.' She pulled away, and this time he let her, but he moved up to the couch. 'That's what this is about, isn't it? They took care of you. Saved your life. And now you're feeling sympathetic.'

'This isn't some twisted form of Nightingale Syndrome.'

But the suspicion burned in his eyes, navy fire. 'I'll give you until tomorrow, and then you're coming into HQ, and I will *take* you to see Dennis.'

He'd left, and she'd spent the next several hours doing nothing but napping and pigging out on marshmallows and oranges.

Now, curled up on her couch with Mickey in her lap, she dug her nails into the skin of a tangerine, working her frustration off on the poor fruit. She didn't need a doctor. Well, she probably did; last night on the way home from the warehouse, she'd suffered another loss of function, the episode leading to people at a bus stop calling paramedics. By the time the ambulance arrived, Tayla had recovered and was long gone.

In a moment of extreme weakness, she'd thought about calling Eidolon on the off-chance that he'd been telling the truth about his ability to help her.

She'd gone so far as to say the words on the back of the card he'd given her, but when her breasts tightened and her thighs quivered at the mere thought of seeing him again, she'd thrown the phone across the room. If her hormones were that out of control when he wasn't around, what would happen in his presence?

She hadn't known her body could react like that to any man, let alone one who wasn't human. If someone had told her a man could make her heart race, her breath catch, her sex ache, she'd have laughed, but that's exactly what happened when Eidolon touched her. She craved him even while she hated him.

She was an addict, the same as her mom. The only difference was that Tayla's drug of choice could be destroyed.

The phone rang, and she nearly jumped out of her skin. Mickey shot under the couch, chattering indignantly. Something cold dripped onto her leg, and she realized that at some point, she'd squeezed the hell out of her tangerine and now had juice and pulp oozing between her fingers.

Quickly, she rinsed her hands in the kitchen sink but didn't bother drying them before picking up the phone.

'Yeah?'

'Tay.' Jagger's voice made her tense. He rarely called, and when he did, the news was always bad. This time, though, he sounded almost giddy, which raised her alert status even higher. 'Get over here.'

'I'm taking today off.'

'Trust me. You want to be here for this.' Silence stretched, but she refused to give him the satisfaction of asking about his cryptic response. 'We caught your demon doc. He's not in good shape.'

Tayla froze. Nearly fumbled the phone. 'What ... what do you mean?'

'I mean that if you don't hurry, you won't have a chance to watch him die.'

ဢ

Tayla couldn't afford a cab, but she took one anyway. She burst through the Aegis HQ back door, startling the half-dozen Guardians watching a movie on the big-screen TV.

Play it cool, Tay.

'Where are they?'

'Basement.' Excitement lit the expressions of everyone in the living room, a far cry from the depressed atmosphere Kynan had led her to believe had taken over. The Guardians were practically bouncing in their seats, throwing off anticipation and bloodlust.

The familiarity of it all came crashing down on Tayla. A demon had been captured and was being made to pay for the deaths of their three colleagues. They enjoyed knowing that Eidolon was being tortured. She'd have enjoyed it, too, a few days ago.

Sickened, she dashed down the stairs. Several Guardians practiced with weapons and fighting techniques in the fitness room, but their half-hearted efforts didn't fool her. They were eavesdropping on what was going on in the Chamber – a room most, including Tayla, had never seen inside.

No, she used to hang out like the others, listening and laughing, because really, they were *just demons*. So what if they got slapped around a little before they were dispatched?

But the knowledge that Eidolon had been slapped around was somehow different, and she had to steady herself with a deep breath as she opened the heavy steel door.

Inside the room, which had been constructed of cement and spells from floor to ceiling, Lori and Jagger sat on stone benches, their gazes locked on the naked, bloody body curled in a fetal position on the floor and chained to the opposite wall. She nearly cried out at the sight, caught the sound with a palm slapped over her mouth.

'You're too late,' Lori sighed. 'Jagger lost his temper.' She turned to Tay. 'We didn't get much out of him. Lies, mostly.'

'Nah. The hot poker up his ass got us some good intel.'

Oh. Oh . . . *God.* Tay stumbled to a corner and retched, splattering vomit all over the floor. Not slapped around. This was what they'd been doing in the room all along.

I'm so stupid. A naïve moron.

Still hunched over, her head swimming, she took in the surroundings, the glowing embers in a brazier in the corner, shelves of barbaric tools, racks of various flogs and whips, a hose, and more things she couldn't identify.

'Tayla?' Jagger had moved to her to gather her hair and hold it away from her mouth. 'You aren't upset, are you? I mean, he was just a demon, right?'

'Yeah,' she croaked. 'Demon. It's just . . . the smell.'

159

The smell, the sight, the thought that Eidolon had suffered like that. What had she done? Dry heaves wracked her, twisting her gut until sweat poured down her temples.

'You've never sat shotgun at one of our interrogations, have you?'

She shook her head. Even if she had, would she have cared what went on? After all, demons were beasts. Evil beasts that slaughtered innocent humans for fun.

Funny how she kept telling herself the same thing over and over, despite the fact that no matter how often she repeated the 'demons are evil' mantra like some sort of protective shield, it didn't seem to make a difference.

'Let me take your jacket.' Dazed, as if she'd taken a punch to the head and couldn't put her rattled thoughts back together, she shrugged out of it and handed it to Jagger.

'Come here,' Lori said, and, knees shaking, Tayla moved to the other woman, who was now crouching next to the body. Tayla averted her gaze as she sat on her haunches next to Lori. 'He's wearing a necklace with a strange medical symbol. Do you know what it is?'

Tayla didn't look. Didn't need to. It was the caduceus. The one that had tickled her skin when he was bent over her. Kissing her. Licking her.

'No,' she lied. 'I don't have a clue.'

Her stomach threatened to spill again. Her eyes did. One tear, small, easily and covertly dashed away by the back of her hand. But that one tear contained more emotion than had all of the tears she'd shed since her mom had died combined.

She exhaled slowly, needing a moment to compose herself before she could look. And she had to. Eidolon deserved as much. When she did, her breath snagged in her throat. The body before her was bloodied, bruised, mangled in places. But the right arm was bare, unmarked by the tattoo that ran from Eidolon's fingertip to his neck. Her mind warned against too much hope, but her heart

160

didn't get the message, pounded as if it wanted free of her chest as she tipped the male demon's face with her finger.

Oh, thank you, thank you, God. Intense relief sapped her strength with such force that she fell back onto her butt. A smile flitted at the corners of her mouth, hidden by a hand placed as though her stomach had rebelled once more.

It wasn't Hellboy, but this demon wore the same dagger caduceus. They must have worked together. Yes ... recognition sluiced over the surface of her mind, not quite penetrating ... She could see him, his face fuzzy.

This is a waste of time. The words rang in her ears, and then she remembered where she'd seen him. At UG when she'd first awakened. What had Eidolon called him? Yuki? No, Yuri. That was it. Yuri. But why was he here instead of Eidolon?

Another voice droned in her ear. Lori's. She was jabbering away about all the ways they'd hurt him, and now that the grief and worry had cleared out of Tayla's brain, Lori's bragging took on new significance. Especially with the way she kept sliding Tayla curious glances as though trying to gauge her reaction to what they'd done. But what kind of reaction was she hoping for?

Tayla's energy returned with savage intensity, as if she'd free-based a bowl of adrenaline, and now she wanted answers.

'I don't care what you did. How did you catch him?'

There was a tense silence. 'Our losses have affected us all,' Lori finally said, as though Tayla's snappish tone could be so easily explained. Her smile was brittle as she answered Tay's question. 'Stephanie latched onto the tracking signal you placed on him, but she lost it for a couple of hours. She picked it up again, exactly where she lost it. Now we know approximately where the entrance to the hospital must be. We traced the signal to a residential neighborhood and picked this demon up in his house. He was a shapeshifter.' She sat down next to Tayla, never taking her eyes off the body. 'What was his name again? He told us, but by then,

161

Jagger had broken his jaw, and it was hard to understand anything.'

She didn't have the luxury or even the desire to feel sorry for the creature on the floor, but she did feel relief that at least it wasn't Eidolon Lori was so casually talking about. She also didn't have the luxury of the truth. If they knew the dead demon wasn't Eidolon, they'd want her to get to him again. Taking out the hospital was one thing, but torturing Hellboy was another. So, as though she were overjoyed that he was dead, she smiled and said, 'Eidolon.'

'And that's him, right?'

'No doubt. Did you get any hospital information out of him?'

Lori shook her head. 'He denied its existence no matter what we did to him. So what we need you to do is get back into the hospital. You said he gave you a way to contact them, right?'

'Yes,' she said slowly, wary of where this was going. 'But I'm not sure what you expect me to do once I'm inside. You said you lost the tracking signal, so we can't find the hospital that way.'

'You'll call us from inside.'

Tayla gaped. 'You're kidding, right? Do you think hell has its own cell towers?'

'Of course not. Jagger will explain when he gets back.'

That's when Tayla noticed that Jagger had gone, but when, she had no idea. The door opened, and he entered, carrying her leather jacket.

'All set?' Lori asked, and Jagger nodded, reached into the coat pocket.

He pulled out a cell phone and held it up. 'This, Tayla, is your secret weapon. Did Lori tell you about it?'

'She said I'm supposed to call from inside the hospital. But what if there's no signal?'

Jagger grinned, and she supposed most women found him attractive, but there'd always been something off about him, something that had never allowed her to look at him with physical attraction. Then again, very few men had ever done it for her. The one who did do it for her wasn't a man at all.

'That's the beauty of this little device. All you have to do is flip it open. There will be a countdown on the screen. Before it gets to zero, dial one-one-nine.' He stuffed the phone into her coat pocket.

'That's it?'

'Yep. When you dial, it'll blast out a tracer spell. Everything within a hundred-yard radius will be contaminated, and as the demons leave the hospital, they'll leave trails that'll be visible to our diviner for days.'

'Kinda like ants,' Lori said. 'And if the hospital is in this realm, we should be able to see it with the spell almost instantly.'

Jagger handed Tayla her jacket. 'Once the countdown is activated, it can't be stopped, and the phone will self-destruct if the number isn't dialed.'

Man, this was crazy. The words 'suicide mission' kept flashing in her head. Shuddering, she shrugged into her jacket. She had to get out of here, get some fresh oxygen into her lungs and into her brain so she could think.

Lori nodded at Jagger, a tiny motion Tayla almost missed, and Jagger came at her as if he'd been launched from a cannon. Before Tayla could get her arms free of her coat sleeves, he grabbed her, slammed her back into his chest, and kept her immobilized.

'Hey!'

Lori's foot crunched into her torso, and Tay's breath exploded from her lungs with such force she couldn't even groan at the searing agony. Jagger released her, and she sank to her knees, cursing herself for being so weak as to show pain, but cursing Lori and Jagger even more.

She clasped her hands over her stitches, felt warm, sticky blood flow into her palms. The wound itself stung, but the pain radiated deeper, so deep it felt as if her organs were shifting and imploding.

Lori knelt beside her, all fuzzy pinks and blues through Tay's

163

watery vision. 'I'm sorry, hon. I figured faster was better. Like pulling a tooth.' She stroked Tay's arm gently. 'I know this seems excessive, but we're at war. War means sacrifice. We're all that stands between humans and hell on Earth. Are you willing to do whatever is necessary to take these beasts down? Are you willing to give your life if it comes down to it?'

Her life, yes. Her spleen, no. She didn't have enough breath to say any of those things, so she jerked her head in a nod.

'Good. I think we all feel the same way.'

Yeah, she doubted that. Lori wasn't the one with the lacerated liver. Which reminded her that someone was stealing demon livers – and other parts. Eidolon was convinced The Aegis was behind it. But he also claimed Tay was half-demon. If he was wrong about one, maybe he was wrong about the other. Oh, please let him be wrong about the other.

'Lori,' she croaked. 'Speaking of war, do you know anything about the demons that are being captured and chopped up for their parts?'

Lori's gaze slammed into hers. 'What are you talking about?'

A twinge of pain made her suck air before she could speak. 'Eidolon. He told me The Aegis was capturing demons. Selling their parts on the underworld black market. Is it true?'

'You're taking the word of a demon?' Lori asked, her tone putting a chill in the air.

'I'm trying to get to the truth.' Of everything. 'I don't care if it's happening, but the demons think it is, and it's put them on the offensive instead of the defensive. If The Aegis isn't involved, it makes sense that we should find out who is, before more Guardians die.'

'If The Aegis is involved,' Lori said, 'it isn't through our cell.'

Jagger snorted. 'Great idea, though. We should get in on it. We could make a shitload of money.'

Lori shot him a dirty look. 'Jagger, have Scott take Tayla to Queens and leave her near that restaurant we've been staking out.

164

She can contact the demon hospital from there, say she was injured in a fight.'

'Okay, you know, screw that,' Tayla said tightly. 'I'm not comfortable with this plan.' She didn't know if her hesitation came from a reluctance to see Eidolon again or if she didn't want to face what he'd said about her parentage, but in any case, something was niggling at her, something she couldn't put her finger on. But she'd learned to trust her gut, even when it was bleeding out.

Jagger bent over her, and when he started to stroke her hair, she shoved him away. Still, he leaned close, so close she could smell the sausage pizza he'd had for lunch on his breath. 'You said you're willing to do what's necessary, Tay. Did you change your mind? You getting chummy with the demons?'

'I just don't think this is the way to go.' She stood, forcing him to straighten and back up. 'And don't you ever question my loyalty again.'

'I guess we could send someone else,' Lori sighed.

Yeah, that was straight out of Manipulation 101 class, but even knowing that, Tayla took the bait. 'It has to be me. They know me, even if they want to kill me.'

Limping, she followed Jagger out of the room, Eidolon's words from days ago ringing in her head.

Brainwashed lemmings following orders without question.

THIRTEEN

❧

'Have you found a mate yet?'

Eidolon pinched the bridge of his nose with one hand and held the cell phone a couple of inches away from his ear with the other. 'No, Mother.'

'You don't have a lot of time, you know.'

'I know, Mother.'

'Your uncle Chuke knows a fiery little Oni who hasn't mated. And you know how gluttonous they are, always eating and drinking and having too much sex. She'd be perfect for you. She'd certainly give you a heads-up when disease or disaster was about to strike the human population.'

Eidolon's head was starting to hurt. Good thing he was at the hospital, where he had access to plenty of pain medication. 'Thanks, but I'll find my own mate.'

'Be sure you do. I don't want to lose you to that horrible change. I won't stand by and watch you be hunted by every male in the underworld. I'll kill you myself. Do you understand?'

'Yes, Mother.'

'Come by for dinner this weekend if you have a chance. Ravan is bringing home her first suitor. We thought we'd put him on the spike and interrogate him before the appetizers.'

'Sounds fun. I'll see if I can make it.'

Eidolon snapped the phone shut and jammed it into his scrub pants' pocket.

'Your mom harassing you about a mate?'

Wraith stood at the ER entrance, arms crossed, shoulder braced against the sliding glass door. He'd pulled his blond hair back and tied it with a leather thong that matched his jacket, an Indiana Jones replica that suited him, given that his job at UG was to hunt down ancient relics and magical artifacts, often from hazardous locations.

Eidolon nodded. 'She threatened to kill me again.'

'Yeah, my mom did that a lot. Only she meant it. Tried, that one time ... '

Eidolon shot his brother a troubled look, not knowing how to respond. Wraith said shit like that just to get a reaction, and it was sometimes hard to tell what kind of reaction the guy wanted. Fortunately, Wraith shifted the focus when he held up a vial of green liquid.

'Think fast.' Grinning, he tossed the vial to Eidolon, never mind that the priceless potion, taken from a lactating acid sprite, wouldn't be available again for another thousand years. 'Busted my balls to get that. Had to seduce a Charnel Apostle and kill three of her knights, but hey, all in a day's work.'

The ER doors slid open, dislodging Wraith. Shade strode in, dressed in black BDUs and ready for his medic shift. He clapped Wraith on the back.

'How was Mongolia?'

'Cold. Bad food. Mongolians taste like yaks.'

'Didn't take long to get the Neural Mana,' Shade noted.

'Twenty-four hours. You so busy with – what's that human's name? Runa? – that you didn't notice I was gone?'

Eidolon cocked an eyebrow. Shade was rarely with any female long enough to discuss her, so this was interesting. Interesting, too, that Eidolon hadn't known about her. Then again, Shade and

Wraith had always shared a deeper connection than what Eidolon shared with his brothers.

'Nah. She walked in on me when I was with Vantha and Ailarca.' Shade shrugged. 'I asked Runa if she wanted to join us, but she freaked and took off. I have a feeling she won't want to see me again.'

'Imagine that,' Eidolon said.

Wraith rolled his eyes. 'Oh, look. E's moral values rear their ugly heads.'

'We're all cursed in one way or another,' Shade drawled. He turned to Eidolon. 'Have you heard from Gem?'

'Not a word.' And he was starting to worry – and not just because the twenty-four-hour deadline Gem had given was nearly up and somehow he had to convince her to give him more time.

He hadn't heard from her or Yuri since they left together after Luc had come out of surgery. Nor had he heard from Tayla, though he hadn't expected to. Still, her genetic issue would only worsen. Her lab work had come back, leaving more questions than answers. The DNA hadn't been identifiable, something that torqued him beyond belief. He'd been adding to the hospital's genetic database for years, requiring that every species, breed, and race of creature that came through the doors be catalogued. But there were thousands of species in the underworld, and only a fraction had been seen at UG. Obviously, none of Tayla's sire's species had been treated.

One thing had been conclusive, however. The demon genes were aggressive, and if she didn't address the issue soon, it would be too late.

'Wraith,' he said tiredly, 'you missed a lot.' He gestured for his brothers to follow him, and they ducked into the empty break room.

Shade plucked the ever-present pack of gum out of his shirt pocket while Wraith went straight for the coffee pot. 'What's up? Did one of you nail Gem?'

'No.' Eidolon dragged a hand through his hair. 'Gem thinks her parents were taken by The Aegis, but not for the black market. Whoever has them is using them for leverage. They want her to perform the surgeries and organ removals. Apparently, the operation is growing, and they need more help.'

'Fuckers,' Wraith muttered, still facing away as he poured his coffee.

A tic pulsed in Shade's jaw, and when he spoke, his tone was glacial. 'They got Nancy.'

Wraith spared no love for the nurse, but when something pained Shade, Wraith took it to heart. 'Is she dust?'

'Extremely.'

Without spilling a drop of coffee, Wraith swung around in a fluid, predatory motion that, even after all these years, still surprised Eidolon. Because despite Wraith's I-don't-give-a-fuck attitude and childish fits, he was a lethal sonofabitch with expertise in every ancient and modern fighting technique known to man or demon. He wasn't about to let anyone hurt him ever again.

'I told you we should have killed the Aegi bitch,' Wraith growled.

'She had nothing to do with it, and she doesn't know anything.' Eidolon was sure of that. She'd been too shocked by what had been done to Nancy.

Shade let out a harsh laugh. 'Sounds like someone is thinking with his dick.'

'Finally.' A thread of amusement shot through Wraith's still-irate rumble. 'Damned inconvenient timing, though.'

No shit.

All he could think about was Tayla, no matter how hard he tried to shake her from his mind and off his skin.

A beeper went off – Shade's, which meant an ambulance run. Palming the device, he glanced at it, then shook his head and did a double-take. 'Fuck me.'

Wraith peered over Shade's shoulder. 'Nope, wrong brother.' He bared his teeth at Eidolon in a cold smile. 'Looks like your little slayer misses you. Got herself all beat up and in need of a lift to the hospital.'

ॐ

Tayla waited in the alley between a Chinese restaurant and a liquor store. Scott had splattered blood in the alley, blood Jagger had collected from a Daeva demon he'd tortured a week ago. Now she sat against the wall, hand pressed to the oozing wound in her side, stomach churning from a combination of pain and the mingled scents of demon blood and cheap takeout.

She'd called the hospital from a pay phone, and the strange thing was, no one had actually answered. She'd heard a click, a growl, and then the line went dead. Really, she had no idea if the call had gone through. If she hadn't been in so much pain, she'd have gone home, screw the assignment. As it was, she could barely walk, so until she regained some strength, she had to sit still and hope the stench of Daeva dim-sum didn't make her puke.

Her patience paid off when, fifteen minutes after the call, Eidolon's brother, Shade, and a female Umber demon he called Skulk arrived. She couldn't decide if she should be happy that Eidolon's brother had been dispatched or not. Clearly, he was no fan of hers, but then again, at least he was familiar. Better the enemy you know, and all that crap.

No one spoke as Shade carried her, not so gently, to the waiting black ambulance that passersby didn't seem to notice. She remembered how Eidolon hadn't worried about his BMW ... maybe whatever spell encompassed his car also protected the ambulance. The demons would be safe; humans didn't see demons unless demons wanted them to see or the human was either trained or gifted.

Like Tayla, who had been able to see the fiends since the day her mother died.

'I'll ride with her,' Shade said to the Umber, as he laid Tayla on the stretcher.

Skulk glared at Tayla from the rear ambulance doors, but she slammed them shut, leaving Tay alone with Shade. The same soft, reddish-gray light she'd noticed in the hospital illuminated the interior of the ambulance, and the same inscriptions were scrawled on the walls and ceilings. Aside from those things, she could have been inside any human emergency vehicle. Any human emergency vehicle staffed by demon paramedics.

When Shade lifted her shirt with gloved hands, she resisted the urge to slap them away. She also resisted the urge to compare him to Eidolon, something that would be easy to do, given the identical tattoo running the length of his arm, the muscular, powerful body, the sculpted features of his face, the lusciously long eyelashes ...

'Didn't Eidolon tell you to take it easy?' he growled, and she rolled her eyes.

'Whatever.'

'Stubborn human.' He wrapped his hand around her wrist, pressed two fingers to her pulse. 'So. You're fucking my brother, huh?'

'Not one to beat around the bush, are you?'

'Not so much.'

A strange warmth washed over her, and when her heart should have been pounding with nervous energy, it slowed, along with her breathing. Relaxation turned her into a puddle. Pleasure tingled through her, as if the blood in her veins had turned to carbonated cream. She hadn't felt like this since she'd been a teen smoking joints with her delinquent friends.

'What are you doing to me?' she asked, hoping the slur in her voice didn't sound as pronounced to him as it did to her.

'I'm slowing your bodily functions and triggering a rush of endorphins. Helps ease the pain.' He hooked his stethoscope's ear-buds in his ears and pressed the bell to her chest. 'It also gives you a false sense of well-being that'll make it easier for me to manip-ulate you.'

'Cool. Can Hellboy do that?'

'Eidolon has a different gift.'

'I'll say,' she sighed.

He made her feel good in other ways. Ways that sent a wave of heat rolling through her lower body just thinking about them. Were all the brothers so alike, and yet so different? She eyed Shade as he inserted an IV line into her left hand, his skilled efforts efficient but relaxed, as if he could do it in his sleep.

Eidolon came across as focused, tense, and in control. Shade, on the other hand, seemed more laid-back, but she wasn't sure it was in a good way. More of an *I can kill you and not care less* sort of way.

Tiny pinpricks of pain spread through her right arm, one of the familiar sensations that preceded a loss of function. She winced, and Shade smoothed a palm over her belly, but she shook her head. 'Not the wound. It's my arm. Right one.'

Frowning, he reached across her body to her shoulder, which had gone numb. 'Make a fist.'

She tried. 'I can't.'

'Has this happened before?' When she hesitated, he tipped her chin toward him with his other hand. 'Slayer? Answer me.'

The command in his voice made her bristle. She did *not* follow orders given by demons. 'I already discussed this with Hellboy. Ask him.'

She caught a whiff of something tangy. Whenever some part of her body gave out, her sense of smell grew more acute – a strange response, and one that lent credence to what Eidolon had said about her demon parentage.

Even though she refused to admit it out loud.

'You smell funny.'

'It's called irritation,' he muttered as he pushed his fingers firmly into her elbow joint. 'The problem is your nerves. They've shut down somehow and aren't allowing control to the muscles.' His large palm moved slowly upward to her shoulder. 'I need you to sit up.' She did, and his hand drifted around to her back, then up

172

her neck. It felt good in a way it shouldn't, good enough that she didn't even notice that the rig had pulled to a stop until the back doors opened.

Eidolon stood there, his expression stony, his eyes nearly black and revealing nothing. Her chest constricted so she could barely breathe, because God, she'd forgotten how beautiful he was in scrubs, the way his broad shoulders filled out the top, how the V-neck revealed tan skin lightly dusted with dark hair. The markings on his muscular arm writhed almost hypnotically, and she nearly sighed at the visual orgasm it was giving her.

Even all Mr. Grimface, Eidolon was the hottest thing she'd ever seen.

'What happened?'

'Yeah, I missed you, too, Hellboy.'

Eidolon pegged her with an exasperated look and grabbed the stretcher. 'What did you do now?'

'She got into a fight with a Daeva.' They wheeled her into the dark ER, where humanoid and nonhumanoid beings glared at her with unconcealed hatred.

'I wasn't looking for a fight,' she protested.

Shade gave her a flat stare, so like Eidolon's. 'You just happened to be taking a walk in demon central and got ambushed?'

'Sort of.'

'What happened to the Daeva?' Eidolon asked. Silence fell like a guillotine blade as everyone waited for an answer.

Pride made her want to say she'd killed it, but not being suicidal ... 'It got away.'

'Uh-huh.' He and Shade settled her into a cubicle and closed the curtains to shut out the gawkers.

'Where's Wraith?' Shade asked.

'Hunting.' Eidolon's deep voice resonated through her with almost the same effect Shade's touch had had on her earlier. She'd forgotten how seductive his voice alone was. 'Why did you call us, Tayla?'

Because my boss ordered me to. Guilt kicked her in the chest for just a second – until she glanced over at Shade, who looked as if he'd rather kill her than treat her.

'I don't need anyone asking questions about this wound and why it won't heal.' That much was true. The thought stung, because she felt herself drawing further and further away from the only family she'd ever known, and if she couldn't count on them, she had nothing left.

'Probably smart,' he said, as he pulled on some surgical gloves.

When he finished, he and Shade moved her to a padded table, where she lay still while Shade gripped her wrist and Eidolon probed her wound, which didn't hurt thanks to whatever Shade was doing to her. In fact, Eidolon's fingers on her skin soothed all her aches, except the one that had started to inexplicably blossom between her legs. That one grew worse, and was it her imagination, or had Eidolon started to lose focus?

His long fingers no longer probed her wound, but were instead gliding over the skin of her stomach in long, sensual strokes. Through the thin latex of his glove, she could see his tattoo pulsing, pushing up on the material. His gaze snapped up to hers, glints of gold punching through the brown in his eyes.

'E!' Shade snapped his fingers in front of Eidolon. He jerked back when Eidolon hissed, the gold in his eyes spreading like spilled paint. 'Shit. E, man, get it together. Do you need to transfuse?'

For a moment Hellboy stood there, chest heaving, and then he closed his eyes and took a deep breath. 'No. I'm fine.' His voice was a low, rough rumble as he returned Shade's doubtful look with a hard one of his own. '*I'm fine.*'

She wondered if the *s'genesis* thing had anything to do with whatever was happening, but she didn't ask, merely watched as Eidolon pressed his fingers over her wound. A tingle ran through her belly, similar to what she'd felt when he healed the facial wounds the Cruentus demon had given her during the sewer battle at Nancy's.

'No response. I'm going to have to suture this again.'

'Why doesn't it heal like the other wounds?' she asked.

'I think it's got something to do with what's going on with your anatomy.'

Shade and Eidolon exchanged looks. 'You told her? What, you ran out of pillow talk?'

'She needed to know.'

Shade spouted something in another language, and Eidolon snapped back.

'It isn't polite to speak in tongues in front of guests.'

'Fuck you, slayer.' Shade released her wrist, and pain tore through her abdomen. She gasped before she could stop herself and bit her lip to keep from doing it again.

'Dammit, Shade.' Eidolon grabbed a wicked-looking instrument and thread off the metal tray he'd pulled next to him. 'Stop her pain.'

'We shouldn't be treating her at all. You changed the refusal-of-treatment clause in the charter to include Aegi scum.'

'It's something I shouldn't have done.'

'Shouldn't have done? Are you forgetting what happened to Nancy? To Luc? She could have been in on it.'

'Who's Luc?' she managed, through gritted teeth.

Eidolon answered, but kept his angry gaze on Shade. 'Paramedic. Werewolf. The Aegis surprised him in his house, where he'd locked himself up for the full moon. They killed his mate, tried to take him alive.'

'Animals,' Shade growled. 'He even said they smelled like animals. Apes. But he took two of you scumbags out.'

Trey and Michelle. She drew a sharp, and painful, breath. Kynan said that the Guardians were ambushed. 'Your were is lying. Guardians chased them—'

'Were you there?' It was more than a question; it was an accusation.

'No.'

'Yeah. Right.' Shadows flitted in Shade's eyes ... actual shadows from within that turned his brownish-black eyes completely black as he looked at Eidolon from across the table. 'What if she was? Would that make a difference to you? Or would you still be panting after her like a—'

'This conversation ends now.' Eidolon's tone was a portent for trouble. 'Numb her.'

Cursing, Shade grasped her wrist again, hard enough to cause pain on its own, but immediately, warm relaxation washed over her.

Something else washed over her, too. Gratitude. Eidolon couldn't hurt her inside the hospital; she knew that. But he also didn't have to relieve her pain. If he wanted her to suffer, she'd suffer. She couldn't help but wonder, if the situation were reversed, would she have done the same?

'No,' she whispered, and Eidolon frowned.

'Are you still in pain?' One hand flew to her other wrist to check her pulse. 'What is it?'

'Sorry,' she choked out. 'Talking to myself.'

He looked at her as if she was daft, and Shade shook his head, but then they went back to what they'd been doing, and she went back to wondering when she'd started feeling something other than blind hatred for the demon.

What terrific timing, given that she was supposed to help destroy the hospital, and him with it.

While Hellboy stitched her up, she got intimate with the lay of the land. Not that she could see much except crimson-splashed gray walls and a ceiling from which huge pulleys and chains hung, but hey, no creepy detail would go wasted. She'd always hated hospitals, but the smell of disinfectant and the sound of equipment beeping actually comforted her now, bits of normalcy in what could otherwise be a terrifying place.

The gentle tugging on her skin stopped. Eidolon snipped the thread he'd been working with.

176

'Done?' she asked.

'Yep.'

Shade yanked his hand away. 'Good. I'm going to go help a patient who actually deserves it.' He stalked out. Pain immediately began to throb in her abdomen.

'Damn him,' Eidolon muttered, so softly she barely heard.

'It's okay. I don't blame him. Not after what happened to Nancy.'

Eidolon's startled gaze flickered to hers. 'I can give you painkillers,' he offered roughly, ignoring what she'd said.

She shook her head. 'I need to stay alert.' Going fuzzy in enemy territory could be disastrous. Besides, after her mom died, she'd sworn never to touch drugs again. Her mother's battle with addiction had caused too much misery, had led her down a dark road where demons were real and not a metaphor.

Drawing the tray closer with his foot, he selected a syringe from the lineup of instruments. 'I'll give you a local to keep the discomfort at a minimum.'

He injected the medicine, and after the initial burn wore off, the wound went numb.

'Thank you.'

Once again he glanced at her in surprise, but didn't comment, because suddenly the room swarmed with tiny, round little demon ... things. A dozen of them, furry and about the size of rabbits, scurried beneath the curtains, rolling and pouncing on each other. One paused to look up, its big eyes blinking at her. It was sort of cute. For a demon. Then again, Eidolon was burning hot for a demon. Or a human, for that matter.

They climbed up her IV pole, onto tables and stools, and she smiled as one dived down the sleeve of her jacket that Shade had draped over a chair. They chattered and squeaked and then one dipped into her pocket – and came out with her cell phone. The creature flipped the phone open. Tayla tore out her IV line and leaped off the table.

'Gimme that,' she said sweetly. The critter scampered away, but Eidolon managed to snare the phone.

The curtain whipped open. What must have been the little ones' mother stepped inside, her clawed feet scraping the floor.

'Apologies, doctor,' she growled through fangs the length of Tayla's index finger. Her gaze shifted sharply to Tayla. 'Is that . . . human?' Her large, catlike eyes went even wider, revealing a silver rim that glowed. '*Slayer.* I heard the whispers.'

Still holding Tayla's phone, Eidolon addressed the demon, a subterranean species that came aboveground around Halloween. 'Gather your young, *flitta*. This is not your concern.'

The *flitta,* whatever that meant, didn't seem to hear, instead took a step toward Tayla. Drool dripped from her fangs. 'You,' she hissed. 'You should die.'

Shade moved up behind her, watched with ill-concealed amusement.

'You killed my hatchlings.'

Tayla frowned at the little demons hopping around beneath her, and the mother roared. 'Not them! My nest before this. All of them. In pieces, smashed as they came out of their shells. You slaughtered my babies.'

'It wasn't me,' Tay said lamely, because it could have been. How many demon nests had she destroyed? Too many to count – or even remember.

'It was an Aegi butcher, same as you.'

One of the babies leaped toward Tay's arms, but Eidolon caught it in midair, tickled it behind its pointy ear, and handed it to the angry mother.

'*Flitta,* it wasn't this Aegi. Gather your brood and go. Bring the *flossa* back next week and I'll remove her cast.'

That was when Tay noticed a quiet baby in the corner, one leg wrapped and dragging behind it. Gently, Shade picked it up and tucked it against his chest. Tayla nearly fell over as he began to make soft cooing noises that had all of the youngsters following

178

him out of the room. The mother speared Tayla with a glare of pure murder before sauntering off after Shade and the babies.

'Wow, she was a little worked up.'

Eidolon swept the curtain closed again. 'An Aegi murdered her young.'

'Because that species comes out at Halloween and eats—'

'Vegetables.'

'What?'

'Her particular breed. They're vegetarians. They mainly raid farmers' fields in the fall because they like gourds.' Still holding her phone in one hand, he dumped his tray of bloodied tools into a nearby container with the other. 'Your Aegis buddies slaughtered innocent younglings that would have grown up to do nothing worse than suck the guts out of a few pumpkins.'

Nausea swirled in her stomach. 'How did the little one get hurt?'

'Stepped on by an adult. If it weren't for the hospital, she would have died. Fractured bones are a death sentence for that species.'

Tay seriously wanted to throw up. Things had gone wrong, so wrong. In a matter of days, her world had been flipped upside down. Everything she thought she'd known about demons was wrong. Vegetarian demons? Demons who cured instead of killed? Her simple black-and-white world had gone about a million shades of gray.

'Tayla? Are you okay?'

She blinked out of her gray world and back to the strange, dark one that was Underworld General. A hospital whose very existence should be impossible. A hospital The Aegis wanted to bring down. She couldn't do it. Right now she was too vulnerable, too unsure of her feelings to commit to the destruction of UG.

'Can I have my phone, please?'

'If you're thinking of calling for help, you might as well know that you can't get a signal here.'

'No extended network, huh?' She stood there as he closed the distance between them, his tall, solid body drawing her as if it had its own gravitational pull, and without thinking, she took a step to meet him. He held out the phone, but when she reached for it, his hand captured her wrist.

'Why do you want the phone?'

She swallowed dryly, unsure what to say, not because she couldn't lie, but because suddenly, she didn't want to. Not when the gold flecks in his eyes had begun to glitter again. She licked her lips, and his gaze dropped to her mouth.

He pulled her close, suspicion and something darker swirling in his eyes. 'What's wrong?'

'Nothing.'

'You keep licking your lips. Are you nervous?'

'They're just dry.'

The darkness in his gaze intensified as he watched her, and then he dipped his head until their lips nearly touched and she could feel the softest draft of air in the span of distance between them. 'I can help with that.'

She moaned and wished he'd just kiss her already. He seemed to be waiting for permission, which was ridiculous. Before, he'd taken what he wanted. Why did he want her assent now?

'Do you want me to help?'

'No,' she said, but she tipped her face up so their lips touched.

His tongue flicked over her lips in a kiss that wasn't quite a kiss, but was enough to heat her blood. 'Are you sure?'

'No.' She opened her lips, nearly panting.

'I don't know how you do this to me, Tayla,' he whispered. 'But I can't help myself.' His hand grasped the back of her head and held her for his possession.

Instantly, fire zipped through her veins, lit her up from the inside. She opened to the penetration of his tongue, to the sweep against her teeth, the roof of her mouth. Closing her eyes, she let her body react, to coil tight with desire that was growing addictive. She'd felt nothing for so long, had been in an emotional void, a

180

cold, deep sleep, but with every touch Eidolon changed that. It was as though she were waking up for the first time in a place where everything was new.

Stepping into him, she gripped his shoulders and pulled him closer. A groan rattled his chest, the sound of a male in need making her pulse spike. Shifting, she rocked her aching mound against his thigh, and he hissed, backed up.

'Fuck,' he muttered. 'I can smell you. My brothers will, too.' He shoved the phone into her hand and turned away. 'You are dangerous, slayer.'

She gaped, because she wasn't the dangerous one in this situation. He could seduce her with a look, a touch, and she was growing weaker by the minute.

She started to close the phone, but a flashing number caught her eye. Looking more closely at the screen, she saw numbers filtering down. *Thirty ... twenty-nine ... twenty-eight ...*

'Tayla? What is it?'

Twenty-two ...

Jagger had mentioned a countdown, but there was no way she was activating the spell. She closed the phone. Opened it again. The screen continued to flash numbers.

Eighteen.

I'm testing a new explosive that's odorless, invisible, and can be hidden inside electronic devices like MP3 players.

Cole's words careened through her brain, and her heart skidded to a halt. 'The exit,' she gasped. 'Exit. Now!'

She shoved past Eidolon, bile rising in her throat as she frantically searched for the doors Shade had brought her in through.

There. She darted toward them, and when a nurse shifted into a panther and pounced, she swung, sent the panther skidding across the floor. Pain exploded in her head, but it didn't matter. The door. She had to get to the door.

'Tayla!' Eidolon's shout chased her.

'Stay back!' She burst through the doors the second they slid open. Outside, she recognized the parking lot, and Eidolon's BMW.

Searing heat burned her fingers. The phone glowed orange, pulsing like a stove element with its own heartbeat. As hard as she could, she threw it toward the far wall.

A hand closed on her shoulder. Wheeling around, she tackled Eidolon and took him to the ground, her body covering his as the explosion rocked the underground facility and jarred her teeth.

A tire flew past them, blasted through the space where Eidolon had been standing. Fire, stone, and metal rained down, pelting her as she lay on top of him. He hooked his leg over her back and flipped her, shielding her instead. Then, as the storm of debris eased up and the rumble died away, a louder noise rattled her from above, and she looked up into extremely pissed-off golden eyes.

FOURTEEN

❧

Eidolon paced outside his office, and if Shade said one more time, *I told you we should have wasted her*, he was going to rip his brother's head off.

Problem was, Shade was right. If they'd given Tayla to Yuri, the parking lot wouldn't be demolished. But Tayla would be dead.

Clenching his fists so hard his knuckles cracked, he wondered why that thought bothered him so much. He'd been ready to kill her himself after the explosion. He and Shade had dragged her to Eidolon's office, shoved her inside, and then left her there while they cooled off.

'You ready to deal with her?' Shade asked. '*Can* you deal with her?'

'Don't start.' Eidolon threw open the office door, more to get away from Shade's accusations than to finally deal with Tayla.

She looked up from where she sat on his desk, shoulders hunched, feet swinging like a punished child. Her eyes were reddened as though she'd been crying, but he knew she hadn't. The effort she'd expended to not cry, however, was obvious in the tight set of her mouth and the way she swallowed repeatedly.

He halted just out of arm's reach and held his fists at his sides to keep from touching her out of anger – or something worse, like comfort. When he spoke, he dug deep to find the impartial, cold Justice Dealer voice he'd used for decades.

'Tell me why I shouldn't kill you for what you've done.'

She looked him straight in the eye, every ounce the warrior he knew she was. 'I can't.'

'That was easy,' Shade said, as he moved to the opposite end of the desk, caging her in. 'Let's take her outside—'

'No.' She pushed her tangled mop of hair back from her face. 'Not yet. There's something you need to know. One of your staff, I think . . . Yuri?'

Eidolon's heart missed a beat. 'What about Yuri?'

'He's dead.' Tayla closed her eyes and took a deep, rattling breath. 'I tagged your pager with sort of a psychic GPS.' She looked at him, the dark circles under her eyes blending with the soot smears on her cheeks. 'You must have given the pager to Yuri—'

'Hell's blades,' Shade breathed. 'The Aegis got him. What did they do to him?'

When she didn't answer, Eidolon's Justice Dealer cool disintegrated, and he grasped her by her collar and yanked her to her feet. His right temple throbbed, letting him know just how close to violence he was. He knew, though, that any roughness he aimed at Tayla wouldn't be to kill her. No, he'd shred her clothes with his bare hands and take her hard, show her what he was, what she was, and that she was his.

Dammit. Grinding his molars, he brought the conversation back to less pleasant violence.

'You tortured him, didn't you?' Gods, he could hear her heartbeat pounding, fragmenting the silence in the room, shattering his thoughts.

'Not me. He was already dead when I . . . he didn't give anything up. He didn't tell them anything they didn't already know about the hospital. I'm sorry. I'm sorry about everything.'

To Tayla's credit, she'd seemed genuinely upset that she'd brought an explosive device into the hospital, upset that her colleagues had tortured Yuri to death. It should have been Eidolon they'd captured. If the *s'genesis* hadn't been acting up when it had, he'd never have given the on-call pager to Yuri after Luc's surgery. And, *oh, shit.*

Eidolon released Tayla and turned to his brother. 'Yuri gave Gem a ride home. See if you can locate her.'

If glares were death rays, Tayla would have been seared to ash by the look Shade gave her as he stalked toward the door. He reached for the handle and paused. 'What are we going to do with her now? Hand her over to the Maleconcieo or do her ourselves?'

Eidolon moved to his brother and lowered his voice. 'I still need to talk to her.' When Shade would have protested, Eidolon cut him off. 'She saved my life.'

'And you saved hers. You're even. Kill her.'

Planting his open palm against the door jamb hard enough to make Shade jump, Eidolon leaned in so close he heard his brother's heartbeat. 'Do *not* argue with me about this.'

'I don't like what's happening to you, E. A year ago you'd have done the right thing.'

'Yeah, well, maybe I'm finally turning into a Seminus demon and doing the selfish thing. Seems to be working for you and Wraith.'

Shade snarled a vile curse and charged out the door, slamming it loudly behind him. Eidolon let out his own snarl of frustration. Low blows weren't his style, but lately they were falling out of his mouth when the last thing he needed right now was to be fighting with his brothers. Shade, especially.

Eidolon's own anger flared bright and hot as he rounded on the cause of the tension between them. 'You came here to lead your Aegis colleagues to my hospital.'

'Yes.'

The betrayal streaked through him, and he had no idea why.

They were enemies. He'd expected something like this. But for some reason, the knowledge that she'd wanted to destroy what he'd worked so hard for tore at him.

'I don't need to ask why. That you hate us is obvious—'

'I don't hate you,' she said hoarsely. Her gaze cut to him, full of misery, slicing him like a scalpel. 'God help me, I don't hate you.'

Shock made him take a step back. 'You're lying.'

'No. If I hated you, I'd have let that bomb go off in the hospital instead of the parking lot.'

He laughed, a hollow, bitter sound. 'You were saving your own skin.'

'I suppose I'd think the same thing.' She studied the floor. 'Was anyone hurt?'

'Yes,' he said, angry again. 'The Aegis didn't destroy my hospital, but it did take out a few staff members. Do you realize, little killer, that your own colleagues set you up to die as well?'

A ragged sob shook her. The tears she'd been holding back fell. 'I was a sacrifice. For the greater good—'

'For the greater good?' Eidolon saw red. Blood red. He closed the distance between them in a single stride and seized her shoulders, fought the urge to shake her until her teeth rattled. 'Do you honestly believe that?'

She looked up at him, the pain in her gaze turning her eyes into a murky mire. 'I have to.'

'Why?'

'Because if I wasn't a great sacrifice, then I was nothing to them.' She blinked, and a tear ran down her blotchy cheek. 'They're all I have. If I'm disposable . . . '

Ah, damn. The anger leaked out of him as if he'd been shot full of holes. He was a freaking emotional sieve. Before he could think better of it, he pulled her against him, held her while she sobbed into his chest.

This wasn't supposed to happen. He was supposed to snarl and strike and draw blood for what she'd done. Cuddling her, pressing his lips to the top of her head, rubbing her finely muscled back ... yeah, bad fucking idea.

It certainly wasn't supposed to feel this good. Nothing felt this good, not anything that happened while fully clothed, anyway.

Her hard body, soft in the right places, tucked against his in a perfect fit, and the way he stood between her legs as she sat on the edge of the desk made him remember that they could fit together even better. His cock stirred at the thought, and gods, he needed to get his head on straight.

'Yuri,' she said, her voice trembling as violently as her hands on his shoulders, 'was he a doctor?'

'Yeah. A good one.' A shudder wracked her body, and even though he shouldn't, he felt the need to alleviate her guilt a little. 'He was also a hyena shapeshifter and a cruel asshole.'

'Still, what they did to him ...'

He'd probably deserved. Eidolon didn't voice that, though. He'd lost a talented surgeon, and replacing him wouldn't be easy.

A noise outside his office drew his attention away from Tayla, and what he saw through the window made him curse.

'I really hope that guy isn't a doctor,' she said, drawing back to watch Wraith, swaying like a sapling in the wind, in the outer office. He stumbled forward a few steps, and then fell back against the wall.

'Fucking perfect,' Eidolon muttered. 'Stay here.'

He threw open the door and crossed to Wraith in four strides.

'Hey, bro.'

Eidolon seized his brother by the throat and lifted him off the ground. 'You idiot. *Secor des unez!*'

Wraith laughed, flashing fangs. 'Oooh, the language of Justice. Big E is pissed.'

'I told you to lay off the humans.'

'Yeah, and I'm pretty fucking sick of the reruns, man.'

With a roar, Eidolon heaved Wraith across the room. His brother hit the floor and rolled into the wall. Before he could sit up, Eidolon was on top of him, slamming his head into the carpet.

'E!' Shade's hands closed on his shoulders. 'Eidolon. Let him up.'

'He's high.'

'Yeah, I know. I brought Narcan.'

'Screw that,' Wraith slurred. 'I ate that junkie fair and square.'

Still straddling his brother, Eidolon ground his molars until they hurt. 'Did you kill him? Is the junkie dead?'

'Dunno.'

Shade knelt, scrubbed a hand over his face. 'Any witnesses?'

'Don't give a shit.'

'Wraith—'

'Give it a rest already.' Wraith used his tongue to caress one of his fangs as though tasting the blood that had flowed over it when he ate the human junkie. 'The Vamp Council won't touch me, and you know it.'

No, they wouldn't. As a Seminus demon with vampiric tendencies, he fell into a gray area between both species, and the Councils had nearly gone to war over the laws he should be required to obey. Punishment for various offenses was an especially sticky and sensitive matter, and both Councils had finally, with Shade and Eidolon's help, agreed to a compromise. Wraith didn't know about the agreement, and if Eidolon had his way, he never would.

'Arrogant asshole,' Shade muttered, as he pinned one of Wraith's arms and then tugged the cap off the syringe with his teeth.

Wraith hissed and struggled. Eidolon roughly slammed his knees onto his brother's shoulders to hold him in place while Shade shot him up with the Narcan, one of the few human medications that worked as intended in demons.

'I'm so sick of babysitting you,' Eidolon said, knowing he should be more understanding.

Eating a drugged-up human – always male, since Wraith wouldn't touch a human female for sex or blood – usually meant something had set him off, made him remember the trauma of either his childhood or his torture. It was something he didn't talk about, other than to say that he'd been forced to watch human females suffer and would not be responsible for doing the same. As a result, he fed only from other demons and human males. The occasional junkies were an escape for him, but Eidolon was the one who would pay for his transgressions.

Wraith snarled, his eyes already losing the glassy sheen of his drug high. 'You should be babysitting your whore.'

'You should have been eaten at birth.' Consumed by rage, Eidolon stood before he killed his brother. 'Shade, did you get hold of Gem?'

'Ah, yeah. And brother, she had a message for you. Said to tell you the twenty-four hours is up. What's she talking about? She was riled. Definitely channeling her inner demon.'

'It's nothing,' Eidolon lied. 'Did either of our ambulances survive the explosion?'

Shaking his head, Shade came to his feet. 'Nope. And the parking entrance collapsed.'

'Shit. Has the glamour spell been repaired?'

'Yeah. The entrance is hidden from human eyes.'

The entrance was generally hidden anyway, since it sat on the basement level of a condemned parking garage Eidolon had purchased, but still, what a fucking mess. He glanced at Tayla, who stood in the doorway, her expression haunted in a way that seemed to go deeper than the immediate situation.

'What the hell are you staring at?' Wraith snapped, the downslide from his high doing nothing to improve his mood. He levered into a sit and leaned back against the wall, head back, glaring at Tayla with hooded eyes.

'I didn't know demons did drugs,' she said, and Wraith grinned coldly.

'I don't. I do blood.' He ran his tongue over the points of his fangs. 'Come here, and I'll do you.'

She snorted. 'Dream on.'

'Ah, so you're selective about the demons you do?'

'Wraith,' Eidolon said, his voice low, edged with warning that his brother ignored.

'What? Seems a little hypocritical. Anyone with as much demon in her as she's going to have—'

'*Shut it.*'

This time Wraith listened, but Tayla had moved closer. 'What do you mean, I'm going to have?' She turned to Eidolon. 'I'm already half-demon. How much worse can it get?'

'You haven't told her?' Wraith laughed and leaped nimbly to his feet, the effects of all drugs completely worn off. 'Allow me.'

'Told me what?'

'Nothing,' Eidolon said, but Wraith was moving toward her, blue eyes as bright as a cat's before it pounced.

Eidolon stepped between them, but Tayla grabbed his arm, swung him around. 'Please . . . tell me.'

He'd wanted to wait until her body had taken her as far as it could go so she'd realize she needed his help, but Wraith was forcing his hand. And maybe now was the right time after all. The Aegis had betrayed her – her own kind had cast her out and tried to kill her when they should have protected and cherished her. Learning she belonged to another world might open her mind up to new possibilities.

'Tayla, let's go into my office—'

'Don't jerk me around,' she said, planting her feet and crossing her arms over her chest. 'Whatever it is, I can handle it.'

Eidolon ran his fingers through his hair. 'Fine. I told you that you were half-demon. What I didn't tell you is that the reason you're having the problems is that when the Alu bit you, it activated dormant DNA.'

'Dormant DNA?' She swallowed and licked her lips. 'What are you saying?'

'Geez, humans are stupid,' Wraith said, propping a shoulder

against the wall. 'He's saying it's taking over. It's either going to kill you or rob you of everything that makes you human.'

She glanced at Shade, who nodded, and then at Eidolon. 'I don't . . . that can't be right.'

The sound of Wraith's cold laughter dropped the temperature in the room. 'Welcome, slayer,' he said. 'Welcome to hell.'

FIFTEEN

❧

Tayla didn't speak a word as Eidolon, freshly changed into jeans and a charcoal sweater, guided her through the hospital's dark halls. Her thoughts were still frozen at the place where Wraith had said she was going to lose everything that made her human, and it was all she could do to stay conscious, let alone talk.

She certainly couldn't think.

Ahead, a sleek, black arch framed a glowing gate like the one she'd seen in the tunnel at Nancy's apartment.

Eidolon uttered something in a language she didn't know and ushered her through it. They came out on the other side in what looked like a cave of black marble, with maps carved into the polished stone wall. Eidolon touched one that appeared to be a crude representation of the United States, and then an even cruder carving of New York state glowed red next to it. After a few taps, another arch appeared.

In two steps, she found herself emerging from the side of a building in the South Bronx. When she turned around, there was no evidence of any sort of gateway or opening in the brick. Eidolon hailed a cab, and within fifteen minutes they were at her apartment.

She still hadn't said a word, and her mind still wasn't working.

'You're coming home with me,' he said. 'We're here to grab your weasel and some belongings.'

'I can't.' Her voice sounded rusty and unused and on the verge of breaking. *She* was on the verge of breaking, trapped inside a nightmare that wouldn't end.

The demon in you is going to rob you of everything that makes you human.

'You don't have a choice, Tayla. You gave up that right when you blew up my hospital.' He paid the cabbie and walked with her into her building's musty lobby, shaking his head in disgust when a hypodermic needle crunched under his boot. 'You're going to need help as your body changes. We have a lot to talk about.'

'There's nothing to talk about,' she said, as they mounted the stairs, because denial went a long way when it came to keeping her marbles together. 'I don't know if I believe—'

The hairs on the back of her neck stood on end. Instinct kicked in, along with a burst of adrenaline, and she crouched. Her eyesight grew sharper as she took in the entire area ... below, above, even the ceiling. Demons had a nasty habit of dropping from rafters and ceiling pipes.

Her hand went reflexively to where she'd normally keep her stang, and she cursed when she felt nothing but cool skin beneath the scrub top Eidolon had given her to replace her bloody one.

He eased up behind her, lowered his mouth to her ear. 'What is it?'

'Something's not right,' she whispered. She crept up another step to peer over the top of the next landing. 'My door is open.'

Menace rolled off Eidolon in a wave that was almost palpable. He started up the stairs, but she threw out an arm to block him.

'I can handle this.' Heck, she needed this. She needed to beat the hell out of someone or something, if only to get rid of the numbness that gripped her.

Through the opening in the door, she caught a glimpse of movement. Humans. Guardians.

Two, from what she could see. Cole and Bleak ... the two who had been involved in the werewolf battle that had killed Michelle and Trey. They were sitting on her couch eating McDonald's.

Territorial rage spun up ... humans, in her lair, uninvited ... Closing her eyes, she tried to get it together. She was behaving as if she'd truly accepted her demon fate, that the Guardians were the enemy. These two hadn't been the ones who'd sent her into a demon hospital with a bomb, and rushing in like a rabid hellhound wasn't going to help anything. Besides, their version of what had happened the night Michelle and Trey died was different from Luc's, and she wanted to believe them. Guardians were the good guys. Saviors of humanity. They did *not* betray each other. They didn't lie. They didn't try to kill their teammates.

But her internal alarm wouldn't stop clanging.

'Don't let them see you,' she said to Eidolon. 'I don't know why they're here, but they're more likely to talk if I'm alone.'

'Slayers?' he asked. At her nod, he inhaled sharply. 'If they so much as touch you—'

'They won't.' Before he could argue or she could analyze the possessiveness in his voice, she stepped inside.

Cole leaped to his feet. 'Tayla. Jesus Christ, what are you doing here?'

'I live here.' She moved fully inside, her heart growing cold at the panic on their faces telling her these two had to have known about her being sent to the hospital as an exploding chump. How many other Guardians had been involved? A chosen few? The entire cell?

No. She refused to believe everyone had turned against her.

'We were told you were dead.'

'Obviously, I'm not.'

Cole and Bleak exchanged glances, and yeah, apparently the fact that she was breathing wasn't great news. 'That's awesome,' Bleak said.

'So if you thought I was dead, why are you here?'

'To clean out your apartment.' Cole shrugged into his jacket, and she didn't miss how he'd loosened the snap closure on his stang holster. 'Let's take you back to HQ.'

Bleak moved behind her. 'Yeah. Everyone'll be stoked to see you.'

The unmistakable whisper of a blade slicing the air broke the oh-so-fake happy reunion. She struck hard and fast, knocked Bleak's dagger out of his hand. Cole's roundhouse kick to the hip spun her into the wall, and then Eidolon was there, tearing Bleak away and leaving her to concentrate on Cole.

Bleak's scream pierced her eardrum as she nailed Cole in the face with her fist. 'Don't kill him,' she shouted.

'Fuck that,' Eidolon snarled.

'No!'

The dull thud of flesh striking flesh told her he wasn't listening.

Cole swung, an uppercut she blocked, and she could no longer pay attention to what Hellboy was doing. Cole was hammering her with blows, and it was time to return fire. Spinning low, she swept her legs in an arc and knocked him on his ass. She leaped on him, straddling his waist as she slammed her fist into his cheek. His legs swung up, catching her around the throat, and suddenly she was struggling to stay on top. They were closely matched in skill, having trained together for nearly the same amount of time, but with the loss of her strength and her injury, what should have been an easy take-down now became a fight for her life.

Gasping, she reached for a candle jar that had fallen from the coffee table during the struggle. Her fingers closed on the rim. His fist drove into her belly.

Pain slashed at her, but she ground her teeth and brought the candle down on his temple. Cole groaned and went boneless.

Holding back her own groan, she rolled off him. Eidolon's low snarl vibrated the room. He lunged away from Bleak, landing on top of Cole, one knee in the Guardian's gut, one hand wrapped around his throat.

'Okay, asshole,' Eidolon growled. 'Time for you to sing.'

She glanced at Bleak's crumpled, bloodied form. He wasn't moving, but his chest rose and fell with regular breaths. Thank God.

'You bastard,' she said to Cole. 'What the hell was that all about?'

He glared up at her, and Eidolon must have squeezed, because Cole clawed at his hand. 'Demon bitch,' he gasped. 'You're a spy. You murdered Janet.'

Oh, Jesus. They knew. 'I-I'm not a spy. I didn't kill Janet.' Her denial came out in a rush she didn't even believe because in a way, she *had* killed the other Guardian.

Her gaze locked with Eidolon's.

'Yuri must have talked,' he muttered.

Did everyone know? She still hadn't come to grips with the fact that demon blood ran through her veins, but her own people had obviously tried to kill her for it.

She tucked her leg beneath her and got comfortable, because she had a lot of questions for Cole. Starting with, 'What were your orders?'

Cole's split, bloodied lips made for a grotesque smile. 'Go to hell.'

Eidolon dropped one finger to a cut on Cole's face. He stroked the skin next to it, gently, slowly.

'Funny thing, medical school,' Eidolon murmured. 'In the process of learning how to patch someone up—' suddenly the cut sealed '—you also learn the most effective ways to hurt them.' The cut ripped open with a sound like torn wet paper, and Cole screamed. Damn, Hellboy knew his shit. She couldn't decide if it was sexy, scary, or a little of both.

'Answer Tayla's questions, or I start slicing my way south.'

Cole swallowed audibly. 'We were sent to pack up your Aegis weapons and clothes.'

'And?'

'And kill you if you survived the explosion.'

Though she'd expected the answer, she still felt the ugly sting of betrayal. No, *sting* didn't quite cover it. These were people she'd fought with, bled with, risked her life for. They'd shared a mission, a calling. How could they have done this?

'Who sent you?' She cursed the tremor in her voice. 'Who gave the order?'

'Jagger.'

'He doesn't have that kind of authority.'

'He said it came from Kynan.'

She rocked backward as if she'd been slapped. *No.* Kynan wouldn't do that. Not to her. Not to anyone. He'd once let a Guardian off the hook for releasing a demon from the interrogation room.

Then again, if he believed she was a demon . . . no, even then, if the information had come from Yuri, Kynan wouldn't automatically believe it. Information from a demon, obtained under torture, wouldn't warrant an execution order, and even if it did, the order wouldn't be issued until an investigation had been completed and the Sigil had approved the action.

Something was wrong. Very wrong.

'So you came here to ransack Tayla's apartment and kill her if she survived the explosion?' Eidolon asked.

'It was supposed to look like a break-in.'

'And if I hadn't come back here but was still alive?' she asked.

A cold grin turned up his bloodied mouth. 'We'd have hunted you down like the demon whore you are.'

'Wrong answer.' Eidolon's voice was low, deadly, and in a blur of motion, he twisted Cole's head, snapping his neck. 'Justice is served.'

Tayla supposed she should be shocked, maybe upset, but all she felt was an empty numbness. Was her demon side affecting her already?

She stood there for a moment, staring at the two Guardians bleeding on her floor, one dead, one alive. What now?

As if Eidolon heard her thoughts, he stood and said, 'Pack some clothes and grab your weasel.'

'Why are you doing this?'

'You aren't safe here.'

'I know. But I can take care of myself.' She'd lived on the streets for years, knew the life, knew the places to hang out.

Then again, so did several Guardians, including Jagger.

He reached for her so quickly she was in his grasp before she could blink. One hand tangled in her hair, and the other gripped her waist. 'Tell me,' he said quietly, in a voice that was far more unnerving than if he'd shouted, 'what did The Aegis do to Yuri?'

She swallowed. Hard. 'I told you. They tortured him.'

'How? Whips? Blades? Fire?' His grip grew firmer, drawing her closer into his hard body as he tugged her head back, not so it hurt, but he wanted her attention. He got it. 'Do you think your friends wouldn't do the same to you if they catch you? I know you can't trust me, but I think I've proven that I won't torture you.'

'You killed Cole . . .'

'I did it so you didn't have to.' He dragged his lips across the top of her ear, making her shiver. 'He would have killed you. Maybe not today, but eventually. Go. Collect your things.'

He released her, but she didn't fall for the distraction. 'You're not killing Bleak while I'm occupied.'

'Tayla—'

'No!' She bit her lip and looked at the guy, curled into a fetal position on the floor. 'He's not like Cole. Bleak is a new recruit. He was just following orders. He thinks I'm a . . .'

'Demon?'

'You bastard.'

'Yeah, I know. You can bitch at me later. Right now we have to get you someplace safe.'

She knew he was right, but it was a bitter pill to swallow. 'I'll get my stuff,' she grumbled. 'Just one second. Do not kill Bleak.'

Forcing her lungs to fill with a calming breath, she picked up the phone from where it had fallen on the floor during the battle, and then she dialed with trembling fingers. Jagger answered his cell on the first ring. 'Your welcome-home squad was a nice touch, Jag,' she said. 'But you'll have to do better than that if you want me dead. Now come pick up your trash.'

She hung up, aware that she'd just signed her own death warrant. But when she turned to Eidolon, his grin was blinding. He said something in a language she didn't know, his eyes boring into hers. 'You are magnificent.'

So was he. Magnificent beyond belief. And she was going home with him. The knowledge that she'd be so close to him in such an intimate environment unnerved her. Terrified her. Excited her.

'We need to go.' They needed to do it quickly, before Guardians showed up to kill her, and as she picked up Mickey, she knew there was no going back.

SIXTEEN

∞

Eidolon's apartment didn't resemble anything even close to the dark, dank lair she'd expected. Then again, after seeing his car and how he dressed, she had no idea why she should have expected anything less than a Manhattan high-rise that probably cost more per month than she'd paid for her apartment in two years.

'This is so wrong,' she muttered, as she set her weapons bag and duffel on the floor.

Eidolon pulled Mickey out of his jacket pocket and closed his front door. 'What is?'

'This. You should be living in a sewer or something,' she said, but her voice lacked conviction, because she'd seen more than foulness in him and it was getting harder and harder to hold on to her principles.

Especially since the people she'd believed shared her convictions had tried to kill her. Twice. Oh, and because she was a demon herself. Small details.

'I couldn't find a sewer with a view.' He put Mickey down, along with his litter box.

'So where's your dog? Did you eat it after all?'

'While you were packing I called the lady who walks him and

asked if she could take the mangy thing for a few days. Wasn't sure how he'd react to the weasel.'

Somewhere in the house, a grandfather clock chimed. 'Mangy thing? Don't like him much?'

'He keeps me company.' The words were casual, spoken with a shrug, but the underlying affection in his voice gave him away. He liked his mangy mutt.

He took her bags, and she followed him down the hall, complete with oil paintings of medieval castles and châteaus on the walls, to a bedroom. The room was huge, richly decorated in masculine shades of brown and burgundy. The four-poster bed had to be custom-made, larger than a king-size. How odd.

Then it struck her, and she bit off a gasp. The bed had been made to accommodate more than two people.

'This is your room,' she whispered. 'I saw a guest room back there . . .'

He dropped the bags on the polished wood floor and in a flash, framed her face in his warm hands. 'We're beyond that.' He brought his head down to her neck, his lips caressing her skin. 'You sleep with me.'

Like a real couple. *Way* too intimate. 'I don't want to.'

He inhaled deeply. 'Don't lie to me, Tayla. I can smell your desire.'

God, that sense of smell of his was a pain in the ass. 'I need space.'

'The bed is big enough to give you that.'

'It's big enough to give an entire cheerleading squad space.'

She felt him smile against her skin. 'You almost sound jealous.'

'You're delusional.'

'And you should get some rest.' He stepped back, surprising her, but one fingertip stroked her jaw line lightly. 'You've had a hard day. If you want to shower, the bathroom is to the right. Robes are in the closet.' He cocked a dark eyebrow. 'You didn't really get into a fight with a Daeva, did you?'

'No.' God, what she wouldn't give for this entire day to rewind and start all over. 'Look, about the half-demon thing ... what evidence do you have? Or are you screwing with me?' It was a measure of her exhaustion that she came right out and asked if he was lying to her, but the day had gone to hell in a handbasket, and she just wanted a straight answer.

'Come with me.'

She followed him back down the hall to a room nearly as large as his bedroom, but cozier. The walls were lined with full bookshelves, many titles in languages she couldn't read. A desk took up one corner, a leather couch took up an entire wall. Black marble tile on the floor reflected light instead of darkening the room as she might have expected.

Eidolon pulled a leather-bound book from one of the shelves and flipped it open to a blank page. Closing his eyes, he waved his hand over the parchment. A glow sprang up under his palm, and when he removed it, a pulsing, shiny – *wet* – picture of bloody internal organs appeared.

'First of all, that's nasty. Second, how did you do that?'

'It's a medical text. I wrote it. On these two pages, I can visualize anything I've seen, and it'll temporarily appear like a living photo.'

'Cool. But eew. What's that supposed to be?'

'That's your open abdomen.'

She recoiled. 'I'm no medical expert, but that doesn't look right. Are you sure?'

'I was up close and personal,' he said grimly. 'These are your organs. They're misshapen. Formed from a union of two different species. And no, it's not a human birth defect.'

She wheeled away as though she could escape what he was saying. 'I still can't believe this. My mom wouldn't have kept me. She wouldn't have wanted me if some demon had—'

'She probably didn't know.'

'But how—' She cut herself off, because yeah, stupid question. 'An incubus.'

'That's a likely scenario.'

The conversation they'd had at her apartment before she knocked him over the head with the pipe came back to her, along with a glimmer of hope. 'Wait ... you said incubi only have male offspring.'

'No, I said Seminus demons produce only male offspring. Other breeds of incubi can produce both males and females.'

She really was a demon, and there was no point in denying it any longer. She hated what he was saying, but none of it truly surprised her, if she was being honest with herself. Even as a child, she'd been different from the other kids. More intuitive. Her vision had been off-the-charts perfect. As she got older, her other senses had become more acute.

And her ability to empathize and sympathize with other humans had taken a dive.

'So what's going to happen to me? Your brother said the demon DNA is taking over. Am I going to turn into some horrible beast?' She'd kill herself before she allowed that to happen.

'I don't know.'

'You don't know? *You don't know?*' A bitter laugh escaped her. 'You're supposed to be a doctor. A *demon* doctor.' She waved at the books on the shelves. 'You have demon sorcery at your disposal, and you don't know?'

'There's something I do know. My brother was right.' He propped a hip on his desk, stretched one long leg out in front of him. 'The demon DNA is aggressive. It's trying to take over rather than merge with your human DNA. That's why you're having problems. There's a question what, exactly, you'll turn into, but you *will* turn. Or you'll die.'

'Dying is better than the alternative.'

He shook his head. 'There's another option.'

'Yeah, I can eat a bullet before either of the other two happens.'

'No. With Shade's help, I think we can integrate your human and demon DNA. Basically, it'll give you the biology and form you should have been born with.'

'Which is what? Right. You don't know. So if I do nothing, I either die or turn into a monster?'

The antique clock on the wall ticked away several seconds of silence. 'That about sums it up.'

'Wow,' she said quietly, 'my future looks pretty bleak.' Worse than bleak. The only thing she had to look forward to was her own death. Then again, she'd never had anything else to look forward to, so this was nothing new. She trailed a finger over the books on the shelves. 'So I'm a ticking time bomb. Any idea when I'll go off?'

'I don't know,' he said, shoving his fingers through his hair in that way he did when he was frustrated.

'For a doctor, you don't know all that much.'

The raised gold lettering on one fat tome made her pause. 'Daemonica.' She drew it out, frowning. 'A demon bible?'

'In essence. It's the other side of the story.'

'So, what do the minions of darkness say happened in the beginning?'

'Do you really care?'

'Yeah.' She weighed the book in her hands, expecting it to burn her, but it just sat there, a cold weight. 'It's always good to know how the other side thinks.'

Except, he was no longer the other side.

Eidolon folded his arms across his chest and stretched his long legs out in front of him, crossing them at the ankles. 'Basically, demon lore says that after Satan was banished from Heaven, he was allowed to create his own races. But, because humans are born good and can be turned evil, God insisted that the same, but opposite, should apply to creatures born evil. Satan created some species from his own twisted imagination, and others ... he used animals as foundations for some, humans for the rest.'

'Which is why demons can appear human.'

He nodded. 'Some species are a cross between animals and humans. Shapeshifters, for example. And some species are more inherently evil than others. There are species and individuals who strive to be good.'

'Good? So ... they don't worship Satan? They aren't walking hand in hand with the guy?'

'Some of us even doubt his existence. Just as there are humans who don't believe in God, there are demons who don't believe in the Lord of Darkness.'

'So you've never seen him?'

'Have you seen God?'

'That's not how it works.'

'Exactly. When humans speak of seeing divine energies, they're talking about angels. We have *dresdiin*. And for the record, many of us consider your God to be the supreme ruler. Others worship – or, at least, acknowledge – both. The *Two Gods*.'

'That doesn't seem possible.'

'That any of us can be less than evil? Do you not see that sometimes, something goes wrong at conception, and some humans are born evil? Or they turn evil?'

'I suppose.'

'Imagine that the opposite happens in the demon world. For every action there is an equal and opposite reaction. Yin-yang. You can't have one extreme without the other. So in the demon world, some of the most heinous races sometimes experience an anomaly. I knew a Cruentus once who wanted nothing more than to work in the hospital. He was slaughtered by his own family for his behavior. The world isn't as black and white as you think, Tayla.'

'Believe me, I'm starting to figure that out.' She rubbed her temples, wondering if her life would ever be normal. Not that she knew what normal was. From the moment she was born on the floor of an abandoned warehouse, premature and addicted to heroin, everything had been out of whack.

'Tayla, let me get Shade over here, and we'll help you.'

She shook her head. 'I can't.'

'What are you afraid of?'

'Afraid of? Oh, well, maybe I'm afraid of losing myself. Of turning into everything I've ever hated. I'd rather die than turn into something I don't even recognize.' He looked as if he understood, and she remembered what he'd said about his upcoming transition. 'I don't see you embracing your own change.'

'That's different. I know what I'm going to become. You don't. You have a chance at becoming something better.'

'Better? How is turning into a demon better?'

'Says the human whose own kind tried to kill her.'

Tayla chomped down hard, her teeth grinding. 'Go to hell.'

'You don't get it, do you? This *is* hell.'

She snorted. 'Yeah, well, you aren't exactly fun and games yourself.'

'I was talking about earth. There are no fires, no burning pits of torment, no levels or rings or rivers of lava. When we die, we get put right back on earth to live our miserable existences over and over and over for all eternity.'

Her head spun at what he was saying, things that went against everything she'd ever been taught at Bible school the few times she'd been forced to go by foster families, and by The Aegis. 'That makes no sense.'

'There is no hell,' he said flatly. 'Not like you mean. Our world works like yours. You die, you go to the Other Side. We die, we go to the Nether Side. We're reborn to earth, though most demon species live far below the earth's crust, in what we call Sheoul. It's where I grew up. It's cavernous, dark, confining. Demons want out, and will do whatever they can to bring about an event that will allow them to live on the surface.'

'An event?'

'Imagine what you call the Rapture. Armageddon. The Apocalypse. According to a variety of human religions, the righteous will go to heaven and leave nothing but evil on earth, which is what we call the Reclamation. Earth will then be hell. There is no need for a fiery pit.'

206

He gestured to the book she still held in her hands. 'The Daemonica tells us that human sinners are reincarnated, given another chance to change their ways so that the next time they die, they can go to what many of you call heaven, or the Other Side. When the Reclamation finally comes, that will be the end of redemption. This is what evil wants. A world where the numbers are static and suffering will be eternal.' He speared her with a flat, black stare. 'That will be demon heaven. At least, for some demons.'

It was all too much. Too complicated. Black, white, shades of gray, an occasional splash of blood red. She wanted simple, and she didn't care how she got it. 'Hellboy?'

'What?'

'Touch me. Make me forget all this.'

He was on her in an instant, took her down to the floor before she could blink.

៚

Hundreds of females had solicited Eidolon for sex. But never in his eighty years of sexual maturity had one desired sex for something other than a release. He didn't know how to offer comfort; his healing skills were limited to clinical knowledge of anatomy. But the way Tayla was clinging to him told him she needed more than just sex, even if she wasn't aware of that fact.

A small sound of desperation escaped her as he tore through the scrub top. He cupped one breast through her bra, running his thumb over the creamy swell that overflowed the cotton cup.

'You're so beautiful, Tayla.' And she was. He'd always preferred humanoid partners, had sought out the most attractive females. Tayla wasn't classically beautiful, but her fresh, earthy looks drew his eyes in a way no other female ever had.

His words must have been exactly what she needed, because she sighed and arched into his touch, the small of her back coming completely off the floor. He should move them to the couch, but she wrapped her legs around his waist and his thoughts of comfort scattered.

Somehow, he managed to get out of his jeans without breaking the scissorlock of her thighs around his hips, managed to divest her of her clothing while her lips were sucking lightly on his collarbone. Her scent rose up, filling his nostrils with the sweet fragrance of arousal. Inhaling deeply, he let the passion high take over until his head swam with lust.

'I love it when your eyes change color,' she murmured, and he suddenly wanted to kiss her, a real kiss, not one like they'd shared the first time they'd had sex, when she was still in a dream state thanks to Wraith's head games. Not like the one they'd shared today in the exam room, when he'd been overcome by *s'genesis* urges.

As though she'd read his mind, her gaze dropped to his mouth, and her tongue darted out to moisten her bottom lip. Gods, he wanted to take her mouth, but there was no way he'd be gentle, what she needed right now.

Careful to avoid her stitches, he dipped his head and tongued a nipple, eliciting a soft moan from her.

'You taste like me,' he said, savoring his dark essence in the salt of her sweat. He hadn't come inside her since that day at the hospital, but her body was still processing his fluids, keeping her primed, ultrareceptive. 'Only me.'

His cock throbbed against her wet entrance, but he resisted the urge to possess her. Not yet. The doctor in him wanted to heal her with his touch more than the demon in him wanted to get off.

That had never happened before.

It scared the hell out of him.

Something scared her, too, because suddenly she was pushing against him. 'I can't do this. Oh, my God, I can't do this!'

He reared back, confused, his body on fire. 'What's wrong?'

She scrambled backward, sliding on the slick floor. 'It's just . . .

I can't . . . I can't want . . . ' She buried her face in her hands. 'The other times, it was different.'

Something inside him went cold, even though his body burned. 'Because the other times you convinced yourself that you were being forced or coerced.'

She nodded. 'I'm sorry.'

'Tayla, look at me.' When she didn't, he reached for her, which sent her into a wild flurry of motion. She swept up her clothes but slipped when she tried to get to her feet, and instead made a mad crawl toward the couch. Her curvy ass flexed as she moved, and her sex, glistening with her arousal, made for a sight that short-circuited his brain.

His blood went south, and animal instinct took over. He pounced, grasped her around the waist, and brought her ass hard against his stomach. His erection pressed against her bottom, and he shook with the need to take her. In his arms, she struggled, and he let her because she needed to think she was resisting and if this was the only way he could have her . . . he sheathed himself inside her in one stroke. She cried out at the sudden invasion, her fingers clawing at the floor as she tried to escape.

The scent of fear, nearly masked by the more potent scent of lust, rose up from her, hitting him upside the head. Sonofabitch, he wasn't healing her, he was scaring her. His mind told him to stop, but his hips ground into her, his body rebelling against what his head was telling him to do.

'Please . . .'

Shit. With a roar, he tore himself away. Instantly, a fire-storm of agony ripped through his gut. Still on his knees, he doubled over, sucking air through his teeth.

'Hellboy?' Tayla's hand came down on his shoulder, and he hissed at the sensation that was only going to get him lust-drunk again.

'Get away from me.'

'But—'

His snarl vibrated the light fixtures on the walls. 'I can't control myself right now! *Stay away.*' Pain screamed in his pelvis. His balls tightened, pulsed as if they'd been caught in a vise. Hands shaking, he reached for his pants. He had to find a female. Fast. Being this worked up was crippling, and the pain wouldn't ease until he found release.

The idea of taking a female other than Tayla only added to the agony.

'What are you doing?'

He spoke through clenched teeth, struggling for every word. 'Hospital.' Oh, unholy hell ... railroad spikes of hurt hammered into his pelvis. 'Sora ... demon ... maybe.' He didn't realize he had been muttering out loud until her fingers gouged his shoulder.

'You're going to ... to be with someone else?'

'Have to. Hurts.' He panted, reining in as much pain as he could. 'Can't take care of it myself.'

'Oh.' She rolled her bottom lip between her teeth, and he groaned. 'I'm sorry. I just—'

'I get it. Fuck, I get it. You can't admit you want me.' Jerking out of her grip, he closed his eyes and prayed he'd make it to the hospital without attacking the first female – demon or human – he saw. 'Next time, do me a favor and decide that before you tell me to touch you.'

He started to push to his feet, but she grasped his thigh, too close to where he really needed her hand, and sweat popped out on his brow.

'Please. Don't go.' Still on her hands and knees, she turned, offering herself to him. Blood pounded in his head at the sight of her, sleek and toned and watching him over her shoulder, ready to be mounted.

'Be sure,' he croaked. 'Because I can't stop again.'

'I'm sure.'

It was all he needed. Going to his knees, he entered her so hard and deep that they both shouted. Her tight walls pulled him inside, her slick heat holding him like a velvet glove. He was already close to the edge, and the way she moved against him, grinding, arching like a cat, drove him to the very brink of insanity.

The friction was electric, the rhythm furious. Heat shot like liquid flame from his balls through his shaft and shit, he was done for.

'*Tayla* . . .'

Gripping her hips, he lifted her so she was helpless, at his mercy as he pumped into her. Her sexy whimpers blended with the sound of his harsh breathing until his roar of release drowned out everything else.

She milked his cock, took it all, and though she wouldn't come, he knew his flow warmed her, caressed her, gave her intense pleasure all the same.

What he'd given her couldn't come close to what she'd given him. Being inside her rivaled the adrenaline rush he lived for at the hospital. The sounds she made, the smell of her arousal, the taste of her skin . . . stripped him of thought and logic and reduced him to a creature of pure emotion and desire. Total body ecstasy such as he'd never known.

Heart pounding, breath erratic, he collapsed onto her back and they both crumpled to the floor. He wriggled so they were on their sides, spooning. He was still inside her, hugged by her tight, wet warmth as he hugged her in his arms.

ও

Tayla shivered despite the steamy heat surrounding her, flowing through her, consuming her. She wasn't entirely sure what had just happened, except that she'd freaked. She'd asked Eidolon for comfort, and when he'd tried to give it, she'd been unable to process the emotions he'd awakened. What she'd assumed would be a hard, fast fuck turned into something else she couldn't handle.

Her signals had been so mixed it was no wonder he hadn't

known whether to stop or go, and he'd chosen to detour. Right into the arms of another female.

Except it hadn't been a choice for him. His physical pain had been obvious. Teeth clenched, cords in his neck straining, he'd been pale, sweating, every vein popping like it was going to burst.

'Hellboy?'

He traced the shell of her ear with his tongue. 'Hmm?' His voice was deep, wonderfully gravelly.

'You can't ever . . .?'

'No.' He began moving again, slow, easy thrusts that built sensation into a slow burn instead of the white-hot, explosive heat they usually shared. 'Release can't come by my own hand.'

Funny, since she achieved release only by her own hand. Even then, reaching climax was always a crapshoot. But with Eidolon, it almost seemed achievable. Even now, every languid stroke massaged her from the inside in ways she'd never believed possible. Her heightened senses tingled, the pleasure streaking through her flesh until she was shaking from the intensity of it.

Eidolon held her tight against him as though afraid she'd run away, but that wasn't going to happen. She'd never experienced a moment so sensual, so pleasure-rich. Never had a man taken the time to hold her, to make her enjoy being naked.

Hot breath whispered over the back of her neck as Eidolon nuzzled her there, and she groaned when his tongue traced a path along her collarbone.

'Beautiful,' he murmured against her skin, and then sank his teeth lightly into the sensitive curve between her shoulder and throat. For a moment he held her like that, restraining her with primitive force as he rocked against her. Then she felt the warm stroke of his tongue soothing the spot he'd bitten. 'I want to try again to make you come. Will you let me?'

She closed her eyes, unsure if she wanted to experience that kind of frustration again, but her body was screaming for release,

212

was already so close ... maybe this time she could go over the edge.

'Yes,' she said, and then she couldn't speak because his thrusts picked up speed until he was pounding into her with enough force to slam her exhalations out of her with audible gasps.

She felt him swell, stiffen, as he dropped one hand to her sex to spread her. His shaft slipped out of her and slid between her spread folds. Moaning at the sudden, sharp, sliding strokes through her cleft, she cupped his sex with her hand, holding him against her as he came. His hot seed creamed over her sensitive tissue in a silken flood.

Behind her, he panted, his chest heaving against her back. His hard length still moved between her thighs, a hot, erotic presence that fueled the desire burning at her core. But like before, she hovered on the precipice that would go nowhere.

'Stop,' she rasped. 'Get it off.'

The sound of fabric rustling accompanied some truly vile curses, and then he was wiping her clean, every stroke against her center a torture that kept her on the verge of climax.

'You should bottle that stuff,' she said, when she could speak again. 'I'll bet normal women would pay a fortune for it.'

He tossed the scrub top he'd used on her across the room. 'No doubt it's a black market commodity somewhere.'

She sensed more than saw the tension that filled him. 'What is it?'

'Nothing,' he muttered. 'But ... what if those bastards start thinking the same thing?'

She rolled to face him. 'You mean, they might take one of your species? And what, keep him chained? Jerk him off a few times a day?'

Scowling, he pushed up on one arm. 'You still don't care, do you?'

'That's not what I meant.' She covered his hand with hers, was glad when he didn't pull away.

'Based on how they seem to get off on torture, I doubt gathering semen would be pleasant. Most likely they'd insert a draining tube and take it as it's produced.'

She shuddered. The thought of their doing something like that to Eidolon ...

He reached over his head and pulled a blanket off the couch to cover her. 'Tayla? Why do you have sex if you don't enjoy it?'

Talk about a mood-killer. She sat up and pulled the blanket around her. 'Why the sudden interest in my sex life?' Or lack thereof.

Eidolon remained stretched out on the floor, but he propped his head up on one fist. 'I'm wondering what makes you tick.'

'There's not much to tell.'

'Then tell me how it began.'

The concern in his voice was enough to remind her that she was messed up in the sex arena, and man, did she hate reminders. 'Tell you what, Hellboy. You tell me first.'

'Fair enough.' He cocked one leg up, drawing her eyes to the place between, where his sex, glistening from her juices, lay heavy and semierect on one thigh. 'I was twenty when the urges started.'

'Twenty? That seems sort of late.'

'When you live to be seven hundred years old, twenty is a drop in the bedpan,' he drawled. 'When the urges start, sex is required to complete the maturation process.'

'How much sex?'

He shrugged. 'Pretty much constant for a few days. It can be hard on a lot of us, but my parents bought me an *orgesu*.' At her blank stare, he elaborated. 'A female to have on hand.'

'A sex slave? Your parents got you a sex slave? To have sex in their house?'

'It was the logical thing to do. They couldn't let me die. And they didn't want me out prowling and raping as a lot of my kind are driven to do during that phase.' He yawned, as if it were all normal. 'Besides, they paid to have her released from slavery afterward.'

She couldn't even come close to imagining how he'd grown up

214

if he could be so casual about the sex slave thing. 'Where did you grow up? Do your parents look human?'

His fingers brushed her cheek in a feather-light caress. 'They are humanoid, but their green skin and antlers keeps them in Sheoul. It's where I grew up, though I slipped away to come topside now and then.' He winked. 'I was the rebel of the family.'

Tayla laughed at that. He definitely didn't strike her as the trouble-making kind. 'When did you join us up here in the sunlight?'

'After my first transition.' He rolled one big shoulder. 'Now, enough about me. Your turn.'

'You mean, when did I lose my virginity?'

'Yeah.'

Well, shit. Her experience with sex seemed so vanilla now. 'I was fourteen.'

He slipped his hand down, trailed a finger over the skin of her hip that peeked through the blanket. 'That's young for a human.'

'Yeah, well, I was a wild child. My mom was an addict and my grandparents were in a nursing home, so I was living in foster care with people who couldn't control me. I did what I wanted, when I wanted, and I did *it* with my boyfriend after we got drunk at a party.' She slid a glance at him, but he didn't judge, merely watched her curiously. 'It kinda hurt. Was over in about three seconds. Earth didn't move. So I wasn't in a hurry to do it again. Right after that, my mom got clean and got custody of me, and I was so busy for two years that I sort of forgot about boys.'

'Then what?'

It went against her nature to talk about this stuff, but his touch soothed her, coaxed her, lulled her into a place that felt foreign ... but somehow right. The way he touched her cut right through all her defenses and left marks on her that couldn't be seen but were there nevertheless. Why he would waste his time with her, an enemy who had clawed her way out of the gutter only because Ky had rescued her from the life of a rodent, was beyond her, but for now, she wouldn't question his motives.

215

'My mom was killed,' she said quietly. 'I went to yet another foster home, and one night, my foster dad came into my room.' Eidolon's hand that had been stroking her hip stilled, and a low-level rumble came from deep in his throat. 'We fought. I took off. Later, he was found dead, and a warrant was issued for my arrest.'

'I'm glad you killed the bastard.'

'I didn't. He was beat up, but alive when I left him. I think one of the other kids he molested killed him while he was incapaci-tated.' She shrugged, and his hand went back to stroking her.

'What did you do after that?'

'I lived on the streets. I did what I had to in order to survive. It wasn't pretty.'

Silence stretched between them. Maybe she shouldn't have told him the truth. Maybe he was disgusted. Yeah, a demon who once kept a sex slave, disgusted. *Please.*

His fingers closed around her ankle, and she found herself lying on the floor again, his heavy thigh pinning hers down, his chest covering hers. 'Is that what you're doing now?' he murmured, his warm, strong hand stroking her cheek. 'Are you doing what you have to in order to survive? Are you fucking me because you need a roof over your head?'

Tay's first instinct was to get angry. But she was suddenly too tired to fight anymore. Especially because he knew she wasn't sleeping with him in order to have a place to stay or to get protec-tion or money or whatever. He wanted her to admit that something had changed between them, that she'd wanted *him,* not what he could give her.

'Please don't make me answer that.'

He drew her close, and for a moment she reveled in his embrace, something she doubted he gave often. It was certainly something she didn't get often. Come to think of it, it was something she'd really never had. She couldn't remember a single instance where even her mother had hugged her. It wasn't that her mother hadn't loved her, but there had always been a wall of guilt between them,

216

one her mother had constructed out of the shame she'd felt for abandoning Tayla, a wall Tay hadn't been able to topple no matter how hard she'd tried to bring her mom into the secret mother-daughter fantasy Tayla had dreamed of. The one where they were best friends. Where they could bake together and laugh at chick flicks while curled up on the couch on Saturday nights.

Yeah, her fantasies had been lame, but anything was better than the reality of cleaning up her mom's puke and hiding her crack pipe from the cops.

Anxious to escape the memories as well as the man who was making her think about them, she pushed away from Eidolon ... and froze as the floor lit up beneath them.

'What is that?' She sat up, found that they were inside a penta-gram, outlined in blue lights.

Eidolon's expression went stony, completely flat and emotion-less. 'Make yourself comfortable for a while. I've been summoned for punishment.'

'For what?'

'For killing a human.'

SEVENTEEN

❧

Eidolon had never liked vampires. Not after what they'd done to Wraith. Not after what they'd reportedly done to their father when Eidolon was just two years old.

The thread of prejudice had woven itself deep into the fabric of his soul, but his upbringing had given him enough of a sense of logic to realize that not every vampire was the same. He'd been fond of Nancy, some of his hardest-working staff members were vampires, and he'd enjoyed all of the female vamps he'd bedded.

But he would never feel anything but contempt for any member of the Vampire Council. Worms and cowards, all seventeen of them. He'd love to get even one of them under his scalpel.

Outside the hospital, of course.

They'd summoned him through his personal portal, as they always did, though they probably hadn't expected him to respond so quickly. This was the first time he'd seen the summons when it came, and he'd taken only a few minutes to shower and don a robe. Tayla had asked questions, but he'd avoided them, telling her only to help herself to whatever she wanted in the kitchen and make herself comfortable.

Now he stood in the Vampire Council chambers, where they

stared at him, their haughty asses planted in gilded, thronelike chairs arranged in a semicircle around the portal that had brought him here. Red and black tapers burned in copper candelabra, adding to the mystical and theatrical atmosphere. If there was one thing vamps loved, it was drama. Hollywood had invented the Gothic vampire melodrama, and the vamps had adopted it as fashion.

Eidolon really, really did not like vampires.

Come forward.

The mental compulsion came from the Key, a silver-haired vampire named Komir. Eidolon resisted the command, willed his feet to remain where they were. He was here to answer for a crime, but this wasn't *his* species' Council, and fuck if he was going to obey as if it were.

'My respect for your work only goes so far, incubus,' Komir said, and Eidolon smiled.

'My medical work, or my work on the females of your species?' It was something Wraith would have said, which seemed appropriate, given that Eidolon was here to pay for Wraith's transgressions.

'Both,' a female to the right said, her voice an appreciative husky murmur he suspected would go even huskier just before climax.

'Silence, Victoria,' Komir snapped, and then gestured to one of the two burly enforcers flanking Eidolon. 'Escort him to the platform.'

The platform that was stained with the blood of countless others, that would soon be stained with Eidolon's. Again.

'Hold,' he said. 'One of yours was recently taken by Ghouls. What do you know of them?'

Komir's eyes narrowed. 'Why do you care?'

'Because the victims end up in my hospital, dead or dying.'

Victoria sighed. 'More vampires are killed by The Aegis every day than are taken by the black market operators in an entire year. We don't care. Neither should you.'

Idiots. Shrugging off his robe, he strode naked to the platform without the aid of the enforcer thugs. He cleared his mind as he mounted the stone steps and stood beneath the reinforced wooden structure from which chains dangled. Numbing himself out was the only way to deal with this and, probably, the only way to survive.

A massive warrior vamp, whose name Eidolon didn't know, stood. 'Your brother Wraith has taken more than his limit of humans this month. Are you here to receive his punishment?'

'I am.' Though he'd really like to know how they always knew when Wraith killed a human. Thousands of vampires existed in the world, and they couldn't all be policed. Yet the Council seemed to keep a running tab of Wraith's kills. Granted, Wraith took pleasure in flaunting them, but still . . .

'The incubus is ready.' Komir's lip peeled back to reveal fangs as sharp as a 33 gauge hypodermic needle. 'Let it begin.'

෴

The twenty-four hours were up. More than up, and since Eidolon hadn't called, Gem was taking matters into her own hands. She'd have done it sooner, despite her promise to the other doctor, but she'd been stuck at the hospital on a sixteen-hour shift.

Shift over, and she was going to confront Tayla, and she was going to do it now.

She took the stairs to Tayla's apartment two at a time. As she topped the second-floor landing, the hair on the back of her neck stood up. She crept to the apartment door, listened.

No noise from inside.

Still feeling the tingle of goosebumps crawling over her skin, she turned the doorknob. Unlocked. The door creaked open.

The rich, fresh odors of blood and death swirled around her, soaking into the walls and becoming another layer of scent in the ancient apartment, which had been ransacked. She entered, noted the boxes in the corner. No, not ransacked. Packed. Someone was moving Tayla's things out.

A bloodstain marred the floor near the godawful orange couch. Humans wouldn't see the soiled area, but it was there. Recent. It had been cleaned up within the last hour.

Where was Tayla?

Voices in the stairwell jammed her heart up into her esophagus.

'Shit, man, did you leave the door open?'

'Don't think so.'

The unmistakable sound of metal blades clearing weapons' housings echoed in the hallway.

Slayers.

A chill went through her, a bone-deep cold she hadn't felt since she was a child and her parents had shared Aegis horror stories. The nightmares had plagued her into her teens, had come roaring back with a vengeance when she learned her own sister had become a slayer. A butcher.

A monster.

Gem shot to the bedroom, which was empty. No furnishings, no boxes.

Nowhere to hide.

'Doesn't look like anyone's been here,' a deep voice said.

'Who would steal anything from this shithole?'

Laughter belonging to several people filled the tiny apartment.

'Let's just get this done. We have demons to string up.'

A wail of terror welled in Gem's throat. There were five of them, at least. She might feel comfortable going up against one, maybe two. But five trained killers? She was outnumbered, outgunned, and she definitely didn't have a death wish.

Quiet as a were-rat, she slipped into the closet. The restraining tats circling her neck, wrists, and ankles burned, making themselves known. Inside, her inner demon was clawing to get out.

She prayed it didn't get its wish.

ତଙ

221

Tayla put her time alone in Eidolon's condo to good use. Mainly, she snooped, partly to learn more about him, and partly to keep from thinking about what had happened between them.

Because what had happened had shaken her to the core. She'd needed him. Wanted him. Had let her guard down and couldn't get it to come back up. He'd exposed every single one of her vulnerabilities, and somehow, she had to find a way to mash them back into the place she'd been keeping them.

Shaking off the thoughts she'd been trying to avoid, she went back to snooping while Mickey followed her, chattering endlessly as he explored every nook and cranny.

Eidolon's living room, decorated in masculine browns, greens, and leather, revealed nothing except that he had expensive tastes.

A search of the den turned up little more than what was on the surface – wall-to-wall bookshelves filled with medical titles and strangely bound texts, most of which she couldn't read.

Her stomach growled before she made it to either of the bedrooms, so she detoured to the kitchen. The contents of the fridge were a surprise; not that she'd expected quarts of blood and Tupperware containers full of brains, but the fresh fruits and veggies, lunch meats, and soy milk didn't match up to her expectations. Then again, mixed in with the ketchup, margarine, and jars of pickles were containers she didn't recognize, marked in languages she didn't know.

Probably the brains and blood.

She reached for a package of sliced ham, but a thumping noise drew her up short. She closed the fridge door, snagged a knife from the block on the counter, and slipped quietly into the hallway. Easing along the wall, she followed the sound of raspy breathing, her heart pounding painfully in her chest.

Knife ready, she stepped into the den. Eidolon was on his hands and knees just outside the circle, every inch covered in blood, his head hanging so she couldn't see his face.

'Oh, Jesus.' She crossed to him in three strides and sank to her knees in front of him. 'Hellboy?'

A shudder wracked his body. She wanted to comfort him with a touch, but where? Deep slashes scored the skin of his back, his arms, his legs ... even the soles of his feet had been laid open like overplumped hot dogs. Bone and muscle erupted from the shredded flesh, and blood dripped to the floor in a gentle patter of grotesque rain.

'I'm taking you to your hospital.' Unsure exactly how she was going to accomplish that, she pushed to her feet because she had to do something.

'No.' His voice was low, gurgling, as if he'd been flogged on the inside as well as the out. 'Call ... Shade.'

'I don't want to leave you,' she said, but when his only response was to shudder again, she ran to the foyer, where he'd left his cell phone on a shelf.

With trembling fingers, she cycled through his address book to Shade's cell number, and dialed.

'What's up, E?' Shade's voice, deeper than Eidolon's, echoed in her ear.

'It's Tayla. Look—'

'Where is he? What did you do to him?'

She lowered her voice and drifted farther away from the den. 'I didn't do anything to him. But he's hurt. We're in his condo ... he went through that portal, and when he got back ... ' He'd looked like he went through a meat grinder. 'He's messed up. Bad.'

'Shit.' The sound of something breaking on the other end of the line was loud enough to make her jerk the phone away from her ear. 'Turn up the heat as far as it'll go. He's probably in shock, but you can't put a blanket on him because it'll wick the blood out of his wounds. I'll be there as soon as I can.'

He hung up, leaving her with the distinct impression that this had happened before. Sickened by the thought, she located the thermostat, set it for eighty-five degrees. As the hum of the heater filled the apartment, she hurried back to the den.

'Hey,' she murmured, as she sank down next to where he

223

shivered on his hands and knees, in the same position as when she'd left him. He said nothing, but the straining muscles in his jaw told her why; he'd clenched his teeth so hard he couldn't speak.

Nausea rolled through her. Who had done this to him? Other Seminus demons? Were they not allowed to kill humans? The questions ate at her, but until Shade arrived, the only thing she could do was to try to take Eidolon's mind off his pain.

'I like your apartment,' she said. 'I snooped. Hope that's okay. Didn't find anything weird.'

She let a teasing note filter into her voice, because as much as she didn't want to admit it, she wasn't surprised at what she'd found in his apartment. Normalcy.

'So, uh . . . when do you think we'll know what kind of demon my dear old dad was? I hope it isn't something really horrible.' She almost laughed, because just a few days ago she'd made no distinction between *really horrible* and *not as horrible* when it came to demons.

Eidolon's breathing grew more regular and less labored, so she kept talking, inane chatter about stupid things like her bad grades in school, her favorite food – oranges – her desire to learn to ice skate. By the time Shade stalked into the room, Eidolon knew more about her than anyone in The Aegis ever had, though she had no way of knowing if he actually heard what she'd said.

Shade didn't spare her a glance as he dropped his medical kit and knelt at Eidolon's head. 'Hey, man, I'm here. You're going to be all right.'

As though his brother's presence had allowed him to feel again, Eidolon moaned, and the pain buried deep in the sound made her heart bleed.

'What did they do to him?' she whispered, and Shade's flat eyes focused on her as if he had just realized she was in the room.

'Looks like a combination of fists and a cat o' nines.' He slid his gaze over Eidolon's frame and added, 'They also used teeth.'

Ice formed in her chest. This was her fault. He'd been defending her when the Guardians attacked her in her apartment. He'd killed to protect her. 'He didn't deserve this.'

'Let it go, slayer.' Shade turned back to Eidolon, his expression softening as he gently took his brother's face in his palms and lifted his head. 'Those bastards really worked you over this time, didn't they?'

'This time? He said he'd never killed a human before.'

'He hasn't.'

She wanted to ask what he'd done to deserve the other beatings, but the cold rage in Shade's expression didn't invite questions.

Shade inspected his brother's face, his touch tender and light. When he finished, he lowered Eidolon's head and spoke in a soothing, low tone as he ran his hands over his ribs, belly, and extremities. Eidolon's teeth chattered, but he didn't make any other sounds even though the exam must have been excruciating.

'Slayer, open my jump bag and hand me the syringe in the right inside pocket.'

Glad to have something to do, she fetched the item and handed it to Shade, who injected the contents into Eidolon's shoulder with professional efficiency. The guy might have the fun-loving personality of a pissed-off pit bull, but he exuded confidence in his medical abilities, and, she couldn't help but notice, a raw masculinity that was every bit as powerful as Eidolon's.

'Was that for the pain?'

'Antibiotic.' Shade pulled some tubing and a bag of blood from his kit. 'Painkillers are against the rules.'

'*Rules?* There are rules for being beaten nearly to death?'

Instead of answering, he started an IV with the blood, and hung the bag from the door handle. When he finished, he laid his large palm on the back of Eidolon's neck, one of the few uninjured areas, caressing in slow circles.

'Bro, your pulse is off the charts, and your resps are all over the place. I need you to relax.' Shade closed his eyes, and for a moment it seemed as though Eidolon's tension had slipped away, but then he convulsed, and his breathing grew labored again.

Without thinking, Tayla covered his hand with hers. Shade's eyes flew open, and at his dark stare, she jerked her hand away, afraid she was hurting rather than helping.

'No,' he said, grasping her wrist. A low growl erupted from deep in Eidolon's chest, and Shade's eyes narrowed. 'Well, now, that's interesting,' he murmured, and very carefully placed her hand over Eidolon's again. 'Your touch seems to calm him. Leave it there until I put him to sleep.'

Gently, she stroked his fingers, the ones that had saved her life and brought her pleasure, and a few minutes later, Shade nodded.

'He's out. He should stay that way for a couple of hours.'

'He'll be all right though, yes?'

'Yeah. We're not easy to kill. Just FYI, Aegi.' He gathered his gear and gestured for her to follow him into the kitchen, where he washed up. 'If Wraith calls, don't speak a word of this. If he comes over, don't let him in.'

'Why not?'

He hesitated for so long she didn't think he'd answer, but as he dried his hands, he said, 'Eidolon was punished, not for something he did, but for something Wraith did. Wraith can never know.'

'So this wasn't about what happened at my apartment? I don't understand.'

'You don't need to.'

'Yeah, I do. I'm not going to hurt Eidolon, or I would have done it instead of calling you, right?'

Shade bared his teeth at her. 'If you hadn't, I'd have—'

'I did,' she snapped. 'So tell me why he's nearly been killed for something your brother did.'

'I. Don't. Like. You.'

'Feeling's mutual, buddy. So spill already.'

Shade blew out a harsh breath, as if that would cool him off.

At least it got him talking. 'Wraith is part vampire. But he's also a Seminus demon. Vampire and Seminus law don't always mesh, and he falls into a crack between the two. Neither Council can agree on how he should be punished for various transgressions. But they both want someone to pay.'

'Why Eidolon?'

'Because Wraith wouldn't survive it.'

This was seriously twisted, and it fired up all her protective instincts, which she hadn't known she even possessed.

'I don't understand why Wraith would allow this to happen. Why doesn't he stop doing whatever it is that gets Eidolon beaten?'

'Wraith thinks he's untouchable ... he has no idea Eidolon is suffering. If he did, if he knew what E has gone through ...' Shade shook his head. 'We'd lose him. He can never know.'

'That's crazy. You've got to tell him. This has to stop. What if next time they kill Eidolon?'

'It's none of your concern. Like I said, not a word. If you even hint to Wraith that this has happened, I'll take you out, slayer.'

She slapped her palms on the counter and leaned forward to snarl, 'Try it, asshole.'

Shade's eyes flared gold, reminding her of the man suffering in silence in the other room, reminding her that now wasn't the time to pick a fight with the demon who had helped him. He seemed to come to the same conclusion, and the gold melted away, to be replaced by the eerie brown-black, which always seemed to shift, as though a shadow lurked behind his eyes.

'You look like Eidolon,' she said quietly. 'But you're so different.'

He grunted. 'All Seminus demons are nearly identical to their siblings, but our behavior varies because we're raised by different species.'

'But ... Wraith. He's blond.'

'Bleached.'

'His eyes are blue.'

'That's because they aren't his.'

'They aren't his eyes?'

Shade slung his bag over his shoulder, done with the conversation. 'E will be healed by morning. Try to get him to drink fluids, and ...' He trailed off, averted his eyes before boring those chips of stone back into her. 'Stay with him. He usually goes through this alone.'

He slammed out of the apartment, leaving her standing in the kitchen, her heart pounding. Emotion like she hadn't experienced in years nearly brought her to her knees.

The brothers loved each other fiercely, something she wouldn't have believed if she hadn't seen it with her own eyes. They protected each other, healed each other, and clearly, they'd die for each other. She doubted anyone but her mother would have died for her, and even then, most of Tayla's life, her mother had been too stoned to lay her life on the line for anything but the next fix.

What would it be like to have family like that? she wondered as she filled a glass with orange juice she'd found in the fridge.

And then she stopped wondering because that road would only lead to the corner of Self-Pity and Pathetic Idiot.

She slipped into the room with Eidolon, where he appeared to be sleeping peacefully despite the fact that he was still on his hands and knees – the only parts of his body that hadn't been beaten. Already some of his wounds had started to heal.

Yeah, his wounds were closing, but hers had just opened up.

❧

The sound of a phone ringing woke Eidolon. Before he could rouse himself, the ringing stopped and Gem's voice ground out over the answering machine. She sounded as if she'd been dragged through a frat party and left to sleep it off on the front lawn.

'E, it's Gem. I think something happened to Tayla. I don't know what, but I spent the night in her damned closet. I'm at UG now. I need to talk to you. It's important. Can you come in? If not, I'll come to you.'

Why the hell had she spent the night in Tayla's closet? She hung up, and Eidolon groaned. His mouth was dry and his muscles were stiff from spending the last twelve hours on his hands and knees. Rolling his head, he worked out a kink in his neck and then looked down to see Tayla, curled next to him on the floor, her fingers covering his. At some point during the night, she'd snagged a pillow from his bed, and now her hair fanned out like a Leonine Beast's mane, begging for his touch.

He'd never seen her sleep before, not peaceful sleep that didn't involve a hospital bed and pain medication or sedatives. The doctor in him measured the steady rise and fall of her chest; the male in him stirred at the push of her breasts against the T-shirt of his she'd put on.

It looked much better on her than it ever had on him.

He inhaled her scent, so brutally feminine, mixed with a tart note of concern, a sharp thread of fear. He vaguely remembered Shade being there, touching her ... had his brother threatened or hurt her?

He scanned her body, tipped her face up off the pillow to check for injuries. Sweet relief sighed out of his lungs.

And then he wondered why he'd worried. Tayla could take care of herself, a fact he'd seen with his own eyes. Maybe it was his brother who had borne the damage.

Shit.

Jerking to his feet, he winced at the creak of aching joints. Dried blood cracked on his skin, but beneath it, he'd healed. He made a quick call to Shade to make sure his brother was unharmed, and then he showered. Still naked, he returned to the portal room to gather Tayla in his arms and settle her into his bed.

He'd barely pulled the sheets over her when she opened her eyes.

'Hellboy,' she rasped in a morning voice that sent shockwaves into his groin. 'Are you okay? I mean . . . '

His lack of clothing had registered, and the way she was staring at his erection made him, for the first time, a little self-conscious. 'Yeah, I'm good. My species heals rapidly. Get some rest. I know you were up all night.'

He turned away, but then she was there, grabbing his arm to bring him back around. 'Are you sure you're okay?' Her hands slipped frantically along the skin of his back, chest, arms, as though she were looking for damage. 'You were pretty messed up. Is that why you have all those little scars?'

'You can see them?'

'In the right light.'

The feel of her hands on his body as she traced the scars was torture, far worse than what the vampires had done. He wanted to pounce on her, but something had changed between them, a subtle, fragile bonding that he was afraid to break by attacking her for sex.

Besides, what she was doing to him wasn't about sex.

It was about her caring enough to make sure he was okay. No one but his brothers had ever truly cared about him. Oh, his Judicia parents and two sisters felt affection for him, but only because it was logical to feel something for someone who'd grown up in the same household. If ever a time came when it would be logical to kill him, they wouldn't hesitate.

No one outside of his brothers had ever taken care of him as Tayla had last night, as she was doing even now. The newness of the situation left him off-balance, tilting toward her physically and emotionally.

In a move that went completely against his nature, he stepped back. 'Thanks for helping me.'

She grinned. 'Consider it partial payment on my hospital bill.'

Her smile sent a jolt of lust through him. His groin filled with heat and blood, and the right side of his face throbbed. This was insane. His control was slipping in a downward spiral that was becoming harder and harder to recover from. Shade had transfused him last night, but the *s'genesis* was rising in him again. It was happening more frequently, so either the transfusions weren't working, or he needed them more often.

They stared at each other for a moment. Slowly, the smile slid off her face. 'Look, ah, Shade said that what happened last night was because of something Wraith did. Is that true?'

'Shade has a big mouth,' he growled.

'So it's true.'

He sighed. She deserved an answer after what she'd done for him last night. 'To keep their existence secret, vampires are allowed a minimal quota of human kills. Going over results in severe punishment.'

She rubbed her eyes and yawned, and he figured Q and A was over, but then she said, 'So why are you their whipping boy instead of Wraith?'

'I volunteered.' Shade had, too, but his curse was more than enough to deal with already. 'Wraith would never survive the torture.' Not with his mind intact, anyway.

Tayla shook her head. 'I still don't understand why you can't tell him to stop doing what gets you punished.'

'It's too late. We kept it from him from the beginning. If he knew he was the cause of my pain ...' He blew out a breath. Wraith would either go insane, go on a rampage, or both. 'That's one of the reasons he's working at UG. Shade and I figured it would keep Wraith busy and out of trouble.'

'I'm guessing the plan didn't work?'

'It did,' he muttered. 'You should have seen Wraith before UG started up. And speaking of the hospital, I need to head there for a while.' He urged her back into the bed and pushed her into the mattress. 'Get some rest while I'm gone.'

She nodded and closed her eyes, falling instantly asleep. He dressed quickly in jeans and a blue button-down he left untucked

231

and took the nearest Harrowgate to the hospital, where he approached Solice, the on-duty triage nurse.

'Have you seen Gem or Wraith?'

'Haven't seen Gem.' Solice jerked her thumb down the hall. 'But I saw Wraith go that way with Ciska.'

Shit. Ciska, the Sora demon nurse, radiated sex like a contaminated nuclear power plant. Wraith couldn't resist her if he was in a coma.

Eidolon took off down the hall toward the cafeteria, following the perfume of arousal that ended at the supply closet door, where a muffled giggle and thumping sounds told him as much as the scents did.

He threw open the door, not surprised to find Wraith's face buried in Ciska's neck, his hands groping her breasts, her scrub bottoms pooled around her ankles. The fly of his jeans was open, but Eidolon tore his gaze away before he saw more than he wanted to.

Wraith lifted his head to look at Eidolon with golden eyes. Blood dripped from his fangs until Ciska licked it off with her forked tongue.

'I need to talk to you.'

Ciska's tail whipped up to nudge the front of Eidolon's pants where he sported a raging hard-on, thanks to the overpowering scent of female arousal. She stroked his shaft through his pants until he cursed and stepped back. With a saucy smile, she swung her tail away and wrapped it around Wraith's cock.

Wraith threw back his head and groaned. 'Bro, either give me a minute or join us.'

It wouldn't be the first time he shared a female with one or both brothers, but for some reason, all he could think about was Tayla. Which wasn't good. 'Hurry up.'

He slammed the door and stood in the hall, his sex heavy, aching. Images of Tayla, her body pliant yet strong beneath his, flashed in his head until he was ready to howl in frustration –

frustration that wasn't entirely physical. The fact that he couldn't bring her to climax gnawed at everything that made him an incubus.

Muttering under his breath, he told the triage nurse to page Gem, and then he settled himself in his office with an IV of his blood set at full bore. Gem arrived ten minutes later. She looked as if she'd just rolled out of bed two minutes ago, her bloodshot eyes framed by dark circles.

'Where's Tayla?'

Eidolon felt a possessive rumble rattle his chest at her tone. 'I told you she's mine. I won't let you hurt her.'

'She might already be hurt. I went to her apartment—'

'She's at my place. She's safe.'

'Oh, thank heaven.'

'Heaven had nothing to do with it,' he said wryly. 'And why are you so relieved?'

'The bastards called,' Gem said, closing the door.

'And?'

'They won't wait any longer. They said they need me right away.'

'What changed?'

'The person they were using can't do the procedures. Apparently, whoever it was was injured in an explosion.'

Eidolon's stomach bottomed out. The organ-harvesting operation could be based anywhere in the world – or underworld – and the individual performing the surgical work could live and work anywhere as well. But Eidolon didn't believe in coincidences.

'The hospital explosion.'

'That's what I'm thinking. How many were injured?'

'Three killed. Seven injured. Two seriously.' He shoved his hands through his hair, ignoring the tug of the IV line. 'Of the seven, four are well enough to work.'

'So that means one of the three is the cutter.'

Rage bubbled up in Eidolon at the thought that one of his

trusted staff could have been involved in something so heinous. Traitorous.

Something pricked his memory. Derc, the male he'd treated a few days ago. He'd been aggressive, rude ... until panic set in when Eidolon asked him about his surgical incision. At the time, it had seemed odd, but now, knowing that someone inside the hospital had been involved ...

And something Nancy had said bothered him, as well. She'd fingered The Aegis, but what if she'd said something else? She'd been whispering. Her voice had gurgled, been mushy.

The three injured staff members ... Reaver, Seknet, Paige.

Oh, *damn*.

'It's Paige.'

'The human nurse?'

He nodded. 'Nancy said something to me before she died. Aegis. But it could have been Paige. Or Paige's ... something. And Paige was present when a patient of mine went into a death panic. He must have recognized her.'

'This might mean The Aegis isn't involved. They wouldn't blow up the person they need to perform the surgeries, right?' Gem's voice went as cold as he'd ever heard it, her eyes went black, and for the first time, he saw the demon in her human-shaped wrapper. 'I want my parents back. We need to talk to Paige.'

'She's in a coma.' He pinned Gem with a hard stare. 'But I'll make sure I'm here the moment she comes out of it.'

Tayla might have blown up the hospital, but now, it seemed, she'd done him a favor.

EIGHTEEN

❧

Tayla woke to the delicious smell of something spicy and Italian. Assuming that a dangerous demon wouldn't have broken into the apartment to cook, she showered in Eidolon's luxurious bathroom – white marble with a shower stall the size of her apartment's bedroom – and when she got out, a plush robe lay on the bed.

Smiling at his thoughtfulness, she donned it and padded to the kitchen, where he was stirring some sort of cream sauce on the stove.

'Hey,' she said. 'You look good for a guy who nearly died last night.'

'Is that what Shade told you?'

'Actually, he said you weren't easy to kill.'

He poured some spiral noodles into a colander. 'I'm not.' He shot her a wink. 'But don't think I'll tell you how to do it.'

That stung. It shouldn't. She understood – she wouldn't tell someone trained to kill her how to go about doing it. But it still hurt.

She climbed onto a bar stool and sat at the island as he scooped pasta and sauce onto two plates. It smelled awesome and looked even better. 'You keep surprising me,' she murmured, as he slid the plate in front of her.

'Because I can cook? I'm a hundred years old. You learn a few things in that much time.'

'I guess I'm just surprised that you're so ... domestic.'

Grinning, he pulled up a stool next to her. 'I do my own laundry, too.'

'I'll bet you have a maid, though.'

His grin turned sheepish. 'Maybe. Now eat. Doctor's orders.'

Smiling, she picked up her fork. One bite, and she was lost to ecstasy. The pasta melted in her mouth, and the cheese sauce exploded with complex flavors that warmed her from the inside.

How long had it been since she'd eaten real food? The Aegis didn't pay well, mainly because funding came from largely private sources and, according to Lori, a few government agencies that siphoned off money where they could. But with so many cells around the world, most of the money went toward supporting the group rather than the individual. Which was why most Guardians lived at headquarters, where they were sheltered and fed as much boxed macaroni and cheese and canned ravioli as they could eat.

She finished her plate before Eidolon was halfway through his, and that was when she noticed the reason he'd stopped eating. His eyes, focused on the gaping openings in the robe that bared the swells of her breasts and one thigh, glowed gold. She became aware of the cool air that caressed her exposed skin, and of the burning stare that negated it. The promise of untamed sex radiated from him, the hunger in his eyes having nothing to do with the food on their plates.

'God, Hellboy, what are we doing?'

Abruptly, his eyes flashed back to their normal color. He closed them with a sigh. 'I don't know.'

She could still feel the heat of his gaze lingering on her skin like an erotic sunburn. 'I wish ... ' What? That she were a kid again? Being abused by druggies her mom brought home? That she were a teen? Living in foster homes and the streets? That this was a month ago, when she was alone with nothing but hate to keep her alive?

Because truth was, she'd never been happy. Until now.

'What do you wish, Tayla?' Eidolon was looking at her, his gaze warm and soft.

'Nothing.'

He took her hands, pulled her so that her stool slid across the tile and she was practically in his lap. 'Tell me.'

'I just wish . . . I wish I had something of my own. I have nothing to my name. I've had very little of value in my entire life. All I have is The Aegis and my word, and now I don't even have The Aegis anymore.'

He dug into his jeans' pocket and withdrew a small silver band. 'You have this.'

'My mom's ring,' she whispered. She slipped it onto her finger, the familiar weight comforting and welcome, and she could hardly breathe for the emotion that clogged her throat.

Next thing she knew, she was in his arms and he was kissing her neck and telling her she was beautiful and sexy and that he would give her anything she wanted.

She wanted to cry. No one, no *human*, had ever said those things to her, had ever made her feel beautiful and sexy.

'This is crazy,' she moaned, as his hands slipped inside her robe and cupped her breasts.

'And?' He nipped her shoulder, where the collar had slipped down. She wanted him to bite harder, but he licked the spot, soothing it, wringing shivers of pleasure from her.

'Just saying,' she sighed, because when he touched her, all other worries and cares flew out his high-rise window.

She shifted to give him better access, her hip brushing against the bulge behind his jeans' zipper, and he hissed against her skin. 'I need to be inside you. I want to take you until we both pass out.'

'Oh, God, yes . . . '

He moved so quickly she didn't have time to blink, and then the robe was gone and she was naked on his lap. Grasping the zipper tab on his jeans, she tugged, releasing his straining erection. It filled her hand, hot and heavy as she wrapped her fingers around the thick length. He was so hard she could feel his pulse slamming into her palm. Her thumb flicked over a drop of liquid at the tip, and he closed his eyes and groaned as she spread the moisture around the smooth cap.

She longed to taste him, something she'd never wanted to do. Before now, sex had been a way to feed herself; she wasn't proud of it, but sex had been about life and death when she lived on the streets. Now she wanted to give pleasure to the one who had given her so much, and her mouth watered.

She shimmied off his lap, but he misunderstood and came to his feet with her. 'No.' She stayed him with the flat of her palm on his broad chest. Dragging her hand down, over steel-cut abs, she fell to her knees before him.

His sharp intake of breath drifted down to her, and another groan followed as she took him in her mouth. Smoky, spicy flavors burst in her mouth, unlike anything she'd ever tasted. Her tongue tingled, and the sensation spread down her throat, to her spine, her very core. When he touched her hair, she felt it everywhere.

Every taste, smell, sound, became magnified. It was as though her body was a huge net, capturing all sensations and funneling them straight to her sex. She clenched her thighs to ease the ache, but the delicious pressure only intensified her need.

She wanted more of him, and she sucked hungrily on his cock, stroking him with her fist.

'Tayla,' he gasped, 'you need to stop.' He grasped her shoulders and tugged.

'No.' Determination and desire kept her on her knees, one hand working his shaft, the other caressing his balls, which grew tight, drawing closer to his body with every stroke. 'I need this.'

'You don't understand—'

'Shut up and let me suck you.' She closed her mouth around the velvety head and flicked her tongue along the smooth ridge.

His curses filled the air as his fluids filled her mouth. She swallowed greedily, moaning at the taste of him ... bold and dark, utterly male. A second later, waves of heat broke over her, and she cried out as her entire body came alive.

Her skin became one big nerve, and where his fingers lay, tiny sparks, mini-orgasms, fired up.

Oh, wow. This was going to be interesting.

∽

Eidolon pulled out of the hot, wet depths of Tayla's mouth, the high of climax tempered with the concern over how she'd react to his seed. Already her eyes had dilated and glazed over.

'Oh, man,' she whispered. 'Oh, boy.'

He hooked her beneath her arms and brought her to her feet. 'My semen is an aphrodisiac.'

Closing her eyes, she cupped her breasts, letting her thumbs graze the stiff nipples. 'Yeah, no kidding.'

Watching her pleasure herself made him instantly hard again. 'My bed,' he croaked. 'Now.'

She didn't seem to hear, instead was running her palms down her belly and between her legs. A low moan escaped her, shattering his control. He swept her up in his arms and strode to the bedroom, thanking the gods when her mouth attached to his neck and began to suck. Before they reached the bed, she wrapped her legs around his waist and impaled herself on his shaft.

'*Damn.*' Her silky passage sucked him deep, going deeper as she ground herself against him. Legs threatening to buckle, he sank down onto the bed before they crashed to the floor. She pushed him back and rode him furiously until he came, but she didn't.

'Another position,' she gasped, and he flipped her, brought her up on her knees, and took her from behind.

Her body shook, trembled with such force that she nearly bucked him away from her.

'Please . . .'

Gods, he couldn't breathe, could hardly stand the force it took to not come again. Grinding his molars, he pounded into her even harder, faster, until her sobs brought him to a stop.

'Don't stop, Eidolon, don't.'

He withdrew and inserted a finger into her slick heat. Her moan drifted up to him, a sound of pleasure and misery. Slowly, he spread the moisture they'd made, the satin lubricant of her desire and his seed, over her swollen knot.

'Oh, yes.' She arched her back like a Halloween cat. 'Now . . .'

He plunged inside her in one smooth motion, and she cried out, her muscles clenching him and holding him inside. He rammed her hard, let her excitement guide his speed and rhythm.

'Come Tayla. Come for me.'

She fell forward on the bed with a scream, but it was one of frustration. She flipped herself, wrapped her legs around his waist and drew him on top of her. Tears ran down her cheeks and sweat dampened her hair and skin.

'It isn't working!' she cried, her anxiety intensified by the aphrodisiac pounding through her veins.

'I'll back off, *lirsha,* and you can make yourself climax.'

Anger lashed at her expression. 'No. No, dammit! I want to be normal! I want to come with a man.'

'Tayla, not all human females—'

Her hand slammed into his shoulder. 'I can. I know I can. I just have to get rid of him.'

He froze. 'Him?'

In the shadows, her eyes sparked. 'Him. The demon.' Suddenly, she was flailing at his chest, pummeling him with her fists. 'I hate them,' she sobbed. '*I hate them . . .*'

He closed his eyes and let her take it out on him, let her strike him until her strength gave out and her sobs became uncontrollable.

Until she lay limp beneath him, little more than a quivering mass of flesh and tears.

Rolling to his side, he pulled her against him, let her cry for what seemed like hours, her body heaving.

'Tayla, tell me what's wrong.'

'I can't ... I can't get it out of my head.' A shudder wracked her body. He was still buried deep inside her, still hard, and her shaking made him suck air.

'What?' he managed, needing to know because alongside the arousal was a fierce need to kill whoever had traumatized her. 'What can't you get out of your head?'

Tayla burrowed into Eidolon's chest, wishing he'd stop asking, stop acting as if he cared. Because every touch, every gentle word, broke down her walls when she should be building them stronger. People who cared about her had a habit of dying ... or trying to kill her.

For a long time, she listened to the sound of his breathing and the beat of his heart. He said nothing, wearing her down with her own thoughts. Finally, she pulled back a little.

'I was sixteen,' she said, her voice sounding raw to her ears. 'I came home from school and heard strange noises from the kitchen. I saw her, my mom. She was on the table. Being raped.'

Eidolon had been stroking her hair, and his hand stilled. 'Demon?'

'Soulshredder.'

'Gods,' he whispered. 'It doesn't get much worse than that.'

No, it didn't. Soulshredders got off on tormenting their victims, slowly, over long periods of time, driving them mad rather than killing them outright.

'I tried to fight, but ... it was strong and I was terrified ... it lashed me to a chair and forced me to watch as it raped her, over and over. She couldn't scream because it had gagged her.' A dish-towel had plugged her mom's mouth, the spaghetti stains from the previous night's dinner distinguishable from the blood. Her flesh had been plowed by serrated claws. She'd looked like a bear's scratching post, and the smell of her blood had been powerful enough for Tayla to taste.

'Then . . . oh, God.'

'Go ahead,' he murmured. 'You can tell me.'

She closed her eyes tight, as though doing so would shut out the images, but they only grew more vivid. 'She . . . came. He was raping her, and she . . . she came.'

Eidolon hooked a finger under her chin. 'Look at me. *Look at me.*' Reluctantly, she did. His expression was one of savage determination. 'That's why you can't have an orgasm with a man, isn't it?'

She tried to wrench out of his grasp, but he framed her face with both hands. 'She liked it,' Tayla said, her voice rough and raspy and on the verge of breaking. 'She was being tortured, raped, and she . . . she got off.'

'Listen to me, Tay. The Soulshredder was messing with you. And her. They have the ability to force someone to feel pleasure in the midst of pain. It's another way to torture them, to humiliate them. And look how it worked. Look how he's been tormenting you for years with this memory.' His thumb brushed her cheekbone in long, soothing strokes. 'Has that scene been playing out in your head every time you have sex?'

A sobbing sound escaped her as she swallowed around the lump in her throat. 'Yes. Sometimes, even when it's just me, all I can think about—'

'Stop. Don't give him that power anymore.' His thumb dropped to her trembling lips, where he traced them, his touch light and gentle. 'Has he returned to torment you since then?'

'No, but I wish he would,' she said fiercely. 'I'd tear him apart.'

'You're so strong,' he whispered. 'So brave. Your fight against demons has been as internal as it has been external. You can win this battle.' He kissed away her tears. 'Let me help you.'

'You want to heal me, doctor?' she asked softly.

Possessive eyes focused on her. 'I've never wanted anything more.'

'Me, either,' she said, and Lord help her, it was true. The events of so long ago had stuck with her for so many years, had ruined her life, had ruined her ability to have a normal relationship with a man. It was time to let it go. Or, at least, try to let it go.

Her mouth found his in an urgent, desperate kiss. He was still inside her, hard and thick, and she ground against him, already losing herself to the passion he coaxed out of her with sinful ease.

A rumble of approval issued from deep in his chest, and he began a slow, sensual rhythm of thrusts. Always before, sex between them had been little more than a violent sprint to the finish, but this ... this was already shaping up to be a marathon. He took her face in his hands and kissed her, deeply, tenderly. His tongue worked hers, sucking and stroking. Between her legs, tension mounted as he changed the tempo and depth of his thrusts, going from shallow and rapid to deep and slow.

'You're beautiful, *lirsha*,' he murmured against her mouth. 'Perfect.'

His words were a caress to the soul, and she felt herself opening up like a night-blooming flower. She no longer cared who or what she was, what he was, or what existed beyond the bedroom door.

She dragged her hands up from his hips to his waist, taking in the taut layers of muscle, the smoothness of his skin. She didn't stop there, let her palms map his back until she reached his broad shoulders. He was a thing of beauty, a creature built to please a woman, from his looks to his scent to his skill in bed, and with every thrust, he took her higher.

'Say my name,' he purred, his voice vibrating through her in an erotic wave.

'Hellboy—'

'No.' He pushed up on his elbows. His eyes glittered, molten gold. He kept pumping though, and the slick friction had her panting, which she hadn't realized until she tried to speak. 'When you

243

get close, look at me. Think only of me, and say my *name*. I want to hear you say it when you come.'

His admission sent a surge of passion roaring through her, as though her heart were connected to her sex by a white-hot wire.

'Yes,' she whispered, even though she doubted she'd come – no, she would. The past had no place in this bed.

He groaned and started to move faster. Sensation doubled, her pleasure climbing higher as the crown of his cock slid back and forth across a place inside she hadn't known existed. Closing her eyes, she concentrated on the feel of masculine weight on her body, something she'd never enjoyed. But now it felt so right, so good, and oh, God, *right there.*

Her orgasm hovered close, hot. He dropped his forehead to hers, and her eyes flew open.

'Come for me, my *lirsha*, my lover,' he murmured, his gaze holding hers so she couldn't look away, couldn't see anything but the promise of ecstasy that rose up as though answering his command. 'Come for me now.'

Quivering with the need to explode, she clung tighter, digging her short nails into his shoulders, scoring his skin. He hissed and arched, and if not for his throaty, 'Gods, yes,' she'd have thought she hurt him.

She burned for him, smoked and sizzled. He was flame and she was fuel and when he did something sinful with his finger between them, she finally ignited. She came, bellowing out his name. He followed, his body going bowstring taut, his head falling back, his hips jackhammering into her. His warm, spurting seed splashed deep inside, triggering another powerful climax that forced her to unwrap her legs from his waist in order to brace herself on the bed as her hips came off it.

As though the air had been let out of him, he sagged on top of her. He was heavy, crushingly heavy, but she didn't care. She'd just had not one, but two orgasms when she'd never been able to come with a man.

Gratitude and something even stronger, an emotion she didn't want to name, tripped through her as she stroked his muscular back, petting him, telling him with her hands what she didn't have the breath to say.

Abruptly, he rolled off her, pulling her with him so she lay on her side, facing him. Male triumph lit his expression, bringing out the gold flecks in his dark eyes.

'That was—'

'Shh.' He pressed a finger to her lips and then drew it down her chin, her throat, her breasts . . . all the way to her core. 'You're not through.'

'But—'

He made a harsh noise, shutting her up as he dipped two fingers inside her. 'Remember what my seed does?' Before she could respond, he spread his moisture through her slit, coating her bud, which still tingled. She groaned, arching into his touch, but he withdrew. One big hand clenched her thigh. Eidolon was looking at her, lids lowered, gaze fierce. Slowly, he squeezed her legs together and pulled her close, the friction threatening to set her off again. He knew, was massaging her thigh to create tiny waves in her muscles.

'No,' she said, grasping his wrist. 'Not alone.' The vulnerability of it all, coming apart while he watched, totally uninvolved, God.

'You're going to come again. Don't fight it.'

But she was fighting it. She felt so stupid, so exposed, and, as he kept tenderly caressing her, so freaking *inflamed.*

He leaned forward so their chests touched, so his lips brushed hers. 'Trust it. Trust *me.'*

'No,' she moaned, but her body trusted him, and it took his words and ran with them. Pleasure spread in a tidal wave from her sex to her scalp. She thrashed, writhed, bit her tongue to keep from screaming.

'Ride it out,' he murmured.

When she came down from the high, she didn't have a chance

245

to feel embarrassment, and honestly, she didn't know if she would. The way he took her in, the admiration in his gaze, wow. Suddenly, she understood feminine power.

'You're lovely when you come. I could watch your pleasure all day long.'

'Not one for TV, huh?'

His laughter rang out, deep and hearty. 'You are much more fascinating than anything I could watch on TV.'

So was he, as much as she hated to admit it. 'Eidolon?'

'Hmm?'

'Thank you.'

He pushed up on his elbows. 'No, thank you.'

'For what?'

He smiled, the one that made her weak in the knees. 'For reminding me why I need to fight the *s'genesis*.'

'So you can heal women with sexual hangups?'

'No,' he said, dipping his head to kiss her, 'so I can be with a female because I want to, not because I need to.' His voice dropped lower, became a hypnotizing purr. 'Let me heal the rest of you. Let me integrate your demon half.'

'Yes . . . no, wait.' She struggled to sit up, but with one hand on her breastbone, he kept her down and still.

'I don't want you to die.'

'That's what it could really come down to, isn't it?' God, she was insane for even considering it. 'If I agree to this, I need you to promise me something.' She couldn't believe she was asking a demon for a promise. A week ago she'd have killed anyone who said she'd ever do such a thing. 'If I turn out to be something really horrible . . . you'll kill me.'

Eidolon's dark brows shot up. Before he could say anything, she pressed one finger to his lips. 'Please. I can't say yes unless I know I won't be a danger to anyone. Can you promise me that?'

After a moment, he bowed his head so his forehead rested on

246

hers. 'I promise. I'll give Shade a call in the morning. We'll do it then.' He palmed her hip and pushed his thick thigh between her legs, making her sigh with contentment. 'Tonight, we have other things to do.'

NINETEEN

᮪

The hazy morning light streaming through the window seared Eidolon's eyes. He didn't think about the reason he was so sensitive. He didn't care. All that mattered was getting to the blinds and closing them.

His feet hit the floor, but his legs didn't work. Rubbery muscles couldn't support his weight, and he crumpled next to the bed. Pain covered him like a blanket of thorns. Everything hurt. His eyes. His face. His entire body throbbed.

Had Tayla done something to him?

Tayla.

A surge of lust shot through him like a burning arrow. He lifted his head, caught the savory scent of the sex they'd had for hours last night. Yeah, she'd been cured. She'd come over and over, in every position, in every room.

Forgetting the blinds, he staggered to his feet, swaying until he caught himself on the side of the bed. Tayla lay tangled in the sheets, her hair fanning out over the pillow, her breasts exposed to the air and his gaze. Lower, the sheet had fallen away, allowing a glimpse of her thighs and the sweet place nestled between.

He wanted her. Needed her.

Growling low in his throat, he lowered himself onto the bed and opened his mouth over her hip.

'Mmm, Hellboy,' she murmured, smiling, her eyes still closed.

She shifted and stretched. Opened her eyes. And gasped.

'Shit!' She scooted toward the headboard, but he grabbed her foot and tried to drag her back down. A kick aimed at his chin nearly connected. 'What is wrong with you?'

'Nothing's wrong with me. What's wrong with you?'

She jerked free of his grip and rolled off the bed, coming gracefully to her feet.

Naked.

The delicious, potent aroma of fear came off her hot body in waves. He had to have her. Now.

'Stay away from me.'

Not going to happen.

Take her.

His nostrils flared as he separated the scents coming from her. Fear, confusion . . . ovulation.

She's ready.

Mingled with her smells, masking the scent of human, was the one of demon. His body answered.

Power rippled beneath his skin, threatening to tear him apart. His brain fogged. Pain crackled through him. The sound of ripping flesh hit him at the same time as the stabbing sensations in his back.

When his vision cleared, he looked down at his hands. No, not hands. Paws. Red, scaly paws tipped with serrated talons.

Impregnate her.

'I'm going to have you now.'

Tayla's scream shot straight to his groin. The sound of terror was a rush, an aphrodisiac for both the mind and cock. Now he needed to taste her, to rip into her flesh with his teeth –

He shook his head. These thoughts weren't his.

Impregnate her.

He lunged. Landed on her, held her shoulders with the claws on the tips of his wings, while his hands grasped her hips to bring her closer to his barbed penis. She brought her knee up, nailed him between the legs so hard he roared. Rolling, she caught him behind the knees with her foot, and he went down.

He snagged her calf, but she wriggled out of his grasp and darted to her weapons bag.

'*Esraladoth en sludslo.*' The words came out of his mouth, but he had no idea what he'd said.

She whirled, a boleadora in her fist. 'If that means kick my ass, then fucker, you're in luck.' She hurled it at him. He felt it wrap around his throat, and the world went black.

❧

Tayla watched the Soulshredder go down, her heart beating so hard her ribs hurt. Terror like she hadn't felt since the day her mom died threatened to turn her into a useless blob of jelly, and she had to fight like hell to stay on her feet. The thing twitched and went still.

The events of the last few moments played back in her head like a horror movie, but no matter how much she paused the video, she couldn't find an explanation for what had just happened. Where was Eidolon? One moment he'd been kissing her hip; the next he'd been sprouting membrane-thin, veined wings from his back. Had the Soulshredder killed him and taken his form? If the Soulshredder had taken someone else from her, she swore she'd make what Jagger and Lori did to Yuri appear tame.

Hand shaking, she drew a dagger from her weapons bag and nearly dropped it. Twice. If this was the best she could do, beheading the thing would be messy. Not that she cared. Oh, no. She was going to work the beast over, make it suffer until she discovered what it had done to Eidolon.

She swung around.

It was gone. In its place, Eidolon was there, the boleadora around his neck.

Oh, shit.

Still clutching the knife, she pulled a set of manacles from the bag and hurried to him. In the gray, cloud-choked light filtering through the window, he looked the same, except for the huge, swirling tattoo on the right side of his face.

And when she'd first seen him in the bed, his eyes had been red.

Cautiously, she shackled his ankles and wrists, and removed the weighted rope from around his throat.

Sitting on her heels, she stared at him, wondering what to do now. Besides get dressed, anyway. She couldn't leave him here, tied up, indefinitely, but neither could she turn him loose and risk his spontaneously shifting into something horrible again. Of course, that was assuming the creature on the floor was him at all.

Maybe one of his brothers could help.

Quickly, she threw on some jeans and a plain black T-shirt from the bag of clothes she'd brought with her, and then she hunted down his cell phone and dialed Shade. When he didn't answer, she found the hospital's number in the phone's directory. A female answered and identified herself as the nurse in charge at Underworld General.

'I need to speak to Shade.'

'He is unavailable.'

'Then get Wraith. It's an emergency.'

'Do you require medical assistance?'

'I require Shade.'

'Ma'am,' came the irritated voice that sounded as if it was being sifted through fangs, 'Shade is busy—'

'You can get him on the line, so do it. Now.' Actually, she had no idea if they could get him, but she was done being nice.

There was a pause, a click, several rings, and then a grumpy, deep voice.

'Shade.'

'Yeah, look. It's Tayla. Eidolon ... he's in trouble.'

'Again? This wasn't Wraith's doing. He's been level. So what the fuck did you do to E?' A vicious snarly sound vibrated through the phone. 'If you hurt him—'

'I didn't, asshole. Something's wrong. He went crazy. He's got this big tattoo on his face, and his eyes were red—'

'Ah, shit.' Curses flew over the airwaves, and she hoped the underworld equivalent of some FCC wasn't listening in. 'Where are you?'

'His apartment.'

'Stay there.'

'Well, duh. Where else would I—'

The line went dead. Demons were so rude.

She didn't want to go back to the bedroom. What if Eidolon had morphed into a Soulshredder again? What if he hadn't, but was awake and wondering why she'd beaten and bound him? What if he'd known exactly what he was doing when he turned into the thing that terrified her most in the entire world?

Nervous energy zinged through her like an electric current as she paced in the kitchen, jonesing for an orange. She finished off the last of the orange juice, and as she drained the glass, someone pounded on the front door.

'It's Shade. Open up.'

She did, and he strode in, completely encased in black leather and steel-toed boots. Wraith entered behind Shade, somehow looking even more lethal than his brother despite the fact that he wore torn jeans and a Hooters T-shirt. Danger followed in his wake ... followed, because it wouldn't dare get in his way.

They both stopped short at the sight of Eidolon on the floor in the bedroom, in shackles and unmoving.

'Overkill, much?' Shade said, striding forward to drop his medic bag next to Eidolon.

'You didn't see him before.'

'What do you mean?' Wraith asked, joining Shade.

'He turned into a Soulshredder.'

Shade let out a low, stunned whistle, but Wraith grinned over his shoulder at her. 'Damn. First time he shapeshifts, he picks something like that. Who knew he had it in him?'

'Is it really him?'

Shade knelt and palmed Eidolon's forehead. 'Yeah, it's him. Tayla, I need you to remove the restraints.'

She tossed him the key, still hesitant to go anywhere near.

'E?' Wraith helped Shade turn him onto his back. 'Bro, you hear me?'

Eidolon groaned. 'What happened?'

'You got your ass whupped,' Wraith said, squatting on his heels and bracing his forearms on his knees. 'Almost sounds like you deserved it.'

'Where's Tayla? Is she okay?' He tried to sit up, but Shade and Wraith pushed him back down.

'I'm fine.' She moved closer, drawn by the concern in his voice. 'I'm not sure what happened.'

'She says you turned into a Soulshredder.'

The blood drained from Eidolon's handsome face. He levered into a sit even with both brothers trying to make him eat carpet. 'I *what*?'

'What do you remember?' Shade asked, as he inserted a needle into Eidolon's hand. His dark hair had fallen down around his face, concealing his expression, but his broad shoulders hunched with tension.

'Not much.' Eidolon's voice turned husky, and his eyes went gold as he looked at her. 'I wanted her. I know that.'

Wraith placed a restraining hand on his shoulder. 'Idle down, man. Now's not the time. And that's something I never thought I'd say.'

Eidolon went utterly still, and then he shook his head as though trying to clear it. 'That's all I know. I wanted to take her. More than I've ever wanted anything.'

Heat washed over her body at the memory of how she'd

253

awakened, ready for him even though they'd spent the entire night engaged in the most amazing erotic play. But then she'd noticed that he looked different. Acted different. Terrifyingly different.

'It was weird,' she said. 'It was like he was possessed.'

'So you refused him?' Shade asked, and she bristled.

'Well, hello . . . he wasn't himself—'

'Chill,' Shade said, his voice softer than she'd ever heard it. 'I didn't mean anything. I'm just trying to get to the bottom of this. For his sake.'

She felt herself blush. Talking sex with Eidolon's brothers was just too weird. 'Yeah, I refused him. That's when he turned into the Soulshredder.' She shuddered. 'We were talking about them last night. Maybe it was the first demon he thought of to change into.'

Wraith and Shade exchanged glances, something ominous passing between them. Eidolon seemed distracted, looking inward, his face still ashen.

'That's why he didn't return,' Eidolon muttered, making no sense. He shoved both hands through his hair and focused on her with an intensity that made her take a step back. 'It bothered me, why the Soulshredder didn't come back to torment you after he killed your mother. That's what they do. They keep at it, driving their victims insane.'

'You don't think the memory of what he did has tormented me all these years?' And why did her voice have to tremble like that? Eidolon had helped her through so much last night, and now she felt as if she was living the trauma all over again.

'I know it has, *lirsha*.' He scooted toward her, slowly, and with every inch, she felt panic rise. 'But now it's making sense. You weren't his intended victim. He didn't kill your mom to torment you. He killed her after tormenting her for years.'

'Years? No. That couldn't be.' She frowned, because actually, what he said made sense. Everyone who'd known her said she'd had goals, a good life, and then she started doing drugs. Tayla remembered how she would talk about getting rid of her demons . . .

They'd been real. The demons had been real, and no one had believed her.

'She'd get clean for a while, and then relapse, going off about demons, how her nightmares had started again. He must have come to her during the times when she was clean, and he drove her back to the drugs.'

'When did she start using?'

'I'm not sure . . . ' Before her grandma died, she'd told Tayla that everything happened at once. Her mom had dropped out of college in the middle of a nervous breakdown everyone assumed had come as a result of stress, drugs, and an unexpected pregnancy . . . 'Oh, God. *God, no.*'

'Yep.' Shade's mouth tightened in a grim line as he connected a unit of blood to Eidolon's IV line. 'There's only one reason E would have turned into a Soulshredder, Tayla.'

Cramps twisted her insides, threatened to double her over. 'Because he sensed it in me,' she said hoarsely.

Eidolon inclined his head. 'The demon who killed your mother—'

'Was my father.'

Eidolon rubbed his cheek where the markings had been. 'That's why you can see scars no one else can. Shredders can see old injuries, even if they've healed. They find weaknesses and exploit them.'

Wraith shot her a look of sympathy she could see through the veil of darkness that started to descend. 'Dude, and I thought I was fucked up.'

'You are, dumbass.' Shade hung the bag of blood from a dresser knob as she backed toward the door. She had no idea where she was going, just that she needed to get out of this room that kept growing smaller with every passing second.

'I, uh, I need some air.' She darted out the door and down the

255

hall, ignoring Eidolon's shouts for her to come back. The sound of footsteps behind her only spurred her faster, and before she knew it, she was running barefoot along the maze of hallways that made up the top floor of the high-rise building.

'Tayla!' Shade's voice echoed after her, distant, but not distant enough. Panic had reached up and taken her by the throat, and right now she just needed to be alone.

She darted down the fire escape stairs and kept going once she hit the lobby. People stared, but she didn't care. The doorman opened the doors for her, and she flew out of the building and into the rain-soaked daylight.

The cool spring shower did nothing to ease her fevered thoughts even as it saturated her to the bone. People dressed in business attire and outfitted with umbrellas gave her a wide berth, no doubt seeing a crazy, homeless waif with tangled hair, hole-ridden jeans, and no shoes.

She didn't give a crap.

The Soulshredder that killed my mother was my father.

The words screamed through her head. She clamped her hands over her ears, as if that would block them out, but it only made them echo more violently off the inside of her skull.

A massive sob escaped her, and she did the only thing she could. She ran.

TWENTY

෬

If nervous energy could be harnessed, Eidolon would have lit up Manhattan with his pacing. Shade and Wraith had gone in search of Tayla, and now, fifteen minutes later, there was no word. He'd stayed behind in case she returned, but he didn't know how much longer he could stand doing nothing but wait.

The front door flew open, and Shade, dripping wet, burst inside. 'She's gone. Wraith is tracking her, but I have a feeling that if she doesn't want to be found, she won't be.'

Pain struck him like a blow, worse than anything Tayla could do to him if she tried. 'I have to find her. If her demon half rears up, she could be incapacitated. And if The Aegis catches her ... I have to go.' He grabbed a jacket from his closet. 'Call Gem. She said she can sense Tayla—'

'E.' Shade grabbed him by the shoulders and shook him. 'Give her some space. She just found out her sire is a species that makes Cruenti go to ground.'

'Why do you care?'

'Because you do.'

In a moment of tense silence, Eidolon let the words sink in. He did care for Tayla, and he might as well stop denying it. 'Is it that obvious?'

'Ah, you're kidding, right? She's the enemy, she blew up the hospital, got Yuri killed ... yet you moved her in with you. I'm thinking all that means you care. A lot more than you should.' He dropped his hands and leveled a hard look at Eidolon. 'That said, she could have taken you out a couple of times, but instead, she called me to help. She might not be a total wench.'

'She's not.' The night they'd shared came back to him in slow motion. He'd fucked a lot of females, but he'd never once made love to one.

He'd made love to Tayla over and over.

'Shit,' Shade muttered. 'Don't do it. Don't bond with her. E? You hear me? She's a slayer—'

'Not anymore.'

Curses fell out of Shade's mouth, creative ones Eidolon had never used. 'You know our blood is toxic to humans.'

'She's half-demon. She could survive the ritual.'

'It's dangerous enough to make a demon your mate, but someone trained to kill you? Twenty years from now, when she decides she wants a divorce—'

'That'll be my concern. Not yours.'

Shade stared at him for a long moment. 'If I wanted to take a mate, would you be worried?'

'Damn straight. But only because of your curse.' A curse that would doom Shade to a fate worse than death if he ever fell in love. 'My situation is different. A lot different.'

Shade shook his head in exasperation. 'Fine. Whatever. You bitch about Wraith being so stubborn, but you make him look like an amateur.'

The phone rang, and Shade grabbed it. He listened for a moment, then hung up. 'We need to get to the hospital.' His sinister grin matched the evil glint in his eye. 'Paige just woke up from her coma.'

❧

It was a monster with a hundred eyes. Some had been smashed, others were so clouded they couldn't be used. The thing stared at Tayla through the rain and fog, mocking her with its silence.

It was The Warehouse, the one where she'd been born, the one she always came back to because the hunting was so good, though now she wondered if there was another reason she kept returning to this place. Maybe she was suffering from some sort of demon compulsion to return to her birthplace, because eight hours after fleeing Eidolon's apartment, she found herself before it once again, and with no memory of how she got here.

All she knew was that her feet were bleeding, she was soaked, and she was angry. She crossed the street, not caring that cars had to slam on their brakes and honk their horns to keep from smashing her. Several drivers cursed at her, then cursed more when she presented them with a middle-finger salute.

She walked into a wall of stench as she stepped inside the building. Human waste, smoke, rotting food. She'd always ignored the odors and the filth, but today she catalogued it all in her mind. This was where her mother had spent a lot of her life. Here, among the graffiti-scarred walls, the discarded hypodermic needles, the rats and cockroaches.

The Soulshredder had done this to her mother.

A sound, faint, female, carried over the scratching of rodent claws on concrete, and Tayla crouched, crept toward the east wing. Several voices rang out behind her – laughter, probably coming from the western offices where crackheads liked to hang out. The dozens of exits in that part of the building provided a safety net for them, especially during police raids.

'Leave me alone, Bryce.' Ahead, a woman sat in a corner, blood dripping from her nose, her stringy blonde hair matted to what looked like dried blood on her cheek. A bulldog of a man stood over her, meaty fist cocked back. The woman scrambled away, but he caught her and punched her hard in the head.

Curiously calm, Tayla stepped out of the shadows, prepared to

259

pound the man into dust. A vampire did the same, at the other end of the room. A large male, it seized the man by the back of the neck, slammed him against the wall, and buried its fangs deep into the human's jugular.

Whimpering, the woman lurched to her feet and fled the room, not sparing a glance back.

The wet sound of sucking cut through the other warehouse noises. Bloodlust shimmered in the air like an electric current, dancing off Tayla's skin. She'd never noticed the sensation before, or maybe she had, but assumed it was part of the adrenaline rush that filled her before battle. It felt curiously good. Seductive, even, and she had to plant her feet firmly to keep from moving closer to the bloodsucker and his prey.

Just a few days ago, Tayla would have taken out the vamp and saved the man, which seemed ironic, given that the human had beaten the crap out of a smaller woman and might have killed her. Now Tayla just watched.

'Funny how sometimes humans prove to be bigger monsters than demons, huh?'

Tayla whirled around. The first thing she saw was a pair of luminous green eyes that were level with hers. The second thing she saw was the fist connecting with her face.

Tayla's head snapped back. 'Ow!' She returned the favor with an elbow in the black-haired woman's jaw.

The woman wobbled on her feet before steadying herself, one corner of her black lipstick-stained mouth tipping up in a half-smile. 'It's good to finally meet you, Tayla.'

Tay touched the back of her hand to her stinging lips. It came away with blood. 'Right. Finally. Who the hell are you?' Whoever she was, she was pretty, with long, thick eyelashes, high cheekbones, black and blue hair braided into two pigtails that would have looked ridiculous on anyone older than seven, but that somehow worked on her. Probably because she was dressed like a Catholic schoolgirl. On crack.

'My name's Gem.'

'Well, Gem, now that we're all buddy-buddy and on a first-name basis, you want to tell me why you introduced me to your knuckles?'

'So many ways to answer that.' Gem studied her black-painted nails. 'How's life in The Aegis treating you?'

'You must be a demon.' Something struck Tayla as being familiar. Gem's eyes . . . so green. Tayla had seen them before.

'Why do you say that?'

'Because demons seem to lack the switch in the brain that warns them when they are about to say something stupid.'

'I knew you'd have a sense of humor.'

'Enough of the cryptic shit. How do you know me?'

'I've always known you.'

'Jesus Christ,' Tayla muttered. 'I don't have time to play games.' She turned on her heel, not sure where she was going but desperate to get away from Cryptic Goth Chick.

'You have very little time for anything, slayer. You're dying. And not slowly.'

Tayla snorted and kept walking. 'Tell me something I don't know.'

A hand closed on her elbow and jerked her around. 'Fool!'

Tayla had Gem flat on her back and was straddling her waist in a flash. 'What the hell is your problem?'

'My problem?'

The sound of approaching footsteps barely registered, but the low, controlled drawl drew a groan from them both.

'That is *so* hot. E, do you think we can talk them into getting naked, too?'

Eidolon stood next to Wraith and Shade, arms crossed, watching Gem and Tayla like a stern father, which was appropriate, because fighting with Gem seemed unnaturally . . . natural.

'She started it,' Gem said, and Tayla snorted.

'What's your issue with me?'

Gem shrugged off Tayla's grip on her upper arm, but didn't try to dislodge her. 'My issue is how you've wasted your life. You could have been so much more than an Aegis slayer.'

'Guardian,' Tay growled. 'And how do you know what I've done with my life or what I could have been?'

'Because,' Gem said, 'we're sisters, and look what I became.'

Tayla narrowed her eyes at the other woman. 'Sisters in what? Half-humanhood?'

'Blah, blah.' Wraith yawned. 'Can you guys start fighting again?'

Gem shoved Tayla off her. They sat in the light from street lamps that streaked through a broken window, staring like rival cats. 'I'm half Soulshredder. Just like you.'

Tayla's breath left her in a rush. 'We have the same father?'

Eidolon moved in, as if he knew she was going to need him, which was good, because she had a nasty feeling he was right.

Deep grooves furrowed Gem's brow as she grasped Tayla's hand. 'We have the same father,' she confirmed. Her gaze locked with Tay's. 'And the same mother. We're fraternal twins.'

The world fell away. 'That ... that's impossible,' Tayla whispered. There was a pause. A long one in which she began to tremble. 'My mom—'

'She didn't know. I was born first. Delivered by demons right here on the warehouse floor while our mother was in a drugged stupor. The demons took me because they sensed demon in me. They didn't sense it in the unborn baby. You.'

And suddenly, Tayla realized why Gem's eyes had seemed so familiar. They were her mother's eyes.

ॐ

Eidolon was just as stunned by Gem's news as Tayla was, and as they all headed back to his apartment, he wondered why he was so surprised. With the exception of the dyed hair and Goth-style makeup, Gem was very nearly the spitting image of Tayla.

And now, the reason he'd been so aggressive in the car with Gem became clear. He'd seen Tayla in her.

'I don't understand this,' Tayla said, as they exited the Harrowgate in an alley near his building. Like all of the gates, it was invisible to human eyes and wouldn't open if humans were within visual range, but Tayla lowered her voice anyway. 'How long have you known?'

Gem picked up her pace, walking slightly ahead of the group. 'My parents told me years ago so I would have the choice about whether I wanted to know you.'

'How special. And what, you just spied on me all this time?'

'I wanted to tell you.' Gem sighed, slowing. 'I went to your apartment once, but you were leaving. I followed you, saw you meet up with some delinquent-looking friends. Figured you'd be drunk in an hour. Turned out you did your partying in the sewers.'

'You followed us down there?'

'Yep. I saw you hunting. Telling you who – and what – I was, didn't seem like a great plan at that point.'

They arrived at Eidolon's building, and inside the elevator, Tayla turned on Gem, though she kept her hand in his. 'Your *parents* left me and my mom to die on the warehouse floor.'

'My mother called an ambulance, but she couldn't risk being seen with me. Please, Tayla,' Gem said softly. 'Stop fighting what you are. Who you are.'

'Easy for you to say.' Tayla's voice was sharp, cutting, and he knew she wasn't going to accept anything without drawing blood first. 'You've known since you were born. You didn't have a choice about what you are. I do.'

They exited the elevator on Eidolon's floor, and as he unlocked his door, he said quietly, so as not to freak out any neighbors, 'You are half-demon, Tayla. There's no choice about that.'

'True.' She didn't look at him, her eyes focused on the door. 'But I don't have to integrate that half.'

'You'd rather die? Because that's your choice, slayer,' Shade said as they entered.

Wraith rubbed his hands together in cheesy horror-movie glee. 'Join us or die.' He grinned. 'I've always wanted to say that.'

'Wraith's demented,' Gem said, 'but he's right. Tayla, let us—'

Tayla whirled, stopping them all in the foyer. 'No.'

'You agreed earlier,' Eidolon reminded her, hoping his voice didn't betray his fear that she'd truly changed her mind.

'That was before I found out what my father was. Before I learned I'm a monster.' Tears welled in her eyes as she looked down at her hands, her arms. 'That . . . that *thing,* is inside me. In my blood. Under my skin.' She began to scratch, and then claw, as though trying to rip off her skin.

'Stop.' Eidolon grabbed her by the shoulders. 'Calm down—'

'Let me go.' She jerked wildly in his grip until he pulled her against him.

Gods, she felt good in his arms. Her struggles had triggered his libido, of course, but as she settled down and just held him, rubbing her face against his chest, something else triggered, something more powerful than an urge to mate – an urge to save her life so he could keep her as his own.

'Listen to me, Tayla. Look at Gem. Look at your sister.' Tayla lifted her head as Eidolon gently stroked her wet hair. 'See the tattoo bands around her wrists and neck?'

Gem pulled down her inch-wide dog collar to reveal the Celtic knots that circled her throat. 'They're on my ankles, as well. They contain the demon side of me. Without them, it comes out when I'm upset or angry. Tayla, you can contain yours, too. Being a demon doesn't automatically make you evil.'

She pulled out of his arms, and he felt the loss in his soul. 'You guys are broken records. Demons aren't all evil. The Aegis is selling our body parts—'

'Ah . . . well . . . '

She dabbed at her eyes with the back of her hand. 'Well, what?'

Shade popped a stick of gum in his mouth. 'While Wraith and Gem were looking for you, we went to the hospital to have a chat with one of our nurses who was injured in the explosion. It was . . . enlightening. Seems The Aegis isn't involved.'

'Then who is?' Tayla asked.

Fury washed through him at the memory of standing at Paige's bedside, her hatred of demons becoming clearer with every vile word. 'Paige wasn't sure. She was human, but not Aegis.'

'Was?'

'She was disposed of.' And unfortunately, she'd known nothing about the status of Gem's parents.

Tayla crossed her arms over her chest and stared toward the kitchen, her gaze distant. Scents swirled around her, confusion, suspicion, and anger. 'Why did she do it?'

'She was addicted to black magic,' he said grimly. The dark arts seduced humans, gave them powerful highs and the belief that they were damned near gods. Paige had considered demons to be nothing more than insects, minions for her to abuse as she wished, and she'd gone willingly into the organ ring not for money, but to harvest parts for her personal use. 'Apparently, she'd receive a message from the Ghouls to meet somewhere. A different location every time. She'd be met by various demons who would take her to a facility outfitted for surgery.'

'She was a doctor?'

'Nurse. But she learned enough working at UG to perform the duties required. It wasn't as though she was removing organs for transplants.'

'Now they want me,' Gem said. 'They took my parents and threatened to kill them if I don't cooperate.'

Realization sparked in Tayla's eyes, flickering like green fire. 'That's why you're here. It has nothing to do with wanting to know me.'

'I'll admit, the kidnapping pushed up my timetable, but I always wanted to know you, Tayla.'

'Yeah. Whatever.' Tayla's self-defense mechanism, disbelief that anyone might want to get close, reminded Eidolon so much of Wraith.

'What's next for your parents?' Eidolon glanced at Gem. 'Are you supposed to contact the Ghouls?'

Gem nodded. 'I'm supposed to meet them at the old zoo tomorrow night.'

'The zoo?' Tayla frowned, turning to Shade. 'Didn't you say your paramedic werewolf was attacked by Guardians?'

'Bastards.'

'So that's a yes.' She twirled a strand of hair around her finger and tugged, thinking. 'And he said they smelled like ... what was it? Apes?'

'Yeah? So? Humans stink.'

Eidolon would have argued that, but he knew Shade was being obnoxious for the sake of being obnoxious.

'It's just ... someone is lying. Luc said he was surprised in his house. The Guardians who survived the battle told our leaders that they chased him into the house. Just for shits and grins, let's say they're lying. Why? Why would they lie to the leaders of our cell? The only answer is that the leaders don't know what's going on. And if your were is telling the truth ... if they smell like apes ...'

Eidolon cursed. 'The abandoned zoo.'

'Yeah.' Despite the fact that she now suspected Guardians were involved, she sounded relieved to know that at least the leaders she'd trusted might be clueless. 'It would be the perfect place to keep demons they caught.'

'But we know demons are involved,' Shade said.

Tayla nodded grimly. 'Sounds to me like they might be working together.'

'*There's* a nightmare scenario. Oh, hey, a weasel!'

Wraith swept up Mickey, who had been circling at his feet.

'I need to contact Kynan,' Tayla said, though she seemed to be talking to herself.

'Kynan? Kynan Morgan?'

Tayla spun around to Gem, who had gone utterly pale. 'You know him? How?'

'He's a slayer?' Gem's mouth worked silently for a moment, as though she couldn't process her own question. 'He's one of them?'

'How do you know him?' Tayla repeated.

'He's a regular at the hospital. Comes in every Tuesday to see a friend.' Gem exhaled slowly, the way Tayla did sometimes, when she was trying to keep it together. 'Oh, my God ... *Holy shit.*'

Tayla hugged herself, shivering even though the heat was on in the apartment. 'Dennis. He's known Dennis for years.' She heaved a grateful sigh as Eidolon wrapped her in his jacket.

Gem moved like a snake, her desperation obvious in the way she clamped her hand down on Tayla's forearm. 'You've got to talk to him. Tayla, you've got to go now. Ask about my parents.'

'I can't. The Aegis either thinks I'm dead or wants me dead. I can't go waltzing into headquarters right now. It'd be a suicide mission.'

'We've got to do something,' Gem insisted.

Tayla casually peeled Gem's fingers away. 'Tuesday ... that's tomorrow. He'll be at the hospital. If you can arrange for me to talk to him in private, I can catch him unprepared. Without backup. That's the only way this will work. I'm still not sure what's going on at The Aegis and who is involved.'

'We'll work something out,' Gem said, her voice barely a whisper. 'Damn, I still can't believe he's Aegis.'

'He's more than that. He's a Regent. The leader of the New York cell. What did you think he was?'

Gem toyed with her dog collar, her fingers trembling slightly. 'He tells everyone he runs a halfway house.'

'That's the cover.'

'Do you ... do you think he'd know anything about my parents?'

'No,' Tayla said fiercely. 'The leaders aren't in on it. They can't be.'

'You're sure that waiting to talk to him tomorrow is the only option?'

'Absolutely.' When Gem nodded, Tayla cocked her head and studied her sister. 'How did you know where to find me tonight, by the way?'

'I sensed you were in trouble.' Gem touched a hand to Tayla's shoulder. 'I've always been able to sense you if you were close enough to me.'

Tayla stood there, avoiding eye contact with her sister and looking more vulnerable than Eidolon had ever seen her. He fought the urge to wrap her in an embrace and protect her from all of this. Which was insane, because he'd never seen a female so capable of protecting herself.

'Eidolon, if I were to do the integration thing, would I be able to sense Gem, too?'

He almost smiled at the wariness in her tone. His little killer had to question everything. 'Probably.'

Her gaze caught and held his for a long moment as she considered what he'd said. 'Okay, but one thing I don't understand ... Gem said her parents sensed demon in her when she was born, but not in me. If we're twins, why did she develop her demon half, but I didn't?'

'I'd probably need to run tests on you both to answer that, but my guess is that since you are fraternal twins, you don't share an identical genetic code, and you developed differently. Her DNA merged. Yours didn't. But we can fix that.'

When she didn't respond, Gem broke the silence. 'You need to decide, and fast. The changes I'm sensing in you are all over the place. You don't have much time.'

Tayla's eyes narrowed into slits, as if she questioned Gem's motives. 'I'm not sure I trust you.'

'I don't trust you, either,' Gem shot back. 'So where does that leave us?'

'It leaves you in what's called a family, girls,' Wraith drawled. 'Get over it.'

TWENTY-ONE

꩜

After spending two hours in Eidolon's den talking to Gem, Tayla decided that she didn't like her newfound sister. It wasn't that Gem had grown up in a mansion, had attended private schools, and had lived an outwardly normal life despite being raised by demons. It wasn't that Gem was smart and educated, having entered college two years early, where Tayla was a high-school dropout who had a GED only because Kynan insisted that all Guardians have a basic education.

No, Tayla hated Gem because she kept saying 'our mother,' when Gem had never known her. She didn't have the right to call *our mother* anything but Teresa.

'You seem distracted,' Gem said, when Tayla pulled Eidolon's medical text off the shelf and began thumbing through it. She couldn't read a word of it, but the illustrations were interesting, if disgusting.

'Maybe I'm just tired of hearing how lucky you are.'

'I am lucky. I should have been slaughtered,' Gem said. 'That's what my parents' species does. They sense demon pregnancies and either ensure that the young are never born or destroy them at birth if a foster family can't be found. But my parents had been unable to conceive a child of their own, and I came along at just the right time.'

'And that's what you do at the hospital? The same thing?'

Gem hooked a leg over the armrest of Eidolon's couch, making the slit in her short leather skirt open over a tattoo of a long-stemmed rose on her thigh. Blood dripped from the thorns – Tayla counted three drops along the length of her leg, the last one half-covered by the top of her combat boot. It made her wonder if Gem had more tattoos, or more piercings besides the six in her ear, the one in her eyebrow, and the one in her tongue.

'Mainly, I work with humans. But I do my best to intercept the odd cases that come through the hospital ... infections from demon bites, illnesses and injuries in those with demon parentage, stuff like that. It's not a big deal if I miss any of it – anything that seems odd to a human doctor is diagnosed as a mystery disease or a deformity. Humans have an incredible capacity to explain away stuff they don't want to know the truth about.'

Tayla understood that. Her mom had tried repeatedly to tell her that demons tormented her, had even described the Soulshredder, but Tayla hadn't believed her, had chosen to believe that her mother suffered from drug-induced delusions. Because at the time, that was easier to believe than the truth. Heck, even after witnessing her mother's death at the hands of a demon, it hadn't occurred to Tayla that her mother had truly been tormented for years by the Soulshredder.

Gem sprawled back even more, making herself comfortable. Too comfortable. She'd been here, in Eidolon's apartment, before.

'Have you slept with him?' Tayla asked, gripping the medical book so hard she was going to leave impressions. Better that, though, than giving in to her possessive urge to bean Gem with it if she gave the wrong answer.

'Who? Eidolon? No.' Gem's eyes glittered. 'But you have. I've smelled you on him.'

Geez, did all demons possess overdeveloped olfactory senses?

271

'He's helping me through something,' Tayla said, and then wondered why she felt the need to explain her sexual relationship with him.

'Yeah, I'll just bet.'

'You sound a little jealous, sister.'

'Jealous? Nah. I could have him if I wanted him.' The way she said it, so sure of herself, made Tayla bristle. 'He's desperate for a mate to head off the *s'genesis*.'

'A mate? I was just talking about sex.'

'That's good, then. Because that's all any incubus is about.' Gem dropped her feet to the floor and propped her forearms on her bare knees. 'A piece of advice, sis. Don't get too close. He'll either go through The Change and leave you behind, or he'll take a mate and lock himself into a lifetime of fidelity. Either way, you're stuck on the outside looking in, and it sucks.'

'You sound like you know a little bit about that.'

'More than I'd like.' Tension vibrated between them, so not the reunion Tayla would have envisioned for something like this. 'Look, just think about the integration. As you can see, I'm not a monster. Our father—'

'Don't call him that,' Tayla snapped.

'It's what he is.'

Realization slapped her upside the head. 'You know him. Dear God, you *know him*.'

Gem regarded her coolly. 'I've met him.'

'Met him? Like, what, for tea and crumpets? He tormented our mom, Gem! For years. He raped her, God knows how many times, and then he tore her apart in front of my eyes. And you *met him*?'

Tayla must have been yelling, because the door burst open, and Eidolon filled the doorway, fists clenched, concern branded in his expression. 'You two all right?'

Gem ignored Eidolon to move closer to Tayla. 'What he did was horrible. But it was his nature. We all do things we're programmed to do . . .'

Whatever Gem was saying melted into a whirlpool of meaningless words. A cry tore from Tay's throat and then she was launching herself at the other woman. Her hands closed around Gem's throat as Eidolon's arms caught Tayla around the waist.

'How can you defend him?' Tayla screamed, fighting wildly against the set of arms – no, two sets, Shade had grabbed her, too – dragging her off Gem.

'You'd better go,' Eidolon told Gem, who nodded.

'Tay, you've got to look at who donated your DNA if you want to know who you are. What you can be.'

Something dark and oily gurgled through Tayla's veins, an evil industrial sludge that threatened to leach the humanity right out of her. 'Oh, I know who donated it. And I want nothing to do with it. Nothing to do with you. I will never – *never* – integrate that shit into myself. *Go. To. Hell.*'

'I'm sorry,' Gem whispered to Tayla, and then she looked up at Eidolon. 'I . . . I have to go. I'm sorry.'

Tayla stopped struggling, and gradually, Shade's hands eased away, but Eidolon only held tighter. Grateful for an island in the middle of the nightmarish sea she'd been swimming in, she folded herself into his embrace and wondered how much longer she could tread water before she drowned.

ᐁ

If Gem had been part Trillah demon she couldn't have run away from Eidolon's apartment any faster. She had really, really messed up with Tayla. As if things weren't bad enough with her parents already, now this.

'Stupid,' she muttered, as she hoofed it down the sidewalk in search of a taxi. Raised among humans, she had a tendency to eschew the Harrowgates in favor of more traditional means of transportation. 'Idiot!'

First, she'd been antagonistic about Eidolon, something that had been totally uncalled for and more than a little childish. Didn't matter that she knew where her behavior had come from – her jealousy. Not jealousy of Tayla's relationship with the incubus – well, maybe a little, since Gem couldn't have the man she loved, someone who might be responsible for her parents' kidnapping – but mostly of Tay's relationship with their mother.

Gem had never had that. She'd seen Teresa from afar, had taken pictures. And once, she'd worked up the guts to speak to her at a bus stop. Gem had been terrified, fifteen years old and dressed like a punk, but Teresa's voice had been soft and musical, with a hint of southern drawl that went down like sugar, a far cry from the clipped, stern voices of her adoptive parents.

Yes, she loved her parents, would always be grateful to them for saving her life and then giving her a great one, but deep down, she'd resented the fact that Tayla had been given sole rights to being Teresa's daughter.

How fucking petty. Especially considering how Gem had grown up wanting for nothing, but Tayla ... she'd suffered.

Once Gem was old enough to venture out on her own, she'd tracked Tayla down, had followed her from school to the rusted-out trailer where she'd lived with three other foster kids. When Gem saw her the next day, she'd been wearing the same clothes. Tayla had bounced around between foster care and the streets so much that Gem couldn't keep track. It wasn't until Teresa got clean and regained custody that, for once, Tayla had a stable home. Granted, the apartment she'd shared with Teresa was a roach motel, but they seemed to be happy for two years.

Until that night.

News reports had blasted the gory details nonstop, had shown pictures of the crime scene and made a big story of how Teresa had been torn apart by a vicious serial killer, and that her daughter, Tayla, was missing. Tay had eventually been found, but she'd never spoken to the authorities about the murder. Afterward, she'd gone again into foster care, but by the time Gem had located her sister, wanted for the killing of her foster father, Tay was already with

The Aegis ... which was around the time the Soulshredder had come to Gem.

She'd known instantly that the creature was her father.

It had slipped into her bedroom in the middle of the night, its goal beyond comprehension. It had intended to sire young on her, its own flesh and blood.

Her struggle to keep her inner beast at bay had been lifelong, something that had required discipline and protective tattoos. But that night, for the first time, she'd let her demon side reign, had used every trick in her book to kill the thing that was her father.

So, yeah, she knew firsthand that 'we all do things we're programmed to do.' Because like it or not, thanks to her sire, she was hardwired to torment and kill.

Every day was a battle, a tug of war between her two halves. And every morning she wondered if that would be the day her human half finally lost.

ର

Eidolon paced in the kitchen while Tayla showered and Shade whipped up some dinner. Wraith lounged on the couch, playing video games on the X-Box, Mickey tucked into one armpit. It had taken half an hour and three shots of Cutty Sark to calm Tay down, and then the adrenaline crash had turned her into a noodle. All she'd wanted was a shower, bed, and food, in no particular order.

In the meantime, he wanted to hunt Gem down and string her up. Gem had been their best shot at convincing Tayla to integrate her demon side. Now that was blown all to Hades.

'Want a beer?' Shade asked, as he pushed a plate of spaghetti across the kitchen island.

'Nah.'

'Suit yourself.' Shade snagged a bottle of Harp from the fridge. 'What a night, huh? I can't freakin' believe Paige was part of the organ thing. And Gem, the slayer's sister? Gives me the jeebies, man. Maybe if we could get them to fight again ...'

Eidolon smiled. 'You sound like Wraith.'

'Come on. He had a point. You have to give him that much.' Shade popped the cap off the beer. 'I mean, twins wrestling on the ground? Hot.'

Maybe, but Eidolon wasn't interested in two women. He wanted only the one. Shade went on about twins, ticking his conquests off on his fingers. Eidolon recommended a calculator and swept up the plate of food to take it to Tayla, though he wished he had some oranges. Her citrus craving made sense now; Soulshredders were a tropical species that required the fruit to survive.

Halfway to the bedroom, his heart skidded to a halt. The sweet, musky scent of Tayla's arousal drifted from the living room.

Wraith.

Eidolon sprinted down the hall, caught the corner with his shoulder, and spilled half the spaghetti onto the floor. Not that he noticed. No, all he could see was his own anger in a filter of red splayed across the scene before him.

Tayla stood in the living room, robe loosely tied and showing way too much creamy flesh. Wraith, his bloody video game on pause, watched her, his eyes glowing, not with the normal gold of arousal or anger, but with the blue-flecked gold of his hypnotic gift.

'See what it would be like with me?' he was saying. 'Bet E won't do that to you. It's not *civilized.*'

The bastard was in her head, feeding her images of gods knew what.

Territorial rage lit Eidolon up like a gas-soaked torch.

'Back *the fuck off,* brother,' Eidolon bit out. 'You don't do humans or Aegi.'

'She's not either. Not anymore.' Wraith smiled, his white fangs gleaming hungrily. 'Fair. Game.'

Darkness swallowed him. Eidolon dropped the plate and launched over the couch armrest. He slammed Wraith into the wall with a hand around the throat. Sober, Wraith could kick his butt, but he didn't give an imp's ass. 'She's mine.'

Wraith's eyes went half-lidded, and if he was bothered by the fact that Eidolon was nearly choking him, it didn't show. 'Look at her, E. She's primed. She'll take us both.'

An image of Wraith brutalizing Tayla with his teeth as he took her tattooed itself into Eidolon's brain, turning his thoughts to poison. 'Don't touch her,' he snarled. 'Don't you *ever* touch her, or I *will* let the vampires—'

'Hellboy?'

They both turned to Tayla, who stood there as though in a daze, her fingertips playing lazily along the edge of her robe where it gaped at the sternum. A blast of lust came from her like a shock-wave, and Eidolon jerked as though she'd grabbed his cock.

'That's never happened before. She should be calling my name,' Wraith muttered. 'And what were you saying about the vamps?'

Ignoring the question, Eidolon released Wraith with a shove and crossed to Tayla. She flew into his arms, climbed him like a tree until she was wrapped around him, rubbing her face on him, writhing against his body.

She was going to take him right there.

The thought made him so hot, so deliriously fuzzy-headed, that he nearly forgot Wraith was watching and let it happen. Instead, he hauled ass to the bedroom. By the time he kicked the door shut, his jeans were unbuttoned. By the time they were halfway to the bed, he was sheathed inside her wet, satin heat.

'Oh, my God, Eidolon . . . oh, my God.' She pelted his face with kisses as she began a punishing grinding motion with her hips. 'I went to get my backpack. Saw your brother . . . and suddenly, my mind just kept seeing—'

'Wraith.' Fuck. He stopped short of the bed, his heart growing cold even as he thrust into her hot depths.

'No,' she moaned. 'You. He was there for a second, but it wasn't right. I concentrated hard, and it was you.'

Pressure filled his chest cavity. A sudden, fierce instinct rose in him, a foreign and yet familiar urge. It didn't matter that her

277

passion had been induced by a mind-seduction. It didn't matter that she was hardly in a position to know what she wanted from him. All that mattered was that he take her. Bond with her. Make her his mate.

'Mine,' he growled into the slender column of her throat. 'You're mine.'

'Yes ... oh, yes.' Her voice throbbed with the promise of what she was saying. That she was his, that all his years of empty sex with empty females was coming to an end, that he would no longer worry about becoming a mindless beast, that there would be no more loneliness for either of them.

The surge of emotion triggered a chain reaction inside him. Fire shot from the fingertips of his right arm, up the tribal pattern in his skin. The designs glowed red through the sheen of sweat that had broken out over his entire body.

Spinning, he pinned her to the wall. He pumped into her, lost to the sensation of the intimate slide of slick flesh on slick flesh. Pleasure whipped at him, and still, it wasn't enough. He needed to possess her, to have her in every way he could.

The thump of their bodies against the wall reverberated in the room, all the way to his balls. Words came out of his mouth, words he'd never heard and didn't even know the meaning of, but he no longer operated on a logical level. Something primal and raw demanded he do nothing but follow a natural course.

Reaching down, he opened his bedside drawer and fumbled for what he was looking for.

Tayla was whimpering and writhing and clenching him to her so hard that he had to wrench his spine to get the space between them he needed. The air around them pulsed with powerful mating magic, cocooning them in their own world as he drew the scalpel across his chest. He felt no pain and was powerless to stop himself. Dropping the blade, he cupped her head and brought her lips to where his blood welled at the thin seam.

She hesitated, looking up at him with passion-darkened eyes.

278

'Do it,' he whispered. 'Taste me. Take me inside you.'

Holding his gaze, which was erotic as hell, she touched her tongue to a single pearl of blood.

Oh, sweet hell. Electric whips lashed at him, spreading from her tongue through his entire nervous system. He was short-circuiting with ecstasy, humming with the energy and hunger. A moan dredged up from the depths of his chest, and as she latched on and began a gentle sucking action, he threw back his head and roared.

His climax hit him with the force of a fire tornado, burning, twisting, turning him upside down and inside out.

Tayla joined him, screaming with the force of her release. She bucked against him, her female muscles clasping tight and drawing on his shaft for every last drop of seed.

For a moment, they shuddered together, panting, and he had to lock his knees to keep from sliding to the floor with her. His muscles quivered, and his insides gelled. Hazy reality filled his mind like smoke, and just as he realized what he'd done, Tayla cried out.

A violent spasm hit her with such force that they were propelled away from the wall. 'Hurts,' she gasped.

'*Lirsha,* oh, gods, what have I done?' Fear froze his marrow as he laid her on the bed and sank down beside her, one hand on her hip, the other threaded in her hair. She writhed, alternately clutching her gut and clawing at her skin. 'Shade!' Shit. He pulled her robe closed and tightened the sash. 'For fuck's sake, Shade! *Get in here!*'

The door crashed open, wood splintering. Shade hadn't bothered with the door handle. Wraith was right behind him, both taking in the scene in an instant.

'Is her DNA—' Shade sniffed the air. 'Ah, man, you didn't.'

Tears streamed down Tayla's face, dampening the pillow. Her eyes were closed tight against the pain as she huddled in fetal position on the silk comforter.

'I did.'

Wraith peeked around Shade. 'Did what?'

'He began the bonding process,' Shade said.

Wraith let out a low whistle. 'I knew you were desperate to get around the *s'genesis,* but I didn't think you were *that* desperate. Have you lost your fucking mind?'

Shade reached for Tayla, jerking back when Eidolon growled before he could catch himself. 'I need to get inside her, E.'

'I know,' he snapped, not wanting anyone, including – or especially – his brothers, to touch the female he wanted as his lifemate.

Warily, Shade wrapped his hand around her ankle. 'Our blood is toxic to humans, you knew that.'

Yeah, he knew that, but he hadn't been thinking, had been too deep in the rut, too driven by pure instinct. The argument that she was only half-human was too lame to bring up, so he stroked her cheek and talked to her as she'd done for him the night he'd taken the vampire punishment.

'You'll be fine,' he murmured, sending a healing wave into her, figuring it couldn't hurt, but she still made little sobbing noises, punctuated by high-pitched cries. Her legs scissored back and forth until Shade gripped both ankles and held them still.

'I'm not sure what's going on,' he said. 'I think it's a combination of the poison she ingested and her body's reaction to the chemical changes the bonding put into motion.'

Damn, he felt so helpless. 'Hang on, Tayla.' He wrapped his arm around her slim waist and dragged her against him, as if, if he held on tight enough, she couldn't die. 'Damn you, hang on. Don't let a demon be the death of you. You've fought too hard for too long.'

Wraith uttered some smartass remark from behind him, but Eidolon wasn't going to leave Tayla for even the five seconds it would take to ram his brother's head through the wall. He'd deal with him later. Right now . . .

'Hellboy?' The sound of her rasping voice was music. 'What's happening?'

'Shh ... we'll get you through this.' He slid a pleading glance at Shade. *Sedate her.*

'I can't. Not until she—' He broke off, nodding at her left hand. 'There. It's happening.'

Eidolon bunched the sleeve of her robe up to her biceps and nearly swayed with relief at the beautiful miracle taking place. A shadowy replica of his tattoo was etching itself onto her arm, temporarily marking her as his. Gradually, she calmed, the tension draining out of her so she melted against him.

Where she belonged.

'Someone get her some water,' he said, not looking away from her. Her strength amazed him, humbled him. She was the fire he'd never had, the spark that had lit his calm, measured existence. He brushed her hair out of her eyes, an excuse to touch her. 'How are you feeling?'

'Better,' she croaked, as she pushed up on one elbow. 'Is this a DNA thing? Is it happening? Am I dying?'

'No, nothing like that.' He handed her the glass Shade brought. 'You guys go make the preparations for tomorrow night. I'll call you in the morning.' After his brothers left, he grasped her empty hand. Gently, he raised her arm so she could see the markings.

Her hand shook as she set the water on the bedside table and pulled the robe open to get a look at the tattoo that ran from fingertip to shoulder. 'This is yours. What did you do?'

'I initiated a bonding sequence. It's not complete yet,' he finished quickly. Gods, she made him feel like a youth just entering his first transition. 'Be mine.' Yeah, that was smooth.

'Eidolon ... '

'You don't have to decide now. You have five days, and then the markings will fade.' Once they disappeared, the window of opportunity would close, but by then, he might have completed the *s'genesis* and wouldn't care, anyway.

'But you said your species doesn't mate with humans because the offspring are half-breeds.'

'We can mate with half-breeds. The young will be full-blooded Seminus demons.'

Tayla was silent for a long moment. 'Is that what the blood was about?' She shot upright and her face, already pale, grew even whiter. 'Oh, gag. I drank your blood. Why did I do that? And why do you keep a scalpel in your drawer?' She narrowed her eyes at him. 'Most guys keep condoms there.'

He bit back a smile. 'I don't need condoms, since I can't impregnate anyone yet.' Though he vaguely remembered wanting to plant his seed in Tayla when he'd shape-shifted, so maybe he could now. The idea that she could right now be swelling with his offspring filled him with a sense of wholeness he'd been missing all his life. He could ask Shade to feel for a pregnancy –

'So what's up with the scalpel?'

Heat flooded his face, probably making him as red as she was white. 'I—' he felt so stupid admitting this '—I've always wanted to be prepared in the event that I found a mate.'

'Are all Seminus demons so sappy?'

This time, he couldn't contain the smile. 'I doubt it.'

'I really, really do not understand demons.' She closed her eyes and breathed deeply. 'I heard Wraith say something. Something Gem said, too. About being desperate to stop the *s'genesis* by taking a mate.'

'We'll talk about it later. You need your rest.' He pulled the sheets up over her, but she stopped him with a firm grasp on his wrist.

'Tell me about it.'

Oh, hell. He swore and looked up at the ceiling. 'Taking a life-mate is the only way to stop the worst of the *s'genesis* changes. We still become fertile and gain the ability to shapeshift, but the insane need to impregnate everything in sight will disappear.'

'And you've been looking? Your brother said "desperate."'

'Yes, but—'

'So am I like, your last resort?'

'No, Tayla.' He climbed into bed beside her and tucked her into his body, her back to his chest. 'It's nothing like that.'

There was a long pause, and then she said in a small voice, 'How close are you to no-return?'

Reaching around her, he tipped her face up to his and sealed his mouth over hers. Her lips were warm, firm, tasted mildly of the salt from her tears. For a moment, she melted, opening to him, shifting toward him.

But she wouldn't be deterred, and she murmured against his lips, 'How close?'

'Close,' he admitted, running his palm down her hard belly, spanning the narrow distance between her hipbones where her womb might be quickening. 'The next time I shapeshift, I might not come back as myself. I'll look the same, but I won't be running the show.'

She pulled away from him. 'And you say that bonding with me now has absolutely nothing to do with the fact that you're on the verge of no-return?'

As much as he wanted to answer that, he couldn't. Had he met her a year ago, he didn't know if she'd have set fever to his blood the way she did now.

'That's answer enough,' she said, lurching to the other side of the bed. 'And my answer is no. I won't be anyone's last resort.'

Shit. This could've gone better.

'Just listen for a minute, okay?'

'I said, no.'

He sat up and stretched across the bed for her hand, which she yanked away. 'Dammit, Tayla, I don't care if my instincts are responsible or not. I want you.'

'Oh, that's one hell of a proposal,' she snapped, tugging her robe tight around her. 'Excuse me if I don't run out and reserve a caterer and a church. Oh, wait. You probably can't set foot in a church.'

'So I need to work on my delivery . . . '

'You need to work on finding someone who doesn't mind being

283

the 3:00 a.m. wallflower. I might not have anything to my name or any place to go, but that doesn't mean you can take advantage of me just so you can hold on to your precious medical degree.' She glared at him, daggers of fury that pinned him in place when he would have grabbed her and held her to him. 'How dare you lie to get me to fall for your shit? You don't want me. You can't. You don't even know me.'

'I'm not lying. I do want you, and I know all I need to.'

'You know nothing. *Nothing*. How am I supposed to believe what I am isn't a problem for you, when it was before? I'm an Aegi butcher. A lemming, remember?'

'I was wrong, Tayla. My brothers are wrong.'

She shook her head. 'See, that's where you *are* wrong. I *am* a butcher. Want proof? Proof that you know nothing about me?' When a tremor entered her voice, she cleared it ruthlessly. 'Let's talk about your brother Roag—'

'Don't say it.' He searched her eyes, seeing an ugly truth in their murky depths. 'Don't. Even. Say. It.'

But she pressed on, leaning forward on fists pressed into the mattress. 'I was there. At Brimstone. I was there and I killed anything that moved. When Jagger set the place on fire, the sound of demons screaming didn't bother me at all.'

Oh, shit. *Roag.* 'It might not have been you . . . ' The desperation in his voice was pathetic, and he hated himself for it.

'Or it might have been. I don't remember seeing a demon like you, but—'

'He could have shapeshifted.'

Eidolon felt his world collapse in on him, felt his chest crack wide open. It hurt. Gods, his heart hurt.

The female he wanted as a mate had killed his brother. Had been involved, at the very least.

'Do you see, Hellboy? Do you see why we can't be together? Can you really see beyond what I was? Can I ever see beyond what you are?'

284

But he was no longer listening. '*You killed my brother.*'

He pushed backward, off the bed, feeling the anger rise in him, feeling something even more horrible churning inside. He could feel The Change pulsing, clawing to the surface.

With a roar, he tore out of the bedroom, out of the apartment, away from Tayla before he did something he'd regret. Because he was pissed, hurt, and he was also out of time.

TWENTY-TWO

❧

A combination of sunlight streaming through the bedroom windows and the sound of the television woke Tayla. A glance at the bedside clock told her she'd slept later than she'd wanted to. Eleven a.m. She'd wasted so much time sleeping. And crying.

She hadn't bothered chasing after Eidolon last night. He'd clearly been devastated, and besides that, his eyes had gone red, just as they had before he'd turned into the Soulshredder, and she was *so* not prepared to deal with a repeat of that.

Instead, she'd cried herself to sleep, something she hadn't done in years. Not since the first night she'd spent at Aegis HQ, when gratitude had overwhelmed her, gratitude that Kynan and Lori had taken her in and given her a safe place to sleep for the first time since her mother died. They'd said they wanted her. Every foster parent had said that, but she'd quickly learned not to believe it.

Her own mother had said it, but if that were true, she would have stayed off the drugs. Yes, she'd had a demon tormenting her, driving her to self-destruction, but Tayla couldn't shake the belief that if she'd only been a better daughter, her mom would have fought harder.

And now Eidolon said he wanted her. If only she could believe him, could believe that for the first time in her life, she was something special. Worth more than what the state paid someone to take care of her, worth more than her fighting skills.

He'd hurt her last night when he'd hesitated to answer her question, and she'd struck back with Roag's death, a low blow, and something he hadn't needed to know.

Desperate to hold off on a confrontation that would surely end in his kicking her onto the streets, she showered, taking a long time to inspect the new decorations on her arm. They weren't as sharply defined or as dark as Eidolon's, but they were otherwise identical – and she knew because she'd traced every one of his with her tongue.

Whatever Eidolon had done to her had also sealed The Wound That Wouldn't Heal. Not even a scar remained, though she'd had to use his scalpel to remove the stitches.

When the water started to run cold, she rinsed and dressed in leather fighting pants and a lace tank top, and when she couldn't stall any longer, she entered the living room.

Where Gem was standing, holding Mickey. The recliner behind her was rocking; she must have heard Tayla coming and gotten to her feet. A map of the abandoned zoo lay spread out on the coffee table, along with photos and a notebook with wildly scratched notes next to it.

'What are you doing here?' Tayla growled.

'Eidolon called me last night. He wanted someone here with you.'

Tayla's heart squeezed painfully. He'd been so angry, probably on the verge of violence and hatred, and yet, he hadn't wanted her to be alone. 'How did he sound?'

'Destroyed. On edge.' Her gaze flickered to Tay's arm, where the markings on her skin itched. 'What did you do to him?'

Why did everyone automatically assume she'd done something to him? *Maybe because this time, she had.* 'That's none of your business. Get out. I thought I'd made it clear that I never wanted to see you again.'

'Yeah, about that . . . ' Gem cleared her throat. Swallowed a few times. That was when Tay noticed her puffy, bloodshot eyes. Gem must have been up all night. 'I killed him.'

'What? Who?'

'Our sire.' Gem sank into the chair, her midnight-blue skirt squeaking on the leather cushion. Always an emotional barometer, Mickey scampered down and under the couch. 'When I was sixteen. He came to me. We fought. I stabbed him. It wasn't pretty.'

'Jesus,' Tay whispered. 'Why didn't you tell me this last night?'

'You flipped out before I had the chance.' She peered up at Tayla through watery eyes. 'And I think I kinda wanted to hurt you.'

'Hurt me? Why?'

'I was jealous. Of how you grew up. Of how you have this "Teresa was my mom and not yours" vibe going on. You knew her. You got to do things with her.' Gem hung her head and played with one of her two braided ponytails.

'All I have are a few grainy pictures taken from blocks away and a fading memory of what her voice sounded like.'

'Gem, I didn't know her that well. She was killed just as we started to mesh.'

'You still . . . you still had a life I didn't have.'

'Yeah. You had everything.'

'Except a mom,' she said quietly.

'But you had—'

'Demon parents who were always disappointed in me.' She sighed. 'Don't get me wrong. I love them. And they love me in their own way. But I couldn't be everything they wanted me to be. I didn't even want to be a doctor. I did it for them. You grew up in one world. It might have sucked, but it was one world. I was the product of two worlds, and they never let me forget it. Even today, I can't tell humans what I am, and I can't tell demons I'm half-human. Only you and the Axis of Evil know the truth.' When Tay raised an eyebrow, Gem elaborated. 'Eidolon, Wraith, and Shade. I've called them that for years, mainly because it annoys them.'

Tayla laughed at that, the discharge of tension and emotion a welcome release. 'You really are my sister.'

Gem tugged on a thick braid. 'So we're cool? Me and you?'

Listening to her instincts, which told her she needed to let her sister into her life, Tayla nodded. 'Yeah. We're cool.' But what now? She was willing to accept Gem into her life, but that was the Gem she saw before her now, the one that appeared human. What lurked beneath the pretty, pierced exterior? 'Can I ask a favor? Can I see what you keep locked away behind the tattoos?'

For a moment Gem looked as if she would refuse, and then she nodded, slowly, sadly. 'I guess you need to.' Closing her eyes, she concentrated. A low moan dredged up from deep in her chest. Her entire body began to vibrate, and then she just ... exploded. Like a kernel of popcorn. One second she was a cute Goth chick, and then next ...

Sweet Jesus.

'Well? This is my other side.'

Gem hadn't spoken in English, but Tay understood her. Knees practically knocking, she forced herself to move closer to the beast in front of her, a strange cross between human and Soulshredder, a terrible, beautiful creature with red skin, black claws, and Gem's eyes.

'I have to change back,' Gem said. 'Every second like this reduces my human instincts.'

The vibration started again. Tayla leaped back, and then Gem was standing there, sweating bullets. 'Man, that stings.'

Shaking a little, Tayla circled the other woman, checking for ... what? Leaks? 'So, you can control yourself when you shift?'

'To some extent,' Gem said, watching as Tayla came around front again. 'I can't when it happens spontaneously, which is why I got the tats.'

'So if I were to integrate, I could control it?'

Gem grinned. 'Does that mean you're thinking about it?'

Tayla looked down at herself, wondering how her body would change should she be integrated. Then she sighed. 'It might not be an option anymore. Eidolon hates me.'

'What happened between you two?'

'Mainly, I killed his brother.'

'But I just saw—'

'It was Roag.'

Gem blew out a long breath. 'God, Tayla. He was devastated when Roag died.'

'Did you know Roag?'

'Not well. Roag wasn't around much. He and Wraith fought like vamps and slayers—' She shot Tayla a sheepish smile. 'Sorry, *Guardians*. Eidolon was always afraid they'd kill each other, especially after Roag went through his *s'genesis*.'

Tayla rubbed her eyes, exhausted and bitterly regretting what had happened between her and Eidolon. She should have kept her mouth shut about Roag. Had she known more about the *s'genesis* and the mating requirements, maybe she wouldn't have flipped out like she had. But then, how was she supposed to have known? The Aegis had an extensive library at its disposal, but anything but the most basic of books had to be ordered from headquarters, approved by the Regents, and now it was too late to do any of that.

'Tayla? Are you okay?'

Not at all. 'I just wish I knew more. About Seminus demons. About Soulshredders.'

'Yeah, well, don't beat yourself up. I grew up with demons, and I know exactly squat.' She straightened her skirt, which had bunched up during her transformation. 'Have you checked out E's library?'

Tayla resisted the urge to thunk herself on the forehead. 'You're a genius.'

In the den, they sifted through the hundreds of tomes on the shelves until Gem found what amounted to an encyclopedia of demon species. Tay sat down with it, started with the section on incubi, and specifically, Seminus demons. The information, while a bit more generic than she'd hoped for, still gave her some insight into Seminus behavior, mating rituals, and dermoire symbols.

'Gem, you've been friends with Eidolon and his brothers for a long time, haven't you?'

Gem glanced up from one of the medical texts she'd been reading. 'Years. My parents took me to UG for most of my medical appointments.'

'Has ... has Eidolon really been searching for a mate for so long? Is he really that desperate?'

'God, Tay, I'm sorry I said that—'

Tayla cut her off with a shake of the head. 'Wraith said something like that, too.'

'Listen to me.' Gem slammed the book closed with such force that Tayla jumped. 'Eidolon isn't an idiot. He's one of the most logical, annoyingly intelligent males I've ever met, human or demon. He isn't so desperate that he'd lock himself into a lifetime of misery with a female who might turn on him or who might be a bad mother to his children. Yes, his life and his hospital mean everything to him, but he'd rather die than be bound to a female he doesn't love. He loves you, Tayla.'

'I don't think—'

'I can see it in his eyes and hear it in his voice. We're Soulshredders, sis, which means that we can sense weakness and pain in others. Eidolon's weakness is you. But you could also be his strength. He loves you, even if he hasn't admitted it, even to himself.'

Tayla slouched in her seat, feeling miserable and lost and guilty as hell. 'Doesn't matter. I hurt him. He wants nothing to do with me.'

'I know how that is,' Gem muttered. She glanced at her watch and laughed, a bitter, scornful sound. 'Perfect. It's time to get to the hospital. Kynan should be there soon.'

'He isn't involved in what happened to your parents.' Tayla spoke with the confidence she *wanted* to feel.

Gem's black-painted mouth tightened into a grim slash. 'I hope to God you're right. If anything has happened to them ...'

Gem didn't have to finish the sentence. Tayla knew what would happen, knew now what lurked behind the cage of Gem's protective tattoos.

'I'm right,' Tayla said. 'Let's go prove it.'

A deep-seated ache throbbed through her. She had a feeling that after meeting with Ky, whatever hope she'd had to somehow maintain her relationship with The Aegis would be as dead as her relationship with Eidolon.

ॐ

Just as Gem predicted, Kynan arrived at Mercy General with two Guardians in tow. Tayla watched covertly from around the corner of the main waiting room, her heart pounding with nervous energy as Gem approached him. Dressed in blue scrubs that looked tame and out of place alongside her funky hair and piercings, Gem said something that lured him away from Tim and Jon, and they disappeared into an examination room.

A moment later, Gem slipped out of the room where she'd taken Kynan. Tay met her near the door. 'I told him Dennis wanted to talk to him privately about one of his guys. He's not expecting you.'

'Thanks. Wish me luck.'

Gem grabbed Tayla's arm as she brushed past. 'I hope he's not involved.'

'Me too, Gem. Me too.'

Sucking in a deep, bracing breath, Tay entered the room where Kynan, dressed in his usual jeans and leather jacket, braced his forearm above his head on the windowsill, looking out at the grassy quad. Tufts of spiky dark hair stood up haphazardly as if he'd been running his fingers through it.

'Hey, Dennis.' He swung around, his combat boots squeaking on the tile.

'Hey, Ky.'

'Tayla. *Jesus Christ.*' He came forward as though to embrace her, but battlewise wariness sparked in his eyes, and he halted a stang's length out of arm's reach. 'You're supposed to be dead.'

His proximity forced her to look up at him, but she wouldn't be the one to back off. 'Disappointed?'

'How can you say that?'

'Oh, I don't know. Maybe because you tried to kill me? Twice?'

To his credit, he looked stunned. But then, in all the years she'd known Kynan, she'd never known him to be anything but brutally honest. If he appeared to be surprised, he probably was. At least, she'd have believed that before. Right now she wasn't so sure. Not when her life was on the line.

'I'm not sure what to say.' His voice was a deep rumble that gave nothing away about what he was thinking. The man was no fool, and his cautious nature had saved his life more than once.

Her temper flared, because she could think of a million things to say. 'How about, "Sorry The Aegis tried to turn you into a suicide bomber"? Or, "Hey, I apologize for putting a price on your head"? Yeah, I can think of a few things you could say. Why don't you start with what you were told about my death?'

For a long moment he took her in, from her feet to her face, until she had the urge to fidget. 'Lori said you were sent to the demon hospital to release a tracking spell. But when you didn't release the spell or return, Jagger sent Bleak and Cole to your apartment. They were ambushed by demons. We assumed you'd been killed, too.'

'You were lied to.'

Ky stared down at her, the calculation in his denim eyes something that had always fascinated her. He could take in information and process it faster than anyone she'd ever known. To her relief, his angular, hard features softened – minutely – and he stepped back in a minor concession.

'Tell me everything.'

She did, leaving out her parentage and her sexual relationship with Eidolon. Kynan listened, his expression impassive, but his golden-tan skin went the color of pale butter when she told him Jagger had given her the phone that had contained the explosive device but no tracking spell, and that the two Guardians sent to her apartment had claimed that Ky knew about the order to kill her.

'Who killed Cole?' he asked, his voice so devoid of emotion and inflection that she couldn't get a good read.

'He tried to kill me, Ky.' She refused to elaborate. Cole's death had nothing to do with what was going on inside the cell.

Ky leveled a probing stare at her. 'Fair enough. And you say Lori was in the interrogation room when Jagger gave you the phone?'

Tayla nodded. 'I don't know if she knew—'

'She didn't,' he snapped. 'Fuck.' He rubbed his eyes. Sank into a chair and put his head in his hands. 'I'm sorry, Tayla. This is just all so unbelievable.'

'Are you saying you don't believe me?'

'Not at all. ' He cleared his throat and brought his head up. 'But something has gone wrong somewhere. This doesn't add up. I don't get why Jagger would want you dead.'

This was it. Positioning herself near the door in case he went crazy was a plan that might have worked had he not noticed exactly what she was doing.

'No matter what you say,' he said softly, 'I'll stay level.'

She wanted to believe him, but two attempts on her life by people she'd considered friends had killed her ability to trust. Not that she'd ever fully trusted anyone, but The Aegis had been good to her, and after years of fighting alongside friends, she'd started to let down her guard.

'Someone is capturing demons and chopping them up to sell their parts on the underworld black market. The demons think The Aegis is doing it.'

'That would be a natural assumption, given that we're the enemy.'

Why did he have to be so logical about it? She'd railed about how The Aegis couldn't possibly be involved, and shame on Eidolon for thinking so. 'Yeah, well, I thought the demons were full of shit. But I'm not so sure anymore. And I think our cell is involved.'

'We're not.'

'You might not be, but what if others were?' She shook her head, because suddenly things were becoming clearer. 'See, up until right now, I thought The Aegis wanted me dead for another reason, but even then, it didn't make sense, because I think you wouldn't have been so hasty.'

Ky leaned forward on the chair and braced his forearms on his spread thighs. 'You're talking in circles. Spit it out.'

She eyed the door, her heart pounding. 'I'm a demon,' she blurted.

Silence stretched, growing more pronounced as tension rose like an ocean swell in the space between them. Kynan's gaze grew sharper, more focused, as though his thoughts had been distilled into a single plan, and his broad shoulders began to rise and fall more rapidly. She recognized the battle mode and braced herself.

'Is this a joke?' he asked in a low, controlled drawl that was more terrifying than if he'd yelled. She hadn't realized until this very moment how intimidating he could be.

Because until this moment, she hadn't been on the receiving end of his dangerous side.

'I wish it were.'

His right hand clenched and unclenched, drifted toward his abdomen, where, no doubt, his weapons were stashed beneath his jacket.

'I didn't know until a few days ago,' she said, eyeing his face and his hand alternately. He was one of the few Guardians who carried a gun, and if he decided to pull it, she had no defense. 'But Jagger knew. The demon doctor he tortured told him. I thought that was why The Aegis wanted me dead.'

'We wouldn't have taken the word of the demon.' He made a sound of disgust, as if the very idea made him ill. 'There would have been an investigation.'

'I know. That's why the attempts on my life didn't make sense. Why would Jagger have trusted Cole and Bleak with the information, but not you? Why them, specifically? It's got to be because they're already involved in something.'

'The demon-snatching thing.'

'Yes.'

Kynan spoke through gritted teeth. 'I'm not sure what I think about all this, but I need you to tell me about you. Everything. Now.'

The military-crisp command tone ruffled every one of her feathers, but now wasn't the time to rebel. She needed Kynan to believe her. He listened, his hand still too close to his weapons harness for comfort, as she shared all she'd learned about herself, from conception to Gem to her most recent breath. By the time she'd finished, the Aegis Regent looked worn out. Before he could speak, there was a knock at the door, and Gem entered.

'Your boys are done with their patch jobs.'

Kynan shifted his gaze to Gem, his eyes devoid of the friendly, warm light that had been there before. 'You're sisters,' he muttered, as though he couldn't believe it. 'Jesus Christ. You're one of *them*. All this time, you've been treating me and my people. And you *knew*.'

Gem's expression fell, and in that moment, Tayla realized that her sister was in love with him.

And now he hated them both. Didn't matter to him that she'd rather die than become a vicious beast. She carried the blood of one in her veins.

'I think I'm done here.' He came to his feet in a graceful, fluid move that reminded her of how he fought, and how the more relaxed he seemed to be, the more dangerous he was.

'What are you going to do?' Tayla moved aside as he strode toward the door.

Pausing at the threshold, he nailed her with a look as savage as she'd ever seen from him. 'I don't know, Tayla. You've got my cell number, so call and leave a message with a way I can contact you. But stay away from headquarters, you got it? You are no longer welcome there.'

That hurt, more than she thought it would. 'I'm the same person I was before, Ky.'

'Yeah?' Ky eyed her arm, where Eidolon's markings throbbed beneath the surface. 'That's new. Demon?'

'It's not permanent. None of it is.'

'You can't change your DNA.'

God, she was sick of hearing about D-N-fucking-A. Then again, she was just plain sick. She'd been tired for days, lightheaded all morning. On the way to the hospital, she'd lost the use of her right arm, but hadn't told Gem. Her demon side was kicking her human side's butt.

She crossed her arms over her chest and hugged herself. 'I'm still human,' she said, probably more to herself than to Ky, but he shook his head.

'You can't be. Not if you have an ounce of demon blood in you.' Ky clenched his fists again, his body so tense he looked as if he could crack right down the middle. 'Stay away from HQ. I mean it. Come near, and there *will* be a price on your head.' Slowly, he swung around to Gem, his expression a mix of sorrow and disgust. 'And you. Stay away from me and my crew. If I catch you so much as breathing on them ... '

Shaking his head as if he couldn't bear one more second in the same airspace with them, he swept out of the room, taking the crushing tension with him.

Remorse darkened Gem's eyes. 'That really didn't go well, did it?'

'It could have gone worse.'

Gem absently rubbed her sternum, as though her heart hurt. Tayla knew the feeling. 'How hard did you press him?'

Tayla flexed and rolled her shoulders, but nothing eased the stiffness in them. 'I didn't. I'm 99 percent sure he doesn't know anything.'

'And if he does?' Gem demanded. 'What about my parents?'

'We'll get them back.'

Gem tapped her tongue piercing against her teeth for a moment. 'Did you tell him about the zoo?'

'Hell, no. If he's working with the Ghouls, I didn't want to tip him off that we know about the meeting place. And if he isn't, I didn't want to tell him too soon. As freaked as he is, I can see him rushing over there and ruining everything. I figure I'll call him just before we go, give him a chance to show up and see for himself what's going on.'

Gem swore. 'I hate this. I hate sitting around and doing nothing while my parents could be suffering.'

'I know,' Tayla said, reaching for Gem's hand. 'But it'll be over soon. Just a few more hours. We have to see what Kynan does now. He'll either uncover a lot of deception within the cell, or, if he's in on everything that's happened, he'll send out a squad to kill me. Either way, the shit is about to hit the fan.'

TWENTY-THREE

❧

Eidolon felt like shit. Utter, stinking, shit. The kind produced by bone devils after gorging on a live meal.

He'd come to Shade's place, the Jackson Heights apartment where his brother stayed when he was working or when he needed a normal place to bring his human sex partners. To his relief, Shade had been gone all night, which was fine because Eidolon had been too juiced to sleep, and even if he hadn't been, he was terrified to close his eyes for fear that when he woke up, he'd have completed the *s'genesis*. Not that it couldn't happen while he was wide awake, but he'd rather not waste a single moment of being who he was.

The downside was that he'd spent the entire night thinking about Tayla and the part she'd played in Roag's death.

'Hey, man.'

He looked up at Shade from where he sat on the balcony, looking out at the garden park below. His brother wore his usual black leather pants and jacket, and not surprisingly, he smelled of sex. 'Hey.'

'Figured you'd be at the hospital with Tay. Isn't she supposed to be talking to her Aegis boss?' Shade came outside, closing the sliding door behind him. 'Aw, E, you look like hell. What's up?'

How to answer that. Shade hated Tayla enough without knowing what she'd done.

'E?' Shade hooked a chair with his foot and planted his ass in it across from Eidolon. 'You're making me nervous.'

'Tayla was there,' he finally said. 'She was there when Roag died.'

Shade sucked air between clenched teeth and looked at Eidolon for a moment. 'I guess it shouldn't be a surprise. We knew The Aegis was responsible.' Shade stood. 'So, you gonna sulk all day? Or do you want to catch a movie or something before the field trip to the zoo tonight?'

Eidolon jerked in surprise. 'Did you hear what I said?'

'Your slayer might have whacked Roag. Bummer. But I'm seriously craving greasy popcorn.'

Eidolon burst out of his chair and right up into Shade's face. 'What the fuck is your problem?'

'My problem?' Shade jabbed a finger at his own broad chest. 'You're the dumbass who has never seen Roag for what he was. Me and Wraith? We're going to thank Tayla next time we see her.'

Snarling, Eidolon seized Shade by the throat. '*He was our brother.*'

'He was a monster.' Shade bared his teeth.

'Shut up!' Eidolon flung Shade against the balcony railing. Shade fumbled for the rail, and for a split second, it looked as if he would go over and plummet the fifteen stories to the ground. Eidolon grabbed his brother's shirt, yanked him so hard they both stumbled backward. The scare broke his anger, but it sent Shade's into orbit.

'You blind, self-righteous fuck!' He shoved Eidolon into the glass door. 'Do you intentionally block out how he was off screwing some whore in an alley while we were putting Wraith back together that night in Chicago? Do you not remember how he went completely batnuts after The Change, how he was raping and killing?' Shade closed his eyes, clenched his fists, and when he opened his eyes again, his expression was softer, and so was his voice. 'You know it was only a matter of time before a demon took him out. The Aegis just got to him first.'

Eidolon swallowed. Looked down at the concrete deck. Rubbed the back of his neck but couldn't stall any longer. Shade had him by the balls with that truth of his. 'Holy hell,' he breathed.

'Man, I know you two were close, maybe because Wraith and I left you out, what with the weird mind connection. I don't know.' Shade clapped a big hand down on Eidolon's shoulder and shook his head ruefully. 'I'm sorry about Roag. Sorry for *you*. But I was never able to grieve his loss.'

Eidolon frowned. He and Roag had been close, but not in the way Wraith and Shade were. Even now, as he looked at his brother who, with his long hair, looked more like Wraith than Eidolon, he could feel the wall between them. A wall that had never existed between Wraith and Shade. Those two were open about everything – the phrase 'too much information,' wasn't in their vocabulary. But Eidolon's more reserved nature had paired well with Roag's secretive disposition. Secretive and . . . cruel. Eidolon swayed, thankful for Shade's bracing hold. Gods, but he'd overlooked so much . . .

'Where have you been?' Shade snarled to Roag, as Eidolon lowered Wraith's shattered body from the ceiling, the chains that held him clanging.

Roag sauntered across the abandoned brewery, kicking through the piles of vampire dust, looking calmly at the two left alive, cuffed to each other in a puddle of their own blood. 'You two handled things well enough.' He jerked his chin at Wraith. 'Looks like you found our long-lost little brother. Not much left. Leave him. We'll go find the whore I just balled.'

Shade and Eidolon had known Roag for ten years before they'd found Wraith, twenty-two years old and nearly dead, but never had they seen the ice-cold side of him until that day. It had only grown worse after that, Roag's strange jealousy of Wraith causing a rift between all of them. Eidolon had played peacemaker for decades, until Roag went through his *s'genesis* ten years ago.

Roag had not come out of The Change well. He'd gone mad, had been unable to control his powers and urges. Shade was right; if Roag hadn't died when he did, he'd either have been killed by other demons, or the Seminus Council would have eventually brought him to heel, and as the next-eldest sibling, Eidolon would have been required to carry out the punishment.

'Shit.' Eidolon sank into a chair and buried his face in his hands. 'I need to talk to Tayla.'

'Has she agreed to bond with you?'

Eidolon looked up. 'She doesn't want me.'

Shade crossed his arms over his chest and braced one hip on the patio railing. 'She's a fool.'

'I can't blame her. She thinks I want her because she's my last resort.'

'Is she right?'

He swore, frustration and conflicting emotions churning in his mind. 'I don't know.'

'What is it about her that has you all wound up?'

A dull ache pounded in his chest. 'She's brave. Strong. What she's lived through.' He shook his head, amazed at her resiliency. 'She does everything with so much passion, something I've never had. For anything – until her.' He rubbed his breastbone as though he could relieve the empty sensation inside. 'Fuck me, I love her.'

'Well, I'd say you have your answer. She's not a last resort.'

'She'll never believe that, and I don't have time to prove it.' He locked gazes with his brother. 'I can feel The Change, Shade. I'm not going to make it through another night.'

A pained light came into Shade's eyes. 'Maybe—'

'Don't. I've already had a taste of how it's going to be, and who I am now is not who I'll be afterward. But I need some favors.'

'Anything.' Shade's voice trembled.

'I want Tayla cared for. She's to have full access to my bank accounts, and I want her set up in an apartment of her own.'

'Done. What else?'

'I need you to give her a once-over as soon as possible.'

Shade's brow furrowed. 'For what? Oh. Oh, man, you think you knocked her up?'

'You've been taking tact lessons from Wraith again, haven't you?' Eidolon muttered. 'I doubt she carries my offspring, but if she does, she'll need to understand that going through with the integration is the only thing that will save them both.'

Shade shook his head. 'I can't do the procedure without you.'

'I've been thinking about that. I believe you can. You'll need Gem, though. Using your gift and her blood, you've got a shot. If you don't do it, she'll die anyway. One more thing.' He took a deep breath and spat it out. 'If I turn out like Roag—'

'You won't,' Shade croaked. 'You *won't.*'

'Put me down.'

'E . . .'

'Promise me, Shade. I don't want to live like that. You have to promise me.'

Swallowing over and over, Shade nodded. Then he turned on his heel and headed inside. Eidolon followed. 'What are you doing?'

Shade drew to a halt in the middle of his living room, head bowed. Something plopped to the floor at his feet. A tear. 'I'm calling Wraith,' he said, his voice shot to hell. 'We're all gonna do the brother thing today, 'kay?'

'Yeah,' Eidolon said, his own voice cracking. 'Sounds good.'

⁊

Kynan was still reeling from his meeting with Tayla five hours earlier. He couldn't decide which was worse: people he trusted being demons, or people in his cell lying to him. Adding to his frustration was the fact that Jagger and four other Guardians were nowhere to be found, and when he asked Lori if she'd seen anything strange going on within the cell, she'd said no and then promptly seduced him. Which wasn't unusual or a problem – he was a guy, after all – but afterward she'd been anxious to go out hunting, when usually, daytime sex sent her into a fit of domesticity. Guardians joked that they could tell how frisky she and Ky and been by how many batches of cookies she baked in a week.

Half an hour before sunset, just as he was preparing to dial Lori for a status check, the phone rang.

'Ky.'

'It's Tay.'

'What do you want?'

Her soft sigh crackled over the bad cell connection. 'I guess you haven't learned anything.' When he didn't answer, because he wasn't about to tell her that his spidey-sense was tingling, she sighed again. 'We think the captured demons are being held at the old zoo. If any Guardians are involved, that's where they're going. Tonight.'

Something tightened in his gut, because as much as he wanted to get to the bottom of this, if only to prove that his people weren't involved, he was terrified that Tayla might be right.

Or it could be a trap. He couldn't trust anything she said. Not anymore.

'Kynan? Did you hear me?'

'Loud and clear.'

'Okay, then. Um, see you around.'

He hung up. Checked his watch. Tonight. It was already tonight. Quickly, he dressed to kill; leather pants, T-shirt, weapons harness, leather jacket, and finally, every fucking weapon he could load on his body. If this was a trap, he wasn't going down easy. He was, however, going alone. If Tayla was right, he couldn't trust any Guardians to go with him. If this was a trap, he couldn't risk getting any of them killed.

One way or another, the truth was coming out tonight.

TWENTY-FOUR

❧

At dusk, the abandoned zoo took on a strange life … one where shadows lurked in the corners of Tayla's vision, disappearing when she'd turn her head, and where crickets chirped only in the distance, probably afraid to reveal their location because something might eat them.

Tay, Eidolon, Shade, and Wraith had come over the wall at the rear of the zoo, the plan being to locate Gem's parents and any other imprisoned demons before Gem entered through the front. With any luck, they could free the demons and Gem would never have to set foot inside the zoo, but if she did, Luc was with her. Tay had never seen anyone as eager to fight as the huge paramedic, and even though he couldn't take beast form without the full moon, Wraith had assured Tayla that he could hold his own. Wraith had been the one to tell her, because Eidolon wouldn't so much as look at her. She didn't blame him.

When she'd first seen him at the back wall, she'd wanted to throw herself at him, to apologize for her role in Roag's death, but he'd kept his gaze averted, his fists balled at his sides. He definitely hadn't invited conversation, and with his brothers standing there, talk would have been awkward, anyway.

As they cleared the back half of the zoo where they'd come in from over the wall, Wraith moved off on his own toward the big-cat habitats, moving silently, all coiled danger on the prowl. A moment later, Shade peeled away, slipping into the darkness and disappearing right in front of her. Eidolon hadn't been kidding when he'd said Shade could turn to shadow in the presence of shadow.

'I'm heading to the bear pens,' Eidolon said, his voice low, scratchy, as if he'd been up all night the night before. 'Be careful.'

'You, too.' As per plan, she'd sweep the bird-of-prey habitat and then head to the place where Gem was supposed to meet her handlers. Tay would hide and wait to see what – or who – showed up. 'Hellboy?' She grabbed his forearm, feeling his muscles tense beneath her fingers. 'Look, I know I have no right to ask this of you, but will you please not kill any humans?'

'After what they tried to do to you, you still defend them?'

'I want them to face Aegis justice for what they've done.'

'What they've done is what The Aegis has taught them to do, Tayla. Do you really think they'll be punished?'

'If they've been operating against the Regents' orders, then yes, they will.'

Eidolon stared over her shoulder, his gaze turned inward where she couldn't follow. Finally, he nodded. 'I'll see what I can do.'

And then he was gone, and she was alone.

For the first time in her life, she didn't like the feeling.

෴

The bird-of-prey cages were a bust. No demons fitting Gem's description were being held there. Some sort of winged demon occupied a cage, but having no idea if the thing was dangerous or not, Tay left it imprisoned.

Disappointed, she used abandoned buildings and trees as cover as she worked her way to the old koala habitat. Quick and sure, she slipped through underbrush and overgrown hedges, easing up to the viewing area, a pavilion built against a glass-enclosed habitat. The rustle of movement and soft crunch of footsteps on pine needles alerted her to the presence of others even before she elbowed aside some prickly branches.

What she saw nearly paralyzed her.

In the center of the pavilion, Gem knelt, head down, while Lori tied her hands behind her back. Where was Luc?

'When can I see my parents?' Gem asked.

'I didn't say you could speak.' Jagger slapped her hard enough to make her nose bleed, and it took every ounce of self-restraint Tayla possessed to keep from bursting out of the bushes and tearing him apart.

Hatred and defiance blazed in Gem's eyes, but when she slid a covert glance directly into the brush where Tayla crouched, one corner of her mouth turned up in satisfaction. Emotion nearly sapped Tay's strength at the realization that struck her. Gem wasn't afraid, wasn't even worried. No, she knew that as grim as her situation appeared to be, nothing bad would happen to her. She had backup. She had Tay and Eidolon and his brothers. She had family.

Yeah, they were all one big, happy demon family. And Tayla needed to put a crush on the sap factor, because the mission hadn't ended yet. It was time to put on the game face and worry about touchy-feely moments later.

Lori finished securing Gem's wrists. Jagger checked the knot, and then, in a move that shocked Tayla to the core, he grabbed Lori by the hair and brought her face to his. 'I wish we could kill her.'

'We have orders.'

'Yes,' he murmured, and ran one finger over her lips. 'But someday, I want to make love to you in the blood of our kill.'

Dear God. They were lovers. Twisted, evil lovers. Though Tayla had to admit that Lori didn't appear to be thrilled at the idea of rolling around naked in demon blood. In fact, when he kissed her, practically crawling down her throat, she struggled against his hold.

'*What. The. Fuck.*'

Oh, *shit.* Kynan stood at the far side of the koala viewing area, his expression a mixture of shock, devastation, and rage. Lori gasped and jumped away from Jagger as if her husband hadn't already seen her kissing another man.

'Kynan—' she said, but he wasn't looking at her. His gaze was fixed on Jagger, and there was murder in his eyes. The men stood deadly still, and then, like two rival lions, they met in a furious explosion of blood and limbs.

'Dammit.' Tay burst from the foliage and darted toward Gem. Sobbing, Lori backed away from the battle, her hand over her mouth as if she wanted to scream. But she didn't. She turned on her heel and bolted.

Tayla grabbed Gem and dragged her out of the way of the two men, who didn't care what got in the way. Ky and Jagger, both expert fighters, were normally graceful, purposeful, beautiful to watch in combat. But not tonight. Tonight was about pain – who could dish out the most and draw the most blood. There was nothing graceful or beautiful about it. This was raw, brutal, a fight to the death.

'Sister?'

Tayla tore her rubbernecking gaze away from the battle. 'Sister?' It was the first time she'd been addressed that way. Sister. It felt strange. But good.

'Yes, sister,' Gem said. 'But yo, I'm the tied-up twin.'

'Right.' Tay whipped out her stang and sliced through the ropes binding her sister's wrists. 'Where's Luc?'

'I made him stay at the front when my parents hadn't made it through the gate by the time I was supposed to meet my contacts here.'

'Find them,' Tayla said. 'I'm going after Lori.'

'But Ky—'

308

'He can handle himself. Go!'

After casting Kynan a worried glance, Gem took off, and Tayla sprinted in the direction Lori had gone.

ॐ

Aside from being extremely annoyed, Gem's parents were no worse for wear when Eidolon released them from the polar-bear enclosure. He sent them on the run with instructions to find Luc out front, and then he released a corpse-eating demon and dispatched a *mamu,* a demon that ate humans and that didn't need to be on the loose in New York City.

As he slipped away from the bear exhibit, he heard a sound. Thumps. Spinning, he came face to face with three Aegi who had leaped from a rock wall to the ground. He recognized one from Tayla's apartment ... the one he hadn't killed, and dammit, he should have, because the slayer recognized him, too.

'He's a demon,' Bleak said, and the three immediately spread out, circling. 'He killed Cole.'

The dark-haired one with glasses looked Eidolon up and down, measuring him, and then, in a coordinated move, launched a morning star as Bleak swung a machete.

Eidolon blocked the machete, but the star caught him in the chest. Something blunt mashed a kidney. Hot streaks of agony rose up from his wounds. He grunted, managed to wrestle the machete away from Bleak. The next few moments were a blur of fists, steel, and feet.

When they came apart, Eidolon was still trapped, his left leg wasn't working right, and blood ran freely into one eye. The slayers were panting, bleeding, but he'd held back, Tayla's plea to spare them ringing in his head. On the other hand, they outnumbered and outweaponed him. If he didn't kill them, they were going to turn him into mulch.

The right side of his face pulsed. An injury ...

He froze. Not an injury, not with the way his face burned as though it had been branded. Not with the way his vision had gone sharp and red, as if he could see the aggression around him as well as smell it.

The Change.

Time was up. Game over.

The urge to shift into something huge and scary made him moan with anticipation. He wanted to tear the slayers apart, feel their bones break between his jaws. And then he'd hunt down their females and –

No. Gods, no. Cold sweat broke out all over his body. He would not turn out like Roag. He would not force his brothers to kill him, or worse, force Tayla to do the deed.

Tayla.

Pain ripped through his chest, pain that had nothing to do with what the slayers had done to him. He hadn't had nearly enough time with her, hadn't opened his heart soon enough. And now he'd never know the feel of her tender touch again. The next time she saw him, he'd be the beast she had believed him to be from the beginning.

A bolt of *hell no* shot through him like summer lightning. Roag should have been put down at the time of his transition. Eidolon would be.

He tore the morning star from where it had lodged in his right pec, and smiled. 'Well, Aegi, seems like it's your lucky day.'

ॐ

Gem raced out the zoo's front entrance, nearly knocking over Shade, who was rushing inside.

'Your parents are fine. I found them wandering around, looking for Luc.' He cocked a thumb over his shoulder. 'They're over there. Worried as hell about you.'

'Thank you.' She grasped his forearm before he could take off. 'Make sure Tayla is okay. Please?'

'It's what Eidolon wants,' was all he said. Like a phantom, he stepped into a shadow and disappeared.

'Gem!' Her father's voice, as full of emotion as she'd ever heard it, called out to her. Within seconds, both parents had engulfed her in a hug, something as rare as the Amazonian orchids her mother collected.

She hugged them back. 'I'm so glad you're okay.'

'What's going on in there?' her mom asked, as they broke apart. 'Can we go home now?'

Gem dragged in a breath. 'I want you to go home. I have to stay. I have to make sure Tayla is okay.'

'*Tayla?* ' her parents said in unison.

'I'll explain later. But you have to trust me.' She glanced at Luc. 'Can you make sure they get home safely?'

'Do I look like a taxi driver?' He growled low in his throat, obviously disappointed that he couldn't kick some ass inside the zoo. 'Yeah. Whatever.'

'Gem, no. You're a doctor. And part human. You shouldn't—'

'Mom.' She reached out, cupped her mom's cheek in a loving gesture she'd never made before. 'I'm also a Soulshredder. I know you've tried to pretend I'm a Sensor, but it's time to face reality. I was built to take care of myself. And I need to do this.'

The demons who had raised her, had taken her in when they should have destroyed her, looked exhausted, worried ... and proud.

TWENTY-FIVE

❦

Tayla lost Lori, but she found Eidolon.

Sig, Warren, and Bleak were circling him, sharp blades drawn. Bleak was limping, and a steady stream of blood ran from Warren's nose, but Eidolon had taken a good beating, as well. Deep cuts scored his back and arms, and his bared teeth were tinged red.

Those sons of bitches.

He said something she couldn't hear. The machete and a morning star fell from his hands, clattering to the asphalt. What was he up to?

The guys backed off, suspicion darkening their expressions, but when Eidolon did nothing, they closed in, smiling, mocking him. Their taunts cut her like any blade, the things they said to him, the vulgar names she'd once used. She launched herself across the span of space. At the same time, Warren struck Eidolon from behind, a scissor kick to the spine. Eidolon crashed to his knees.

'No!' she screamed, and four heads whipped around. 'Take them, Eidolon! Forget what I said!'

But he stayed where he was, a willing sacrifice. 'Go! Get out of here.'

Good God, was he insane?

'This is my choice.' His voice throbbed with something sinister and foreign even as the swirling glyphs on his face began to glow and set in his skin. 'Better them than you.'

A chill went through her, jerking her to a halt. The Guardians all paused, their curiosity temporarily overriding their training.

'I won't force you to have to kill me, *lirsha.*'

'How fucking sweet,' Warren said. 'Now kill them both.'

Oh, Jesus. That was the wrong thing to say. Eidolon's face contorted with possessive rage. The air around him practically shimmered with menace.

'Touch her and die.' Eidolon exploded into action, came to his feet in a flash. His red-eyed glower lit the darkness, and then Bleak was flying backward, crashing into a fence before crumpling to the ground, momentarily motionless.

She joined the fray, striking Sig in the jaw before nailing him with a hard kick to the gut. The bite of a blade in her shoulder made her yelp and miss a step. As she careened off a tree trunk, an inhuman roar shattered her eardrums.

Eidolon had morphed into some sort of horned demon she'd never seen before. Shredded clothes hung from a frame that was taller by half, twice as wide, and his sharp-toothed jaws held Warren between them, dangling off the ground.

Sig launched himself at Eidolon. Bleak leaped to his feet and came at her, his fists crunching into her ribs. Screams tore into the night, accompanied by wet ripping sounds, and then Bleak was lifted violently into the air. Eidolon held him in his jaws as he'd done Warren ... who was now in pieces on the ground, something she could have gone her entire life without seeing. Sig lay crumpled in an unnatural position at the base of a nearby oak tree.

'Hellboy,' she said gently. He swung around to her, hell on two thickly muscled legs. 'Drop the human. He's not a threat anymore.'

He raised his head and sniffed the air, his red eyes going to the cut on her arm. A low growl erupted in his chest, and his jaws tightened until Bleak cried out.

'I'm okay.' She moved toward him, her arm outstretched. Gently, she laid her palm on one leathery biceps. 'Please. Put him down.'

Abruptly, he opened his mouth, and Bleak plopped on the ground. Eidolon's arms came around her, and his hot breath fanned over her neck. Behind him, Bleak stirred, but didn't make any stupid moves.

'Thank God, Eidolon. I'm so glad you're okay.' She stroked his massive back as he hunched over her, long, slow passes to calm him. That she was petting a beast, the very type of demon she used to slaughter with relish, struck her so hard it reverberated to her soul. She loved this beast. It didn't matter what he was, what she was, or what either of them had done in the past.

Eidolon's weakness is you. But you could also be his strength. Gem's words from earlier in the day rang through her head. *He loves you.*

And yes, he'd been ready to die rather than hurt her, proof, perhaps, that he really did want her. Tears stung her eyes, and she began to shake.

'Please, Hellboy,' she whispered. 'Come back to me.'

The next time I shapeshift, I might not come back as myself.

Beneath her fingertips, she felt his skin soften, his body grow more supple. 'Tayla . . . '

She gasped as he palmed her ass and hauled her hard against his arousal. He was back, but his eyes still glowed red, and the swirling tattoo on his face remained. One hand tore at her shirt, but she didn't resist, lesson learned during the Soulshredder disaster. This would be her last chance to save him, and herself.

'Eidolon, it's not safe here. We need privacy.'

Growling low in his throat, he swept her up and carried her to a nearby building, a veterinary clinic, if she had to guess. The door was locked. In one powerful move, he kicked the door open. It crashed into the wall behind it, and before the building had stopped vibrating from the impact, Eidolon had placed her on a desk. When

314

he stepped between her thighs, her legs came up to lock around his of their own accord.

'I want you,' he said, his tone a rough command, and her body heated, went wet at her core as though it had become trained.

'Yeah, that's pretty clear.' She grasped fistfuls of his torn, bloodied T-shirt and pulled him close, needing full body contact as her skin came alive.

'That's it, Tayla.' He tore her pants in his haste to remove them. 'Show me what you want.'

She wanted him. Whatever it took.

Her voice shook as she blurted, 'Bond with me.'

He reared back, breaking her leglock. 'Bond? No.' Red eyes glowed in the darkness. She thought she saw a flicker of gold break through, but then it was gone, and his guttural rasp drifted down to her. 'Fuck? Yes.'

Shit. He'd warned her that if they waited too long it would be too late. Desperation clawed at her as the reality set in. She couldn't lose him now. Remembering what she'd read about his breed and their mating rituals, she tore off her shirt, fumbled with the fasteners on her ankle holster, and withdrew her stang. Before he could blink, she sliced through the front of her bra and drew the blade across the top of one breast. Pain surged through her, followed by a double burn of lust and love.

'Taste me.'

His chest heaved as he lowered his gaze to her breasts. Reaching up, she threaded her fingers through his hair and pulled him toward her, but just as the heady sensation of his hot breath fanning her skin hit her, he jerked away, eyes wild. He palmed the cut, and the familiar vibration shot through her as it sealed up. Every one of her injuries knitted together before she could pull away.

'Please, Eidolon,' she whispered. 'This is what you've wanted your entire life. You want a mate. Children. You want to be a doctor. Take me. Claim me.'

He groaned, and this time, when he looked at her, his eyes were gold, molten brilliance. 'Be . . . sure,' he panted. 'Can't hold on . . . much longer . . .'

'I'm sure.' She toed off her sneakers and pulled him tight between her thighs again. 'Hurry.'

Instead, he kissed her. Gently, leisurely, as if they had all the time in the world. Then, as though to make up for time wasted, he hauled her off the desk and yanked down her pants. As she stepped out of them, he settled on the desk and lay back. One hand gripped the edge with white-knuckled force, and the other released his arousal from his jeans.

'Climb up.' His voice was a tense rumble, spoken through clenched teeth, and she knew they had not a second to spare. 'This has to be voluntary. You must initiate it and offer it, the way I did with you in my room.'

Anticipation made her sex clench and weep as she straddled him, knees braced on the desk, hovering over his rigid shaft. His hands opened and closed at his sides as though he wanted to grab her. In one quick motion, she sat on him, burying him deep. He shouted and bucked, and the expression on his face could have been ecstasy or misery.

He bit his lip so hard he drew blood as he strained to remain still.

'Hurry, *lirsha,* hurry,' he rasped. 'Your wrist. Feed me.'

She'd dropped her stang on the floor along with all her other weapons when she'd undressed. Shit. Thing was, she knew better than to not have a weapon within reach. That was what he did to her, made her so crazy with lust and love that all her training, all her hatred, disappeared.

She looked down at him, at the way he was watching her with a laser focus. Little flecks of red broke through and she knew they'd reached critical mass. She tore his caduceus pendant from his neck and stabbed the tiny dagger into her right wrist. It hurt; the blade was dull, but it did the job. Quickly, she forced the cut against his mouth. His right hand, the tattooed one, closed on her left. He threaded their fingers together so that from shoulder to shoulder, they were one long, sinuous piece of artwork. The connection, wrist-to-mouth, hand-to-hand, pelvis-to-pelvis, created a circuit, an electric path that made her scream with the intensity.

She rocked on top of him, writhing with no sense of rhythm or regularity. Her body did what it wanted. Every nerve ending tingled. Her head spun. Eidolon surged against her as she churned above him. The loss of control barely registered in her mind, should have been frightening, but nothing had ever been so intense, so good. She was falling, and Eidolon would be there to catch her.

Sensations popped all over, on her skin, in her veins, and when he pulled deeply on her wrist, it felt as though an erotic string connected her wrist to her sex. She whimpered her approval as he sucked harder and her sex clenched with each draw from her vein.

'I feel you inside, Tayla ... Gods, I love you.' The fingers on her hip tightened. 'Oh ... *damn!*' He threw back his head and shouted, slamming his hips upward with such force that she came off the desk. Their tattoos glowed red fire and then she came, a full-body orgasm that went on and on.

Heat flowed through her body, her lungs burned, and the blood in her veins sizzled as she collapsed on top of him, panting, dizzy.

'Hold still,' he said hoarsely, and a mild buzz vibrated her wrist. He was healing her cut.

'Is it over?' she asked.

'Yes. Can you feel it?'

'Everywhere.'

On her skin, in her body, in her soul. She could sense him, could almost touch his thoughts, and she knew exactly what he was feeling.

Peace.

She knew, because she felt it, too.

ॐ

Tayla and Eidolon's peace was short-lived. The sounds of battle and screeches of pain rang out in the night. She didn't even have time to fully explore the way the markings on her arm had darkened and set, shimmering on her skin. Quickly, they dressed. At the door, Eidolon stopped her with a hand on her shoulder.

'You weren't a last resort.'

Emotion nearly choked her as she reached up to cup his cheek, where no sign remained of the facial tattoo, though there was a new one on his neck, two connected rings circling his throat. 'I know. And for what it's worth, I'm sorry about Roag.'

'Shh.' He made a sound, a near-purr, and his hands came up to hold her palm against him in a gesture so tender and loving she felt it in her soul. 'The future is what matters now. Because of you, I have one.'

'Because of you, I feel like I finally belong somewhere.'

He crushed her to him, his mouth finding hers in a demanding, dominating kiss that nearly made her forget where they were. The hold he had on her, a cage of safety and devotion, anchored her love for him firmly in her heart.

This was what being wanted felt like.

'We have to go,' he murmured against her lips, and she nodded.

Reluctantly, they headed for the zoo entrance, where, they hoped, Gem would be waiting with her parents. Instead, they found Lori, arms wrapped around herself and looking lost, standing beneath the gate arch. When Lori saw them, she paled, and Tayla watched the woman who had been her leader, her mentor, as she backed up against the wall of the abandoned gift shop.

'Leave me alone,' she said. 'You don't understand.'

Tayla snorted. 'You're right. I don't understand how you could cheat on Ky.'

Shame flashed in Lori's eyes. 'I didn't mean to hurt him—' She blinked at Eidolon as though she'd just noticed him. 'You ... you look like Wraith.'

Eidolon nailed her to the wall with hard eyes. 'How do you know Wraith?'

Lori didn't seem to hear. 'Are you an Elder, too?'

'Elder?' Tayla asked. 'As in, all-powerful Guardian Elder? A member of the Sigil? You think Wraith is an Elder?'

'He charged me with organizing a team to bring in demons. Our orders came directly from the Sigil. It was to be kept secret . . .' Crimson splotches mottled Lori's pale skin. 'Why am I telling you anything?' She turned to Eidolon. 'She's a demon. A traitor. She infiltrated The Aegis.' She turned back to Tayla. 'You'll be executed for that, you know.'

Tension cracked in the air around Eidolon, snapping so she could almost see sparks. 'What made you believe Wraith is a Guardian Elder?'

Lori huffed. 'He said he was.'

Eidolon and Tayla exchanged glances, and she knew they were thinking the same thing; that Wraith could have used his mental powers to make Lori think he was whoever he said he was.

'Anything else?' Tayla asked.

'You don't speak to me, demon bitch.'

'Okay,' Tayla snapped. 'I've had it with you. Eidolon, do you have some sort of truth serum at your hospital?'

'We have something better,' he ground out, but he didn't finish, because Wraith burst out of the foliage – apparently the roads and walkways were too easy – brushing off his hands.

'Wraith,' Lori whispered. 'Thank God.' She moved toward him, shooting a withering glare at Tayla. 'They don't seem to under-stand. And someone is releasing all the demons. Were you aware that Tayla is a demon?'

Wraith glowered at her. 'What are you babbling about, human?'

A patient, worshiping smile curved Lori's mouth. She reached for him, and he leaped away from her with a hiss. Frowning, she advanced. He retreated.

'Let her touch you,' Eidolon said.

'What? Hell, no.'

'Wraith! *Do it.*'

Wraith let loose a nasty curse, but he planted his feet and braced

319

himself, going stiff as a rod, as Lori folded herself against his chest. She seemed to be in an almost druglike stupor, melting into him, as loose as he was strung tight.

So. Weird.

'Is it him?' Eidolon asked quietly, and whoa – thanks to their bond, Tayla felt his fear like an icicle in the heart. He was terrified that his brother might be involved in the black market organization. 'Is he the one who enlisted your help to capture demons?'

Lori rubbed her cheek on his chest, ran her hands up and down his body, each touch making Wraith grow even more rigid. 'Touch me like before ...' She sounded intoxicated, and Tayla suspected she was affected by the incubus magic that seemed to emanate from them. Tayla knew the feeling.

'E ...' Wraith said, his voice a strangled plea.

'Just hold on, bro. It'll be over in a minute. Lori, is it him?'

God, Tayla hoped not. If Eidolon's own brother was involved ...

'*Jesus Christ!* Is one lover not enough?' Kynan, bruised and bloody, stood behind Eidolon, gaping at Lori and Wraith. Battle-lust burned in his eyes, and Tay wondered what had happened to Jagger. Ky sat solidly in the camp where thought had fled and only rage remained. He lunged for Wraith. Eidolon tackled him, one thick arm going around Ky's waist, the other jammed against his throat.

They tumbled to the ground, Kynan shouting obscenities, Eidolon doing his best to calm him while pinning him to the pavement.

'We need to know what she knows!' Eidolon said, a few times, and gradually, Kynan grew still, though his nostrils flared and his lips peeled back as if he wanted to take a piece out of Eidolon with his teeth.

Breathing hard even though she'd just been standing there, Tay turned back to Lori and Wraith – and gasped. Wraith's fangs were buried in Lori's neck, and she'd gone limp. One of his arms was wrapped around her waist, and the other had dropped between them, his hand working her jeans zipper.

'Uh, was that supposed to happen?'

Eidolon twisted around and cursed. 'Wraith. Shit.' He eased his forearm off Ky's throat and looked him square in the eye. 'I'm going to let you up. Don't make me regret not killing you.'

'You've got to trust him, Kynan,' Tayla said.

Aggression permeated the air, and strangely, Tay could feel it on her skin, as though the battle-rage the two males were throwing had raised the temperature ... not enough to register on a thermometer, but enough to jack up her body a little. It was sort of ... arousing. She couldn't wait to get Eidolon somewhere private so she could discover more neat perks of the bonding.

Kynan's only response to Eidolon was a low growl and a nearly imperceptible nod, but it was enough. Eidolon pushed up from the ground, and after making sure Ky wasn't going to leap on him, he inched toward his brother. 'Release the human.'

Wraith's gaze shifted to Eidolon, his eyes fierce and golden, his nostrils flaring. As Eidolon drew closer, Wraith pulled back, bringing Lori with him, a feral animal protecting its prey from approaching scavengers.

'Wraith,' Eidolon said softly, 'easy. Release the *human female*.'

That did it. Wraith's eyes shot wide, his teeth disengaged, and he stumbled backward. Eidolon caught Lori as she sagged to the ground.

Panting, his pupils dilating and contracting wildly, Wraith collapsed against a gate. When Kynan rushed forward, Eidolon handed Lori off to him and went to Wraith. Footsteps and screeches still rang out in the night, so Tayla kept watch while the drama she didn't understand played out between the four humans and demons.

Kynan settled Lori against a tree, more gently than Tay would have expected, given the circumstances. He said something to her, but Tayla moved away, not wanting to intrude. Besides, she was dying to know what the thing with Wraith was all about.

'It's okay, bro,' Eidolon was saying. 'It's okay. You didn't hurt her.'

Didn't hurt her? Something was seriously off here. Wraith had been perfectly willing to kill Tayla, yet he hadn't wanted to hurt Lori?

Wraith shivered, rocking back and forth, his expression a combination of shell-shock and horror.

A chuffing sound brought her around, gold-plated dagger in hand. Kynan came to his feet, stang at the ready. Just like old times, they moved in sync toward the noise, and when she saw the demon trotting down the footpath, she sighed with relief. Kynan assumed an attack position.

'No!' She grabbed his arm. 'Let it go.'

'What?' Kynan stared at her as if she'd gone mad. 'Jesus, there's nothing left of your humanity, is there?'

'Actually, I think I'm more human than ever,' she said, because ironically, mating with a demon, becoming a demon ... those things had allowed her to finally feel something other than blind hatred. 'That demon won't hurt anyone. It's not violent. It's even a vegetarian. They're like, happy Halloween demons or some crap.'

'Even if you're right, it's evil—'

God, she'd sounded like that to Eidolon, hadn't she? 'We need to talk. There are a lot of things you should know.'

Though Kynan's fingers tightened around his weapon, he didn't make a move. The demon slipped away. They turned back to Lori ... who was gone.

'Dammit!' Agony screamed from every one of Kynan's pores, and Tayla fought the urge to console him. Words meant nothing right now, not when his wife had betrayed him in so many ways. Not when the words came from a demon.

Kynan took off at a dead run, heading into the zoo once more. She let him go, and silently wished him luck.

෧෨

Eidolon was still confused as hell about what had gone on with Wraith and the human female. His gut told him that Wraith wasn't

322

involved in the black market operation, but shit, the human had been sure of it.

'Come on, bro,' Eidolon said, as he helped Wraith to his feet. 'I'm taking you home.'

Wraith swayed on wobbly legs. 'No,' he croaked. 'I need—'

'Don't,' Eidolon said fiercely, grasping Wraith's elbow and swinging him around so they were nose to nose. 'Don't you fucking do it. You come home with me, got it? We need to talk about what happened, and if you're stoned out of your skull, we won't get very far. I want to know how involved you are with the Ghouls.'

Wraith hissed. 'I'm not.'

'Why should I believe you?

'Because I said so.'

Eidolon fisted Wraith's T-shirt and yanked him nose to nose. 'And you'd never lie, would you?' Eidolon had lost count of the number of times Wraith had lied about going over his monthly limit of human kills, and Eidolon had the scars to prove it. Still, doing something as heinous as what the Ghouls had done wasn't in Wraith's makeup, not after how he'd suffered. Though Wraith had no problem with killing, he did it quickly and efficiently.

A growl rumbled from deep in Wraith's chest. Tayla eased closer, probably intending to pummel Wraith if he so much as twitched.

'What are you going to do, bro? Spank me for fibbing? I don't think so. The big-brother card ain't playing today.' He jerked out of Eidolon's grip. 'Happy fucking honeymoon.' He stalked away.

'Lay off the junkies, Wraith,' Eidolon warned, and Wraith flipped him the bird before disappearing into the darkness.

Eidolon looked skyward and counted to ten, ignoring everything around him until Tayla's hand on his arm brought him back down to earth.

'What was all that about?'

He pulled her into his arms, wrapping her in a firm embrace. He squeezed his eyes closed and let himself feel the opposing sensations of her hard body and her soft touch as he stroked her hair.

'Wraith's messed up, in case you hadn't noticed,' he said. 'He hates himself, and he does whatever it takes to forget. Remember how he was at the hospital?'

'Hard to forget.' She ran her hands up his back, and he felt the tension inside him ease a little. 'What was going on with him and Lori? Why didn't he want to touch her? And why did he freak after he bit her?'

'Wraith never feeds from human females.'

'Why not?'

Eidolon pressed his lips to her forehead and wished they could stay like this forever, could enjoy their new bond without having to deal with whether or not Wraith had betrayed his entire race. 'Because he can't control his urges. Feeding on females leads to sex, and he'd rather die than have sex with a human.'

'So ... why did Lori act like they've slept together?'

'His mind power. If he wanted her to believe it, she would.' *Someone* wanted her to believe it, anyway.

'Like he did to me in your living room,' she murmured, and yeah, he still wanted to kick his brother's ass over that. 'Do you think he's involved with the organ thing?'

'I don't think so. But the alternative is nearly as bad.' Someone with a grudge against Wraith could cause an underworld of trouble.

The sound of a throat clearing brought them apart, but Eidolon kept her hand in his as Shade and Gem stalked toward them.

Shade frowned, looking extremely put out. 'Man, I missed all the good stuff, didn't I?' His gaze settled on Eidolon's bond glyph on his neck and then slid to Tayla's arm, deeply etched with Eidolon's dermoire. 'I'll be damned. Cool.'

'Congrats, you guys.' Gem's grin lit her up, made Tayla draw a sharp breath.

'You look so much like Mom,' Tayla said, smiling at her sister. 'Are your parents safe? Where have you guys been?'

'They're fine. I sent them home with Luc and then found Shade out looking for you two.' Gem glanced around. 'Where's Wraith? Kynan?'

Tayla and Eidolon exchanged glances during the long, tense silence that fell between the four of them. The grin slid off Gem's face, and Shade went taut.

Eidolon scrubbed a hand over his face, relishing the burn of his palm over his tired flesh. 'We have a problem. An Aegi claims Wraith is involved with the Ghouls.'

'He's not,' Shade said fiercely.

'I know.' And Eidolon meant it. 'But someone is trying pretty damned hard to make it look like he is. Looks like they're tricking local Guardians into thinking Aegis leaders are in on it, too.'

'Hell's fucking bells.'

'That's exactly what I was thinking.' Well, he was thinking a lot more than that, mainly because Tayla was standing next to him, her hand squeezing his, and all he wanted was to be alone with her. They could deal with Wraith later.

Right now, his entire world was Tayla, and he wanted to make sure she knew it.

୭

Gem shot through the zoo at a dead run. Tayla, Eidolon, and Shade were making one last sweep of the park to make sure all loose demons had been ushered away and the dangerous ones destroyed, as well as to capture any remaining Guardians.

Gem couldn't care less about dangerous demons and rogue Guardians.

When Tay told her what happened with Lori and Kynan, Gem hadn't waited around. All she could think about was finding Ky, and as she moved swiftly through the zoo in the direction he'd gone, she prayed he was okay. That his bitch of a wife hadn't injured him. That Jagger hadn't done worse.

When she reached the old tiger habitat, she came to an abrupt halt at the sight of the Aegis leader standing there, shoulders

325

sagging, head bowed. His pain rolled off him in seismic waves, vibrating through her at regular intervals, nine-point-oh-my-God on the anguish scale.

'Kynan?'

He didn't appear to have heard her, but she knew he had, and she approached carefully.

'She's gone,' he said, when she eased up next to him. 'I can't find her. Even if I could . . .'

She didn't think. She simply wrapped her arms around him. The contact made something break inside him, and his legs gave out, dropping them both to their knees. And then he was sobbing and she was holding him, and even though she knew he hated her for what she was, she didn't care.

For now, the man she loved was in her arms, and somehow, she couldn't feel guilty for being glad.

TWENTY-SIX

❧

They met up at UG.

Shade had finished mopping up with E and Tayla, had then sent them ahead to the hospital so his brother could get patched up from his encounter with the slayers who'd tried to kill him. Shade had remained behind to find Wraith and Gem.

Wraith had gone MIA, but he'd found Tayla's sister standing near an old fountain, watching as the man she'd called Kynan walked away. She'd seemed upset, but Shade had no idea why, and really, he didn't care. Touchy-feely-mushy crap made him uncomfortable.

They traveled through Harrowgates to the hospital, where E and Tayla were tangled together on the couch in the staff lounge. Talk about touchy-feely-mushy crap. They practically glowed with some sort of after-bond bliss, and her new dermoire stood out starkly on the creamy skin of her left arm. Eidolon, dressed in scrubs, sported his own new marking; mated, post-*s'genesis* males lost the face tats but gained a linked circle around the throat. He had no idea when they'd completed the mating ritual, but it had obviously happened at the zoo – what, somewhere between the apes and the hippos, between fighting demons and slayers? – but

Shade was glad. He still wasn't sure he trusted the Aegi, but she'd saved E from a fate he'd been dreading, had given Shade his brother back.

And speaking of brothers . . .

'Has Wraith shown up?' Shade asked, grabbing a Coke from the fridge.

E shook his head. 'He was pretty messed up. I've been ringing his cell, but . . . '

'Yeah.' Wraith had probably sucked some junkie dry and gone to ground. If Shade focused, he'd be able to feel his younger brother's energy, but Wraith would feel it, too, and he'd dig in deeper. 'I hope he's okay.'

The very idea that some sonofabitch might be impersonating Wraith left him wanting to take someone apart. Too bad they hadn't found any Guardians who were still breathing. Shade wanted answers, and he wanted them now.

He'd never been a patient sort.

'Hey,' Tayla said, extracting herself from E's embrace. 'I guess I need to do that integration thing, huh?'

Her attempt to steer the conversation away from the black hole that was their brother couldn't have been more obvious, but E grinned. 'How about now?'

'Hold on.' Shade moved to the couch. 'Can I have your hand?'

E tensed, probably some sort of instinct the bonding had released, but Shade couldn't be sure. Mated Seminus demons were so rare that he'd never met one and had no idea how they were supposed to react when their mates were near other incubi. Considering how horny incubi were, a protective instinct probably wasn't a bad idea. Then again, the bonding made it impossible for either one of them to willingly have sex with anyone else.

Tayla reached out, and he took her palm in his. Warmth washed over him as he probed her body, moved through her bloodstream to her womb. This was his specialty, the ability to manipulate a female's reproductive organs – he could trigger ovulation in order

328

to ensure conception, though he was not yet fertile. His heart rate spiked as he probed, his instincts firing up because even though she was E's mate, she was female, and she was ovulating. But she hadn't quickened with his brother's seed.

'Well?' E asked, his voice husky with emotion.

'Sorry. No little Es in there.'

Tayla pulled her hand away, and he winced at the sudden loss of sensation. 'Was there supposed to be?'

'Would it be a bad thing?' Eidolon asked quietly, and Shade shrank back, noticed Gem did the same thing. This situation was *way* too intimate for either of them.

'No,' she said, smiling with such radiance that Shade felt himself drawn to her, for the first time seeing what E had seen all along. 'I just, well, what kind of lifespan am I looking at? How long do we have to make a family?'

'Soulshredders live for somewhere around two thousand years. Being a half-breed, you'll probably live a fraction of that, a few hundred, maybe?'

'Good,' she said, sliding Gem a glance. 'I have a lot of family time to make up for.'

Gem grinned, and Shade gagged, more of a self-preservation response to the aching yearning he felt for the same thing than true disgust. But no way in hell would he admit that, even to himself.

'Hell's teeth,' Shade muttered. 'Can we do the integration now, before I puke? There's so much grinning and adoration and sweetness in here that the place should smell like fucking candy-covered roses.'

The door opened, and Skulk stepped into the room. Cocking her head, she stared at Tayla, her gunmetal eyes glinting with curiosity. 'You're fixed. Your aura. It's bright.'

Tayla bit her bottom lip, and E shifted toward her, his need for her rising up in a cloud of scent. They'd require privacy soon, something Shade would be happy to give them. The little jaunt through Tayla's reproductive organs had stirred him into his own state of arousal.

'It was dark before?' Tayla asked.

'Oh, yes. Very. But you're all better now.' Skulk jammed her fists on her hips and scowled at Shade. 'Now we just have to work on you.'

'No hope for me, little sis. Give it up.'

'I'll never give up on you,' she said quietly. 'We're going to banish that darkness.' She slipped away then, as quiet as a shadow.

Gem looped her arm in his. 'Come on, brother-in-law. Let's turn my sister into a full-fledged demon. And then we'll go out for margaritas.'

Yeah, tequila and salt sounded good right about now, both burning, stinging elements to put to a wound. He was happy for E. He was. But his brother's success at finding a mate and keeping the life he'd always wanted only reminded Shade that his Change was coming.

And there was that little matter of the curse . . .

ॐ

Lori found Jagger where she knew he'd be if he still lived; the two-bedroom house they'd rented nearly a year ago. Only the Guardians chosen to work with them knew of its existence. It had always been considered a safe house, a place to come when and if the worst happened.

The worst had happened.

'Jagger!' She flew into his arms, right there in the middle of the living room. He looked as if he'd gone ten rounds with a hellhound. He'd definitely come out on the losing end of the fight with Kynan. How he'd escaped alive and intact was a question she doubted Jagger would ever answer.

'Hey, babe,' he said, locking her against him with one arm around her neck. 'I'm really frickin' sorry.'

'I know. But I'll go to Kynan, explain—'

Jagger stepped away, and at the same time, a sharp cramp in her gut nearly doubled her over. She palmed her abdomen ... wet, warm stickiness coated her fingers. Stunned, her head light, she looked down. A knife hilt jutted from her belly.

'Like I said, I'm sorry. But you can't go to Kynan.' Jagger caught her as she stumbled, her legs no longer working.

'Son of a ... *bitch.*' Her words came out on a gasp.

'Yeah, my mom was a bitch. A whore.' He lowered her to her knees and sat on his heels in front of her. 'I thought all women were whores, until I met you.' Her vision fuzzed as he lifted her chin with one hand, held her steady with the other. 'I mean, you did fuck around on Ky with me, but shit, who wouldn't?'

Anguish, physical and mental, washed over her. She'd cheated on her husband, who she loved more than anything. She'd betrayed him on so many levels, and for what? To die in the shithole where she'd screwed the man who was killing her?

If only she'd listened to Kynan that night, one year ago, when she'd been feeling ill but insisted on hunting anyway. He'd said she shouldn't go, that sickness left humans vulnerable to spells and demon magic, but she'd kissed him and laughed, and had headed out on her own.

Wraith had come to her in Central Park, where she'd been hunting a Nebulous demon that had sucked the soul out of a cabbie a few blocks away. He'd merely looked at her and she'd experienced a rush of desire so strong her knees had trembled.

He'd worn an Aegis ring, had claimed to be an Elder, one of the Sigil who oversaw all Aegis cells worldwide. When she asked about his arm-length tattoo, he'd said that all Elders were similarly marked. Since no one knew the identity of the twelve Elders, she couldn't very well ask for proof. But he had known a lot about The Aegis, and a lot about her.

Such as how she liked to be touched. How she liked to be licked. And he'd shown her new things to like when she met him at a hotel the next day.

She'd never cheated on her husband, not once in their eight-year marriage. But for some reason she hadn't been able to resist the man, who'd asked to be called Wraith.

He'd brought a money-making proposal to the table, and she'd agreed, but then, she'd have agreed to anything if he'd only give her one more orgasm.

'I know what you're thinking.'

Startled, she opened her eyes. Darkness ringed the edges of her vision, but the pain was gone. She was bleeding out. Jagger trailed a finger down her arm. 'You're thinking about sex. With me. How it started. Your life is flashing before your eyes,' he said, and only Jagger, with his mammoth ego, would think that in her last moments she'd be thinking about him.

No, she was thinking about how she'd betrayed her husband, how sex with Wraith seemed to have triggered some sort of addictive response, and after their second encounter, she'd come home, her body pulsing, her skin hypersensitive. Any pressure at all made her womb spasm, and the tiniest vibration made her orgasm where she stood. She'd come three times on the cab ride home.

Jagger had flirted with her yet again, and in her heightened state she'd responded, had let him take her on the library floor while Kynan had been out hunting.

Guilt plagued her; she loved Kynan. But her body hadn't felt like hers in a year, was a slave to her hormones, and although she'd craved Wraith's touch, she couldn't have it as often as she'd like. Hell, she'd been with him only half a dozen times. Kynan could keep up with her sex drive, but he wasn't always around.

Jagger had been there when Kynan wasn't.

'Don't worry, Lori. I'll keep the operation going. Obviously, we'll have to move it here, unless I can take out Ky.'

'No,' she gasped.

'I have to. I can take over the cell—'

Mustering all her strength, she pulled the knife from her gut and buried it in Jagger's.

He yelled, fell backward, and then suddenly, he was flying across the room.

Kynan.

She heard muffled grunts, bellows of rage, and the sound of fists on flesh. Her vision had dimmed to nearly nothing, so she couldn't see, but when she heard the crack of bone, she knew someone had died.

'Lori.' Kynan's strong hands rolled her from her side to her back. 'Hold on. Please hold on.'

'No.' Weakly, she grasped his wrist. 'It's over. Just ... know ... ' She sucked in a gurgling breath. 'I did it for the cell. The money.'

'You were in league with demons for *the money*?'

Demons? She shook her head. 'Orders came from an Elder. We caught the demons. Left them at the zoo. Money was wired into our account.'

Kynan cursed. 'It wasn't the Elders giving the orders and paying you ... it was demons. You were taking orders from fucking demons.'

'No,' she whispered, 'no.' Oh, God, to have gone through all of that, to have betrayed The Aegis, her cell, Kynan ... for demons ...

She shivered. 'Cold ... so ... cold ... '

Kynan pulled Lori into his arms as her life drained away. When he'd arrived at the house, led by the tracking signal he'd planted on Jagger at the zoo, he'd thought he hated Lori. Thought he could kill her. But when he saw her bleeding, on the verge of death, all he could think about was saving her.

As an Army medic, he'd seen it all, had breathed in the foul stench of lifeblood and bowels as he patched up guys he knew damned good and well weren't going to make it for ten more minutes. As a Guardian, he'd sewn up wounds as horrific as any caused by IEDs. But nothing had prepared him for seeing his own wife holding in her guts with one shaking hand.

She went limp and her eyes glazed over and goddammit he wanted to cry like a fucking little girl. Instead, he set her gently on the floor. He didn't spare a glance at Jagger's crumpled body in the corner of the kitchen as he pulled a cell phone from his pocket. With a flick of his thumb, he popped it open.

Thirty-nine, thirty-eight, thirty-seven . . .

He dropped the phone next to Lori and strode out of the house.

TWENTY-SEVEN

⁓

Three months later ...

Working for Aegis demon-slayers while being a demon had, surprisingly, not caused Tayla many problems. Then again, no one but Kynan knew what she was, and she no longer hunted. Her job with the New York cell was to educate the Guardians, to teach them the difference between harmful demons and those who would rather not cause trouble.

So far, so good.

Kynan had been wary of her and her motives, but he'd needed help to make sense of what Lori and Jagger had done, and the deeper he dug, the more he'd distanced himself from The Aegis.

He'd discovered the bank account where she and Jagger had been hiding the money earned from the demon captures, and he'd questioned Bleak, who'd confessed that Jagger had come to him and several others, wanting them to work on top secret missions that were handed down from the very top – from the Sigil. Those involved had truly believed that all orders came from The Aegis ... including the order to kill Tayla.

Kynan's mission – or rather, obsession, in Tay's opinion – since then had been to hunt down those behind the organ-stealing operation, those who had corrupted Lori and taken her away from him. He'd had little success; with Aegis Guardians no longer capturing demons, traffic had slowed. No suspicious injuries or deaths had come through UG, either. The operation had been crippled, but neither Tayla nor Eidolon was naïve enough to believe that it had been shut down.

There would always be a market for demon parts, so someone would always be selling them.

Then there was Wraith. He'd disappeared for two months following the incident at the zoo, and when he returned, he'd behaved as though nothing had happened. And none of them had been able to make headway on who might be impersonating him, or why.

He hadn't stopped taking more than his monthly quota of humans, either, though Eidolon had begun asking the vampires for an accounting of the kills – always men, usually violent gangster types in all parts of the world. Apparently, Wraith liked a challenging hunt, and Tayla had been forced to watch Eidolon suffer three more times on the floor of his den. If one of Wraith's enemies didn't kill him, she might. Soon.

She hadn't tried shifting into her new hybrid-Soulshredder form, not once in the three months since Eidolon and Shade performed the integration and had the protective bands tattooed on her wrists, ankles, and neck, but Wraith was just asking for a taste of Soulshredder torment.

One of these days she'd try the shift with Gem's help, but for now she'd enjoy the benefits of enhanced strength, vision, and hearing that were even more pronounced than they'd been before the integration.

The benefits of the bond with Eidolon were even better. She could feel him in every cell, a comforting, warm presence. Every emotion, every sensation was magnified when they were together, and their arousal was always in sync. Sex had been amazing before the bond, but after . . .

Explosive.

Intense.

Beyond incredible.

Tayla heard the front door to Eidolon's apartment open, and speaking of arousal ... She darted from the kitchen to the hall. Eidolon had better have remembered to wear scrubs home as she'd asked.

She rounded the corner and squeaked with surprise. He'd worn them home, but he'd also brought Gem with him. His eyes flared wide at the sight of Tayla standing there in nothing but a hospital gown. 'Uh ... your sister was at the door ... '

Gem's face went as red as a Sora demon's butt. 'I'll come back later. You two go ahead and play doctor.' She grimaced. 'I so didn't need this trauma.'

She slipped out, and Tayla laughed. She and Gem had grown close over the last three months, especially now that Gem had started work at UG to replace Yuri. Her sister seemed content enough with the job, but Tayla knew Gem mooned over Kynan, who remained cool to both of them.

Eidolon grinned. 'I wondered why you wanted me to wear my scrubs home.'

Tayla put on her most serious expression. 'Well, I didn't want to come to the hospital, but I have something you need to see.'

Instantly, the smile fell from his face. 'What is it?'

'I seem to have a new mark.' Turning, she let the gown fall open.

'My caduceus,' he whispered, trailing his finger lightly over the tattoo she'd had inked just above her tailbone. 'You have a tattoo of my caduceus.'

She threw him a seductive look over her shoulder. 'It's still kind of sensitive, doctor ... maybe you could kiss it and make it better?'

A wicked gleam sparked in his eye as he bent his head to her ear and whispered naughty, raw things in it until she was breathless and on fire.

'Why, doctor,' she murmured, 'do you really want me to do those things to you?'

In a heartbeat, he swept her into his arms and strode down the hall. 'Oh, yeah. Consider it partial payment on your hospital bill.'

'You know, that's really one heck of a bill.'

'Yeah,' he said, nuzzling her throat. 'It'll take about six hundred years to pay off. You up for it?'

Oh, yes, she was. She was definitely up for it. And by the feel of things, so was he.

Also available now from Piatkus

DOWNPOUR
Kat Richardson

After being shot in the back and dying – again – Harper's recovery
has been hard. She's lost many of the powers she'd acquired since first
becoming a Greywalker, and knows that if she dies one more time,
she won't be coming back. Her only respite from the chaos is her
work . . . until she sees a ghostly car accident for which there are no
records. Worse still, the victim of the fatal wreck insists he was
murdered, and that the nearby community of Sunset Lakes – called
'Blood Lake' by locals – is to blame.

The picturesque area is an unlikely a haven for conspiracy but Harper
soon learns that the icy waters of the lake hide a terrible power and a
host of hellish beings. And both are held under the thrall of a sinister
cabal that will use the darkest of arts to achieve their fiendish ends . . .

978-0-7499-4086-7

FIRED UP
Jayne Ann Krentz

More than three centuries ago, Nicholas Winters irrevocably altered his genetic make up in an obsession-fueled competition with alchemist and Arcane Society founder Sylvester Jones. Driven to control their psychic abilities, each man's decision has reverberated throughout the family line, rewarding some with powers beyond their wildest dreams, and cursing others to a life filled with madness and hallucinations.

Jack Winters, descendant of Nicholas, has been experiencing nightmares and blackouts – just the beginning, he believes – of the manifestation of the Winters family curse. The legend says that he must find the Burning Lamp or risk turning into a monster. But he can't do it alone; he needs the help of a woman with the gift to read the lamp's dreamlight. Jack is convinced that private investigator Chloe Harper is that woman. It doesn't take long for Chloe to pick up the trail of the missing lamp. And as they draw closer to the lamp, the raw power that dwells within it threatens to sweep them into a hurricane of psychic force.

978-0-7499-5266-2

DESTINY KILLS
Keri Arthur

When Destiny McCree wakes up beside a dead man on an Oregon beach, she knows only this: she has to keep moving, keep searching and keep one step ahead of the forces that have been pursuing her from the heart of Scotland to this isolated spot. Why? The death of her lover has left her alone, with little memory of her past. A glimmering serpent-shaped ring is the one clue she has – and a bargaining chip in a most dangerous game.

Enter Trae Wilson, a master thief with a sexy, knowing grin and a secret agenda of his own. Destiny and Trae both have powers far beyond human – and both are running for their lives. Together they're riding a tide of danger, magic and lust . . . but with killers stalking their every move, they must use any means necessary, even each other, to survive – until the shocking secret of one woman's destiny finally unravels.

978-0-7499-5302-7

Do you love fiction with a supernatural twist?

Want the chance to hear news about your favourite authors (and the chance to win free books)?

Keri Arthur

S. G. Browne

P.C. Cast

Christine Feehan

Jacquelyn Frank

Larissa Ione

Sherrilyn Kenyon

Jackie Kessler

Jayne Ann Krentz and Jayne Castle

Martin Millar

Kat Richardson

J.R. Ward

David Wellington

Then visit the Piatkus website and blog
www.piatkus.co.uk | www.piatkusbooks.net

And follow us on Facebook and Twitter
www.facebook.com/piatkusfiction | www.twitter.com/piatkusbooks

piatkus